MW00948417

LOGAN - A PRESTON BROTHERS NOVEL

A More Than Series Spin Off

JAY MCLEAN

Copyright © 2017 by Jay McLean

All rights reserved.

No part of this book may be reproduced in any form or by any electronic or mechanical means, including information storage and retrieval systems, without written permission from the author, except for the use of brief quotations in a book review.

Cover Art: Jay McLean

Editor: Tricia Harden (Emerald Eyes Editing)

For Kelli Ann Basil Collopy

PROLOGUE

FRIDAY NIGHT, and it's my first date with Mary since before what my dad likes to call an "episode." She's so deep in my lungs, in my blood, in my thoughts, in my mind that I can feel myself losing to her, giving in to her touch, to the way her fingertips stroke against my flesh. She's whispering words in my ears, from all angles, all spaces, *"Because you never asked, Logan."*

I've been to Aubrey's house, been to her shop, been inside and around and over her, and she's right; I never asked, but she's wrong because she never told me. Never hinted. And that's what Mary's so good at; this mind space, these circles, and I can't get enough, because I inhale and inhale and chop, lick and roll, chop, lick and roll just so I can inhale and inhale and inhale some more.

"Because you never asked, Logan."

"No," I say aloud.

Mary calls to me again, warns me of what's to come: *You're nine years old, and the leather cracks beneath your weight...*

PART 1

LOGAN

THERE ARE two types of people in this world, the fakers and the realists, and I'm pretty sure I hate them both.

Even as Joy sits in my truck, her long, bottle-blonde hair blowing in the wind, I get this tingling inside me, like pins and needles, only worse. She's as fake as they come, but she's also the closest thing I've had to a girlfriend, excluding Mary, of course. Mary, short for Mary Jane, aka *marijuana*.

Joy's laugh is as obnoxious and as fake as the smile that accompanies it, and she's giggling at something I said, something I can't remember, but I'm willing to bet wasn't funny.

Joy... what a name. It's so weighted. As if it's her life's goal to bestow *joy* amongst everyone she comes across.

Poor Joy.

She reaches across the front seat, her hand going to the back of my neck, to the hair there, and she digs her false nails into my scalp while she fakes a moan. I turn to her, smirk, and she bats those inch-long, stuck-on lashes at me. It takes everything in me not to pull over and get my fill of the only thing that makes me enjoy anything other than Mary. Her hand moves from my neck to my shoulder, down my chest until the warmth of it spreads across my stomach, and I internally beg, pray for her to go lower, lower, lower.

Instead, she stops completely and says, "We have to pick up Aubrey."

I grasp her wrist and push it away.

Aubrey: her friend, also known as the most annoying person in the history of existence. If I had to create a graph of fakes versus realists, these two girls would be on opposite ends of the spectrum.

I say, "I thought it was just you and me tonight."

Joy scoffs, and I hate the sound. "And about fifty other people. We're going to a house party, Logan."

It's Friday night, and I've been up since 5 a.m., and at nineteen, I'm too young to be too old for this but too agitated to care. I'm tired and I'm antsy and I just want to spend the night getting the week's worth of aches and pains and frustrations out of me and just blow off steam. Or just blow… a few times… inside the girl who's sitting next to me. But now Aubrey's in the mix, and "I don't want to hang out with Aubrey tonight."

"She's my friend," Joy whines, as if I'm stupid, as if I don't know. I've been with the girl for almost three months, the longest I've spent with anyone. I've kept my dick in my pants. Kept my eyes from drifting. Kept it all in check while slowly losing my goddamn mind.

"Besides," Joy adds, "she didn't have plans tonight."

Can't say I'm surprised. "So now we have to join her pity party?"

"Just be nice."

Be *nice*?

"And if you're a good boy," she says, grabbing my wrist and placing my hand between her legs, "I'll make it worth your while."

And this right here is why I tolerate *people*. Why I tolerate Joy.

AUBREY'S SITTING in her driveway when I get to her house. In a long skirt, white tank top, and an oversized fucking granny cardigan, the girl looks like a hobo.

Joy flips the visor and checks out her made-up, flawless face. "Can she get in on your side? I don't want to get out."

Arguing would be pointless, and so I step out, leave my door open for Aubrey to get in the middle. "Hey, asshole," she says.

I roll my eyes. "I must've missed the memo for the party tonight. Didn't realize it was Hobo Dress Day."

She stops a few feet in front of me, smiles that wicked grin I've come to hate. "That memo was for the girls. The guys' theme is High School Reject Stoner." She claps once. "And look, you didn't even have to dress the part!" She passes me, tugs on the brim of my hat to cover my eyes.

After adjusting my cap, I follow her in and put my truck into gear. And because I'm only slightly affected by her dig, I say, "Your skirt's ugly as shit."

"Awesome," she deadpans. "Matches your face."

Joy sighs, applies more lipstick to her already pink lips. "Can you guys at least pretend to get along?"

"Nope," Aubrey and I say at the same time.

Welp, at least we agree on something.

I reverse out of her driveway and make it back on the road before Aubrey's voice grates on my nerves again. "Besides, you need me. I got us the invite." She's lying, of course, because besides Joy, Aubrey has no friends. Given, she's new in town, but still…

"It's open house, smart-ass."

"Nope." Aubrey shakes her head. "There's a big sign on the front lawn that reads '*No Dogs Allowed*,' so I had to convince Brittney to let you come."

"Then I guess you must be some super unique breed of bitch."

Aubrey murmurs, "Let's just go to this stupid party."

"Look," I start, "if you don't want to go, then, by all means, I can turn around and drop you back home."

"Please do," she says.

I flick on the blinker.

Joy reaches across the seat to switch it back off. She turns to her friend. "We're doing this. All three of us. And we're going to enjoy it."

Joy: The giver of joy.

Sucks to be her.

OUR TOWN IS SMALL, socially split in two by Main Street.

On one side are the Haves, on the other are the Have-Nots.

Cliché, right?

The Preston "estate," so the assholes in town like to call it, is situated at the end of Main Street. Geographically, socially and economically, I consider my family to be right in the middle. Aubrey lives somewhere closer to the Have-Not's, while Joy's basically the queen bee of the Haves, which means the people she acquaints herself with are exactly like her. Both the girls graduated from high school a few months ago. Joy from St. Luke's, the only private school within fifty-miles. Aubrey—I don't even know. Neither of them is off to college. Joy is spending her time doing nothing because she can, because her daddy's money allows it, and because why the fuck not? Aubrey—I don't know what she's doing with her life, and I don't care. The point is, up until I met Joy at one of my regular parties on the *other* side of Main Street, I'd barely even seen this side of town unless I was working construction for my dad. The parties, though, are in a world of their own, and I love them for one reason and one reason only:

Free weed and booze.

I don't even drink.

THE BASS FROM THE DJ—AN actual DJ brought in from somewhere much cooler than here—rattles the windows, the walls, and I inhale all Mary has to offer while I sit back on the couch, watch my girl dance with another girl who looks identical to her. Or maybe I've smoked too much. Maybe my vision's blurred.

Ruby-red satin clings to Joy's curves, ending just past her ass. Long, tanned legs atop black, six-inch stilettos, tiny diamonds on the heels leading up to the red bow on the back, and I'll be sure to have her keep them on later—let them dig into my hips while I dig into her. I lick my lips, take another hit of the blunt, and watch the ribbon of smoke rise to the ceiling, disappearing into nothingness, the same nothingness that lives and breathes inside me.

The couch cushion shifts as someone sits down next to me, and I keep my head back, eyes on the light show cascading on the white ceiling. Flecks of red, blue and green reflect off my irises, and I love this—this feeling of weightless, free euphoria that takes away the darkness, the moments I hide from... the *memories*. This is what living should be... and on Friday nights, every Friday night, I start to exist again. If only for two days. If only for me.

"Your girl's looking fine." I recognize the voice as Denny's: the town's supplier of all things recreational, the dealer of my drug of choice. "Yo, you want to stock up? You may as well while you're here. That Brittney girl's got everyone covered."

I choke on another inhale and nod at the same time. Something light falls on my lap: another ounce of green to get me by. *Thank you, Brittney.* Whoever the fuck you are. "Thanks, man," I mumble, rolling my head to face him. But he's already gone, walking toward the corner of the room. It's only when he stops there that I see who he was following: Aubrey.

I sit up higher, blink hard to fight the high.

She's up on her toes, her hands on his chest, her neck craned to whisper something in his ear. The girl's so fucking naïve, she's borderline stupid. At a party like this where dank smoke overpowers the smell of expensive perfume, cologne and hairspray—where the drug is *free,* she doesn't need to be pulling him away to ask for what she wants.

Denny nods, reaches into his pocket while she reaches into hers. She pulls out a twenty. He's ripping her off, and I'm on my feet to tell her, but then he pulls out a bag—*pills*—and she's not here for the weed and *what the fuck is wrong with you, Aubrey?*

In all the forced hanging out we've done over the last few months, she's never once taken a toke of my joint, and neither she nor Joy have ever mentioned ecstasy. Weed is one thing, pills... *nope.*

I move my feet to stop the exchange, but I'm too late. By the time I get to them, they're already breaking apart and walking in opposite directions:

Denny to the left.

Aubrey to the right.

I should follow Denny, ask him if she's a regular.

I should follow Aubrey, ask her what's up.

Really, I should do neither. I'm not her boyfriend, and it's not my place, and I don't give two shits.

Only I do.

I go right, follow Aubrey past the sea of bodies in the kitchen and out to the patio, more people (ugh), and stop next to her. Elbows on the railing, she looks out into the yard. Summer nights mean twilight until around ten. Parties around here last until twelve. Until some old person who can't handle kids decides to call the cops. Same old, same old.

I say, still standing behind her, "What's up?".

Aubrey turns to me, her eyebrow quirked. "Where's your leader?"

"My *leader*?"

"Joy?"

"Ah."

"So?"

"She's dancing." After shoving my hands in my pockets, I motion with my head to her hand. "Watcha got there?"

"Nothing."

"Didn't look like nothing when Denny gave it to you."

Red lips to match her fiery-red hair, her mouth parts while her eyes narrow to a glare directed right at me.

"You poppin' pills now, Red?"

"Red?"

I tug her hobo hair.

She taps my hand away with a flick of her wrist. "I don't recall when *my* life became *your* business, but you can fuck off now." Another wrist flick to shoo me away.

"They're bad for you," I say, shrugging, because this is fucking awkward, and I *hate* this girl.

Aubrey laughs, right in my face, and I wish I'd never cared enough to come out here. "And what you inhale into your body is okay, because why? Because it cures cancer?"

With a heavy sigh, I shove my hands back in my pockets, and rock on my heels. "I don't know that weed *cures* cancer, Red. But it sure as hell takes away the pain of treatment like chemo, and if I'd known about it back when my mom was going through it, I'd have blown this shit down her throat so she wasn't in agony when she fucking died."

AUBREY'S A BITCH, and I need to get her bullshit out of my head.

I need to get out of my head, period.

I leave her on the patio with her ugly clothes and her stupid hair and her fucked-up opinions and go in search of my kind-of girlfriend so I can get us the fuck out of here and take out my frustrations in the form of wild and pointless fucking.

The living room is the same as I left it, only Joy's not there—neither is her apparent twin. I check the kitchen, the laundry, the entire downstairs. She's nowhere to be seen, and so I check my phone, make sure she hasn't called. She hasn't. Fear and restlessness fill my already paranoid bloodline, and I see Denny by the front door, ask him if he's seen Joy leave the party. He shakes his head, shaggy brown hair covering his red, raw eyes. He slurs when he speaks, and it's too low to hear over the thump, thump, thumping of the bass.

"What?" I shout, pointing to my ear.

He raises a hand, slow as hell, his finger pointed to the staircase.

The first two bedrooms on the second level are empty. The third has a couple on the bed, on top of the sheets, and I can't make out much, just the sounds of rhythmic ball slaps and him telling me to shut the door. He's between her legs, his boxer shorts to his knees, jeans and shoes still on. He's thrusting, and she's moaning, and he's groaning, and she's whimpering, "Please please please please."

Please please please please.

I know the words.

Know the voice.

Know the fucking six-inch heels on the end of fake diamonds and fake bows and fake, fake, fake emotions and desire, and I'm no longer high.

No longer floating.

The guy's nameless, faceless, but he's full of joy when he grunts, "I'm coming!" And Joy's full of him when she chants, "Please please please please!"

She's begging and panting, and I switch on the light. My name? It's never been screamed as loud as it is at that moment, neither from pleasure nor fear. The fuckers are separated now, hustling to find their clothes, and I feel everything at the same time as I feel nothing.

Nothing but the strangled air filling my lungs and then closing my airways.

Just like my feelings, I see the same way: everything and then nothing. Nothing but red-hot rage laced with fury and deceit. I turn swiftly, and head out of the room before I do something pathetic. Joy races after me, panting my name like she panted for a release only seconds ago. And I don't know why I'm so mad. It's not like I loved the girl, but—

But—

But *nothing*.

I'm pissed because I thought she was mine, and who the fuck knows how long this has been going on? I don't want to know, but apparently, she wants to tell me, because she's grasping my arm while I sprint down the stairs, apologies flying out of her mouth faster than I can catch them. "It just happened!" she screams, and the music stops, and my ears fill with silent judgment from everyone here.

I turn to her, watch her too-thick mascara streak down her cheeks along with her liquid regret.

She's wearing his shirt to cover her shame, but those heels... those heels are still on, and I want to say *so many things*.

Instead, I reach into my pocket, pull Mary out and bring her to my lips. From next to me, Denny sets her ablaze, and I wait for the repercussions of Joy's mistakes and my choices to hit me right in my lungs, right in my mind, where all my old memories fog the new ones.

And then I leave.

Because I should've known better.

Joy wasn't and will never be mine to have.

2

LOGAN

My strides are long, my inhales longer. The cool air outside hits my lungs, and I whisper, "Please please please please." I don't beg for release like Joy did; I beg for hope—hope that Mary will do her job. Make me forget. My truck seems so far away, too far, and I can hear footsteps behind me, and please please please please don't let the footsteps bring me Joy.

I don't want joy.

Don't need it.

"Logan!"

"Fuck off!"

"Just wait!" It takes a moment for me to register that it's not Joy. It's worse: *Aubrey*. "Are you okay?"

I stop immediately, turn on my heels. "I'm fine." I'm standing on the sidewalk, and she's nothing but a silhouette moving toward me. Stopping a few feet away, she cranes her neck, looks up at me, and I hope she doesn't mistake the redness of my smoke eyes for tears, for weakness.

Her eyelids open, close, in rapid succession, once, twice. "Are you sure you're okay? I saw… I mean, I didn't *see* it, just the end of it, and I just—" Her breaths are short huffs, and she must have run after me.

Sweet.

Stupid.

"I just wanted to make sure you were all right."

I take another drag, stare her down. She's small. I never realized how small she was. Maybe we've never stood this close to each other for this long, or maybe her offensive words heighten her physique, either way... she's *small*, like a damn mosquito that just keeps buzzing in my ear, stinging me without my knowledge, the reminder of its damage lasting days.

Minuscule.

Pesky.

I ask, "Shouldn't you be in there consoling your friend?"

"Why?" she asks incredulously. "She fucked up. She deserves to cry."

My head tilts to the side while my gaze stays on hers. She steps closer again, and I see her eyes for what seems like the first time.

Green like olives.

Freckles on her upturned nose.

"You look like a leprechaun."

"You smell like a venereal disease."

"You want to get out of here?"

"Yeah."

AUBREY SITS in my truck with her legs crossed, hidden beneath her giant skirt, inhaling loudly through her nostrils, sucking all the air out of the cab. *Suffocating.* She doesn't speak. She just sits; big eyes and ratty, red hair she refuses to do anything with. She's a version of Emma Stone from *Easy A*, back when she was cute, not *sexy*. I regret asking her to come with me, and I don't know why she agreed to it. But it's awkward, and she's awkward, and I break the silence with the only thing I can think to say, "Are you hungry?" I offer her food even though I don't want her here.

"I'm starving," she answers, and I swerve the car around, head back into town and toward the gas station.

She says, her nose scrunched, "I wouldn't trust anything they have to offer."

"You have little faith, Red."

In the store, she watches me fill two Styrofoam bowls of ramen noodles with the water from the coffee vending machine. I tell her to get anything she wants, on me.

"Anything?"

I'm trying to be chivalrous. She takes it as a dare. There's a gleam in her eye, and I nod, accept the challenge.

Bring it, Red.

I wait for her by the counter, and through the security mirror by the front door, I see her with a basket, perusing the aisles as if she has all the fucking time in the world. It takes five minutes for her to finally join me, her basket filled with Pringles and other random snacks. She's buying food and drinks and nothing else, and I roll my eyes at her. "That all you got?"

She dumps the basket on the counter and spins the rack of sunglasses next to her. Bright red, star-shaped lenses sit on the bridge of her nose when she says, "I feel like Marilyn Monroe." And then she giggles.

Breathy.

Husky.

Only *slightly* attractive.

I tell her she looks like an idiot.

She ignores my comment, turns to the guy behind the counter. "And condoms. Two twelve packs. And lube, too." She backhands my chest. "This one has a hard time getting me wet."

I shake my head, but I won't let her win. "You better give me three extra bottles of lube," I tell the guy. "You ever see the Grand Canyon, bud?"

The guy watches our exchange, bored, as if he sees this amount of stupidity every night. "Not in person."

"That's what her vagina's like: a dry, giant, gaping hole of emptiness."

"So… four bottles of lube?"

I nod. "Thanks."

"And this," she says, pulling a magazine from somewhere in her giant skirt: *Shemale Playboy.* "It's the only thing that gets him hard."

WE SIT on the bed of my truck, our legs hanging off the edge while I spread out our food between us. She's still wearing those stupid glasses, her face directed at the empty parking lot in front of us. Her legs kick back and forth when she says, "You know, with any other guy, this might be perceived as romantic."

But I'm not any other guy to her. She knows me, or at least her preconceived notion of me. She hates me. I hate her. And I remember that when I hand the bowl to her, shove a forkful of noodles in my mouth and say, "Romance is dead, Red. Lower your expectations."

"Stop calling me Red."

"Why?"

"Because it's creepy as hell that you have a pet name for me. I don't like it."

"Whatever you say, Red."

She shivers, runs her hands along her bare arms. Her nails aren't painted, but her fingers are covered with rings, all sizes, styles, and colors.

I ask, "Where's your ugly sweater?"

"I must've left it at the party."

"You want to go back and find it?"

"Nah. I'm sure it'll find its way back to me."

"That's because no one wants to claim such a horrid thing."

"Asshole," she murmurs, rubbing her arms again. She looks so small, so compact. I'd break her in half if we ever...

I blame the thought on the weed I've smoked, but maybe...

Just *maybe.*

She asks, "Is this what you plan on doing for the rest of the night?"

"Pretty much. Why? You disappointed?"

"I just thought you'd be out breaking shit."

"I'm not a violent person."

"No?"

"Nope."

And then it's quiet again, and I'm not a big fan of quiet, never was. I'm not a big fan of chatter, either, which is why I choose to spend most of my time with earphones on, music no doubt killing my eardrums. But, I don't have earphones tonight, not expecting to need them. I could leave her sitting in the back of my truck while I go into the cab, listen to music. She'll probably follow, and maybe that won't be so bad, but I don't like being in the confines of that small space with just her, no buffer between us. She's a *girl*, which means she'll want to talk about things I don't want to deal with: *feelings* and shit. So instead, I break the silence and say, "When did you move here?"

"Right after graduation. An hour after that diploma was in my hand, I was on a bus on my way here."

"Oh yeah?" I ask, unable to hide my surprise. "What are you running from?"

She removes the sunglasses and faces me. "Nothing."

"Okay, so... *where* are you running from?"

"Raleigh."

My eyebrows rise. "And you moved to this shithole of a town? You're definitely running from something," I say, shaking my head. "There's no other explanation."

"You know why I like it here?" she asks, changing the subject.

"Why?"

She points to the sky. "The stars are better here."

"Bullshit, you moved here for the stars."

"No, it's just something I've noticed."

"You spend a lot of time looking up at the stars?"

She shrugs, places her empty bowl next to her, and turns back to me. "I came here, alone, with a single suitcase and moved into a house I'd never even seen in person. I know no one here, I *am* no one here, so yeah, I spend a lot of time looking up at the stars. I didn't realize the sky was so vast. Back home, there was too much light, too much going on, the stars didn't look like they do here... so bright and *powerful*. And that's just from Main Street and my backyard. I'd love to find somewhere around here that has nothing for miles and just stand under the starlit sky and…" She stops there, her eyes widening. "I'm totally rambling."

I inhale deeply, coming back to the present. Because I'd been lost, drowning in her words, in her voice. *What the fuck?* I blow out a heavy breath, try to see the world through her eyes. Then I allow my gaze to settle on hers.

One second.

Two.

"You want to see the stars, Red?"

"Why?" she says, a slight smile breaking through. "You want to *show* me the stars?"

3

LOGAN

AUBREY WANTS to see the stars, and the pain or longing or whatever it is I heard in her voice makes me want to give her what she wants, and so I take her to a place I swore I'd never take any girl.

During the drive, she sits completely still, stoic. It isn't until we get to the property fence and I hop out to open the gate that she starts to come to. Once back in the truck, I watch her from the corner of my eye while I drive down the narrow path. She seems to be taking in everything all at once. The trees first, then the open expanse of green grass hidden beneath a sheet of dusk lighting, followed by the ripples in the lake. She sits higher when the water comes into view, her eyes widening, her lips parting just slightly.

For a moment, I want to trade places with her just so I can experience this view for the first time. "It's beautiful," she whispers, and I nod, agreeing. It's one of the few things in this world with true beauty left in it. I stop by my "shack," an old shipping container I converted to a semi-livable space containing a mattress, a fridge, a few pallets, and —since Lachlan went snooping in my room a few months ago and found my stash—a safe that holds all my weed.

"You live here?" she asks.

"Not here." I point in the general direction of my house. "The main house is over there somewhere."

"So... what? This is like, your *sex den*?"

"My *sex den*?" I repeat through a chuckle.

"Is this where you take girls to fuck? It's kind of skeazy."

"It's not a sex den." I shake my head as I step out of the car, listen to her following me. "And no. No one knows it even exists, so I'd appreciate it if you didn't tell anyone."

She marks a cross over her heart with her index finger, then walks around a little, taking in the space around us. Besides the shack, I have an old truck with no engine and a couple of four wheelers. Her already red hair seems to glow beneath the setting sun, like embers set ablaze. She gravitates toward the four-wheelers, her fingers strumming against the handle bars. "Are these yours?"

"Yeah."

"I've never been on one before."

"Big city girl."

She smiles. "Small country boy." Then she clings on to the sides of her long skirt and lifts, lifts, lifts. Black, leather combat boots, pale legs, thick thighs made for gripping.

Fuck.

She straddles the four-wheeler, her skirt bunching around her hips but still hiding her most intimate parts. "Vroom vroom," she growls, and I find myself laughing. Not at her. But *with* her. Her shoulders lift as she grins over at me. Then she bites down on her bottom lip as if to stop herself, as if that reaction directed at me was a mistake. An error. An uncontrollable emotion. Her eyes are no longer green but almost a mirror image of the setting sun.

I kick off my truck. "You want to go for a ride, Red?"

"Why? You want to take me for a ride, Lo?"

"Lo?"

"You keep calling me Red, so I'm going to call you Lo."

"Lo, huh?" I cross my arms.

She nods.

I say, "If we go for a ride, you're going to get dirty."

"I don't mind getting dirty."

Now I'm the one trying to hide my reaction. "Are you flirting with me, Red?"

"Fuck off. I find you repulsive, *Lo*."

I HAND her the only helmet I have. She asks if I'm good without one. I don't tell her that I could ride this property with my eyes closed. Instead, I help her with the helmet, clip it beneath her chin. "Hold on tight, okay?"

Nodding, she shifts back a few inches to make room for me. Her hands settle on my hips, soft, warm, *delicate*.

I repeat, over my shoulder, "I said hold on tight."

She wraps her arms around me, squeezes so hard she forces an exhale from deep in my gut.

"Not that tight. Jesus."

"Did you miss the part about me never doing this before?!"

Sighing, I pull her arms in front of me and settle her hands on my shoulders. "Like that. Don't let go."

HER SCREAMS ARE DEAFENING but not in a way that makes me want to cower and flip her off the damn thing. It's exciting, almost *satisfying*, and the laughter that follows has the same effect. Mud catches on the wheels, flicks all around us, and she lets out a squeal, her cheek pressing firmer against my back. "Do you want me to stop?" I yell.

"No way!" She grips my shoulders harder. "Go faster!"

I slow down instead, and when we come to a stop, I shift around so I can see her face. "You want to see some tricks?"

Her eyes widen as she bounces on the seat. "Why? Are you going to show me some tricks?"

I grin from ear to ear, her excitement causing my own. Then I reach up, wipe the mud off her cheek.

She flicks my hand away, her nose scrunched. "Quit flirting with me."

———————

THERE'S something to be said about showing a girl a good time. And I don't *just* mean in the back of my truck. Though there's that, too. But seriously, listening to Aubrey laugh and squeal between comments of *more, faster, harder*—it's comparable to sex. It may even be better. Or maybe I'm too fucking lit to think straight. Because when her arms are around me, gripping tight, dependent on *me* to keep her safe... It's...

An unexpected pleasure.

A high without the drug.

"Do you want to get wet?" I shout, revving the engine just a tad.

Even over the sounds of the motor, the vibrations of it beneath me, I can hear her slow giggle build to an all-out laugh. "I told you to quit flirting with me!"

"You got a filthy mind, Red." And without waiting for a response, I do a full one-eighty, and head for the lake. We don't get far in the water before she's squealing again, her small breasts pressed against my back. She's laughing, and she sounds like my little brother—back when I used to take him for rides on this thing—before he got old enough to learn how to ride himself. The sun's almost set now, and I have no idea how long we've been here.

After a while, it becomes too dark to keep riding, and so I reluctantly take us back to my truck. I kill the engine, hop off first, and then watch as she removes the helmet. There's dirt all over her shoes, her calves, her thighs. Even on the skirt that's bunched higher on her hips. Her combat boots hit the ground with a thump when she jumps off the four-wheeler, shaking her hair out. She looks like she's auditioning for a shampoo commercial or a really bad beginning to a horrible porno. "Thanks for the ride," she says, handing me back the helmet. I clutch it to my side, busy my hands, because even though she's upright, her skirt's drenched, and it hasn't moved from its position. I take in her legs again: smooth and—"Pervert!"

I chuckle, not bothering to deny it. "Your clothes are ruined."

"That's why they invented washing machines."

I reach out, finger a strand of her hair. "You got dirt caked all over you."

Her grin breaks through, and I can tell that it's real. *Genuine*. "And that, my stupid non-friend…" she starts, stepping closer, "…is why they invented *lakes*."

And then she's stripping.

Or I'm tripping.

I blink hard, wait for the high to pass in case I'm imagining it.

But nope.

Off with her shoes.

Off with her top.

Off with her skirt.

Until she's standing in front of me in her underwear. *Matching underwear*. With… I squint to get a better look. "Are those unicorns and rainbows on your—"

"Shut up! It's cute."

"If you're ten, maybe."

"But there's glitter, too!" She points to her boobs.

I squint harder. "I ain't seein' any glitter, Red."

Another step closer and I can almost touch her. But she doesn't move toward me; instead, she starts running the opposite direction. Toward the lake. And the girl might just be as crazy as I thought she was. As crazy as me. "Are you coming?" she shouts over her shoulder.

Dear God, I hope so. Not right now, obviously, but maybe tonight. And maybe inside her.

If I'm lucky.

Or unlucky.

Fuck.

Make up your damn mind, Logan!

I spark up another joint, try to clear my head, or maybe create more fog. I only take a few drags before butting it out, and then I strip out of my shirt and jeans and dump both our clothes in the bed of my truck. Then I run toward Crazy, smiling when her laughter fills my ears. She's waist deep in the water, splashing around, spinning in circles. The girl's acting as if she's five years old and having the time of her life. I've almost caught up to her when realization strikes me like a bolt of thunder. "Yo. Did you take that ecstasy?"

She stops spinning immediately, pins me with her glare. "No. I trashed it. I don't think I ever really *planned* on taking it. Why?"

"Nothing."

"*Why?*"

"You're just acting… like… like…"

"Like what, Logan? Like I'm having *fun?*"

"I guess."

"What's wrong with that?"

"Because you're with me. You *despise* me."

"No, I don't."

"You don't?"

She shakes her head, wet strands of hair falling around her shoulders. "I don't even know you." Her hands are moving again, side to side, ripples of liquid blue making their way over to me. Suddenly, she stops, her eyes wide. "What the fuck was that noise?"

AUBREY

I can't describe the sound with words, and I sure as hell won't replicate it, but it's terrifying. So terrifying that if I was still wearing my boots, I'd be shaking in them. Fuck it. I am shaking. And Logan's looking at me as if I'm hearing things. "What noise?" he says, looking down his nose at me.

"You didn't hear it?"

"Are you trippin'?"

"I haven't—" The noise sounds again, like a squealing or grunting. "Holy shit, there it is again!"

"I can't hear shit, Red."

The worst possible thoughts run through my mind. Like, I'm going to die. Or, less extreme, but just as terrifying: Logan really does have a sex den, and there's a girl in there, tied up, bound, and blindfolded.

Another squeal from somewhere behind me, and my skin crawls, and fuck it. I don't care if he has a girl in that room. Right now, I feel like he's my only hope. I rush toward him, throw my arms around his neck. "What the hell is that?"

LOGAN

"I can't hear anything," I lie. Because as much as I want to put her mind at ease, I like having her this close more. Even in the cool water, she feels so warm. I remind myself that she's just a girl. Like any girl. And there's really no need to be confused about my body's reaction to her pressed against me, her breasts to my chest, her arms around my neck, her legs around my torso, her breath against my ear, my cock against her—

"Logan!"

"What?"

"What is that?" She's shivering. Or maybe shaking from fear. I can't tell. "The sound's getting louder. Is—is something in the water?"

My hands have a mind of their own when they trail down her back, lower.

Lower.

Lower.

Until I'm cupping her ass, and *Jesus*. Where the hell has she been hiding this ass?

"Logan!"

"Huh?" I rear back so I can look at her face, but my eyes go straight to her tits, and she wasn't lying: *glitter*. There's glitter on her bra and probably her panties, and I picture removing them both with my goddamn teeth.

"It's in the water, Logan!"

"What is?"

"Whatever is making that sound! It sounds like a monster! Or an alien. Holy fuck! How can you not hear that?" She's whispering loudly, and it's part adorable, part *stupid*.

"I hear it," I whisper back. "It sounds like… like… a pig squealing or something."

"Yes!"

I could play this game forever: faking that I have no idea what she's talking about just so she keeps holding on to me the way she is. Faking that I'm not at all attracted to her. "Logan." She says my name the same way she held on to me on the four-wheeler; as if she's relying on me. As if I'm going to be the one to save her.

I hate the feeling.

About as much as I want to inhale it into my bloodline.

"You're okay," I whisper and shift so I can move the hair away from her face. It means moving a hand away from her ass, but... like my old man says: sometimes in life, you have to make sacrifices. Not that seeing her face clearer is a sacrifice. *At all.*

You've gone soft, Logan Preston.

Actually, I've gone hard.

And now I'm having internal dialogue, and she yells, "Why are you not freaking out right now? We could die! This is some fucked-up *Lost* kind of shit, and you're there all calm and... do you have a *boner*?"

"Shut up!"

"Logan!"

"What?!" I grab her ass again, nuzzle her neck.

"Quit it!"

I sniff her hair. "Why do you smell like this?"

"Like what?"

"Like... summer?"

Aubrey tugs on my hair. Hard. So hard I yelp.

The pig-grunting sounds again.

I watch her eyes as they take in mine, left to right, left to right.

She sighs. "How stoned are you right now?"

"I don't know," I answer honestly. "A lot?"

Pig grunts.

Ass grabs.

Head spins.

"Logan!"

Mind blurs.

Ass squeeze.

Summer sniffing.

"Logan!!!"

"Jesus! What?!"

"What. Is. That. Fucking. Sound?!"

"Relax, would you?"

"How am I supposed to relax?" She climbs down my body, and I instantly miss her warmth.

I cup water in my hands, splash my face, try to stay somewhat clear-headed. "It's just Chicken."

"What the hell is a chicken?"

"It's our pet pig."

"Your pet *what*?"

Rolling my eyes, I coo, "Here, Chicken Chicken." A moment later, Chicken sidles up next to me, rubs his snout on my hand. "He must've heard us out here and wanted to see what's up." I pat his head. "He won't hurt you."

Aubrey stays silent for so long, I have to tear my gaze away from the pig and look over at her to make sure she's still there, that she wasn't just a figment of my Mary-induced mind.

"Can I get high from second-hand smoke?" she asks slowly.

"Yes. Why?"

"Because right now, I'm seeing a giant pig named Chicken swimming in a goddamn lake, and you're petting it as if it's a dog."

I chuckle under my breath. "I got him as Mayhem."

"Mayhem?"

"A prank. He was for my brother Leo when he went off to college. I had him sent to his dorm. It was supposed to be one of those toy pigs, you know? The tiny ones? I guess I ordered the wrong one. Anyway, Leo kinda got attached to the little guy, and he and his roommate hid him for as long as they could. Then they realized he wasn't going to stop growing, and he brought him here. We let him wander the property. He comes and goes as he pleases."

Aubrey laughs, low and slow from deep in her throat. "He's a beast, Lo."

"Yeah, but he's had Leo as his parent for a while, so he's a giant softy like my brother." I let Chicken rub his snout on my hand again. "Aren't you, buddy?"

The water shifts as Aubrey comes closer. "So he's real? I'm not imagining it?"

I o*ink*.

Chicken *oinks* back.

I ask, "That's the sound you heard, right?"

Aubrey nods. "Can I—can I pet him?"

My smile is stupid. "Sure."

AUBREY

I hesitate a beat, two, and then I'm moving toward them, both my hands out. I cup Chicken's face, and the pig grunts in satisfaction. "This is the craziest night ever," I say. I'm giggling. Smiling. More than I have in what feels like forever.

"You're telling me," he responds.

I swallow my nerves, my pride. "I mean it, Logan." I lift my gaze to his. "I never thought I'd have this much fun with you." I'm lying. The truth is, I *did* know. And I knew because in the past, when we've been together, it'd been so hard holding back every smile, every little giggle at his sarcasm, every high-five at his comments that had Joy gasping, wondering where the hell his filter was. Filters are for people who live their lives trying to impress other people. Yeah, there are manners, politeness, common decency. But Logan has all those things. He just doesn't have a problem saying what's on his mind.

Logan lowers his gaze, focuses on Chicken. "Feeling's mutual, Red."

"So..." My smile widens when Chicken rubs his cheek against my hand. "Should we call a truce, you and me?"

He licks his lips, takes way too long to answer. "Sounds good."

I clear my throat, look at the amazing scenery around us. "So... tell me again why you don't bring girls here?"

"Because there's nothing here."

"I don't know about that," I tell him honestly. "There's you, and there are four-wheelers and dirt and a lake and... and a *pig.*"

We're both patting Chicken now, using him as a distraction, so we don't have to look at each other. An eternity passes, filled with silence, and I shouldn't have said anything because now everything feels too real. Too raw. Too naked. But then he says, "The girls who are into guys like me are in it for one of two reasons."

I glance up at him. "Sex and money?"

"Ding, ding."

"And you offer them both?" I ask.

"I offer them one."

"Sex?"

"Winner, winner." The tone in his response is as real and as raw and as naked as I'd felt only seconds before he'd spoken, and I wonder... *what's beneath the bravado, Logan Preston?*

"Sucks for them," I say, our eyes meeting. "I have a feeling you have a lot more to offer, Logan."

He keeps his stare locked on mine, almost challenging. He's probably expecting me to be embarrassed, to take back my words, but just like him, I say what's on my mind. The truth. I lift my chin, unabashed, dare him to crack first.

He doesn't. Instead, he goes one step further, moves one step nearer, until we're so close I can hear every one of his exhales. "Hey, Red?"

"Yeah, Lo?"

"Look up."

I tear my eyes away from him, and then slowly, I tilt my head back, look up at the night sky above us, to the stars lighting the atmosphere. "Wow," I whisper.

"Yeah," he agrees, but when I lower my gaze to his, he's looking at *me*...

Like he's never looked at me before.

4

LOGAN

Aubrey waits out by my truck while I head into the shack to grab some towels. We dry off as much as possible and assume the summer night will do the rest. She runs her hands up and down her arms, and I grab a blanket from my toolbox, and haphazardly place it on her shoulders as we sit in the bed of the truck. She asks, "Will this blanket make me pregnant?"

"The odds are fifty-fifty."

She laughs at that, and I watch her, entranced, like those movies they show you in driver's ed: slow motion of a car crash, right at the point of impact.

She's an accident playing out just for me.

My own personal disaster.

She taps my leg with her foot. "Thanks for the blanket."

"You're welcome."

We're both still in our underwear, but neither of us seems to care.

She ends up on her back, staring up at the sky. But... there's a reason why I've never stargazed before. It's boring as shit, and I've got way too much energy and *confusion*, and silence sure as shit doesn't help with either of those things. She must sense this somehow, because she asks, "Are you bored?"

"A little." It sounds like an apology. "You mind if I put on some music?"

"Please don't," she groans.

"Why?"

She's laughing again, all to herself, like there's an inside joke I'm not privy to.

"Why are you laughing?" I hover over her, narrow my eyes in an attempt to intimidate.

"Your taste in music blows, Lo."

"It does not!" I say, defensively. "How would you even know?"

"Because I've heard what plays in your car."

"And?"

She settles her laughter to a simmering giggle before saying, "I swear there was a song you played and the lyrics were *my balls, my balls, put it in your booty hole.*"

I try to keep a straight face. "What's wrong with that?"

"So many things!"

I grab my phone, play the song through the Bluetooth speakers I keep in my toolbox, and sing the lyrics obnoxiously loud while Aubrey switches from eye rolls to giggles.

"This is *not* music," she admonishes.

"What do you consider music then?"

She grabs my phone out of my hands, and I watch her thumbs move swiftly over the screen. She chooses a song I know. A song I like. I don't tell her that. Otis Redding croons, his voice soothing, his words making me want to take Aubrey a mile or so down to the dock so we can live through the lyrics.

She lies back down, my phone clutched to her chest. Her eyes are closed, no longer fascinated with the stars, while her foot tap, tap, taps at the metal beneath it. She whistles in tune, in sync, and I ask, "So you like the classics, huh?"

Her head lolls to the side, her eyes opening on mine. "Do you know this song?"

I nod. "My favorite of his is 'These Arms of Mine.'"

"Oh, my God! I love that one," she rushes out, handing me my phone. "Play it for me."

I find the song, hit play. Her eyes close again, and she says, "There's something so innocent about this kind of music. Before fast beats and auto tune and abusive lyrics... it's literally a love letter from one person to another. Listen..." She pauses, lets Otis's words fill the stillness. "His arms can't live without her. His *arms*, Logan. God, what I'd give..." she trails off.

"What you'd give for what? For a guy to feel that for you?"

"Is that so wrong?"

I shrug. "I mean, it's unrealistic to expect that kind of shit now, Red. The days of giving your girl a letterman jacket, asking her to"—I air quote—"'go steady' are over."

"So, romance really is dead, huh?"

"I hate to be the bearer of bad news, but yeah, it is."

She's quiet a beat, and when I look over at her, she's staring down at her hands resting on her stomach. I say, "Sorry." Because I feel like I just ran over her dog, ruined every one of her hopes and dreams.

"For being honest?"

"I guess."

"You don't need to be sorry."

And then it's silent again, and I don't know how to act or what to say, and so I reach into my pocket for another blunt, spark it without a second thought. She sits up then, my vision of her blurred by the ribbon of smoke between us. She asks, "Feel like sharing?"

My eyes widen—as much as they can when I'm this high. I shouldn't be an enabler, but she's her own person, and so I pass it to her, watch her take it between her thumb and forefinger. Stub to her lips, she keeps her eyes on mine, her lips forming a pout when she inhales and then—

Then she coughs out her lungs, and I'm patting her back, reaching for a bottle of water we got from the gas station. The joint's still in her hand, and her eyes are red, filling with tears, and *I suck*. I should've warned her. I unscrew the lid and hand her the water. "Drink. It'll help." She's coughing and coughing and she doesn't stop, her hands like vices as she grips my arms, hanging on for her next clear breath. After a moment, she takes the bottle from my hand, and like a little red-headed rag doll, she tilts her head back, chugs half the liquid. She's still gasping for air, and fuck me, she's *cute*.

I move the hair away from her face, strands stuck to the tears on her cheeks. She's on her knees, and I'm doing the same, both my hands holding her face. Each of her exhales hits my chin, warm and welcoming, and I ask, "Are you okay?"

"Yeah," she breathes out. "I wasn't expecting it to hit so harshly."

"I don't mix it with anything; it makes the high come faster. Sorry."

She shakes her head out of my hands and sits back, her ass on her heels.

She offers me the joint, and I take it from her fingers. "Are you done? You don't want to try again?"

"I don't know…" Her hands are on her knees, fingers spread.

A slight smile tugs on my lips. "Do you trust me?"

"Not even the slightest."

My grin widens. "Come here."

"What?" Her eyes narrow. "No."

I reach around her, place my hand on the back of her head. She shifts quickly, moves away from my touch and slaps my chest. "Jesus, Logan, I'm not going to blow you!"

"You're an idiot. Just come closer."

She hesitates, the moment stretching longer than I'm comfortable with. Finally, she rises to her knees, shuffles closer until her legs touch mine. When she sits back down, I take the joint between my lips, pull hard on the end, and hold it deep in my lungs. One second, two, then I lean forward, rest my forehead to hers, and say through my soft, burning exhale, "Suck in slowly."

She nods, her lips forming a perfect O. The sound isn't there, but the rising of her chest is, and I pull back, watch her breathe in a ribbon of Mary: the source of my hazy escape.

When she releases a breath, smoke filters from her lips and floats high, high, high through the air, the wind taking it away. Her eyes are closed, and she whispers, "Again." And through my own high, I do as she says, this time moving closer. Her hands are on my legs, the weight of her tiny frame pressing down on me, and without preempt, without thought, I touch my lips to hers. She makes a sound,

as if she's choking, as if she's surprised by the touch, and believe me
—no one is as surprised as me. Because there's something strange
about our connection, about the softness mixed with strength. And
it's more than just her hands, her lips, her breaths—all of them on
me. I have pins and needles again, only this time, they're not in my
head, or my heart; they're lower, in my gut. My stomach twists, and
I pull back, take another hit. I don't share this one with her. I need it
all for myself. Because my mind's starting to go places I can't
control.

My eyes drift shut when I feel the effects of Mary fill my blood, and
I roll my head back, let it hit the rear window of the cab. Her hands are
still on my legs, and the touch is warm, too warm, and too damn
powerful, and I feel it everywhere. *Everywhere.* The stirring below feels
magnified, and I reach out, find her wrist, tug, and murmur, "Come
closer, Red."

"Mmm."

My eyes open slowly, one first, then the other. Aubrey's watching
me, her head tilted to the side, blink, blink, blinking. "What?" I ask.

"Are you too high to know what you're doing?"

I shake my head, lick the dryness off my lips, and tug on her wrist
again. "I *always* know what I'm doing." The girl doesn't budge, and I
meet her resistance with a smirk. "So stubborn," I murmur.

"So cocky," she slurs. "You got one more for me?"

"Are you sure *you* know what you're doing?"

"I *always* know what I'm doing," she retorts.

I smile around another pull of the joint, feeling the heat of the butt
between my fingers, then I push off the rear of the cab, move closer to
her while holding my breath. I release slowly, just a tad, before closing
my airways. The girl sucks in a breath, but there's not much to inhale,
and she pouts, sounds off a quiet, little whine. I do it again. And again.
And she's getting annoyed, frustrated, and with every one of her
whines, I'm getting more turned on. I blow a ring of smoke between
us, close off my airways again. "How badly do you want it?" I manage
to get out. I don't know when I went from insults to whatever the hell
this is, and right now, I don't care.

The girl takes the bait, *challenge accepted,* and climbs onto my lap.

Her hands are on my shoulders and her mouth is *barely* touching mine, and she whispers, "Logan..." And then...

Then she licks the seam of my lips, and that's when I lose it. The dizziness caused by my held breath makes me part my mouth, exhale into hers, and I don't know if she takes the smoke in because I'm too busy *kissing her*.

Slow and soft, every touch, every connection is intensified by the high, and my hands are on her waist, and Aubrey Whatshername has unbelievable curves. And just like that, a second, maybe two... she's gone... off my lap and too far away that I can't bring her back. "I'm sorry," she says. "I shouldn't have done that."

"We both...*why*? What the hell just happened?"

She's yanking at the blanket, trying to cover herself, as if it's the first time she's realized that we're *both* almost naked. "Do you think you could drive me home?" She's refusing to look at me, but I watch her, confused, trying to figure out when the hell it all went wrong.

"Not right now," I tell her honestly. "I'm too lit. Wait a little for the buzz to fade, and I'll take you wherever you want."

She nods, starts reaching for her clothes.

"Red?"

"What?"

"You've been in your underwear for ages. I've seen everything—"

"But it's different now."

I shake my head again. "Trust me, it's not."

"Of course, it's not," she whispers, and I don't understand what the fuck she means. I hoover the rest of the joint and flick it out onto the grass. Knees bent, hands at my sides, I lean back against the cab, eyes barely open, and get lost in the weightless euphoria. Minutes tick by, one after the other. I don't break the silence. I don't know how to. She's leaning against the side of the bed, her legs out, blanket completely covering her. Eventually, she says, her voice low, distant, barely audible, "Earlier, you asked me what I was running from..."

"Yeah...?" I close my eyes because I don't think I could stand to look at her.

Rejection is a bitch.

Denial is worse.

"I wasn't lying when I said *nothing*. I literally had nothing there. My dad passed away when I was nine." My eyes open then, as if on their own, and I make sure to focus them on hers while my heart beats wildly beneath my chest, building pressure on my ribs, and I don't know what more she has to say; I just know that I want to hear it. "He was in a car accident. He crashed head first into a tree. Died on impact."

"I'm sorry," I tell her, my voice breaking.

She shakes her head. "He was drunk. It was pure luck there was no one else on the roads."

"Did you guys get along?"

Her eyes are red when they meet mine, and I regret giving her the weed because now I don't know if she's opening up because she's high or because she wants to. She clears her throat, looks down at her hands, and continues to speak as if she hadn't heard me at all. "After he died, everything changed. His mistakes became mine, and my mom —she left her job, moved us to Raleigh, pulled me out of public school, and homeschooled me. We spent so much time together that I think—I think that's part of the reason we couldn't see eye-to-eye on a lot of things. So when it came time for high school, I *begged* her to let me go, and she caved. But high school… high school was horrible. For the first year, I was a complete outcast. It was like everyone knew about my dad, and people couldn't see past what he did—or at least that's what I assumed. But, maybe I was just weird, you know? Like there was something about me that just couldn't fit in with everyone else." Her voice is distant, as if the memory had been cast away, put aside.

I should tell her I know what that feels like.

She adds, "And then sophomore year, Carter showed up at my school, and he didn't seem to know anything about me. He was only there a few weeks before we started dating. He was my heart, my world, my everything, because I *had* nothing. I had no friends, no hobbies, no extracurricular activities. And maybe that's why I fell so hard for him…"

"Did he…" I clear my throat. "I mean, did he die or something? Is he okay?"

Aubrey smiles, but it's sad. "He broke up with me a month before graduation. He said that I was too needy, too clingy, that I loved him *too* much, that he didn't feel the same way I did, that he *never* did..." Aubrey shrugs, and that one simple movement is as painful as this Carter guy is pathetic. "That weekend, he went to a party and slept with someone else. He broke my heart..." She sniffs once. "He broke *me*, Logan. And that same night, I went online, found this town, found a house, sent through applications and used every cent of my grand-mother's inheritance to start this new life where I was back at the beginning. Alone and afraid. And at the start, every day was like that first year of high school all over again." Her chin rises, her gaze pene-trating mine. "And then Joy walked into my work, and within minutes, she asked if I wanted to be her friend. No pretenses, not a single clue about me. She was just willing to be that one person for me, and now... God, I left that stupid party with *you*. And I just kissed you. What the fuck kind of person does that?"

"Aubrey..." I start slowly, carefully. "What happened between Joy and me has nothing to do with you. What she did... I mean, it's over, so..."

"You say that now," she whispers.

"And I'll say it forever. There's no going back. And it sucks—what all you've been through to get here, to now, but honestly, it's just bad fucking luck that it was Joy who walked into your work that day. You deserve better friends. You sure as hell deserve a better ex. And that means a lot coming from me considering that before you followed me out of that party, I'm pretty sure I fucking hated you."

She laughs once: the sound of heartbreak, relief, and something else I can't put my finger on. "So... the whole kiss thing, can we *please* never bring it up again?"

"If that's what you really want."

She's quiet a moment. Then: "What do *you* want, Logan?"

"Trust me. What I *want* and what I think should happen are two *completely* different things."

"So... what do you *think* should happen?"

"I think we should get dressed, and I take you home, walk you to your door and leave you for the night."

She nods, swallows. "And... what do you *want* to happen?"

"I *want*… I want to know what your body feels like beneath mine. I want to know what it feels like to be deep inside you, and I want to hear what sounds fall from your lips when I make you come."

Her breath catches, and the blanket shifts as her legs do the same. "I think…" She exhales loudly. "I think I should get dressed, and you should take me home and walk me to my door."

5

LOGAN

I DON'T REALIZE how late it's gotten until we're sitting in my truck in her driveway. The clock on the dash reads 2:18., and neither of us has made a move to get out. Maybe she feels the same way I do… that the night feels unfinished. The problem? I don't think either of us knows how we want to end it.

"I have a question," she says finally.

"I don't know if I have the answers, Red."

"Did you… I mean, when you kissed me… were you thinking about Joy?"

"Fuck no." When I turn to her, she's shaking her head.

"I don't mean kissing Joy instead of me, but… was it, like, revenge?"

"Double *fuck no*. Honestly? I haven't thought about Joy once since we got to my place and you rode on the back of the four-wheeler."

Her smile is slow, real. As real as she is.

"Was it *revenge* for you? To get back at your ex or something?"

"No," she says with a giggle. "I've already had my revenge."

"You slept with some—"

"No," she cuts in. "I went to his house in the middle of the night and keyed his car."

I scoff. "Amateur."

"No!" She giggles harder, louder. "I didn't key it for keying's sake. I actually wrote something."

"Yeah? What'd you write?"

"Pathetic Dick."

I bust out a laugh, let it fill the space between us. "You must've been there for hours."

Her laughter joins mine. "No shit. The Cs were the hardest... getting that curve right was tough." I shake my head, grip the steering wheel to stop myself from reaching out, gripping her hair and pulling her mouth to mine. "I have another question," she says, and I lean back against the door, get comfortable.

"Sure, but after this one, I get to ask you some things."

"Do you..." She bites down on her lip, her cheeks blooming the same shade as her hair.

"Do I what, Red?" *Please, please, please ask me to come in.*

"Do you um... do you talk dirty... like you did before, during umm... when you..."

"When I'm sexing?"

"Yeah," she says, refusing to meet my eyes.

I shrug. "Sometimes."

She nods. "My boyfriend—"

"Ex," I interrupt.

The corner of her lip tilts, but she doesn't give in all the way. "Right. *Ex.* One time, he asked me to do that... to spice things up, I guess. And um..."

"Oh no..." I chuckle. "What did you say?"

"I don't..." She's giggling again. "I don't want to say it."

"Say it, Red!"

"I said..." We're both laughing, the silent, unconfined type that makes you lose your breath, hold your stomach. "I said..."

"Red! You're killing me!"

"I said..." And with her teeth clenched, she grunts, "I'm going to fuck your dick off!"

I laugh so hard, the loudness scares even me. I'm slapping at the dash, trying to catch my breath, while she sits up on her knees, grasping my arm, trying to get me to quit laughing at her. But she's cackling, too, the same way I am, and my cheeks hurt, my eyes are watering, and goddamn, this girl is something else.

"Quit laughing at me!"

"I can't," I wheeze.

"I mean it, Lo."

"So do I!"

And then, maybe to get me to shut up or maybe because she wants to, she kisses me. Rough and hard at first, then it switches… slow, soft, *purposeful*. Her hands are in my hair, and my hand's on her waist, the other on her jaw, and she's so imperfectly wild but perfect for *now*.

"Red," I say against her lips, "I have two questions."

"Mmm," she responds. Kisses me again.

I tug on a strand of her hair. "What shade of red is this?"

"Scarlet. Next question?"

Without moving, I mumble, "What do *you* want to happen next?"

Her smile widens against mine, and I *think* I have the answer. Her lips move across my jaw and toward my ear. She whispers, the warmth of her breath causing a shiver up my spine, "I want to fuck your dick off."

AUBREY

I wonder if I should tell him that I saw him first.

The very first night he hooked up with Joy, *I saw him first*.

We were at a party.

I pointed him out to her.

He caught us watching him.

And he saw *her* first.

PART 2

6

AUBREY

In sneakers and running shorts and a cap pulled low on his brow, the kid's a pint-sized thief dressed for business. He's wringing his hands, standing on the other side of the counter. He seems innocent enough, and for a second, I almost let him go. But these punks have to realize that shoplifting might be a thrill for them, a *joke*, but this shop is mine; the profit is my livelihood, and the product they take comes out of my back pocket. I'd caught the kid trying to leave the store with a small notebook in his pocket. Twelve dollars. Not a lot in the big scheme of things, but it's also my dinner. So…

Sorry, kid.

"Cops or parents, dude."

"You can call the cops," he says, squaring his shoulders. "Just ask for Misty, please."

"Misty?"

"Yes, ma'am."

I stop writing down *Misty* and look up at him. "I'm not a ma'am."

"Sorry, miss."

Pencil to paper again, I ask, "What's your name?"

"Logan."

My pencil snaps in half, my surprise unmistakable, and I fake innocence, grab a pen instead. Pens are safer, sturdier. More resilient to my emotions.

"Logan…" I trail off, unable to finish my train of thought. It's been three weeks since that one night with Logan Preston, and I can't even get his name out without losing my breath. "Last name?"

"Preston."

I drop the pen, rub my hands across my face, and make a sound that could only be classified as a grunt. The kid's full of shit. I know it. He knows it. "What's your *real* name?"

The boy sighs, his shoulders slumping in defeat. "Lachlan Preston."

Of course. I really should have put two and two together considering the evidence and the uncanny resemblance, but the second he said *Logan*, my mind fled, head-dived right into a sea of memories. I take my cell phone from my back pocket, find Logan's number from when Joy entered it "in case I couldn't get a hold of her," and use the store phone so my number doesn't show up on his. Logan answers on the third ring, and I forget who I am and what I'm doing. I also forget to breathe. "Hello?" He pauses a beat. "Who is this?"

I anticipate the next few words to be random girls' names:

Tricia the Teacher.

Bella with the Boobies.

Maybe Lesbian Girl.

All names from the text messages he'd gotten that night. I know, because he let me read every single one.

"Hello?" he says again.

"Hey, um… it's uh…"

"Aubrey?"

"Yeah," I say through a sigh.

Silence passes a moment. A really looong moment. "I was wondering if you'd ever call."

He was wondering if I'd call?

"How are you?"

I clear my throat, my thoughts, my memories of his hands and his teeth and his mouth and his tongue and—

"Aubrey? Are you there?"

"Yeah. Sorry." I dig the tip of my pen into the notepad so hard it tears the paper. "Listen, I'm calling from work—Penultimate on Main Street—and I think I have your little brother here."

Lachlan stands taller again, his palms on the glass counter. "Who did you call? Which one?! Please not Lucas or Leo. *Please*?" The kid's in panic mode, his face red. I show him my phone—Logan's name on the screen—and he flops back on his heels. "Oh, thank God."

Through the phone, Logan says, "Which brother? Is it just the one? That means Lachlan. Shit. What did that little punk do now?"

WHEN THE BELL above the door chimes, I try not to look up, swear it I do, but Logan's presence in any room is as tall as his frame, as big as his ego.

He's wearing his work clothes: boots, khaki pants, gray tee beneath an open *Preston, Gordon and Sons* shirt. But what catches my attention the most is the ball cap: his trademark.

He looks *good*.

Better than good.

And I internally slap myself for thinking it.

The gold chain around his neck reflects off the store lights, and I push away the memories of the cold metal gliding up my thighs, of how the flattened penny pendant left a cold trail across my chest when he was on top of me, his hips between my legs. Logan's eyes dart around the store, pausing on me for just a moment, before going to the armchair next to the counter. Lachlan gets to his feet, runs toward his big brother. "Please don't tell Dad!"

Logan's gaze catches mine as he squats down so he's eye-to-eye with his brother. I focus on the receipts on the glass countertop, pretend to be working. "Shoplifting?" I hear, but don't *see* Logan say. "What the hell were you thinking?"

"I was just out for a run and I saw this store and I wanted to get something nice for my girl."

"No girl's worth shoplifting for, bud." Logan's voice is louder now, clearer, and I glance up through my lashes, catch them walking toward me. I quickly drop my gaze, concentrate harder on my fake task.

"Thanks for calling." Logan's hand rests on the counter: large, calloused, *rough*.

I swallow nervously, ignore the rapid thumping beneath my chest, and flip through the receipts so I have something to do with my hands. "It's no problem."

After a long stretch of silence, Logan clears his throat, says, "You know, it's really bad service to not make eye contact with your customers."

I lift my gaze, ready my glare, only to be met with the smirk I love to hate. Why I've had the slightest tingling of anything that resembles longing for him, I have no idea. Logan Preston is cocky, obnoxious, *rude*.

"You look like a garden gnome."

Self-righteous ass.

I look down at my clothes: high-waisted and ripped boyfriend jeans, pink half shirt, floral blazer. I look cute. Fuck him.

"That's mean, Logan," says Lachlan.

"It's not mean," Logan says, rubbing his kid brother's shoulder. "It's *flirting*. Right, Red?" He winks.

Puke.

Winking is for douchebags and assholes with small dicks, and Logan is... well, he's one of those things. I shake my head, grab the notebook that caused all this from under the counter and drop it between us. "Your boy tried to take this. You want to buy it or not?"

Logan shoves his hand in his pocket, the other removing his cap. He runs his hand through his hair, messes it up, and replaces his hat again. Then he shrugs. "I guess." He picks up the offending notebook, looks at the price tag. "Twelve dollars?" he says, looking down at his brother. "You get more than this for your weekly allowance. You couldn't afford to buy it?"

"I didn't have any money on me."

Logan takes his wallet from his back pocket. "This girl better be worth it."

Lachlan grins for the first time since I've seen him, showcasing the gap in his two front teeth. I wonder if Logan ever had that. I wonder if he had to wear braces. I wonder if—

Shut up, Aubrey. Quit wondering about stupid shit.

Lachlan breaks through my thoughts, my trance, by bouncing on his feet, his excitement evident. "You have no idea, bro."

I crack a smile.

Logan dumps his wallet on the counter but doesn't make a move to open it. "Oh yeah?" he asks his brother. "What's her name?"

"Scarlett."

Logan's eyebrows lift, just a tad. "You know scarlet's a shade of *red*, right?"

Lachlan nods.

My heart skips a beat.

Two.

Stupid double-crossing heart.

"She got red hair?" the older Preston asks.

"Nah. Brown."

"Damn shame." Without looking at me, Logan opens his wallet, dumps a twenty on the counter and grabs the notebook. "Redheads are fire." He starts to maneuver his brother toward the door. "Keep the change, Red," he says to me. To his brother: "Say thank you, Lachy."

Lachlan glances over his shoulder. "Thanks, Miss Red!"

7

LOGAN

HERE'S A TRUTH ABOUT ME: I have no friends.

I know, I know. Poor Logan Preston. But when you drop out of high school and start working full-time and the only things you have in common with your school friends are other school friends and all those friends have stories about shit that goes on in a school you no longer attend, those friends start to die off pretty quick. Also, I don't know if they were ever truly friends. Pretty sure they hated me; I'm not even mad about it. And, sure, I have the people on Dad's crew. Thirty-to fifty-something-year-olds who like to complain about their lives, their wives and kids, but they're not *friends*.

And then there's my family: Luce and Luke have Cam and Lane, and the twins have each other. Leo—he was probably the closest thing I've ever had to a best friend (regardless of the fist fights growing up), and when he started focusing on school over *everything* else, I knew it would end. Then he went to college. And I was left with a nine-year-old punk. A punk currently sitting in the passenger's seat of my truck, his stare burning a hole in the side of my head. "What are you looking at, dude?"

"Your car smells like your bedroom."

No arguments there.

"Hey, you know that girl at the store?"

I shrug. "Kinda."

"You sex her?"

I turn into our driveway while wondering how much honesty the kid can handle.

"Kinda."

"You sex a lot of girls."

"Kinda."

"I'm going to sex one girl and one girl only for my whole entire life."

I shake my head, let the chuckle fall from my lips. "Wait till you're my age; you'll change your tune."

"Nah uh."

"Yah huh."

"You don't think I can do it?" he challenges.

"Nope," I say honestly, fingers tapping on the steering wheel.

"Why not?" He raises his chin. "Cam and Lucy have only ever sexed each other."

"That's different."

"Why?"

After a sigh, I tell him, "Because Cam's a Gordon, not a Preston." I throw him a smirk. "Preston men are studs."

"Leo doesn't sex a lot of girls."

"Leo's different, too."

"How?"

How? How the hell did I get myself into this conversation? "Because... because he's more of a Harvey than he is a Preston."

"What's a Harvey?"

I park just outside the house and turn to him. "Mom's maiden name."

"So... you're saying he's more like a girl?" he asks.

"No. I'm saying he's more like Mom. His heart," I say, tapping at my chest, "it overpowers all other organs."

"What other organs?"

And that's where I stop. "Hey look, we're home. Get out."

"Are you going to sex her again?"

I shrug, stare out the windshield. "I don't know."

"Why not?"

"You ask a lot of questions, Lachy."

"Why won't you answer?"

"Because I don't know."

"Why not?"

"Because..."

"Isn't that what you do with most girls?"

"Lachy..." I sigh.

"What?"

I turn to him, lock my gaze on his.

He rolls his eyes. "I'm *nine*, Logan. Not a baby. You can tell me the truth."

The truth? I'd thought about Aubrey beyond that one night. Days beyond it. Maybe even weeks. Aubrey—she was different. *Easy.* And not in the way that draws me to most girls.

So the truth about Aubrey?

"She's not most girls."

8

AUBREY

IN THE FEW months since I've moved here, I've worked out three things:

1. Everyone knows everyone.
2. Baseball is bigger than big.
3. Friday night is *the* night.

I have no idea what happens on Saturday nights, but the town is dead. Mom says I probably moved to a church town and I just don't know it. Either way, every party I've ever been invited to happens on Friday nights. And while the town may be different than home, the parties are the same. The people are the same. The classic jocks with the classic soon-to-be-too-drunk girls, the smaller groups of misfits just happy to be here, and the stoners who keep to themselves, smoke weed openly as if they're smoking cigarettes. And every party, every circle, has that *One Guy*. You know, the one who shows up on their own and finds a way to blend in. Invisibility clings to him like a second skin, and in the next breath, he's the center of everyone's universe. In this town, everyone knows who that One Guy is, and he just walked into the house as if he owns it.

Logan Preston flops down on the couch, right in the middle of the living room, his cap pulled low on his brow, hiding his eyes. A second later, there's a joint between his lips, and he doesn't look up when he sparks it, doesn't even look up when a girl approaches him, whispers something in his ear. He smiles, or smirks more like it, and I lean back against the wall, hope I can blend in as well as he does.

I reach into my pocket, pull out my phone. If he notices me, I sure as hell don't want him to catch me *watching* him. The second I unlock my screen, a text appears:

You think she'll want to fuck my dick off?

A smile breaks through—unwanted—and I glance up at him just long enough to see that smirk directed right at me. The girl's in front of him now, shaking her ass right at his eye level, but he doesn't notice, or maybe he chooses to ignore it. I type out a reply:

That's a given. The real question is: will she let you put it in her booty hole?

I look up so I can watch his reaction before I hit send. Mid drag, his phone lights up his face, his eyes squinting to read my text. Then he chokes out a laugh, white puffs of smoke emitting from his open mouth.

He sits up straighter, still ignoring the beautiful girl in front of him.

What do you think my odds are?

I reply:

I don't know. Why don't you ask her?

I raise my eyebrows in challenge when his eyes meet mine.

Without hesitation, he taps the girl on the shoulder, talks into her ear. She slaps him across the cheek and storms off, all while Logan keeps that same smirk on his face. He writes:

I think that's a hard no.

I reply:

The night's still young.

He reads the text but doesn't respond. He simply watches me from across the room, his eyes moving from my boot-covered feet, slowly trailing up the rest of me. And that's my cue to leave, move as far away from him as possible. I find my way to the keg, fill a Solo cup.

Down it.

Three times.

Because I know how easy it is to fall, and not the good kind of falling.

The kind of falling that's unexpected.

Like a trap in the middle of the woods.

Logan Preston is a trap.

Three weeks ago, I was lost in those woods.

9

LOGAN

AUBREY'S DRUNK. Or, at the very least, extremely fucking tipsy. I watched her down three beers at the keg before filling up her fourth and exiting the house. She's here on her own, or maybe with a friend, but she's not here on a date—or, if she is, he's nowhere to be seen. Now, she's out in the yard, dancing on her own.

There isn't even any music.

She's wearing cowboy boots and denim cut-offs and a loose tank with the armholes cut low, and I can see her bra. Everyone can see her bra. But I haven't been close enough to work out what's on it. If I had to put money on it, I'd say they were donuts or maybe rainbows. I know she owns pairs with both those things on them because that night with her, when we were both high on weed (and maybe each other), she paraded around in them. For me. My own private fashion show.

Fuck, she was cute.

She's *still* cute.

I take another hit of Mary and lean against the brick wall of the house while I watch her lift her cup, sway her hips, move her head from side to side with the music only she can hear. I smile; at her, and at me for being a creep and watching her from a distance. I'm still smiling fifteen minutes later when she's *still* doing the exact same thing. But that smile fades instantly when a guy approaches her from behind, puts his hands on her waist. Before I get a chance to think straight, I'm making my way to them, my jaw clenched. "A little close, no?" I grind out. I don't know why I'm pissed, and maybe a little jealous, but I've had my hands where his are, and I don't like it.

"Sorry, man," the guy says, and I recognize him from school, but I don't know his name. "Is she yours?"

"She sure as fuck isn't *yours*."

His hands leave her to go up in surrender, his apology quick to come. I wait for him to be out of earshot before taking a step toward Aubrey. "You look like Miley Cyrus. The "Wrecking Ball" hammer-licking Miley, not at all like the cute "Party in the USA" one."

Her eyes narrow to a glare, her gaze moving to somewhere behind me. She shouts, her words slurred, "Yo, Guy! I can be yours for the night if—"

I cover her mouth, her lips wet against my palm. "You're wasted."

She mumbles something beneath my touch, and I release her slowly, my hands going to her hips, pulling her closer. And swear to God, three weeks have never felt so long. She's exactly how I remember her. Every dip, every curve. Every expanse of space between us. I close the gap, hold her to me.

Her arms lift, her fingers linking behind my neck, those olive green eyes blinking up at me. "You didn't call me."

"I didn't have your number."

"You *just* texted me."

"I stole a business card from your work."

"Oh."

I sniff her hair, listen to her giggle. "You smell different."

"And you *still* smell like a venereal disease."

I press my mouth to her neck, re-familiarize myself with her flesh. "Let's get you home, Red."

"I'm not fucking you tonight, *Lo*."

I rear back but keep my hands on her. Anywhere on her, so long as

I'm touching her. "As tempting as that is, I'm not into taking advantage of drunk girls. Which you clearly are. And who are you here with, anyway?"

"Joy."

"And where the fuck is she? Shouldn't she be taking care of you?"

Her lips press tight, and I already know the answer. She's with some guy who's no doubt balls deep inside her. "Sorry," Aubrey says, her loose features attempting a cringe.

"Like I give a shit. And on the topic of giving shits, why didn't *you* call me?"

She shrugs. "I didn't have your number."

"Liar," I laugh out. "Lachlan told me it was on your phone." More like I beat the details out of him, but whatever.

She says, "You know why I chose to move to a small town?"

"Why, Master of the Deflect?"

"Because in small towns, everyone knows everyone, which means that if you wanted to find me, you could have. You know where I live, Logan."

I smirk. "Did you *want* me to find you, Red?"

Her eyes narrow, but her hands stay put. "I find you vile, Lo."

I kiss her neck again. "Let's get out of here."

"No."

"So stubborn."

"So cocky."

"Even if I wanted to find you, I couldn't have. I've been in Cambodia for the past three weeks."

She scoffs. "Of all the excuses in all the world, you had to—"

I pull back, reach for my phone. I scan the photos until I find the one I want, then practically shove it in her face. On the screen is a picture of me, standing beneath a sign that reads *"Welcome to Cambodia."*

Her eyes shift from the picture to my face, again and again. "What the hell were you doing there?"

"Working."

"You have contracts in Cambodia?"

"Long story."

She sighs, and I don't know if she means to pull me closer, but the second she does, my hands find her waist again. We stay like that, silent, for seconds that turn into minutes. She's still swaying, and I wish I knew what song was playing in her head. I wonder if it's Otis Redding or Obey Trice. Crowded House or Cypress Hill. Or any one of the songs we listened to that night, back and forth, while we lay naked in her bedroom, on her couch, at the kitchen table when the munchies got the best of us, in between moments of laughter, and the greatest mind-blowing sex I've ever had. Which is saying a lot. Because I've had *a lot* of sex.

"Are we dancing?" she asks.

"Um… you're swaying, and I'm pretty sure I'm just holding you up."

She continues to sway, her nose pressed against my chest, her breath warming every inch of me. "You left me a stupid note."

"At least I left you a note." *Which I've never done.*

"You said you had to be somewhere. That was it."

"I did. I had to be at the airport. Laney called me just after five, freaking out because they realized I wasn't home. I forgot we were leaving that morning. Correction. You *made* me forget we were leaving."

"Who's Laney? The girl trapped in your sex den?"

"What the fuck?" I guffaw. "Laney's my brother's girl, and please, don't ever, *ever*, say her name and sex in the same sentence again." An involuntary shiver runs through me, literally shaking my bones.

"Still. Your note was stupid. You could've elaborated."

"I had five minutes to go home, pack, and get on the road. I was in a rush. You're lucky I managed to find a pen and a piece of paper."

She pulls back then, looks up at me. "Your note was stupid, Logan."

"My note was stupid," I reluctantly concede, because she's drunk and this is *clearly* going nowhere.

"Good." She nods. "Will you take me home even if I tell you I'm not sleeping with you?"

I crack the tiniest of smiles. "Will you *let* me take you home even if I swear I *won't* sleep with you?"

"I have to tell Joy."

"Fuck Joy."

10

AUBREY

"Trust me, you'll feel better after a shower, and I'm not here *just* because I'll get to see you naked. What if something happens?" Logan's in my bathroom, leaning against the counter, his arms crossed, staring down at me. In his presence, in the confines of this room, I feel *tiny*. It's not as if I'd forgotten how tall he was, how built he was. It's not as if I'd forgotten every slope of his body, every dip of his abs, every inch of his co—"Quit fucking me with your eyes and get naked," he orders. "Quick. Before the hot water runs out." The first thing he did when we walked into my house was take off his jacket, walk to the bathroom, and run the shower. He made sure to set it to his version of scalding, because that's how I had it when we were both in there the first time he was here. He sighs, frustrated. "Are you going to make me get in there with you?"

"No." I kick off my boots and remove my top in the sloppiest, most childish, most brattish form. "I'll get in." I strip down to nothing and narrow my eyes at him when he gives me a crooked smile. He watches me through the glass screen, never once making a sound, never once taking his eyes off me. At any other time, I'd probably feel exhilarated, *sexy*. But honestly, I just feel light-headed and worn the hell out. This week has drained me, physically and emotionally. But he's right. The shower does help, at least physically. When I dry off, I tell him that he can leave, that I'm fine. At least my feet are steady. He offers to make me something to eat before he goes, and I don't argue. Once I'm alone, I take a long, steady breath and recall the events of the day.

I wonder if he'd bother to find me if it weren't for his brother.

I wonder if he'd be here if chance hadn't brought us to the same party.

I wonder if he thought about me at all in the past three weeks.

I decide the answers are no.

I also decide that for tonight, just like our first night, I don't care.

LOGAN

Aubrey's sitting on the bathroom floor when I get back with the peanut butter sandwich. She still has the towel wrapped around her, tapping the end of a hairdryer on her palm. "It's broke," she says, pouting up at me.

I sigh, place the sandwich on the counter and bend down to grab the cord. "It's not plugged in, Aubs."

"Oh."

I plug the cord in, switch the hair dryer on and off to test it. Then I hand her the sandwich. She eyes the plate as if it's poison. "What is it?" she asks, as if I've set out to kill her dead. She has no idea.

"It's peanut butter. It's all you had. And FYI, I'm allergic to nuts, so I could've died making that for you."

She doesn't respond, simply takes the hairdryer from me and tries to eat and blow dry at the same time. Which, going by the way the hair dryer is aimed at the wall and not at all on her head, is clearly a struggle. I take the hair dryer from her, start drying her hair.

It's almost dry by the time I realize that I'm turning into one of *those* guys. The one I'd promised I'd never be. I switch off the dryer, practically throw it on the counter. "You're good," I tell her, and she looks up from her half-eaten sandwich, smiles lazily.

"That felt so nice," she says. "I almost fell asleep."

I don't tell her that, yeah, it felt nice for me, too. Because I'm not a goddamn pussy. I'm not my brothers or my brother-in-law. "Finish your food and let's get you to bed."

She rushes through the rest of her sandwich, and I watch her crawl into bed, ignoring the fact that she's fucking naked, that she's on her hands and knees while she pulls down the covers, that those thick thighs of hers are what I envisioned while I jerked off into hotel towels the first week I was in Cambodia. The covers are to her chin now, while scarlet fans across her pillow. She blinks up at me. Once. Twice. Her lashes are the same color as her hair, a few shades darker than her freckles. "Are you leaving now?"

I tap at my pocket, nervous energy crawling, nipping at my fingertips.

"You can smoke in my garage," she tells me.

"Sure?"

"Or you can leave; whatever you want."

I want to leave.

I want to smoke in her garage.

I want to stay in this room and watch her fall asleep the way I did three weeks ago.

Obviously, I don't know what the fuck I want.

"I'll be back."

I go to her garage.

Spend time with Mary.

Inhale her as if she's my last breath.

And then go through every single emotion I've felt the past three weeks.

I didn't want to wake up thinking about her. I didn't want to fall asleep lost in thoughts of her. Because remembering her meant that it was real, whatever I'd felt, whatever we had, and then today...

I heard her voice.

I saw her.

I held her.

I allowed my lips to touch her.

For a second, I allowed myself to want her.

The problem with wanting something, or *someone*, is that you can't control how long you keep them for. Or the hurt it might cause when you lose them. And *that*… that's the reason why I go back to Aubrey's room, just to the doorway, and lean against it, my hands shoved deep in my pockets.

I ignore the twisting in my gut when I look at her. "I tried to add you on Facebook."

"No, you didn't."

I nod. "It's a fake name. Long story."

She reaches for her phone. "The only friend request is sitting in purgatory. From *Bing Bong*. The profile says, *Contact me for cheap Ray Bans*. That's you?"

I nod again.

"Oh."

"I just wanted you to know that I tried, Aubrey. I tried to contact you, but the only way I could think to do it was through Joy. And I didn't care whether or not she knew, but you guys are friends… she's your *only* friend and—"

"I get it," she cuts in. "I'm not mad about it…"

Another nod. "Anyway… I'm pretty jet-lagged… so…"

"Yeah?" She scoots over, making room for me. She's hopeful.

I crush her hope. "So, I think I'm just going to head home."

She stares at me, right into my eyes, into my insecurities. "Okay." She scoots back to the middle of the bed.

I turn to leave, but she calls out after me. "Logan?"

My body stills, but I don't turn around. "Yeah?"

"Can you make sure you lock the door?"

11

AUBREY

FOUR BEERS DO NOT a hangover make. Thank God. Because I'd be further into Struggle Town at work today if it did. It's quiet. I've had a total of three customers walk in. I guess people here don't like stationery as much as they do in Raleigh. I should've opted for a different shop, but this was my job back home, and so I know the suppliers, know how to run the place. What I don't know is how to market it or bring in the customers.

I stand behind the counter, check my phone.

Bing Bong.

What the fuck even is that?

I don't go on Facebook often, because social media is a place where exes go to die. Here's an example of what I know since I left Raleigh:

Carter is working full-time at his dad's BMW dealership.

His sister turned sixteen.

His mom turned forty-five.

His new girlfriend is a knockout.

He loves her already.

He loves her.

He loves her.

He loves her.

He loves her more than he ever loved me.

I know, because he posts about it right there, for the world to see.

He never posted about me.

And when I realized that, I felt dead inside.

Hence, social media is a place where exes go to die.

So do friendships.

This morning, just as I was opening the shop, I got a DM from Joy. Attached, a screenshot from someone's profile with a picture from last night's party. In the background, Logan is holding me, aka: helping me stand. She asked if I fucked him last night. I said no. She asked if I've fucked him ever. I said yes.

She didn't respond.

She didn't have to.

And now I'm back to square one.

WHEN I'D FIRST TOLD my mom my plans, she asked me why I chose here. Besides the fact that I'd been fascinated with small towns (thank you, CW Network) the names of the towns around here were kind of familiar. When I was around seven or eight, we lived in a town similar to this. I don't remember exactly where, and my mom refuses to talk about anything "Pre-Dad-Death," so this was as close as I could get. It's nothing like I imagined. Yes, everyone knows everyone, people wave in the streets, greet using their names... *if* they've lived here forever. They're not so welcoming to the newbies. It feels almost as if they think I'm a threat. To what? I have no idea. It's not like I'm out to steal people's boyfriends or businesses.

I'm just here.

Existing.

Barely.

Soon enough, I'll run out of the money from my inheritance. And then... then I don't know what I'll do.

I PULL up a map of the town on the computer and look at the aerial view. There are too many trees, so you can't make up much. I zoom in. Roofs. Trees. Lake.

Lake.

I shut the browser when the bell above the door chimes, put on my fakest smile, and with the cheeriest voice I can muster, I say, "How are you today?"

I'm one of *those* shop owners.

Lachlan Preston is poking his head inside. Just his head. Not an inch of anything else. Outside, a huge, Goliath of a man in a flannel button-up stares down at the boy with his jaw set, his eyes narrowed— eyes bluer than blue.

Lachlan shouts, "Hi, Red! Bye, Red!" and then he's gone, his shoulders lifting when the man ruffles his hair.

The man looks in through the shop window, offers a smile, a head nod. And maybe I'm slow, because I don't realize it until I see his profile that he's Logan's dad. Jesus. Mr. Preston is a silver fox.

Gross? Maybe.

Truth? *Definitely.*

THREE HOURS and a single customer later, I get a delivery. A huge, heavy delivery contained in five large boxes. I don't remember ordering that much stuff, but sometimes, when my insomnia hits, I order random shit online at four in the morning. The delivery guy's name is Peter. I know, because I see him almost every day. He calls me Audrey. He rushes me to sign off on the delivery and farts in my store before leaving. He couldn't have waited until he was outside where the wind can travel the stench away?

Seriously, my life is *so* fascinating. If they made a show about it, they'd call it, *The Girl Who Breathes* or *The Girl Who Blinks* or *The Girl Who Is Pathetic.*

I don't check the boxes. Not until an hour later when a woman walks in; tiny, shiny, perfect, like a porcelain doll made of diamonds and crystal. She looks at the boxes I haven't bothered to move off the showroom floor. What's the point? Then she looks at the small box she carried in with her. "I think Peter gave you the wrong delivery," she states, not looking at me: *The Threat*.

"Well, that makes sense," I mumble.

"Did he fart in your shop, too?"

I laugh at that, and her eyes snap to me. Her head tilts, taking me in. Head to toe. Head to toe. "You're cute." She says it so matter of fact that for a second, I believe her. "You're new, right?"

"As of, like, four months ago."

"This town..." she says, dropping my delivery on the counter as she jerks her head toward the door, "...we don't get a lot of new people. Stragglers, yes. Visitors, yes. Tourists, fuck no. But no one ever stays."

I nod, bring my package closer to me. "So, how long do you think I have to stay before I stop being 'new'?"

"Until someone else comes along. You look young. Are you here with your parents? Is this their shop?"

"I'm eighteen," I tell her, "and it's *my* shop."

"Good for you." She doesn't say it in a condescending way. It's more like encouraging.

"Thanks."

"Okay, I better get going." She walks over to her boxes piled higher than her head and attempts to lift one. It doesn't budge. "Jesus fuck, what the fuck is in this?"

"Dead bodies?" I suggest. A joke, obviously.

"You'd think they'd chop them up into limbs to make them easier to carry, right?" She smiles. Genuine. Her hair's the shade of auburn I wish I had. She looks like a littler version of Rory Gilmore from *Gilmore Girls*. Stars Hollow. Small Town. *Irony*.

"Right," I answer. "Maybe if we both try... I'm not very strong. Where's your shop, anyway?"

"A couple doors down."

I get on the other side of the boxes, wait for her to get into position. We both try. It lifts... about a quarter of an inch.

We laugh it off.

"I hate to say this…" she starts. "But I think we need a man."

"I think you're right."

"You got a man?"

I shake my head. "Not even close to one."

She eyes me up and down again. "Shame."

I like her.

Not *like* like her, but… and maybe I'm jumping the gun here, but *maybe*, just maybe, I could possibly gain a new friend.

She's on her phone, typing out a text.

"So…" I begin, "I take it you're one of the forever here-ers?"

"Pretty much."

Just then, a man walks in, tall, masculine, rugged. *Hot*. If this woman is Rory, this guy is Dean.

Dean and Rory were a disaster (sorry).

I was always Team Logan.

Fuck me. I can't escape the boy.

The man's eyes glaze over me, goes straight to the woman. "You raaaang," he says, his voice Lurch-like.

The woman points to the boxes. "Carry them for me, dear husband?"

He picks up the top one as if it's filled with feathers.

I giggle. "We suck," I say to the woman.

"No," she says, squeezing her husband's arm. "He's just strong." Then she points to me. "This is—I never caught your name."

"Aubrey."

And before I get a chance to ask them for theirs, she says to her husband, "Isn't she cute, babe?"

As if the husband needed permission to actually *look* at me, he sizes me up, just like his wife did. "Yeah, babe, she's cute." He kisses the top of her head.

I blush like mad, look down at my hot pink Doc Martens.

"Like, *really* cute," she says.

"Sure, babe. *Really* cute."

"You made any friends since you've been here?" she asks me.

"Not really." It comes out a jumbled whisper.

"You should come over for dinner tonight. Right, husband?" It's kind of adorable that she calls him that instead of his name, even though I really want to know what it is.

"For sure. I'll cook, though, babe. You've uh… worked hard today. I'm going to get the hand trolley from the shop so I can get these boxes out of the way." He kisses her again.

Gosh, they're sweet. And Logan (mine, not Rory Gilmore's) says that romance is dead. The woman takes a business card from the holder on the counter. "I'll text you the time and address!" she says, already walking out the door with her husband. I wave goodbye, a little too enthusiastically.

When the man returns with the trolley, he doesn't speak, except to say, "I'll see you tonight?"

"Sure."

And then he's gone.

And I'm back to existing.

Barely.

Two hours, no customers later, a text comes through with an address and the time. I save the number in my phone under *Rory*.

An hour after that, I close the shop. Walk home. It's on that walk home that I play over everything in my head.

The woman.

The man.

The way she looked at me.

The way she kept insisting that I was *cute.*

The way she asked her husband if *he* thought I was cute.

The way she'd asked if I'd made any friends.

The instant invite to dinner at *their* house.

Oh.

Shit.

All the warning signs were there.

How did I not see them?

The Girl Who Is Pathetic.

Oh.

My.

Shit.

I've just been invited to a threesome.

I freeze in the middle of the sidewalk, grab my phone out of my bag, and text the only person I could possibly classify as a "friend."

Aubrey: *How do you feel about threesomes?*

Logan: *Yes.*

12

AUBREY

Logan is being... *Logan.*

Sitting behind the wheel of his truck, he's giving me the glares he used to give me *before.* "Red, when you said threesome, I thought you meant me plus two girls."

"And that's why you're here?"

"Well, I wouldn't be here if I knew I was driving you to get fucked by some other guy."

"I am most certainly not getting fucked by anyone."

"Then why am I here?"

"A friend? A buffer?" Then I whine, "I'm scared, Logan."

"How did you not realize that's what they wanted?"

"Because I'm stupid and naïve and pathetic. I thought she was being *friendly.* I didn't realize until—"

"So what? You want me to sit in on this dinner with you and... what...?"

"I don't know!" I shout. "Pretend like, like, like we're dating and you don't want me to do it."

"This is crazy, Red."

"I know, and I'm sorry I dragged you into it. But they seemed like nice people—"

"Besides baiting an unassuming teenage girl into sexcapades, yeah, sure, they're *real* nice people."

"I'm sorry." I giggle. I can't help it. "Did you really think you were going to get two girls tonight?"

He shrugs. "Maybe."

"Have you ever had—"

"Give me the damn address."

I read out the address.

He asks me to repeat it.

I repeat it.

He gets on his phone.

"You don't know where it is?"

"I'm just making sure."

I'M PRETTY sure we're lost, because when I Google Mapped the address, it said it was ten minutes away. We've been on the road for almost thirty. I *think* I've seen the same area three times. But what would I know? I can tell you the roads, the houses, the cracks in the sidewalk from my home to work. Besides that, I really don't know the area at all. Sucks to not have a car. Or a license.

Finally, Logan slows the car down, checks the area around him. "This is it," he says and then pulls into a gravel driveway surrounded by trees, trees, and more trees. Sunlight filters through the gaps, but besides that, nothing. I try to stay calm, for him, for me, but fear—it's slowly eating away at my insides, turning my stomach to stone. I can hear my pulse in my eardrums, and this driveway is looong. Like, wherever this couple lives—it's secluded. *No shit*. It has to be so people don't hear their sexcapades. "Think they'll answer the door naked?" Logan asks. "Get right to it, you know?"

"Fuck off."

He laughs. I don't know why he finds this so funny.

Swear, it's at least a mile until we get to what can only be described as a cabin. Or, at least, it feels like a mile. The porch light is on, even though it's still light out, and there are two cars in the driveway. One's a small Honda; the other looks like something that doesn't belong on this planet. Logan cuts the engine. "Shall we?"

"Let's just eat and then get the hell out of there."

"Whatever you say, Red."

Logan doesn't open my door for me. He waits by the porch steps as if he's comfortable with the whole scene. I bet he thinks he can turn this into a four-way. He's disgusting, repulsive. *Stupidly hot.* I get out of the car, run up to him as if there's something on the ground, nipping at my heels, ready to destroy me. Discomfort builds a fortress in my lungs, making it hard to breathe. I reach for his hand. He looks down at it, shucks his hand away. "I don't hold hands."

"But we have to pretend—"

"We can do that without holding hands, Red. I can make out with you, feel you up, strip you naked and go down on you in front of them if that's what you want, but I *don't* hold hands."

I cross my arms over my chest, tuck my hands away. "Let's just do this."

He sighs. "You're pissed."

"I'm not."

"Red."

I face him, try not to reveal the hurt in my face. I'm not hurt by what he said, but because I know how he must see me:

Clingy.

Needy.

You love me too much, Aubrey.

All the reasons Carter broke up with me.

"You could've said no," I tell him.

"What?"

"If you didn't want to do this, you could've said no."

He takes the two porch steps until he's standing in front of the door. "And therein lies the problem," he mumbles.

"What problem?"

"Nothing." And before I can stop him, he's knocking.

The couple doesn't seem phased by Logan's attendance, because their attention goes right to me. "Still as cute as I remember," the woman says, smiling that smile I once thought was genuine.

"Super cute," the husband agrees.

Logan takes a step in, hands in his pockets.

The woman says, "So should we eat first, fuck after, or the other way around?"

My eyes go huge.

The husband answers for me, "Eat first. I need the energy to keep up with you two." He eyes Logan. "Or three, if you're joining us."

"I can't do this," I shout and literally *run* away.

Behind me, Logan's laughing.

I think I hate his laugh.

"Aubrey!" he shouts after me.

I've already passed all three cars. "I'll find my own way home."

"Aubrey!" he says again, his footsteps hitting the gravel. He catches up to me quickly and grabs my arm, forces me to stop. "Red," he says, calmer. "You know the good thing about small towns?"

"What?" I grind out, my back still to him.

"Everyone knows everyone. And, a lot of the time..." His laughter suspends his speech.

I hate him.

He tries again. "A lot of the time, the people in small towns, they're related."

I finally face him, glance at the couple waiting by the door. "Like incest?" I whisper, hoping they don't hear me. Logan smiles, mocking. It's part breathtaking, part I-want-to-punch-it-right-off-his-goddamn-face. I lean in closer, whisper quieter, "You mean they're brother and sister?"

"No." He takes me by the forearm, practically drags me toward them. It would be less effort just to hold my stupid hand. "Aubrey, I'd like you to meet my sister, Lucy, and her husband, Cameron."

Lucy laughs so hard, her eyes water. Cameron shakes his head. "Lucy has these hot lesbian tendencies, but I swear, we did *not* invite you over for that. She honestly just wanted to get to know you."

With my eyes wide, I turn to Logan. Punch his arm. "You *knew*?" He and his sister have the same laugh. One high-pitched. One low. They have the same smile, too. Same eyes. God, I'm stupid. "You knew!"

"Not until you told me the address."

I turn to Lucy. "And you knew he was coming?"

"He texted me as soon as he found out."

"Why did it take so long to get here?" I'm half shouting, half crying, half embarrassed, half relieved.

Logan says, "I drove around town because I thought you might recognize the area from that time you were here."

"You were here before?" Lucy asks, then narrows her eyes at her brother. "You took her to the sex den?"

"Ha!" I yell. "I knew it was a sex den!"

"It's not a fucking sex den," Logan mumbles, sobering and shaking his head.

Cameron chuckles. "So now that Little Logan's out of the picture—with the whole sex with his sister thing—should we eat first, fuck later?"

Lucy backhands his stomach. "In your dreams, asshole."

"Wait." I look at Logan. Not his face. Not his chest. *Lower.* "Little Logan?"

"Shut up." He shoves me into the house, closing the door behind him. "He has a friend called Logan. That's how they differentiate between us. No fucking way that's the reason, and you *know* that."

I shrug, sit down at the chair Cameron offers me. "I wasn't of sound mind to confirm nor deny."

"Logan," Lucy says, sitting opposite me while Cameron works in the kitchen. "Is Aubrey the first girl you've brought home?"

"Semantics, Luce," he murmurs, tapping on his phone. A second later, a song comes on from somewhere in the living room. I don't realize its purpose until the chorus hits: *I think you're cute.*

"You're a jerk," I tell him.

He laughs.

Lucy giggles. Then she winks at me.

Cameron sets down a platter of tacos in the middle of the table.

I declare, "I love tacos!"

And Logan says, "And according to you, Lucy loves *your* taco."

LOGAN

Tonight, Aubrey's wearing a dress, no bra. It's the kind of dress I'd see on any number of girls walking down Main Street. It doesn't suit her. Not that it doesn't look *good* on her, it's just that... it's not *her*. "I love your sister!" she all but squeals the second we're back in my truck. She's smiling. Wide. The same smile that's graced us almost the entire night. She waves to Luce and Cam, standing on their porch, their arms around each other.

"Yeah, she's pretty cool," I say, tapping at my pocket. I haven't had time with Mary all day, and I'm jonesing. *Bad.*

"Is it just you three?" she asks as I start the car, roll away, letting the gravel crunch beneath the wheels.

"Who three?"

"You, Lachlan and Lucy?"

I shake my head. "I'm one of seven."

"Is it, like, a Brady Bunch type thing?"

"Nope." I tap at my pocket again. "We have the same parents. Lucy's the only girl. She's the oldest."

"Where do you fit in?"

"Smack bang in the middle."

"Typical," she says.

"What is?"

"You're like a poster boy for middle child syndrome."

"Fuck off. I am not."

"I'm kidding! I don't even know what middle child syndrome is." She laughs. That same laugh that knocked me back a step the first time I actually paid attention to it. Breathy. Husky. *Hot.*

I wait until we're out on the road, where the trees aren't so close, and not so inconspicuously check out her legs. I remember how they felt in my grasp, how her flesh turned white when I grabbed onto them. I remember how she looked, naked, sprawled out on her bed, her legs spread, waiting for me. "So..." I start. Then trail my gaze from her legs to the hem of her dress. "Why are you dressed like that?"

"Like what?"

"Like *normal*."

She scoffs. "Like every other girl?"

I shrug, turn right onto Main Street, past her work, past Lucy's. "Who were you trying to impress tonight?"

"You think me dressing like this is me trying to *impress* someone?" This is our game, Red's and mine. We talk in circles, never really coming up with answers to satisfy the other. She adds, "My washing machine's broken. This is all I had. Which reminds me, I need to get home. I have about fifteen browsers open on how to repair it."

I side-eye her. Her face. Not her legs. Maybe her tits. They're small. Not quite a handful, if my memory serves me correctly, but definitely a mouthful. "You got the tools for that?"

"I have enough."

Before I know it, before I *want* it, I'm pulling into her driveway, cutting the engine. I step out first, wait for her at the front of the car. I've noticed that she does this a lot: takes forever to get out. She should really leave a porch light on, not just for her own safety but because it's too damn dark out here, and I can't see her face. I can't see what the hell it is she's waiting for. Eventually, she steps out, one pale leg after the other. She bypasses me, as if I'm not here, as if I haven't been waiting, and goes right to her door. I follow, settle my hands on her waist from behind. "Logan." My name is a frustrated grunt. She spins in my arms, and I take the opportunity to push her against the door, move in on her. Her hands are on my chest, her eyes on mine. "What do you want, Logan?"

"You."

"You could've had me last night."

"You were drunk."

"I was fine by the time you left."

I press my lips to her bare shoulder. "Why are you acting like you're not going to invite me in?"

She doesn't exactly invite me in, but she opens the door, keeps it open. Then she opens the door leading to the garage, already knowing what I want. What I need. The thing is, I crave them both. Mary *and* Aubrey, and as I watch Aubrey walk down the hallway, lifting her dress over her head as she moves toward her bedroom, I question whom I crave more.

I take advantage of Mary in Aubrey's garage and call out, "You want some of this?"

"I'm already naked in bed!"

SHE LOOKS like she did last night: naked beneath the sheets, scarlet surrounding her face. Her bed is a four-poster with a white canopy draped along the sides. Our one night together, she told me it was the only luxury she allowed herself when she moved here. She said it right before I used the drapes to tie her hands to the posts. I spent the following half hour with my face between her legs, getting what I wanted: hearing the sounds that fell from her lips when I made her come.

I kick off my shoes, remove my shirt, and move to the bed. "It's a shame you're so repulsive," she says, and I chuckle, take off my jeans. I climb into bed with her, and for some reason, I don't feel the need to get on her right away. I try to tell myself that I'm not ready. Or that I'm one step too lit to perform the way I want. I push away the truth—that one of the best parts of our night together was just existing with her—under the same roof, under the same blanket. Touching. Even if the touching led to nothing more than just touching.

She turns to her side, faces me.

I do the same.

"Lachlan came by the store today."

"Oh yeah? Did he steal anything else?"

"No," she laughs out. "He popped his head in, said hi and bye and then he left. Your dad was with him."

I blink, slowly, feeling the effects of Mary start to swarm my insides, making everything crack, disintegrate, liquify, all at once. "They were probably going to see Cam and Luce."

"I love your sister," she says.

"You said that already."

"And Cameron. He's so dreamy."

I get on top of her now, settle between her legs. "Shut up," I mumble into her shoulder. Her skin is so warm, heating my insides. Fuck, she feels good.

I feel her silent giggle against every single inch of me. "And speaking of dreamy, your dad is a fox, Lo."

"Shut up," I say, louder, stronger, and bite down on her shoulder.

"Why?" she asks, her fingers stroking my hair. If my eyes weren't already closed, they would've drifted shut at the touch. "Are you jealous?"

"No. I'm just not into girls I've fucked telling me about their daddy issues."

Her hands freeze, then disappear completely. Underneath me, her entire body is solid. *Cold.* She doesn't respond, and when I look up at her, her eyes are wide open, staring up at the ceiling.

"What?" I whisper, moving up and kissing her jaw.

It takes her a long-ass minute to respond, "You can be so fucking offensive, and you don't even realize it."

I lean up on my elbows, look down at her. "What the fuck did I say?"

"A: you called me a girl you've *fucked.*"

"You *are* a girl I've—"

"And then you teased me, said I had *daddy issues,* when you know that he's dead, and that, yeah, he caused a lot of issues for me."

Fuck.

Fuck fuck fuck.

"I'm sorry," I breathe out. "I didn't mean it." I try to kiss her, but she moves her head to the side. "Red," I murmur. "I'm sorry." I kiss her cheek, her jaw, her neck, whispering apologies with every one. She's stiff for a moment, refusing to give in. *So stubborn.* I finally find her lips in the darkness of my closed lids. My tongue meets hers, and the longing and the craving and the hunger that's coated every breath, every organ, is finally satisfied. Beneath my touch, my whispers, Aubrey cracks, disintegrates, liquifies.

We are one.

One movement.

One sound.

"I'm sorry," I say, one last time. "Forgive me?"

Against my lips, she nods, her fingers finding my hair again.

I am lost.

I am high, floating.

I am low, beneath the earth's surface.

I am night.

She is day.

I am darkness.

She is light.

I am nine years old, and the leather cracks beneath my weight...

"Logan?"

I blink, shake.

"Logan?" Something tugs at my hair, and I open my eyes to hers. Green, like the trees lining my driveway. Freckles, half the shade of scarlet. "Are you okay? Where'd you go just now?"

I am conflict.

Aubrey kisses me again.

And she is *hope*.

AUBREY

LOGAN FIXED MY WASHER. He also scratched the itch I hadn't been able to do myself for the past three weeks. I woke up this morning, and he wasn't there. I wish I could say I was surprised, but I wasn't. What did surprise me, though, were all the texts on my phone:

Logan: *Have to be somewhere. Sorry, Red.*

Logan: *It's a family thing.*

Logan: *Sunday Family Breakfast, to be exact.*

Logan: *Sunday: the day of the week before Monday and following Saturday, observed by Christians as a day of rest and religious worship and (together with Saturday) forming part of the weekend.*

Logan: *Family: a group consisting of two parents and their children living together as a unit.*

Logan: *Breakfast: a meal eaten in the morning, the first of the day.*

Logan: *Elaborate enough for ya, Red?*

I SPEND the morning doing laundry. Mom calls to check in on me. Grandma calls to tell me that she's been thinking about me, that she hopes I'm meeting new people and having the time of my life. I keep her on the phone for as long as she'll let me. Then I make a list of meals to cook for the next few days. I do everything I can to not think about Logan. Because even though I got a hint of what I saw three weeks ago last night—there was nothing more on his end. He said it plain as day. I was a girl he fucked. Nothing more, nothing else. If I'd met the current version of me a year ago, I'd probably slut-shame myself. But the truth is, there's nothing wrong with a girl wanting a guy to pleasure her. And there's nothing wrong with what we're doing. It's not as if we're hurting anyone.

Two weeks ago, I found a bike on the curb in front of a house I pass on the way to work. It had a sign that read "Free to a good home." I can't exactly say that my home is "good," but I took the bike anyway, left a note in the mailbox letting the previous owners know that I appreciated it. I really did. It was probably manufactured sometime before I was born, but hey—beggars can't be choosers. Besides, it has a basket on the handlebars that can hold my groceries. Which means that I can buy ingredients for dinner more than just a day in advance. Seriously, I'm so weak I can't even carry groceries. I remember what Lucy said about needing a man, and I smile to myself as I press down on the button that lifts the garage door. Gripping the handlebars, I wheel the bike out, then press the button again. While I wait for it to lower, I get out my phone, ignore Logan's texts (not thinking about him) and change *Rory* to *Lucy*.

I send her a text:

Aubrey: *Thanks for the orgy last night. Dinner wasn't bad either.*

Lucy: *OMG! Lol. That was so fun. We should definitely do it again. This time, I'll bring the butt plugs.*

Aubrey: *Sweet. I found a great deal on Amazon for a sex swing. Shall I?*

Lucy: *No. We already have one. We forgot to bring it out. (Not kidding)*

Aubrey: *OMG! I'm actually not at all surprised.*

Lucy: *Hey—come by the store tomorrow, okay? I have a list of books I want to lend you.*

Lucy: *...if you want to read them. No pressure.*

Aubrey: *I'd love that! Thank you so much.*

Lucy: *You like romance, right?*

Aubrey: *I love the idea of romance, sure.*

Lucy: *Logan wants to know why you haven't responded to his texts.*

Sigh.

Because I'm too clingy.

Too needy.

I pocket the phone and take my time peddling toward "downtown." I stop by my shop, look at it from the outside: large windows, brick walls, enough stationery to last a lifetime. I make a mental note to study product display and merchandising when I get home. And, maybe if I have time, look at opening an online store. Entering the inventory would be insane, but at least I *might* sell something.

The town is dead on Sundays, besides the few stragglers. I worked this out after opening on Sundays for the first three weeks and not having a single customer.

The grocery store is the same on the inside as it is on the outside.

There's one register open, and I'm pretty sure the old lady behind the counter is asleep. I take a basket from the few they have by the entrance and pull out my list. Then I take my time perusing each aisle, because really? What else is there to do? I don't see a single person on my walk, and I wonder if everyone is at church. Is church an all-day thing? I've never been to church besides three weddings and a funeral (a horrible movie, FYI). I grab everything I need and then head for the freezer section, contemplating whether or not ice cream is a suitable dinner. *Fuck yeah, it is.* There's a guy standing at the floor freezer—a guy I hadn't noticed before—and I slow my steps. Is the ice cream freezer in a grocery store like the men's urinals? Is it weird if I stand too close? Should I come back? *What is ice-cream freezer etiquette?* My feet carry me to the other side of the freezer. This seems safe. Less awkward.

The guy looks up, smiles a half smile. He's probably my age, maybe older, and he's cute. In that quiet, unassuming way. Not at all like the boy I'm *not* thinking about.

Chewing my lip, I eye the tubs of ice cream as if they're a work of art.

The guy hasn't left, hasn't made a move to open the sliding door and pick one out.

I glance up, catch him staring at me.

I drop my gaze, try to hide my blush.

"Are you new?" he asks.

"Apparently," I laugh out.

"Sorry." I look up to see him shaking his head. "It's just that I haven't seen you around before. Where are you staying?"

"Asks the stalker serial killer."

He chuckles, short and deep. "Sorry," he says again. "Is it less stalk-erish if I ask where you're coming from?"

I nod. "Raleigh."

"I live in Raleigh," he says, thumb pointed to his chest. "Well, sort of. I'm studying at NC State. Living in the dorms."

"That's cool. You home for the weekend?"

"Yeah. I don't get—"

"Dude," a familiar voice says, and I cringe at the sound. "They finally brought in flavored condoms!" Logan's walking toward us, his gaze fixed on the back of the packaging. "Mint flavored for extra stimulation," he reads. Then he looks up, sees me standing there. A cocky smile splits his face in two. "Hey, Red."

"You know each other?" the guy asks.

Logan raises his eyebrows at me, as if he's waiting for me to either confirm or deny. I press my lips together.

"I didn't catch your name?" the guy says.

"Aubrey."

"Aubrey, huh? Pretty name for a pretty girl."

"Shut up," says Logan.

"Hey," I interrupt. "He can tell me I'm pretty if he wants. It's not like anyone else does."

Ugh. Needy. Clingy.

Logan glares at me. "You don't need anyone telling you you're pretty, Red."

The guy chuckles. "I'm Leo." He thumps the back of Logan's head. "This punk's older brother."

I ask Logan, "Are you related to *everyone* here?"

Logan readjusts his hat, ignores my question. "Our parents had me because they failed so badly with him."

Leo shakes his head, focuses his smile on me. "So maybe we can get together sometime, and you can tell me all the good places in Raleigh to see."

"That sounds—"

"Like a giant fucking snore fest," Logan cuts in, and Leo's laughing, silent.

"Call it," Leo says. I assume he's talking to Logan because I have no idea what that means.

"This isn't high school, Lee. I'm not calling shit."

Leo winks at me, pulls out his phone. "What's your number, Aubrey? I'll call you la—"

Logan interrupts, "Let's get this ice cream and leave."

Leo says, "I haven't picked one out yet."

Without looking, Logan slides the door open, picks out a tub, and slams it against Leo's chest.

Leo laughs again.

"There," says Logan. "Now we have one. Let's go."

Leo takes the ice cream, glances down at it. "Do you have a death wish?"

"What?" Logan looks as confused as I feel.

"This is Peanut Buttah Cookie Core."

Logan groans.

Leo looks at me. "So, your number?"

Logan slams the tub of ice cream back in the freezer, picks up another one. "Let's go."

"Call it," Leo tells him. "Or I call her."

Logan turns his back to me, his shoulders squared.

After a second, Leo's smile takes up half his face. "I'm sorry, little bro. I couldn't hear you. What'd you say?"

Logan shakes his head. "Dibs! Okay? I call dibs!"

I frown on the outside, fist pump on the inside. "What the hell, dude! I'm not property," I say, the same time Leo teeters on his heels, smiles over at me.

"It was a pleasure to meet you, Aubrey. Have a pleasant day."

And then they're both walking away, Leo laughing, Logan attempting to trip him over with his foot.

I go back to existing, wishing I had a marketing team similar to Ben and Jerry's because the names for these ice creams are—

A hand tugs on my sleeve, and I follow it up to Logan's chest. "Hey," he says.

I meet his eyes. "What's up?"

"This." And then he's kissing me, both hands on my face, forcing me to rise to my toes and release my basket. He's everywhere around me, inside of me. My eyes open the second I feel him pulling back, but his eyes stay closed a second longer. I kiss him one more time. Quickly. And his lips lift at the corners. "You need a ride home?" he asks.

I shake my head, breathless.

"Sure?"

"I rode here."

His eyebrow quirks. "On a bike?"

"No. On my gigolo."

He laughs. "We can put it in the back of my truck. The bike or your gigolo."

"I'm good," I tell him. "Honestly, I could do with the exercise."

He smirks. "Your stamina seems fine to me." He kisses me again, this time slower, softer, more powerful. He has my back against the freezer, his hands in my hair, my hands wherever they land as long as they land on him.

"Oi!" the store clerk shouts at us.

Logan pulls away, adjusts my clothes, keeps the smile on his beautiful face.

The old lady behind the counter yells, "Quit groping the poor girl, you damn Preston Punk."

Logan rolls his eyes. "She was groping me!"

I look over at her and nod enthusiastically. "I was totally groping him!"

Logan chuckles, runs his finger along my palm. He doesn't hold my hand, but he comes pretty damn close. "I'll see you later?"

"Okay."

And then I spend the rest of the day failing at my task of *not* thinking about Logan Preston.

14

LOGAN

SOME PEOPLE HATE MONDAYS. I actually don't mind them. Fridays are the hardest to get through, because everything is so close, yet so far. Lucas, my oldest brother, calls me a functioning stoner. I'm not. I don't smoke during the week. I make up for all that non-smoking between Friday and Sunday. He stopped making me piss in a cup when I stopped caring that they came out positive. My dad stopped trying to lecture me, as long as I somewhat *function*.

Working helps with that—the *functioning*—more than he probably knows.

On Monday mornings, my dad, Lucas, Brian (Dad's head foreman, aka Laney's dad, aka my boss) and Cameron (the Gordon in *Preston, Gordon and Sons*, who also happens to be an architect) have meetings before the work day begins. Six a.m., they'd sit down together at the diner and talk about the work schedule for the rest of the week. A few weeks ago, Dad asked if I wanted to join them. It may not have been a big deal for him (considering I'm part of the *Sons* that makes up *Preston, Gordon and Sons)*, but it meant something to me. I don't allow myself high hopes of taking over his role in the business, and I don't want it—that's all Lucas, and that suits everyone. Luke's got that business sense in him. I don't know shit. But, I wouldn't mind taking over

Brian's job when he retires. It'd be tough, being the youngest on the job and expecting the same respect, but honestly, I think I could do it. If Leo hadn't gone off to college, he would've been client relations, for sure. He's good with people. Shows respect even when respect isn't earned. I'd both suck and blow at that job. The twins have no plans of joining the family business, and besides, they make more money than I do on YouTube views alone. *Punks.* Lachlan... I can't even think of Lachlan beyond his current age. The kid's growing up way too quick. I wish he'd slow down, stay a kid forever... for everyone's sake.

"So, we should be finishing up on the site on Fifth tomorrow, which means the Baker site should be ready to go first thing Wednesday," Dad says, then looks up from his compendium. He should really go digital like I've been trying to show him for years, but he's old-school, and I respect that. "Lucas, can you organize new portables for the Baker site for Tuesday morning, that way Logan can get in and set up all the equipment ready to go for Wednesday."

"Yes, sir," Lucas says, typing away on his laptop.

Dad asks me, "You need anything for the setup?"

I sip on my coffee, shake my head. "I got it."

Lucas looks over his laptop screen at me. "You aren't taking notes."

I tap my temple. "Set up computer equipment in portable office on Tuesday. Got it."

"What about passwords and—"

"Lucas," Dad interrupts. "If Logan says he's got it, then he's got it." Dad's the only one who seems to have any faith left in The Family Fuck Up: me. I wonder if it's a father-son thing. Like, our shared blood is the only reason he still believes in me. But then again, Lucas and I share that blood, and he treats me like a dumbass. Can't blame him. I am a dumbass. A self-deprecating one, apparently.

The meeting goes on; Cameron giving us timelines for drawings, Dad and Brian talking about the roster.

I pull out my phone, send Aubrey a message:

Logan: *I had a dream about your boobs last night.*

Aubrey: *I hate my boobs, and I'm asleep. Why are you up so early?*

Logan: *I'm in a work meeting.*

Aubrey: *Thinking about my boobs?*

Logan: *I like your boobs.*

Aubrey: *They're too small.*

Logan: *I like your boobs, Red.*

Aubrey: ...

Logan: *And your nipples.*

Aubrey: *I'm going back to sleep.*

Logan: *They remind me of cookies.*

Aubrey: *My nipples?*

Logan: *Your boobs and your nipples. Together. They remind me of Subway cookies... the strawberry and white chocolate chip ones.*

Aubrey: *Really? My boyfriend says they're too small. Not proportioned to the rest of me. He says he likes me better from behind.*

Logan: **Ex-boyfriend. Also see: Motherfucker. *Said/used to say. *Liked... Unless you're still talking to him, in which case, I'll kill him.*

On the screen, three little dots appear, showing that she's typing. They disappear. Appear. Over and over. A whole minute passes before I get her response.

Aubrey: *When are you coming over again to eat my cookies?*

I laugh.

Logan: *Friday.*

"Logan," Dad says. "Focus, son."
I shove my phone in my pocket. "Sorry."

HALFWAY THROUGH THE WORK DAY, Dad calls another "managers' meeting." Niall, an old-timer on Dad's crew, finds it necessary to announce everyone's entrance onto the site by shouting their name three times. Like a warning siren. Only he doesn't use our real names. Dad is *Bossman*. Brian is *Big Man*. Lucas is *Junior Boss Man*. Laney (when she comes on site) used to be *Baby Big Man*. That changed when she and Lucas (finally) started going out. Now she's *Junior Boss Lady*. Cameron is *Suit*.

"Suit! Suit! Suit!" Niall shouts. His warnings used to annoy me when I first started. Now, it's kind of *cute*. Like, old man cute, you know? I don't know what he actually does on the job. I haven't seen him with a tool in his hand yet. I'm pretty sure Dad just keeps him on to help him out. Plus, Mrs. Niall provides lunch for everyone at least three times a week. That's always a bonus.

Cameron offers Niall a lip tilt, then walks over to me, already loosening his tie. Unless he's in a meeting or taking measurements or talking to clients on-site, he normally works in his office above Lucy's bookstore. He meets with clients a lot. I guess that's why he's stuck wearing a suit and tie. Sucks for him. "You coming?" he asks.

"Where?"

"To the meeting."

"It's a managers' meeting."

He's on his phone before I know what's happening. "Hey, sir." He still calls my dad sir. Not Tom, not Dad, not Mr. Preston. *Sir.* "You want Logan in on this?" I don't hear Dad's response, but Cam nods, jerks his head toward Dad's office. I guess since I've started sitting in on the meetings, I'm now management.

Rad.

I don't mean to walk with a swagger in my step, my head held high, like I'm fricken royalty, but it feels good. Luke and Brian are already in Dad's office, leaning against the wall, and another guy sits in the chair opposite Dad, facing him. If they asked me in here to fire someone... but then the guy turns around and it's Garray, aka Dumb Name, Luke's best friend.

"What's up?" he says, standing up to slap my back, kick the back of my knee. He and Luke have been friends since I can remember, so it's no surprise he treats me like a brother. He does the same for Cameron, minus the kick, then sits back down opposite Dad.

I lean against the now closed door, Cameron next to me. There are too many people in such a small space, and the air already feels thick. I say, "Aren't you supposed to be in your fifth year of college?"

Dumb Name looks over his shoulder at me. "I deferred."

"You mean dropped out."

"Shut up, Logan," says *everyone.*

Dumb Name looks to my father. "You heard they closed down the tile plant, right?"

Dad nods. Then his eyes widen. "How's your mother?"

"That's actually why I'm here," Dumb Name says. "Ma—she's been having a hard time trying to find a job. She's worked there all her life, and now she's too under-qualified for anything. So, I *deferred,*" he says, the final word directed at my smart-ass, "to help her out with the rent and stuff." I feel like an asshole. "I know it's not the same as working for you over a few summers, but if you got any positions—"

"Can you start today?" Dad cuts in.

"Yes, sir."

"And tell your mom to come and see me. I'll see if I can find anything for her." In high school, back when I went, I'd hear people talk about my dad a lot. Some would call him the Coach Taylor (of *Friday Night Lights* fame) of our town: the man with all the answers. I didn't really understand it until now. Niall should've been the first clue.

"I really appreciate it, sir," Dumb Name responds.

"Kiss-ass," I say, because it's expected of me.

"Shut up, Logan," says everyone. Again.

Dad sighs, tells Dumb Name while pointing at me, "Say hello to your supervisor."

I kick off the wall. "Seriously?"

"Dad," Lucas interjects, using the same tone he's always used when it comes to decisions about me. Luke thinks he's my dad—or at the very least—believes he has more power over me, a higher morality. "Do you think that's the best idea?"

Dad shrugs, asks me, "Do you think you can handle it?"

"Yes, sir." Now I'm the kiss-ass.

He says to Luke, "If Logan says he can handle it, he can handle it."

I reach for my phone, send Aubrey a text:

Today is a good day, Red. And I'm pretty sure it's all because of your cookies.

"What kind of cookies?" Cameron asks, reading over my shoulder. "And is that Aubrey?"

"Who's Aubrey?" Lucas asks. "Is it that girl from the store Leo told us about?"

I open the door. "Get back to work, ya slackers."

15

AUBREY

I NEED to come up with a name for Logan's penis. Preferably food related. And something more creative than any make of sausage.

It's been two days since he deemed my boobs cookies, and I've narrowed it down to Pork Sword or Yogurt Slinger—both things I can barely type, let alone say aloud.

The bell above the door chimes and Lachlan Preston is there. "Hi, Red! Bye, Red!" And then he's gone again.

I release the breath I'd been holding, startled when I saw him, as if he could somehow sense that I'd been thinking about his brother's penis.

A half hour passes—I've added Meat Popsicle to the list—and Lachlan Preston is back. He doesn't just pop his head in this time. His entire everything walks through the door, hands grasping the straps of his backpack. "I'm watching you," I say, doing that lame two-finger point from my eyes to him.

He laughs, mumbles, "Sorry about the other day. Swear, I won't do it again." He drops his backpack by the counter and looks up at me with those blue-blue eyes of his.

"How old are you?"

"Nine."

"Huh. You getting your girl something else?"

"We broke up," he says matter-of-factly.

"Sucks. I'm sorry."

He shrugs. "She's going with Snot Eater now, so whatever."

"Snot Eater sounds like a *real* stud. And she picked him over you?"

"I don't really care," he says, his head tilting. "I mean, I'm *nine*. It's not like I'm going to marry the girl."

I lean on the glass counter. "So, you're going to play the field, huh?"

"Nah. I'm a one-woman kind of man. Like Cameron. Or Leo. I'm *not* like Logan."

Well...

"My dad makes me come to Lucy's shop after school until he gets off work. He says I'm too young to stay on my own. Lucy just sits there and reads books, and Cam's always working. You think I can hang out here?"

"With me?" I ask, my eyes wide.

"Unless you're busy."

I shake my head. "I'm not busy."

"Cool." He smiles that gap-toothed smile. "You need any help with anything? I can, like, clean or dust or something."

"Dude, it's so quiet here, all I do is clean and dust."

He giggles the way nine-year-olds are supposed to and picks up his backpack, points to the armchair next to the counter. "Can I sit there?"

"Sure."

"Thanks, Red. You're a good friend."

Friend.

I now have multiple friends. Too bad they all share the same genetics.

Lachlan sets himself up on the chair, school books on the table next to him.

"They got you doing homework young, huh?"

"Tell me about it," he says, rolling his eyes.

"Do you know what you want to be when you're older?"

He shrugs. "I'm nine, Red. Don't be asking me such hard-hitting questions," he says through a smirk.

"Right on." I get on the laptop, open Spotify. "You want some music on while you work?"

He gets to his feet quickly, starts tapping away on the keyboard. A second later: "*My balls. My balls. Put it in your booty hole.*"

I LET Lachlan choose the soundtrack for the afternoon. Maybe I should filter what he listens to, but it's obvious he's heard them all before. And maybe I shouldn't be playing that kind of music in my store, but it's not like I have any customers. I let him go on with his homework while I rearrange the window display, the order of the pens, the angle of the notebooks. When I get back to the counter, his textbooks are gone, replaced with a sketchbook. His eyes are narrowed, his bottom lip jutted out in concentration. Between his fingers, he holds a graphite pen. "Whatcha doin' there?" I ask.

He looks up, dazed and confused, and slowly turns the sketchbook my direction. On the page, in gray lead, is an anime drawing of a kid with shiny hair, a scarf around his neck, thick jacket, hands shoved in his pockets. It's so detailed, shaded to almost perfection, that I gasp at the sight of it. "That bad, huh?" he asks.

"No. Dude. This is…" I take the sketchbook from him, lift it higher. "This is insane. Did you copy this from somewhere?"

"No. I just thought it and drew it. Do you like it?"

"Dude…" It's all I can say. "You're amazing."

"Yeah?" He sounds surprised.

"You've never been told how good you are?"

He shrugs.

"Do you draw a lot?"

"When no one's looking, yeah."

"What do you mean?"

Another shrug. "I'm a jock."

"So?"

"A jock can't be an artist."

"Don't do that, Lachlan. Don't stereotype yourself. Ever. You are who you are, and you like what you like."

"But Lucas was a jock."

"And Lucas is…?"

"My oldest brother. Two above Logan. We're both sprinters. He trains me. My family—they all come to watch my meets. It's like… the *only* time they come together when they're not forced to. So…"

"So… you like the attention?"

"No," he says, taking the sketchbook and closing it. He shoves it back in his bag, as if it's something that needs to be hidden. As if it's a secret. With his back to me, he adds, "I like seeing them all together, though. I was, like, super young when Lucy went off to college, and then Lucas moved out, and Leo moved to Raleigh."

"You still have Logan… and the twins, right?"

"The twins have each other, Red, and Logan's not home much on weekends, so…"

I get between him and his backpack, knowing he's about to leave. "Can I ask you something?"

"Sure."

"What do you like more? Running or drawing?"

"It doesn't matter," he says. "Drawing doesn't bring my family together." He moves around me, shoulders his backpack. "I better get back before Lucy knows I'm missing."

LOGAN

"You'd love college," Dumb Name says, helping me nail up a frame. Being on supervisor duty means getting back to basics. "The girls there —they'd eat you alive."

"I do fine right here," I tell him.

"Yeah, but the options are limited here."

No shit.

"Besides, they're all the same here."

Not always.

Luke approaches, checks out the frame sitting in the yard, then gets out his measuring tape. "I know how to frame," I mumble, annoyed. "You gotta give me room to breathe, bro."

Luke pockets the tape measure. "Sorry," he says, then: "Have you guys seen my phone? I can't find it."

"Have you tried calling it?" Dumb Name asks.

That question earns him an eye roll from Luke. "Why didn't I think of that?"

"You ask stupid questions, you get stupid answers," I tell Dumb Name. Then to Luke: "You play stupid games, you win stupid prizes."

"What the hell does that even mean?" he murmurs, and then he's off—probably to annoy someone else. As soon as he's out of earshot, Dumb Name asks, "Where's his phone?"

"In my pocket."

He cracks a smile. "What are we doing with it?"

"We're dry walling the bathroom this afternoon."

"You're putting it *in* the wall?"

I shake my head. "I have no idea what you're talking about."

LUNCH COMES AND GOES. Luke asks everyone at least three times if they've seen his phone. Dumb Name and I hang the drywall in the bathroom, patch it, paint it. The best part of the plan is that Luke will be so embarrassed he let it happen to him, he'll repair the work himself when he finds the phone. *If* he ever finds it. Just as Dumb Name and I take a break to admire our work, Dad walks in, tells us he has to take off early. "Hot date?" Dumb Name asks, waggling his eyebrows.

Dad sighs, then smirks. "Yes. With yo mama!" And then he does this strange old man dance that he really only ever does with Lachlan. It's rare that I get to see this side of him—the jokey, carefree side—and I laugh so hard, it makes me breathless.

"Seriously?" Dumb Name asks. His mom's been single forever, about the length of time Dad has, but the idea of either of them moving on with each other, or *at all*, makes me a little uncomfortable. Not that I don't want to see my old man happy. I just can't imagine him with anyone else. And I sure as shit can't envision anyone replacing my mom.

Dad taps at the doorjamb. "I'm introducing her to a friend of mine. I think she might do well in an office environment, answering phones and such."

"She's not very good on a computer," Dumb Name says.

Dad smiles. "She'll do just fine." He switches his focus to me. "You can finish up early. I need you to pick up Lachlan, take him to training with that specialist sprint coach."

"Isn't that Lucas's thing?"

"Lucas doesn't know about it." His words are meant for me. "We'll talk about it later." Then he points to the wall. "I hope you at least left the ringer on before putting it in there."

My eyes go wide.

Dumb Name yells, "It was his idea!" *Fucking traitor.*

Dad just laughs.

I say, removing my tool belt, "So I'm getting him from Lucy's shop?"

"Nah. Lucy mentioned that he's been hanging out at some new store a couple doors down. Stationery or something. Do you know it?"

AUBREY

"Should I be calling your dad or something?"

Lachlan looks up from the pile of notebooks he's counting and shakes his head. "Lucy already did."

"And it's okay that you're here?"

"Lucy told him you were good people." He goes back to counting, from the beginning. He'd come in after school again, backpack in tow, and *made* me come up with a task for him. To help *me*. As if he could sense that I needed help. I do, just not in the way he thinks. Besides Logan's occasional text message, my phone has sat stagnate all week. I'm both lonely and alone, and there's no remedy for that. No cure. There is, however, Lachlan Preston.

I get back behind the counter, pretend to be working as hard as he is. "What do kids around here do for fun?"

His shoulders lift with his heavy inhale, and he looks over at me, his eyes narrowed. I've screwed up his counting again. He's clearly taking it seriously. Maybe my little speech about shoplifters, stock control and loss prevention really got to him. *Oops.* "Don't worry about counting the books. Come talk to me."

"You sure?"

"Yes!"

A smile breaks through, glorious, and there's no doubt the kid's destined to break hearts. "There's a lot to do around here," he tells me.

"Like what?"

"Like swimming, fishing, jet skiing, camping."

"And where must one go to do all these?"

"Our house." His eyes are huge. "You should come over to our house! Yeah! On Saturday! Please?" He's nodding, hopeful.

"I work on Saturdays." *And that's stage-six clinger activity*, I don't say.

"Then Sunday?"

Tempting… "Anything that doesn't involve your house?"

"Batting cages. Movies. If you drive a little bit, trampoline park, rock climbing…"

"Hmm. I don't have a car. Or a license."

He eyes me warily. "Aren't you, like, *old*?"

I flick the brim of his cap. "I'm not *that* old. What else? Any hidden gems?"

He adjusts his hat, but it's clear he's losing his momentum. "All the fun things to do are at my house. You should just come over. Lincoln—"

"Your friend?"

"My brother, one of the twins… he and Liam—"

"The other twin?"

He nods. "He just got a girlfriend."

"Liam?"

"No. Lincoln. Come on, Red. Keep up."

"Got it," I laugh out. "Keep going."

"Linc and Liam have been inseparable their entire lives. Like, for real. They even have this weird scar on their elbows, Liam on the left, Lincoln on the right. Or maybe it's the other way around. I can't remember. Some days, I can't even tell them apart. Anyway, these scars —no one knows how they got them. *No one.* And so everyone thinks they were conjoined twins separated at birth. Dad says they weren't, but I don't know. Seems pretty suspect to me."

A giggle falls from my lips. "I bet they were."

"So anyway," Lachlan continues, and I lean against the counter, loving the company. "Lincoln got a girlfriend recently. His first. And now he's doing all this stuff *without* Liam. Which, I mean, I don't really get it. Why can't Liam go on the dates with them, right?"

"Right."

"So Liam's like, lost without Lincoln. He wanders around the house, and sometimes I catch him talking to himself, like Linc is right there next to him. The other day, I saw him have an entire conversation with Linc in the kitchen while he was making a snack. Linc wasn't even home. And then last night, at dinner, he took two glasses out of the cupboard and set one next to him—"

"Where Linc normally sits?"

"Yeah. He poured the juice and everything. Even said 'you're welcome', even though Linc wasn't there to say thank you."

I'm smiling so wide my cheeks hurt. "Your family is fascinating."

"Not really." He shrugs.

"Tell me more?"

"Hmm…" He's tapping his chin. "Did you know I killed my mother?"

My stomach drops. So does my jaw. He said it so matter-of-factly that I stumble over my next words. "I thought your mom died of cancer."

"Yeah. Right after *I* was born. Six kids before me, she was in perfect health. I come along, boom, *dead*."

"Lachy…" I start, and that's all I can get out because he's looking at me with those blue-blue eyes, and I'm looking at him like he's a poor, lost soul.

"It's true," he whispers, dropping his gaze.

"Lachlan, you know cancer… it's just a really sucky disease, and there's no—"

"Cure?" he cuts in.

"I was going to say *reason*. There's no reason. And if there was, if one day someone really, really smart finds that reason, I can guarantee it won't be *you*. It won't be having a child. Especially one as great as you."

He's looking at me again, as if he's trying to work out if I'm telling the truth. I keep my eyes on his, hoping he finds whatever he's looking for. I refuse to be the first to look away. I won't. I don't. Not even when the bell above the door chimes, my first customer for the day. I'll lose the sale if it means this little boy understands that he did *not* kill his mother.

Lachlan looks up at the sound of a short, sharp whistle, so I do the same. Logan's a foot inside the door, his hands in his pockets. "You playing that staring game?" he asks. "I used to love that game."

"Yeah," Lachlan answers for the both of us. "The staring game."

"Dad had a thing, so I'm taking you. Get your shit," Logan says, even though Lachlan's already picking up his backpack. Logan hasn't looked at me. Hasn't said a word. Apparently, I'm invisible in the presence of *anyone* else. When Lachlan gets to him, Logan hands him his keys. "Wait for me in the truck."

"Why?"

"I'll let you choose the music."

"Deal! Thanks, Red! Bye, Red!"

Logan's still standing just inside the store when his brother moves around him, leaving us alone. As soon as the door's closed, Logan focuses on me. He doesn't say anything, just trails his gaze from top to bottom, back again. "What?" I say, crossing my arms. "Let me guess. I look like a unicorn? Or a peacock?"

His smile is faint. "Fuck, Red. You look good enough to eat."

It's only four-thirty, and it's the first time I've ever thought of closing the shop early and maybe walking around town. Maybe catch a movie. I'll probably be the only one there on a Thursday evening. Scratch that. I'll probably be the only one there on a Thursday evening *alone*. For some reason, the idea of this doesn't completely suck, and so I start switching off all the displays. I take what little cash is in the register and bring it with me down the short hallway to the small office. I'm at the safe when the bell chimes, and shit, I forgot to lock the door and flick the sign to closed. "Sorry," I call out, rushing out onto the sales floor. "We were just closing up."

Logan smirks as he turns the sign to *closed*, locks the door. "We sure were."

"What the hell are you doing?"

"I'm hungry," he says, and then he's stalking toward me, his lips lifting at the corners, ending on a smirk. He looks over my shoulder, his footsteps slow. I take a step back. He asks, "What's down there?"

"My office." My voice is a whisper.

His smirk gets smirkier, and then his hands are on my hips and his mouth is on my neck and I *try* to fight him, try to push him away.

"You can't just come in here and do this. I have plans."

"Like what?" he says against my skin.

"Like, like..." I'm sure I had plans, but now he's kissing me, and even if I could remember those plans, I can't voice them. I can barely breathe. He tastes different. Like *him*. No aftermath of marijuana. And my feet are no longer on the floor, and my hands are no longer pushing. They're in his hair, holding him to me while his arms hold me to him, and then we're in my office and he's moving shit off my desk, clearing it. I reach for the buttons of his work shirt the same time he goes for the zipper of my dress. As soon as my dress is on the floor and my hands are on his bare chest, he unsnaps my bra from behind, and his eyes go straight to my breasts. "Me love cookie," he says in a Cookie Monster voice. I laugh so hard, so free, and I want to tell him that I've missed him, missed *this*. Not the fooling around, but the laughing. With him.

"You're an idiot."

His face goes serious. "I've missed ya, Red."

My heart stops. One beat. Two. And when it starts again, it's racing, climbing, *soaring*. "Me too." It's barely a whisper, because anything more means he'll definitely hear it, and I don't know that I want him to. I lean back against the desk and reach for his belt, and then his lips are on my nipple, his tongue flicking back and forth.

Logan keeps his gaze on mine the entire time he pays attention to my breasts, moving from one to the other, his eyes bright against the store lighting. I continue to work on his belt, his fly, until he's completely free and in my grip. A moan escapes me when my hand circles his hard, hot length, and he smirks against my skin, moves from my breasts to my collarbone, up my neck, finishing on my lips. He kisses me deep and slow, while his fingers gently skim up, up, up my thigh, stopping at the apex. He pulls my panties to the side, and I inhale his groan when he realizes the effect he's had on me. Slowly, so fucking slowly, he slides two fingers inside me, and we're nothing but hands and mouths and tongues and heated breaths caused by pure ecstasy. My head throws back when his thumb finds my clit, and he goes back to my neck, teasing, tempting. He kisses his way up to my ear, at the same time he pulls his fingers out of me. "I've been dying to taste you again, Red. It's all I can fuckin' think about." And then he wipes my pleasure off his fingers with his lips, with his tongue, and my breath... my breath is gone. My vision blurs from need, my core pulsing at the sight of him. Then he does something wild—something *completely* him. He offers that same taste to me, his index finger strumming on my bottom lip, waiting for me to open for him. And so I do. He smiles, his eyes glazed with the same need swarming through every one of my cells. "Tell me how good you taste," he demands.

The second I start to shake my head, he covers both his fingers and my lips with his mouth, and I taste his tongue, taste myself on his fingers.

Everything is slow.

Everything is frantic.

Like we're trying to fuck the evidence of my pleasure with just our mouths alone. "Logan," I whine, pulling his fingers away with my free hand.

"What, baby? Tell me what you want."

I grip his cock tighter, start working faster. "I need you inside me."

He smirks. "Soon."

"Now!" I barely recognise my own voice.

"Fuck, I love it when you get like this." He takes a step back, his hands going for my panties.

"What are you doing?" I breathe out.

His eyes narrow. "You want me to do you with your panties on?"

Pushing off the desk, I shake my head. "No, Logan," I say, dropping to my knees in front of him. I take his cock in my hand again, run his head along my wet lips. "I *need* you inside me." And then I take him in my mouth, my eyes locked on his.

"Jesus fuck, Red," he groans, his head tilting back while his hands find my hair. He grips the base of his cock, his gaze lowering to meet mine. "Play with your tits."

I do as he asks, tweaking my nipples, and I'm *lost*. So damn lost in my pleasure. Logan—he makes me feel sexy, makes me feel wanted, needed, like no one has before.

His hips pump, short movements, not wanting to hurt me. "Now your pussy," he orders.

I lower my hand down my stomach, beneath my panties. My moan vibrates against his length when I slide two fingers inside my warm center.

"Fuck," he spits out, pushing me away. "I can't fucking take this." And then he's lifting me off the floor until my back's on the desk, and he's sliding my panties down my legs. His every move is calculated, yet frantic. He takes a moment to look down at me, naked and spread out on a table, just for him, as if he's a king and I'm his feast. "You have no idea what you do to me."

I grasp his hand, bring it to my wetness. "I think I have some idea."

His face pinches, as if he's in agony. "Dammit, Red. I think... I think I'm stupidly attracted to you."

A laugh emits from deep in my throat. "Sucks to be you."

He shakes his head, eyes moving from where his fingers play with my folds, up to my eyes. "You know what? It actually doesn't suck at all." He grips my hips, pulling me down to the edge of the table. He stands between my legs, his cock at full attention. "You're not doing this with anyone else, right?"

All air leaves my lungs, and I hesitate a beat, wondering why he's asking me this... especially now... when we're so damn close and my need is heating my entire body. "*Only* you."

The corners of his lips lift. "Good."

It's one simple word that means more than it should, and I feel my heart beat wildly throughout my entire body.

"Good," he says again, and then he's on his knees, his face between my legs, and I stare up at the ceiling, gripping the edge of the table. The harsh lights blur my vision while Logan and I blur the lines, and my hips rise, his mouth and fingers bringing me closer and closer to the edge. My eyes water from the brightness of the lights, and I feel like I'm in heaven… and if this is heaven, I don't ever want to come down to earth.

I've barely recovered from my release before he's rolling on a condom, finding a home deep, deep, deep inside me. He holds his weight up on his elbows, while he slowly pumps into me, his eyes right on mine. His thumb strokes against my temple, shifting the wetness there. His movements slow, but he stays inside me. "Are you crying, babe? Do you want to stop?"

"No," I breathe out. "Please no."

He stops completely.

"Aubrey, if you don't want to do this…"

"It's the lights," I say, kissing him gently, tasting my pleasure on his lips. "They're bright, that's all," I lie. Because that's not all. And going by the way he's staring at me, at the way his hips move, his pelvis slowly and achingly grind into mine, the way he never takes his eyes off me, the way he whispers my name with his release right into my neck… he knows it, too.

Something's happening between us.

Something *more*.

He settles on top of me, his breaths sharp, short.

"I never want to hurt you, Red," he whispers. "Don't let me hurt you, okay?"

"You haven't," I assure, running my hands through his hair.

He rears back, his eyes on mine again. "Promise me?"

"I swear."

He kisses me again, slow and meaningful, as if he's trying to convey the unspeakable words hidden between the blurred lines of what we created.

I break the kiss, smile up at him, and try to find our level ground again, because it feels as though my world's been rocked, shaken, tilted off its axis. I tease, "So… you're attracted to me, huh?"

He chuckles, his lips meeting my collarbone. "Shut up."

I run my hands through his hair again. "It's a shame you're so repulsive, we could've had some really cute little red-headed babies."

"Oh, my god…" he says through a chuckle, his entire body shaking with the force.

I lift my head. "They'd be born with abs of steel like yours."

He smiles down at me. "We could call our firstborn Leppy."

"Leppy?"

"Little Leprechaun."

The back of my head hits the table when I burst out laughing. He tries to drown out the sound with a kiss, but all it does is merge both our amusements. "Are you okay?" he asks, his hands going to the back of my head, soothing the area that landed on the table.

"I'm good."

He rolls his eyes. "You're so full of yourself."

I laugh again. And for a moment—just one—I forget the meaning of loneliness.

LOGAN

"Why are you so smiley?" is the first thing Lachlan says when he's back in my truck.

I school my features. "How was practice?"

"Same as always." He wipes the sweat from his brow and replaces his running shoes for his everyday Air Jordans—my old ones. "What'd you do while you were gone?"

"Not much."

"You're smiling again."

"Am not."

"Are too."

"Am not."

He sighs. "You think Red will still be at her shop?"

"It's not *her* shop."

"Yes, it is."

"Not, it's not."

"Yes, it is. She owns it. She told me."

I pull out of the park once his seatbelt's on. Lachy trains three times a week, plus whatever Lucas has him doing. The training with his specialist coach is at the high school—the facilities are better here. I make my way out of the familiar grounds and onto the road, wondering how it is I never worked out that it was *Aubrey's* shop. I always assumed she managed it. Now the whole calling me for Lachy shoplifting makes sense. I just assumed she used it as a way to get to me. Obviously, I've assumed a lot of things about Aubrey. Truth is, I don't really know her. I should probably change that if I expect her to keep giving me the best blow jobs in the history of the world.

"So," Lachy says, pulling me out of my thoughts.

I adjust in my seat, push away memories of her mouth. "So, what?"

"You think she'll still be at work?"

She's probably still trying to find her underwear. They're in my pocket, just FYI. "Maybe. Why? Did you leave something there?"

He shakes his head. "Yesterday, I was telling her about the pizza place. You know, the one with the taco pizza?"

"Yeah."

"And she said she would love to try it, so I thought... I mean, maybe we could order it and bring it back to her. Have dinner with her. I think she's lonely."

At his final word, my foot slips on the accelerator and we get jolted forward. My arm instinctively extends, pushing Lachy back in his seat. "Sorry."

"All good. So? Can we?"

I shrug. "We can drive past, see if she's there. If she is, then sure. Why not?"

AUBREY IS STILL THERE, and so I give Lachy a twenty and get him to order the pizza. She's at the corner of the store counting a pile of books, and even though the sign says closed (because I made it that way), the door is unlocked. I open it, and the second I do, my ears are filled with the sound of her horrible singing. There's no music playing, but I can see the cord of the earphones hanging from her head. She's obviously listening to Ed Sheeran and echoing his lyrics, as if she *can* sing, as if just anyone can *actually* sing Ed fucking Sheeran. I should move. I should let her know I'm here. I should do something more than just stare at her, smiling like an asshole. Now she's screaming the lyrics, and I'm holding back a laugh because she's *that* bad. Finally, *finally*, the singing stops, and she drops the books on the floor, creating a loud *thwack* that echoes off walls. She moves to the right, picks up another stack of books, and starts counting them, too. She starts singing again. No. She's *rapping*. Snoop and Dr. Dre to be specific, and *what the hell kind of playlist is this*? She's dropping F-bombs as naturally as I breathe, and now I'm laughing out loud. I can't help it. But she doesn't hear me, the bass through her earphones loud enough for me to hear. My legs eventually move, as if on their own, one foot in front of the other toward her. I jump back when she starts moving again, rapping louder, her hips swaying quicker, throwing up gang signs that could possibly get her killed. My hands settle on her hips, their favorite place, and she turns swiftly, screams, holds a pen like a knife raised in the air. "You asshole," she shouts, and I laugh harder.

When she removes the earphones, I say, "You got some voice there, Red."

"What the hell are you doing?" she's clutching at her chest, the freckles on her nose a shade darker than normal. "You scared the fuck out of me. And, hey"—she swats my chest—"did you take my underwear?"

"Memento."

"More like *trophy*."

"You say potato, I say tomato."

"That's not how the phrase goes." Her eyes narrow on mine. "Have you been smoking?"

I shake my head. "Lachlan's getting us some food. We're having dinner together."

"You and me?"

"And him."

"Oh." Her gaze drops. "That's cool. But seriously, can I have my underwear? I'm not digging this breeze."

I reach into my pocket, hand them to her. She puts them back on in her office. She does *not* allow me to watch.

AUBREY LOVES THE PIZZA, and Lachy says, pointing to her, "I knew you would!"

We're sitting on the cold tile of her shop floor, pizza between us, soda can each. She says, "You did say that. I was going to order it tonight, but by the time I walk home, it would've been cold. I checked online. They don't deliver." She frowns.

"You gotta call Peter," says Lachlan.

She asks, "The guy who delivers my packages?"

Lachy nods, finishes chewing. "He delivers everything. He's the town's only Uber, Lyft, Curb, and taxi driver, too."

"He farts in my store," she tells him, and he laughs.

"He says it's a medical condition," Lachlan replies.

They continue their conversation as if I'm not here, and to be honest, I'm not even mad about it. If Lachy is right, that Aubrey is lonely, I'm glad Lachy's spending time with her. Time I can't. As if Peter heard us talking about him, he enters the shop—the door still unlocked—and Aubrey gets to her feet, signs off on the package.

He *doesn't* fart.

Aubrey inspects the small, square box and sits down again, her legs crossed.

"Stock?" Lachy asks. "If you leave it until tomorrow, I can unpack it for you."

She smiles at him, the kind of smile that's normally followed by a pat on the head or shoulder.

"I ordered them yesterday," she tells Lachy. "I didn't think they'd get here so fast."

"What is it?" he asks, and her gaze flicks to mine for half a second. She uses my keys sitting next to me to cut the tape, then open the package. Inside are a bunch of markers, all different colors. Nothing spectacular.

"Are they Copics?" Lachy rushes out, sitting up on his knees to get a better look.

"You know what they are?" I ask him.

He shrugs, sits back down. "I've seen them on YouTube or something."

"What are they for? Drawing?"

Aubrey answers for him. "Yeah. Something like that."

"You draw?" I ask her.

She ignores my question. "I was thinking of setting up a desk in the corner, having them out for kids to use when their parents come in here. The longer they're here, the more chance I have of actually making a sale." She sets the markers to the side, picks up another slice of pizza.

I sip my soda.

Lachlan watches her. After a while, he says, "Aren't they, like, really expensive?"

Aubrey shrugs. "They're worth it."

I'VE NEVER SLEPT with a girl sober. I mean, I've had sex with girls without being under the influence of Mary, but I've never *slept* with one. And I have a feeling that if I take Lachy home first, then Aubrey— she's probably going to expect that, and if I do, then there's the possibility of what happen *while* I'm asleep. Dreams are too vivid and memories are too real, and I wake up constantly, my search for answers and reasons making it impossible to sleep again. When I smoke, I sleep through the night. When I smoke, I never have regrets. When I smoke, I am weightless. Not just physically, but mentally.

There is no burden to keep me down.

I am liquid, ebbing, flowing.

I am pulling into Aubrey's driveway.

"Thanks for the pizza," she says, looking at Lachlan.

"No problem. I'll walk you to your door."

Aubrey's finger runs along my palm as it sits between us. She doesn't hold my hand. Doesn't squeeze it. "I'll see you later?" she asks, and I don't know if she means later tonight or tomorrow—like our original plans—but I nod anyway. When she starts to leave, I grasp her finger. Hold it. It's as close as I've ever gotten.

Lachlan walks her to her door, and he's smiling like an idiot, and I'm smiling at him smiling like an idiot, because never in my life did I ever think that Lachlan and I would be after the same girl. Leo: plenty.

Lucas: just to piss him off. The twins: only celebrities. Lucy: well... that's to be determined.

Their mouths are moving, but they're speaking so low I can't hear what they're saying, and then Lachlan's hugging her. Not in the way Liam hugged Laney right before he went for the boob grab—so I've heard, I wasn't there—but he's hugging her like how he hugs Dad or how he hugs Lucy.

Like how I used to let him hug me.

BACK IN THE CAR, Lachlan faces me as he buckles himself in. "I think you should do more than just sex Red."

Me too, buddy. Me too. I keep that thought to myself.

17

AUBREY

LOGAN DIDN'T COME BACK, which is fine; I only half expected him to. I spent the night trying to come up with more names for his penis. I switched from ideas of food and combined the two things he told me are his favorite things in the world. Weed and sex. I've replaced the sex with masturbation. I now have an ongoing list comprising of the following:

Weed Whacker.

High Jacker.

Toke and Stroker.

Stoner Boner.

Masterbaker.

I'm pretty happy with all of them so far.

I WALK TO WORK TODAY, because the bike has a flat, and knowing me, I'll never fix it. I plan to draw up a sign offering it to another good home. The Copic markers are still where I left them in the middle of the shop floor, and so I pick them up, put them in the safe. Before Lachlan gets here this afternoon, I plan to bring the desk from the office out to the shop floor so he can draw on that. Obviously, I made the plans before his brother and I had sex on it. I'll wipe it down. He'll never know.

After doing my opening checklist, I go back to my usual spot behind the counter and check my phone. Nothing. No surprise. I send my mother a text:

All good here. What's up with you?

I send my grandmother a text:

All good here. What's up with you?

I write out a text to Joy: *Why the fuck does it even matter? You cheated on him.*

I delete the text.

For a few minutes, I watch people walk past the store one way. Then the other. They never look inside.

I jump on Facebook, and I'm bombarded with status updates from Carter—the ex.

I love her.

I love her.

I love her.

That's not what they say, but that's how I read them, and that's okay. It doesn't hurt like it used to. Then I remember Logan's friend request sitting in purgatory. I accept the request from *Bing Bong—seller of cheap Ray Bans* and smile when a picture of him replaces the generic white silhouette and blue backdrop. The night at Lucy's, they mentioned how the twins are YouTube famous, and that's why they all have their accounts on lock down. Their dad even had to put up a security gate at their property because teenage girls were starting to show up. I've watched a few of their videos. Logan's not in any that I saw.

There isn't a lot going on in his profile. Mainly pictures of him in what I assume is Cambodia, building a house. There's a picture of him with another guy, who I assume is Lucas. Lucas has his arm around a girl with thick, black glasses. She's beautiful. He's beautiful. Everything is beautiful. Especially the picture of Logan holding a banner that reads: *Habitat for Humanity,* and now it all makes sense, at the same time it doesn't, because I'm pretty sure that no one could force Logan into doing something like this unless he wanted to. Logan is *nice,* and he treats it as though it should be a secret.

I go through more and more of his profile, because I have my own secrets: I *like* Logan Preston.

I'm smiling, and I shake my head at myself, but I can't stop my face's reaction to my admittance.

I *like* Logan Preston.

Every time I say it in my head, I scroll down a little more.

Then stop.

The girl is beautiful: long, blond hair, and bright brown eyes, and the kind of smile that's hard to fake. Logan has his arm around her, and they're both smiling at the camera. The background is the house they're building, the Habitat for Humanity banner hanging above where the front door will eventually sit. Her name is Casey Allen, and it's her photo, and he's tagged in it. The caption reads: *More like Habitat for Hotties.*

I click into her profile—completely public—and feel the pierce of my heart cause my entire body to deflate. *We weren't anything,* I convince myself. We were a one-night stand that meant nothing.

We *still* mean nothing.

Because three weeks ago, Casey Allen was in a hotel room, and this boy she's dubbed "hottie" is under a sheet, covering just his junk. He's reaching out, likely telling her not to take the picture, but she does it anyway, and she posts the photo to show off to her friends, to show off to me, because social media is the place where *hope* goes to die.

It would be stupid to cry.

I cry anyway.

And send another text to my mother:

I miss you.

By early afternoon I've convinced myself that it's not a big deal. Really. I just... I need to understand the meaning of casual sex, that's all. This is what happens: Boy meets girl. Boy and girl have sex. The end. I've never done casual before, and so this is normal. This feeling is normal.

My mom hasn't called or written back. According to my grandmother, she's away for business somewhere where there's no signal. It would've been great if she let her daughter know.

There are two girls in the store (possibly the only bright side to my day), and it's taking all the power in me not to follow them around, beg them to buy something. I've seen them around at the parties Joy used to take me to, but I've never said a word to them and doubt they have any idea who I am. They're talking about their plans; plans for the future, the weekend, tonight. All things I *don't* have.

Jealousy is a petty emotion.

"Will's taking me away for the weekend," the brunette says.

"Oh. Em. Gee, Bree!" says the blonde, clutching a hand to her heart. "You're so lucky. Will's such a nice guy."

"I know, right? I did good with him."

"Totally." They move from the notebooks to the pens, and the blonde says, "There's this party tonight, but I'm not sure if I'll go..."

"Why not?"

"I'm waiting on a call."

"From a guy?"

"Yep."

"Who?"

"I don't want to say."

"No, Bella!" says Bree.

Bella?

Why does that sound so...

Bella with the Boobies.

She does have boobies.

"No, Bella, what?" Bella mocks.

Her friend rolls her eyes. "Your not wanting to say can only mean one thing."

"And what's that?"

"Logan Preston."

My heart sinks to my stomach, and I rise a few inches, flex my hands at my sides. "He called me last week," she says. *Liar.* He was gone last week. "On Thursday," she adds. "As soon as he got back from Cambodia."

My eyes drift shut. I force myself to breathe. In through my nose. Out through my mouth.

"You're such a sucker for bad boys," Bree says. "I take it you slept with him... *again.*"

"Hell, yeah, I did. And I have no regrets. Not everyone gets to have a Will in their life."

Bree sighs.

I glance down at my hands, at the freckles, at my unpainted nails, and the half-dozen silver rings on my fingers. I try to name each stone, just so I have something else to concentrate on other than their conversation. But they're talking louder now, coming closer, and when I look up, Bella has two notebooks and a pen in her grasp. She smiles at me, the kind of All-American-Girl smile that makes you fake smile back without realizing. She dumps her items on the counter and turns to her friend. "And then he found me at the party on Friday."

The party on Friday. I was at the party on Friday.

"I thought he left," Bree says.

He did! With me...

"He did," Bella confirms. "He says he had to take care of some business. But he came back and found me. We spent the night in one of the rooms." She turns to me, but I can't see her expression beyond my pain. "Can I get these?" She's pointing to the notebooks and pen. "You take debit card, right?"

I nod, ring up her purchase. "Sixteen dollars and fifty cents, thank you." My voice breaks.

I break.

As soon as they're out the door, I flip the sign to closed and go to the office, where I take out the Copic markers from the safe and put them in a nicer box that still hides its content. Then I flick off all the lights and lock up the shop. I don't bother putting a note up. It won't make a difference. I take the markers to Lucy's bookstore. She's sitting in an armchair at the end of one of the aisles, a place where she likes to "hide" from customers. I leave the markers on the counter, and as soon as I'm back out on the street, I send her a text:

Aubrey: *Left a gift for Lachlan on your counter. Tell him he must keep them and USE them, no matter what.*

Lucy: *You're not at your shop today?*

Aubrey: *Heading home for the weekend.*

I delete my Facebook app, and switch off my phone. Then I walk to the bus stop and prepare to go to an empty house where silence will greet me and loneliness will consume me.

18

AUBREY

MY MOTHER BURNED every single item belonging to or resembling my dad the day after his funeral. I have no physical memory of him. Not even a single photograph. When I was younger, I'd scour the house for anything that reminded me of him: a plate, a towel, a DVD. One time, I found an old sock of his. She burned that, too. She said I was too young to understand, that I might never understand. Now there are zero chances of me finding anything of my father's. The house she owns now—the one I'm currently in—is *not* my home.

Neither is *my* house.

Or the town I live in.

LOGAN

We try to preserve as much of my mother as possible. Every item, every scent, every memory. In the living room, she used to sit on this giant armchair next to my dad's recliner. When I close my eyes, I can still see her there; a blanket on her knees, knitting needles between her fingers. *Smiling.* She was always smiling. When she did frown, it was because one of us kids was sad or hurt. Her chair's still in the living room. Over the years, the smell of her has faded. No one sits on the chair. No one but Lachlan. I don't recall the conversation. It's not like we all sat down and said, "We have to preserve this piece of her. Only Lachlan can sit in her chair, smell her perfume left behind, so that he can feel somewhat close to her. If we all sit there, we'll take a piece of her with us every time we leave it. Let him have this tiny piece of her." When I was kid, I'd watch Lachy sitting in the same spot I'd always find her. Even now, seeing him there makes my breath catch.

He's sitting with his legs crossed, headphones on, iPad in hand. It's Friday night. I've already had my fill of Mary, and so I rush through the house, hope he doesn't catch onto it. I make it to the front door before he calls out, "Where are you going?"

My shoulders slump, and I lick my lips, try to act straight. I turn to him, shrug. "Just going to hang out with Aubrey."

"At her house?" he asks, removing the headphones.

"I guess."

"In Raleigh?"

"What?"

"She's gone home for the weekend, dude." He sighs, puts his headphones back on. "Sheesh, don't you and your girlfriend communicate?"

"She's not my girlfriend." *I think.* Or maybe she's closer to it than I let myself believe, because she should've told me, right? I mean, we made plans. *Didn't we?*

I go to her house anyway, just in case Lachlan was talking shit. The house is dark, no sign of life, and so I try calling her. Her phone goes directly to voicemail the first time, so I don't really know why I try three more times. I go to her shop. It, too, is closed. But there's no sign on the door saying she's closed for the weekend. I call home, ask Lachlan how he knew Aubrey was going out of town. He says Lucy told him. I call Lucy. She confirms. I call Aubrey *again*. I'm officially *that* guy. Surprise, surprise: straight to voicemail.

I've lit up another joint before I even make it to my shack, my phone on my lap in case she calls. I'd be lying if I said I wasn't looking forward to seeing her even though I managed to satisfy my craving yesterday. Yesterday was intense, sure, but it was rushed. I like to take my time with Red. Like to build her up just to pull away, tease her. She hates it. I love it.

The sun's setting earlier now than it did the one time she was here. I get out of the truck and instantly look up at the stars. They're still the same in my eyes: dots of light surrounded by darkness. Some rustling sounds from beside me, and I know who it is without turning. I click my fingers, mumble, "Come here, Chicken."

Aubrey wasn't exaggerating; the pig *is* a beast. He walks—waddles?—over to me, his snout instantly going to my hand. He loves the smell of weed. Sometimes, when I'm really high, I think about blowing smoke in his face. I'm not that cruel. Plus, if he's anything like other stoners, he'll probably get the munchies, and that's not a good idea when he's 350 pounds, and I'm the only thing in front of him. He searches around us, as if he's looking for something, *someone*. "She's not here," I say aloud.

Chicken squeals.

"I know, dude. Me too."

I smoke three joints in a row, because there's fuck-all to do, and I don't feel like partying. I call Aubrey again, and this time, I leave her a voicemail. "Thanks for letting me know you were heading out of town. I could've made other plans." And then I hang up, because I'm annoyed and I'm disappointed, and I'm alone on a Friday fucking night when I don't have to be.

I call Aubrey again. I've memorized her voicemail message, memorized her voice. "Can you please call me when you get back? Hope everything's okay. I'm missin' ya, Red."

19

LOGAN

I DON'T CALL Aubrey again the next day, but I drive by her store (still closed) and her house (still lifeless). There's a bike on her front lawn with a sign that reads "Free to a good home." I question whether it was there yesterday, and I decide that it had to be; I was just too annoyed to notice it.

The next day, I *barely* make it through Sunday Family Breakfast. Dad senses this and tells me to get some rest. Meaning: *Go to your room so your brothers don't realize how fucking stoned you are.*

I go up to my room, shut all the blinds, lie in bed in the darkness with my phone resting on my chest. If she calls, I don't want to miss it. Only a few minutes go by when there's a knock on my door. It can only be Lucy—she's the only one who knocks. "Come in," I say, and the door opens slowly, slightly.

She pokes her head inside. "Okay?"

"Yeah."

"Sure?" Lucy was in college when I first started smoking, so she missed the beginning, the middle, the peeing in the cup that led to what everyone hoped would be *The End*.

"Yeah, Luce, I'm all good."

She steps into the room. "So…" she starts, then looks around my room as if it's the first time she's seeing it. She's still in her pajama pants (pages of books) and probably one of Cameron's hoodies because it goes past her knees. She's so short. Shorter than Aubrey. Maybe even shorter than Mom was.

"You're so little and cute," I tell her, pressing my cheek against the pillow.

She smiles over at me, sits down on the end of my bed. "Do you know when Aubrey gets back?"

"I didn't even know she was leaving."

"She didn't tell you?"

My answer is to look up at the ceiling.

"Well, it's not like you guys are… you know… are you?"

"Sexing?"

"Logan, you've sexed nearly every girl in this town, some of the women, too. Even a couple of the lonely housewives—"

"False."

She rolls her eyes. "I hear things, you know. A *lot* of things. I think this town sometimes forgets that there's a vagina amongst all the Preston testosterone."

"That's probably a good thing," I tell her.

"Maybe." She shrugs. "So, Aubrey…?"

"Luce." I sigh. "When have we ever talked about this stuff?"

"We could start," she says, hopeful.

I crush her hope. "I'd rather not."

My phone vibrates on my chest, and I'm quick to unlock it.

Bella with the Boobies: *Where the hell have you been?*

20

LOGAN

I COULD BARELY FOCUS during Monday morning's meeting because Aubrey's phone's still off and she still hasn't called. Even when Dad called me into his office halfway through the morning to tell me he was proud of my work lately, it still didn't take the edge off. My mind is scattered. Lost. I mismeasure three times. Garray cracks a joke about how I should've finished high school. The glare I give him lets him know that it's the last time I'll let him get away with it. I'm an asshole to everyone, and I know it. I just can't help it. I watch the seconds tick by, but they feel like minutes, and as soon as lunch break comes along, I'm out of my tool belt and into my truck and making my way to her shop.

Still closed.

I drive to her house, knock on the door.

AUBREY

I came home Saturday morning. I wanted to leave within an hour of getting to Mom's place, but unfortunately for me, the buses had stopped running. When I left, I was sure to make it look as though I hadn't been there at all.

I didn't go to work on Saturday. I didn't have it in me to plaster on a smile, talk to the two, maybe three people who might walk through the door. Besides, I didn't want *him* to know I was home. Hence why I never answered the few times he came knocking and why I haven't bothered to switch on my phone. But I'm answering now, because I should, because I deserve to have my say, and because it's time.

I don't let him step foot in my house.

"Where the hell have you been, and why didn't you call me? Did something happen to your phone?" I imagine the hint of worry in his tone. "Aubrey?" He rarely calls me Aubrey. "Why won't you look at me? Is something wrong? Did something happen?"

I shake my head, but I keep it lowered, because looking at him is like looking at the sun: pure agony. "I don't want to do this anymore." My voice wobbles, and I hate that it does.

"What?" He steps forward, tugs on the end of my sweatshirt. "I couldn't hear you."

I look up now, my eyes focused on his shoulder. I'm weak. Pathetic. I force eye contact. Blue-blue eyes stare back at me. I think I'll miss them the most. "I said '*I don't want to do this anymore.*'"

"Do what?" he asks, his eyes narrowing, head cocked to the side.

"Whatever it is we were doing." My voice is stronger, more certain, mirroring how I feel on the inside. "I don't want to do it anymore."

His eyebrows rise. "What the hell happened over the weekend? Did you get back with your ex or something?"

"*Definitely* no." If I were *that* desperate, I'd simply continue to have meaningless sex with the boy in front of me.

Logan takes a step forward, and I take a step back. "Don't."

"Red, what's going on?"

I drop my gaze, stare down at the rings covering my fingers. I clear my throat, ready my words. "I added you on Facebook."

"So?"

When I'd thought about this moment, all the things I would say, I ran through every single response he might possibly have. "So" was on top of that list.

"So" meant "So what?"

"So" meant that he didn't care.

"So" meant that I was doing it all over again: falling for a guy who didn't feel the same.

"So, Cambodia was fun, huh? Building those houses and sleeping with Casey Allen?"

He sighs, rubs his hands across his face. "Jesus. *That's* what this is about? We weren't even—"

"And Bella with the Boobies?"

His eyes widen now. "That was before—"

"Before what, Logan? Before you gave me the excuse that you were jet-lagged? That you were going home to crash? Before you left me alone in bed and you went *back* to the party *you* dragged me away from and spent the night with someone else?" I'm fucking crying. I'm crying and he's watching me, watching every single emotion pass through me, watching me wipe away every single tear. I hate myself for feeling this. I hate him for making me.

"When did…?"

"People talk. *Girls* talk. Girls walk into my store and touch my shit and talk about fucking a guy the night *before*…" I choke on my words, my pain. "I don't want to do this anymore," I repeat.

His eyes drift shut, his hands balling at his sides. "Aubrey," he whispers. "This is—"

"Nothing," I finish for him. "This is nothing. *We* are nothing. And it's my fault for thinking that it was more, just like I did with my ex. It's like history repeating itself."

"Don't compare me to him," he grinds out.

"But you are. You're just like him. Maybe that's why I fell for you. Maybe that's why…"

He shoves his hands in his pockets. "Why what? Say it."

I swallow my nerves, my pride, and lean back against the door, the weakness of my knees unable to hold me up. "Maybe that's why I saw you first."

Logan's head moves from side to side, but his eyes stay on mine. "What are you talking about?"

"That night," I finally admit, tears threatening to fall again. My heart's racing, thumping, beating on the walls of ribs. "The first night you and Joy hooked up… I saw you first. I pointed you out to her, and when you noticed us watching you, you didn't even… it's like I was invisible to you. And I let all that go because, I swear, sometimes…"

Sometimes *what*?

Sometimes he looked at me as if… as if… as if *nothing*.

"You can't be mad at me for that," he says, his voice so quiet I barely hear him.

"I'm not mad at you for that. I'm not even mad about the girl in Cambodia. I'm mad because you…" *You made me feel wanted when you didn't want me at all.* "I'm *not* mad, Logan. I'm just… just *sad*. God, I'm so sad," I cry out. "And I'm allowed to feel that way. I'm allowed to want out of this mess, and I'm allowed to want to be with someone who *sees me first*."

He shakes his head again, his eyes boring into mine. His jaw clenches. His brow furrows. Right before he says, breaking me completely, "Later, Red."

LOGAN

I cut out of work as soon as it's time and head right for my shack where I let Mary fuck me over the way Aubrey did. Before I know it, day turns to dusk, turns to darkness. Mary is a part of every inhale, every reluctant exhale. I consume enough of her to make Aubrey's words disappear, make the vision of her crying get lost in the jumbled puzzle pieces of my mind. I let Mary fill every nerve, every vein, every heartbeat until the world begins to spin, just how I like it. I hate it when everything is still, frozen in time, like memories.

I hate it as much as I hate silence.

I grab my headphones from my truck, plug them into my phone, and then I drown out the silence the only way I know how. I lie down on the bank of the lake, Chicken next to me, and look up at the stars again.

I wonder if I'm broken.

I laugh at the thought.

Of course, I am.

But Mary fixes me. She's my glue, putting the *right* pieces back in their designated place. She rewires my insides until nothing works, and everything is how it should be.

I put out the glowing embers of her soul and light up a new version of her. Then I close my eyes and hope sleep gets me before *It* does.

Minutes pass before I feel the affects:

I am weightless.

Buoyant.

I am high, high, high above the surface.

I am floating on clouds the color of scarlet.

I am nine years old, and the leather cracks beneath my weight. The car still smells new, even though I've been in it for months...

My body goes limp, and Mary becomes sleep's ally: they work together, fighting to scare my demons away.

21

LOGAN

I ACCIDENTALLY SKIPPED dinner last night and breakfast this morning, so when the horn of the food truck sounds, I immediately drop my tools, make my way over to it. Dad's the first one there. I'm right behind him. After ordering his standard turkey sub, he says, eying me over his shoulder, "You didn't come home last night."

"I accidentally fell asleep at a friend's house." The lie comes effortlessly. "Sorry."

Dad nods, turns his entire body toward me. "Come see me after lunch, okay?"

UNLESS IT'S WORK RELATED, Dad's lectures are few and far between, so I'm not really looking forward to whatever it is he has to say. I knock on the door of his portable office and wait, hands in my pockets. He doesn't respond verbally, just opens the door, motions for me to come in and take a seat.

Jesus. This is going to be a long one.

It's not that he cares what we do, especially once we're grown-ass men, but he doesn't like to worry, and going by the look on his face, the darkness around his eyes, he's probably spent half the night worrying.

"Sorry," I say again, because I truly am. The man has seven kids to take care of; the last thing he needs to worry about is my not coming home because I was stoned off my fucking face.

"For what?" he asks.

"For last night, not coming home. For not calling."

He waves it off as he takes his seat on the other side of his desk, the cheap plastic of the chair bending beneath his giant frame. "That's not why I asked you in here."

"It's not?"

Dad shakes his head, leans forward on his elbows. "You've been doing great on the job, Logan. And I mean it when I say I'm proud of you."

"But...?" There's always a "but" when it comes to me.

"But we had a deal."

I sigh, pick at my work pants. "I know."

"The deal was, you leave high school, you work for me, and you get your GED. It's been three years, and I haven't seen you—"

"I know. I'll do it, it's just..."

"Just what?"

I'm a dumbass, I want to say. Instead, I tell him, "I don't know."

He sits taller. "You have until the end of next year."

"School year?"

"Calendar."

"Okay."

"Okay." He starts messing with some paperwork on his desk.

I don't make a move to leave.

He lifts his gaze. "Anything else?"

"No lecture?"

"Don't do it again?" It comes out as a question, as if he doesn't know if it's the correct thing to say. He does that a lot in these moments. Like, he questions his own parenting without my mom around. Like he hopes he's doing right by us.

He is.

"I was thinking..." I start.

Dad drops the papers, gives me his full attention. "Yeah…?"

"I was thinking of going to trade school."

His eyebrows shoot up. "Instead of getting your GED?"

I shrug. "I was thinking I could do both." What the hell else am I going to do with my life?

"What trade?" he asks. "You know everything there is to know about construction."

"Electrical."

"Really?"

"Yeah. I mean, it can't hurt to know that stuff as well. And I enjoy it so…"

"Taking things apart and putting them back together… You've always been good with that stuff." He's smiling. "I'll cover the costs on one condition."

"I can cover the costs." Seriously, I can. He pays me more than any other guy my age, and everything I use, everything I own is covered by the company. Truck, gas, phone. I literally have *zero* expenses.

"One condition," he repeats, and I sigh. "You do it during the day as part of your work hours. No night school. You need to be a nine-teen-year-old boy, Logan. This job—it can't be your life like it was mine."

"But look where it got you."

"Yeah. But look at all the time I missed out on," he says, and I know he means time with my mother. Time with us. His throat bobs with his swallow as his gaze drops. "Just trust me on that, okay?"

I nod.

He motions to the door. "Get back to it."

I get up, start to leave, but pause with my hand on the doorknob. "Dad?" I say, turning to him. When he looks up, his eyes on mine, I tell him, "You're doing just fine. With us kids, I mean. Mom—she'd be proud of you, like you are of me."

I DON'T REALIZE the work day's over until Lucas slaps my back, tells me it's time to leave. Everyone else is already packing up their tools. "I think um… I think I'm just going to hang back, finish up on a few things."

He taps his pockets, probably searching for his phone. He thinks I'm planning another Mayhem. I'm not. Truth is, if I don't keep my mind busy with something, anything, I'll only think about Aubrey. And then I'll end up back at the shack, letting Mary have her way with me.

I can't do that shit again.

"You sure? We're on schedule."

"Yeah, man."

"All right, you got the keys to lock up?"

I'm here every morning before he is to set up for the day. Of course, I have the keys. I give him a look that tells him exactly that.

"Of course, you do. Sorry."

"You don't need to keep me on a leash, Luke," I sigh out. "I'm not fifteen anymore."

He nods, responds with a look of his own—one I can't figure out. "I'll see you later, then."

AUBREY

No one took the bike, because everything I touch turns to shit.

23

LOGAN

DURING WORK, my mind is focused. Super, ultra, hyper focused. So focused that I can't switch it off. Even when the work day's over, all I can think about is the job.

The problem is, it's only my mind that's like that. Everything else is a mess, in pieces; shards of glass too fine to repair, scattered in places too far to reach.

My hands don't follow my mind, my legs move only through a lifetime of repetitive motion. My stomach is a roller coaster: dipping, sliding, swirling. And my heart?

My heart belongs to Mary.

24

LOGAN

I'VE HAD a date with Mary every single night for two weeks. Mary is my comfort. My *joy*. Mary is the only girl who understands who I am, *what* I am, and the best part? Mary gives zero fucks about any of it.

But.

Mary also makes me feel things I don't want to feel, makes me think things I don't want to think. And the down side? Most of those thoughts are layered in scarlet:

Scarlet is bad.

Scarlet is dangerous.

Scarlet is the reason you're back to using me.

I want you to use me, Logan.

Use me!

Scarlet needs to go.

Besides, you don't need another girl.

You just need me.

Mary.

Mary is a fickle bitch.

But.

Mary is right.

She always is.

25

AUBREY

So maybe not *everything* I touch turns to shit, because Lachlan still shows up some days after school, sketchbook in hand. He goes right to the desk I set up in the corner for him, pulls out his markers, and gets to work.

The boy's skills are beyond talent, and even though we don't talk much while he's drawing, I know that I at least did something right. And eating toast for dinner every night to make up for the cost of the markers has totally been worth it.

I print off an email from a supplier with a list of things I've asked to return to them. It's the fourth time I've done it this week. Soon, my store will be empty. Soon, *I'll* be empty.

I start going through the stock on the shelves, dumping products into a box haphazardly, ticking off items one by one.

Tick.

Tick.

Tick.

"Do you not want me here?" Lachlan asks out of nowhere.

My eyes snap to his. "No. I mean, *yes*. Of course, I want you here. Why would you say that?"

He scratches the side of his head. "You've just been, I dunno"—he shrugs—"*different* the past couple weeks."

"Different how?"

"Well, for one, you stopped dressing cool."

I look down at my clothes: sweats. Because I decided this morning that it didn't matter how I dressed. It's not like anyone was going to see me. I replay his words in my mind. "Wait. You think I dress *cool*?"

He grins, as if he knows he just complimented me. He has no idea that besides Logan saying I didn't need anyone to tell me I was pretty, it's probably the nicest thing anyone has said to me since I moved here. "You totally dress cool," he says, nodding. "So... is everything okay with you?"

I *could* lay it all out there: I could tell him his brother hurt my feelings. That if my heart wasn't already partially damaged, Logan had the power to break it with a simple "Later, Red." I could tell him that the image of Logan with someone else right after spending time with me keeps me up at night. Or the fact that he was with someone the night before we reconnected. I could tell him that even though I'm hurting, most of my thoughts are still about a blue-eyed boy who made me laugh more than anyone, who made me feel *something* beyond loneliness and insecurity. I *could* open up to him, considering he's the only person I have in my life who knows to ask if I'm okay. But... Lachlan's *nine* and not at all ready for any of that, so instead, I muster a smile and make my way over to him. "My washer's broken," I lie. "That's why I haven't been wearing my normal clothes. And you,"—I pull down on the brim of his cap, making him giggle—"you being here is absolutely the highlight of my day. So *please* don't ever think that I don't want you here."

"Okay, Red," he says, offering a smile of his own. "I was just worried that something happened with you and Logan."

My heart skips a beat, and I stumble over my words. "Why—why would you say that?"

Lachlan shrugs. "He's been coming home late, which isn't a big deal on the weekend. But, during the week, he normally goes to work and comes right home."

I *try* to play it cool, but the images are back, only this time, it isn't just Bella with the Boobies. It's so many various nameless, faceless girls. "Oh yeah?"

"He's probably just been hanging out with you, right? Sexing or whatever?"

My eyes widen at the last part, and I shake my head. "No, Lachy. He hasn't been with me. But, that's not to say he hasn't been with someone else."

"Oh." He drops his gaze. "But I thought you two were…"

My lips thin to a line.

"I'm sorry, Red." He goes back to his drawing, shaking his head. "I don't ever want to be a stud," he says, and I laugh for the first time in what feels like forever.

"I don't think you have a choice, dude."

"WHO'S SUPPOSED to be picking you up tonight?" I ask, looking out the full-length windows of my store. Most nights, Lucy or Cameron collect him when they leave work at five. Other times, Lachlan's brother's girlfriend, Laney, gets him. But it's past seven now, and he's still here.

"Dunno," Lachlan says, shrugging, too preoccupied with his drawing.

Thunder claps, and I look up at the dull, gray sky, wait for the clouds to open up. A few seconds later, they do, and the atmosphere is coated with heavy rain.

"Dude. I don't drive, so… maybe I should call Cam or Luce for you?"

He's paying attention now, looking out at the thick sheets of rain falling from the sky. "How will you get home?"

I turn to him, and without replying, I reach for my phone and pull up Lucy's number. The bell above the door dings just as I hit call. I hit end just as fast, turning as I do. Logan's standing outside, cap backward, soaking wet. He has the door open just enough to whistle into the room. He doesn't look at me. "Let's go."

"I'm just finishing something," Lachlan rushes out.

Logan snaps, "I don't feel like standing out in the fucking rain!"

"So don't stand outside," Lachlan tells him, not bothering to look up. "Just come in. I'll be five minutes."

Logan shakes his head. "Now, Lachy," he says, frustrated. His focus switches to me, his eyes red… he's stoned. He balls his fists, his eyes locked on mine. "Pack up your shit, Lachlan, and say goodbye to your *friend*. This is the last fucking time you come here."

"What?" Lachlan's on his feet. "You can't do that. You're not the boss of me!"

"Yeah?" Logan laughs. Cynical and deranged. He walks into the middle of my store. To Lachlan, he says, "Dad shouldn't be letting you spend all this time here. He doesn't even know Aubrey. For all we know, she could be a kiddy fiddler." His gaze moves to mine, holds it there. "Is that it, Aubrey? Is that why you let him spend all that time here? Buying him gifts when you barely fucking know him. Do you like little boys?"

It's hard to find your voice when everything inside you shatters. It's one thing not to give a shit about me, but this—this is too much. My voice cracks, and I hate that it does, "Jesus Christ, Logan. Don't be vile."

"And don't talk to her like that!" Lachlan yells.

And that's when Logan loses it. He reaches over, grabs Lachlan by the arm, picks up his backpack, and drags him across the store.

I run after them, trying to save Lachlan from Logan's path of destruction. "Don't you dare make him get in the car with you!"

Logan halts on the sidewalk, me beside him, and we let the rain drown out our anger, our hurt. He turns to Lachlan, hands him his keys. "Wait in my truck."

"No."

Logan glares at him, a silent warning. After a beat, Lachlan's eyes find mine, worried. *Tearful.* "I'm not saying goodbye," he mumbles, and my heart cracks against the weight of longing and loss for something I never really had. When I don't say anything, just stand there, shivering against the temperature, Lachlan runs across the road and toward Logan's truck. As soon as he's inside, I brace myself for Logan's words, his *attack*.

"I'd never put Lachlan in danger. Ever. So, don't tell me what to do, Aubrey. You don't fucking know me." His eyes stay on mine, his words meant to slice, severe, destroy. "You *thought* you did, but you don't. And you had no fucking right to say the things you said to me—to make me feel *guilty*. I did nothing wrong. That girl in Cambodia—she snuck into my hotel room. Luke gave her the key. It was a joke. Nothing fucking happened. And Bella—she says she sleeps with me every other week. She doesn't. Did I leave you that night and go back to the party? Yes. You were drunk, Aubrey, and I knew if I stayed that I'd give in to what *you* wanted, and I didn't want to take advantage of you. I went back to the party and bought weed. Then I left. I fucking left. I haven't been with *anyone* since that night with you. And if you'd stopped to *ask me* about any of the things you accused me of, then maybe you'd know that. But you didn't. I was right fucking here if you wanted the truth, but instead, you judged me. You decided I was a disappointment, and instead of coming to me, you just fucking *left*."

LOGAN

Because we lived by the lake, most of us kids learned how to swim from an early age. For some reason, I just couldn't get the hang of it. By the time the twins were older and experienced enough to swim without floaties, I was still wading on the edge of the water, afraid of dying.

When I told my mother that, she said I had two options:

A: be afraid for the rest of my life.

B: take swimming lessons.

I wish I'd opted for option A. Because option B only made things worse.

After she died, there was a moment when I no longer feared death. In fact, I wanted to be a part of it. So, a few days after her passing, I left the house in my pajamas and walked through the darkness of the night toward the lake. I got to the end of the dock, and I jumped. I couldn't reach the bottom. I didn't care. I stayed under the water until my lungs burned, and I'd heard her voice—my mom's—telling me to rise, to get some air.

So, I did.

But then I'd go back under, do it again, just so I could hear her voice.

I was nine years old, and all I wanted was to hear my mother's voice.

Lucas found me that night, and he stripped me out of my wet clothes, gave me the shirt off his back. Literally. He walked me back to my house, his arm around my shoulders.

I lied when I told him I just wanted to feel *something*.

Truth is, I wanted to feel *nothing*.

He swore he'd never tell anyone.

He never did.

Now, I fill my lungs, my entire insides, with everything Mary has to offer. Mary is my whore, and she never once tells me what we're doing is wrong, that we shouldn't. I walk toward the lake, my hands at my sides, and continue until the water reaches my nose. And then I keep going farther and farther under so I can hear her voice. My mother's...

But I don't.

Instead, it's Mary's voice.

Aubrey's.

And it's not just voices.

It's visions, too.

Aubrey's eyes.

Aubrey's tears.

And then Mary's back, begging me to take her. To *love* her.

Aubrey's crying.

You don't need her, Logan. You have me: Mary.

Aubrey's breaking.

I rise up from the bottom, gasp for air as soon as I hit the surface.

Aubrey.

Aubrey.

Aubrey.

I go back down.

I am tied.

I am bound.

I am sinking.

Low, low, low.

I am liquid.

I am drowning.

I am disappointment.

I am nine years old, and the leather cracks beneath my weight. The car still smells new, even though I've been in it for months. The dash is gray. I can barely see over it...

I am nine years old, and I am fucking terrified.

IT'S two in the morning when I make it back to the house. Dad is up, pacing the living room. He takes me in from head to toe while audible droplets of lake water fall to the floor beneath me. I try to calculate how many times I've seen him like this: unsettled eyes and a tired mind and a soul too forgiving of me.

I should really cut this shit out; it's not fair that I do this to him. I know that. Deep down, past the bullshit, past *Mary*, I know he worries.

He's expecting me to say something, *anything*, but the only thing I can think to say is "Mary made me do it." I don't say that, obviously, and so we stare each other down, waiting for the other to speak first.

But it's neither of us who do.

"I'll get a towel," Lachlan says. I didn't even notice him sitting on the stairs, pajama pants, no shirt, and he shouldn't be up this late, or early, whatever. He comes down a moment later, towel in hand. There are tears in his eyes, but no sound to accompany them. "Bend down," he whispers, and so I do, and then his towel-covered hands are on my head, patting my hair, and I fight back my own tears, because I've never treated him the way I did tonight. I need to apologize. I need to get rid of Mary, to get her out of my system, to stop letting her control me. I'm about to speak, to say sorry, but Lachlan beats me to it. "I'm not saying goodbye to her."

And I say, "Okay."

And then Dad is pulling him away, handing me the towel to dry myself off. He says, his voice soft, but his words hard, "I'll make the call tomorrow."

And I say…

I say…

"Okay."

26

AUBREY

My heart drops when he walks through my door, hat backward, clothes disheveled, his backpack dragging on the floor behind him. His tired gaze finds mine, and I shake my head. "You shouldn't be here," I tell him, slowly moving toward him.

Lachlan lifts his chin, his lifeless eyes squinting. "I'm not saying goodbye to you," he says, his voice wobbling.

It's the exact same words he said last night, and I wish I didn't have to fight him on this, but: "I don't want that, either, dude, but I have to be the grown-up here, and if your brother—"

"There's something wrong with him, you know?"

"What do you mean?" I rush out, my heart pound, pound, pounding. "Is he... is he sick or something?"

Lachlan shakes his head, drags his backpack across the floor, and slumps down on the chair. "Not like my mom was sick, but... Dad says you can't see it, and sometimes, Logan can't even see it himself." His voice is so soft, so desolate, my stomach turns at the sound of it. "Dad says that he's... he's *self-destructive*. Do you know what that means, Red?" His gaze drops. "Because I don't. I tried to look it up, but it didn't make sense to me. And it should. Because we're buddies, you know? He's my best friend. He's my favorite of all my siblings, and I know I shouldn't say that, but it's true. And I should be able to help him. But…" He looks up, his eyes clouded with unshed tears. "But I don't know how."

I stand in the middle of the store, wordless, my heart torn to pieces. Not for Logan, but for a boy who sees too much and feels too much and aches in ways I can't even imagine. Logan and I slept together. That *was* it. But Lachlan… *God*. Logan is someone he loves, someone he looks up to. My breaths weaken. So do my knees. So does my will. "You can stay," I tell him. "But I need to speak to your dad." .

He nods. "He's picking me up tonight. He wants to speak to you, too."

I KEEP STARING at the clock, the door, the clock, the door. Lachlan never said what time his dad was coming, and he's been so quiet, so focused on his drawings that I don't want to interrupt him. At 5:30 p.m., Mr. Preston shows up, his giant frame *barely* fitting through the doorway. I instantly heighten a few inches and smile so stupidly wide; my cheeks sting with the force. Hand outstretched, I make my way over to him. "Mr. Preston," I greet, and his smile is warm and genuine and everything mine isn't.

"You must be Aubrey."

His hand dwarfs mine.

Lachlan's chair scrapes when he stands, quickly moving his sketchbook behind him. *Hiding it.* My smile drops. "I didn't realize the time," he tells his dad. "I'll get my stuff."

Mr. Preston pulls out his wallet, hands over a fifty to his youngest. "I just ordered some pizza. Can you go get it? Give Aubrey and me some time alone."

As soon as Lachlan leaves the store, Mr. Preston turns to me. "I should've come here earlier."

"It's fine."

"Lachy's told me a lot about you. He also tells me that you don't mind having him here, but I just want to make sure."

"Honestly, sir, Lachlan is basically the only person I see all day, so having him here keeps me sane."

He nods at that, a slight smile appearing beneath his facial hair. "It's quiet, huh?"

"Understatement."

"It'll pick up, just give it some time."

I nod.

He does the same.

Then we just stand there, awkwardly. I shuffle on my feet while he rubs the back of his neck. We're looking down at the floor but glancing up at each other. He breaks the silence just as I'm about to. "Lachlan also told me about last night... with Logan."

"Yeah...?"

"I want to apologize to you on behalf of my son."

"I appreciate it, but it's not necessary."

"Logan... he's—"

"Self-destructive?" I finish for him, repeating Lachlan's words from earlier. Without waiting for a response, I turn, walk behind the counter so I can get some distance and clear my head. I'd expected to speak about Lachlan. Not Logan. I don't want to speak about him, don't want to think about him. If I do, the tears will return. Because I'm angry at myself, and angry at him, but neither of us can take back the words we dropped like bombs set to destroy. "Like I said, I appreciate it, but we don't need to talk about it anymore."

Mr. Preston sighs, the single sound filling the entire room. "Okay," he says, nodding. "Okay. Well"—he looks behind him—"what time do you close up here?"

"Nine, normally. But I'll probably hang back."

"Got work to do?"

I shrug. "The store's smaller than my house. It feels less..." I trail off, catching myself before I give him too much.

"Lonely?" he asks, and I press my lips tight. "Young lady, at one point, I lived in a house with seven children, and I still had moments of loneliness. Having people around doesn't take the loneliness away. You know what does?"

"What?"

"Pizza."

"Pizza?"

He opens the door. "Are you coming?"

"To your *house*?"

"Well, unless you want to take one of the pies home and eat alone, then yes. My house."

"But..."

"Are you expecting customers?"

My eye roll makes him chuckle.

"All retail stores close at five here. Restaurants at nine. You won't be seeing anyone else tonight. And if it's Logan you're worried about, he's not home. Won't be for a while. So?" He tilts his head to the side, his eyes focused on mine.

I succumb to his offer. "I'll grab my stuff."

His smile widens. "I'll wait."

WE WALK side by side toward the pizza shop, my three steps for every one of his. "I know you don't want to talk about this," he starts, staring right ahead, "but Logan—he's the most carefree of all my kids. He walks around this town giving zero shits—pardon my language—about what anyone thinks of him, and to me, that's a good thing, because people here like to talk. You understand?"

"Yes, sir."

"It takes a lot to affect him, to get a reaction out of him, and so when something or *someone* does, it's because he *cares*, Aubrey. He takes out what little emotion he carries on the people he cares about, which is normally his family. He says a lot of things he doesn't mean. And we know that. But, I thought it important to share this with you—just in case you don't know him well enough to know that, too. And because... well, because he's my boy, and I want to see him happy."

LOGAN

Guilt.

Sorry.

Disappointment.

I write down all three words on the notepad my therapist handed me—our standard routine—and pass it back to her. She looks down at what I've written, then up at me. "Guilt and sorry are too similar," she says. "You're going to have to do better, Logan."

With a sigh, I lean back in my chair. "But what if they're about two different things?"

"Interesting." She taps her pen on her chin a few times. "Tell me about the guilt first."

I've been seeing Amanda as her patient for a couple years now. Before that, I saw her as Lucy's friend… who also happens to be Big Logan's girl, and I know she's not going to like what I'm about to say. "I was an asshole to Lachlan."

Eyes wide, pout protruding, she whines, "How? Why? But he's so cute!"

"I know." I sigh again. I have a feeling there'll be a lot of sighing in this session. Guilt, sorry, and disappointment can do that. "I don't know what got into me. I was just… I was so mad."

We're in the pool house behind Big Logan's dad's house—where she and Logan live. The pool house has been converted to her out-of-hours office. She doesn't allow a lot of people beyond the high brick fence and barbed wire. It's almost prison-like, security cameras and everything. But, knowing what all went on with Big Logan, it makes sense. She asks, "Was your anger linked to the disappointment at all?"

I shrug. "I guess."

"Who disappointed you?"

"A little bit of me, and maybe…"

"Maybe…?"

"Well… see, there's this girl…"

"Ahh." She scribbles down a few words on her notepad. "There's always a girl."

I shake my head. "That's the thing, there's never been a girl. I mean, besides Mary."

"Mary is a drug, Logan. She's not a person. She has no emotion. No say. No control over your life... unless you let her. Did you let her?"

I quirk an eyebrow. "You mean *again*?"

"How are your flashbacks going?"

"Wow. Straight to the point, huh?"

"I'm trying to work out if anything's linked. That's all."

I'm not here to talk about the flashbacks, so I change the subject. "So, this girl..."

Amanda presses her lips tight but nods for me to continue, "I guess she assumed some shit about me that wasn't true."

"Like what?"

"Like, that I'd been screwing around with other girls."

"Are you two exclusive?"

"No," I say quickly, then take a breath. "Okay, so we hooked up before I left for Cambodia, right? Three weeks pass and we don't see each other—"

"Because you were gone those three weeks?"

"Yes. And then when I get back, we bump into each other again and... you know..."

"Have sex?"

"Yes."

"And she thinks you were with someone while you were away?"

"Yes. And with a different someone when I got back. I guess she overheard things and jumped to conclusions."

"And I just want to confirm, you *weren't* exclusive?"

"Right."

"So... why the guilt?"

"Because..." I shrug. "Because it upset her, I guess, and I didn't like seeing her upset, even though I didn't do anything."

"Have you told her you didn't do anything?"

I nod. "Last night, after the whole treating-Lachlan-like-shit thing."

"And that's the first time she mentioned it to you?"

"No."

Her eyebrows rise. "When did she tell you about what she *thought* she knew?"

"Like, two weeks ago."

"And what did you do then?"

"I..." I look down at my hands and sigh again. "I walked away."

"And is that where the *sorry* part comes in? Are you sorry for walking away?"

"Part of it, I guess."

"What's the other part?"

"I treated her worse than I did Lachlan. I said some shit that... *Jesus*." I scrub my hands across my face, frustrated that it had to come to this. "I said some horrible shit."

"Why?"

"Because *Mary*."

She exhales loudly. "Mary's not a reason or an excuse, Logan. *Why*?"

I rush out, "Because I was mad at her for thinking those things about me."

"Logan," she says, her voice stern enough for me to face her. "Can you blame her for thinking those thoughts?"

Another sigh. "I guess not."

"Right." Amanda nods, focuses on the pen scrawling across her notepad. I sit up higher, try to read what she's writing, but she just smiles, turns the page closer to her. "Your dad seemed pretty worried when he called me this morning."

"Yeah, I had um..."

"He likes to call it an *episode*," she murmurs. "And, we, in the psychology world, like to call this" —she points to me—"a break-through."

"How the fuck is this a breakthrough?"

"Because you *like* a girl, Logan. You *care* about someone that isn't a member of your family. And that's a big deal for you. Your guilt, sorry, disappointment—they all have one thing in common."

"And what's that?" I ask.

She smiles full force. "They all belong to *you*. Which means, *you* have the power to change them."

AUBREY

The Preston estate (according to Google Maps) is huge. The Preston house? Not as extravagant as I thought it would be. Why I pictured crystal chandeliers and white marble floors, I have no idea. It's big, yes, but it's also cozy. Warm. Familial. Framed pictures of every one of the kids (from every year, I suspect) hang on the wall next to the staircase, the lower as infants, leading right up to what I assume is now, but I can't see from just inside the door. Mr. Preston's walking ahead of me, boxes upon boxes of pizza in his grasp. Behind me, Lachlan says, "You can go inside, you know?"

"Right." I put one foot in front of the other, while I look at the pictures, trying to work out who each one is, trying to remember all their names.

"It's in age order," Lachlan says. "Logan's right in the middle, if that's who you're looking for."

I was, I realize too late, and the admission has me disappointed in myself. "I was looking for you, you goofball."

"Sure."

I pass a dining room that looks like it hasn't been used as its purpose for a while. Computers and camera equipment sit on the table instead, and I assume it's where the twins do their thing. The kitchen is about the size of my entire house, with a large table in the middle. I count ten chairs before a boy I've only ever seen through a computer screen says, "Lachy's bringing his girlfriends home now? Starting young, huh?"

Mr. Preston laughs, and Lachlan shakes his head. "She's my *friend*," he says and then points to the other boy. "This is Liam."

I raise my hand in a wave. "I've seen a few of your videos. You guys are so entertaining."

He smiles wide. "Thanks." And then Mr. Preston dumps the pizzas on the table and they all sit down and begin to eat like boys do—as if it's a race to the finish. I'm barely through one slice when Mr. Preston's on his fourth, and I smile to myself when Liam pours two sodas in a glass and sets one next to him. "You're welcome," he says, and I giggle out loud. I can't help it.

Lachlan says, "I told you."

And Liam asks, "Told her what?"

And Mr. Preston states, "Linc's not here."

And Liam says, "Oh."

And then the back door opens, and my heart drops, and Logan's walking into the house, head lowered, Chicken by his side. He says, "Whose turn is it to wash the pig? He stinks." When no one answers, he looks up, his eyes immediately finding mine.

I stand. "I'll leave."

"Stay," begs Lachlan.

Mr. Preston says, "I thought you had an appointment."

Logan responds, "I did. We finished up early." He doesn't take his eyes off me.

Liam says, picking up his plate, "We're going to the editing room."

"Linc's not here," Lachlan says.

"Oh."

I pick up my phone and keys off the table. "Thank you for dinner," I tell Mr. Preston. "It was very nice of you to invite me." I'm tapping at my phone, loading the Uber app.

"I'll give you a ride home," he says.

Lachlan tugs on my sweatshirt. "Stay."

And then Logan's clearing his throat. "You should stay," he says. "I'll go."

"No one is going," Mr. Preston mumbles. "Sit down. Everyone. Eat your food."

I hold up my phone. "My Uber's already on its way."

"What the hell's a Goober?"

"*Uber*," Liam laughs out. "It's the new taxi cab, or in your case, horse and carriage."

"Watch your mouth," Mr. Preston warns, but he's kidding, the smile on his lips proof.

Logan opens the back door, lets Chicken out. Lachlan says, "It's my turn to wash him. I'll do it after dinner." He turns to me. "You want to help?"

"But my Uber…"

"Cancel it." Logan jerks his head toward Lachlan. "He wants you here. I'll get the bath ready."

As soon as we hear the front door close, Lachlan turns to me, whispers, sadness linked to his words, "You should talk to him."

Liam asks, "You know Logan?" Then he rolls his eyes. "Of course, you know Logan. What girl doesn't?"

"Liam," his dad says. Another warning, only this one's serious.

I cancel my Uber and eat another slice of pizza while the boys devour multiples, and then Lachlan stands, puts his hand on my shoulder. "You ready?"

INSIDE THE PRESTON garage is a large kiddy pool already filled with water. Around the pool is some kind of contraption like they have at dog groomers with a belt that goes below the dog's tummy to keep them in place. Next to the contraption stands Logan Preston. Usually tall, proud, and cocky, he stands with his hands in his pockets, his head lowered. He's not wearing a cap. Instead, his dark hair sways in all different angles, directions, chunks of it higher than others, as if he's been pulling, tugging on the ends. He asks Lachlan, his voice low, "Where's all his bath stuff?"

"Shoot," says Lachlan. "I'll be right back."

"I'll come—" I start, but he's already gone, sprinting away, and the kid's *fast*. Super-human fast. There's no way I could catch up with him. There's no way I'd even try.

"Red?"

"Don't call me that."

Logan sighs. "*Aubrey*, then. Will you talk to me?"

I shake my head, cross my arms. "I don't think there's anything left to say."

"There's a lot to say."

"Like what?"

"Like… I don't know. I'm glad you're here."

"Yeah? Because that's an absolute contrast to the words you spoke yesterday, and if this is your version of an apology, it's not good enough." My voice is strong, unwavering. It should be. I've practiced these words on repeat all night. All day. I add, "If you were simply angry that I made assumptions without speaking to you first, then that's fine. I'd understand that. But the things that you said to me, *about me*—they were horrible, Logan, *vile*, and I won't ever understand it. And honestly, I don't think I'll ever be able to forgive you."

He licks his lips, tugs his hair, locks his eyes on mine. "I can't be the only one to blame here, Red—I mean, *Aubrey*. You assumed that stuff and then you were gone, and not just *gone* gone, but, like, off-the-grid gone. Do you know how many times I tried calling you?"

I stay silent, because I have nothing to say.

"And I wasn't with anyone—"

"It doesn't matter," I cut in.

"Why? That's how all this started, right?"

"Because even if you did that stuff, it's not like I could..." I exhale loudly and admit a truth I've been trying hard to deny. "It's not like I could be *that* mad about it, you know? We never... you and me... we were never..." My words die in the air, while my insecurities come to life. "I don't want to talk about this anymore." I look over my shoulder. "Where the hell is Lachlan?"

When Logan doesn't answer, I turn to him, my breath catching when I realize how close he's gotten. He's so close he could easily reach out, touch me. *Please, God, don't touch me.*

"Did you see what I was carrying the day I went to see you?"

I shake my head, annoyed, my heart thumping wildly. *Where the fuck is Lachlan?*

"Red, I—"

"*Don't* call me that."

Blue eyes blink, blink, blink. Then: "I had my work jacket."

"What?" I huff. "What's that got to do with anything?"

He shrugs, his thumb going between his teeth, his lips moving around it. I *think* he says, "I don't have a lemmami yacki."

"What?" I ask again, my eyes narrowed.

He clears his throat, drops his hands. His words are clearer when he says, "I was never an upperclassman, so I don't have a *letterman* jacket." My heart, my world, stops the second realization hits. My mouth opens, but there's no air in the atmosphere to jump start my pulse. Logan scratches the back of his head, and he's nothing but wild hair and wild eyes and wild words. "I wanted to ask you to *go steady*, you know? Like you said that night. I wanted to ask you on Friday night, but... but you left."

"I don't know what to say." It's barely a whisper.

"Say *yes*, Red." He steps forward, his hand reaching for me. Not my hand, but my wrist. "Please say yes."

My eyes drift shut when his fingertips brush my skin. "You called me a *kiddy fiddler*, Logan."

His touch is gone. "I should *not* have said that. I have... I have... *issues*."

"Maybe you should lay off the weed, then."

He laughs once. Bitter. "No shit."

Lachlan returns, bucket filled with bottles in his hands. His gaze switches between Logan and me when he says, "I can come back."

"No," I rush out. Then look at Logan, repeat the same word, but with a completely different meaning. "*No*."

AUBREY

WHEN I WAKE up the next morning, there's a text waiting for me.

Logan: *Friends, then?*

Aubrey: *No.*

There's a reply almost immediately:

Logan: *You're friends with my brother. So, that means... friends by association? That's how we do it in the Preston house. It's all of us or none of us.*

Aubrey: *Please stop.*

Logan: *One question.*

Aubrey: *No.*

Logan: *Last Thursday, after dinner with Lachy... if I'd come back that night and given you the stupid jacket, would you have said yes?*

I grip the phone tighter in my hand, release my frustration in the form of a moan. He's asking all the right questions, but he's asking at the wrong time, because it's too damn late.

I flip the script, switch the focus.

Aubrey: *Why does your dad call you self-destructive?*

A minute passes with no response, and so I get out of bed and into the shower, pretending not to be focused on my phone sitting on the counter. I stare at it, wait for it to light up, to vibrate. As soon as it does, I switch off the water, step out, and read the text.

Logan: *He said that, huh?*

Dripping wet and too anxious to care, I write:

Aubrey: *Answer my question.*

Logan: *You answer mine first.*

"So fucking stubborn," I mumble to myself, my thumbs flying across the screen, leaving a trail of water in their wake.

Aubrey: *Yes.*

…

…

…

I chew on my thumbnail, tap my feet.

…

…

…

Aubrey: *Why does your dad call you self-destructive, Logan?*

…

...

...

Logan: *Because it's true.*

28

LOGAN

THE PROBLEM WITH WANTING SOMETHING, or someone, is that you can't control how long you keep them for.

Even when my eyes are closed, scarlet replaces the darkness. I see her everywhere. Even in the places of my mind. The grocery store isn't the same anymore. There are shades of scarlet in every aisle, taking up every inch. The ice cream freezer is nothing but Red, and every single tub of ice cream is Peanut Buttah Cookie Core. The roads are different somehow, and every sidewalk reminds me of her desolate face, the tears she shed when I ripped her apart. Her tears, too, are scarlet. Which is probably why when Dad asks me to pick Lachlan up from her store to take him to his specialist training, the first thing I do is tap my empty pocket in search of my mind's only reprieve. My dad's the one who thinks I'm "self-destructive," and yet here he is, handing me the directions and a trigger to a ticking bomb. When I don't respond, he adds, "I have an important meeting I need to get to, Logan. Please do this for me?"

"Why can't he just go to Lucy's? I can pick him up from there."

Will says, smirking, "Is Aubrey an ex? I thought you and Joy—"

I shake my head, glare at him. Will's only a year older than me, and since Garray joined the crew, Old Man Niall has dubbed us "the fear-some threesome," which is as dumb as Garray's name.

"He likes it at Aubrey's," Dad says with a shrug. "So? Will you get him or not?"

When I don't respond, Garray says, "I can pick him up for you, sir. Who's Aubrey, anyway? Is she cute?"

"I'll go," I say. "It's fine."

It's not fine. And with every second that ticks by, the *un-fine-ness* of it all gives me more and more anxiety. A half hour before I have to leave, I call Lucy. "Can't you just pick him up from there, like, five minutes before I have to get him?"

"I'm busy."

"Luce," I sigh out. "You're not fucking busy. You're never busy. That store is your own personal library. No one even reads for pleasure anymore, and half this town is illiterate."

"Aubrey reads for pleasure. She's part of our book club. Last week, the girls and I all went to her house."

In my mind, Aubrey's house is the brightest shade of scarlet. So bright it's almost blinding.

I sigh again. "Just pick him up for me."

"No, Logan. You play stupid games..." she trails off, and I don't need to hear the rest to know the ending: *you win stupid prizes.*

THE GLASS DOOR to Aubrey's shop is heavy—as heavy as my legs that unwillingly dragged me here. Aubrey looks up from her spot behind the counter, her eyes widening when she sees me. I nod at her, switch my focus to Lachlan. "Are you ready, buddy?" My gaze fights to stay on him, but it deceives me, moving to Aubrey again. She's wearing a white blouse beneath a mustard sweater, suspenders, and when she moves around the counter to help Lachlan pack his shit, I notice the short skirt attached to said suspenders, and black thigh-high socks. Her hair's up today; like a librarian's bun—scarlet upon scarlet upon scarlet—and she looks so fucking cute I almost tell her that. *Almost.* I stop myself at the last second and take Lachlan's backpack when he hands it to me, but I can't take my eyes off Aubrey. I want to say so many things in such little time and I want to *be* so many things in such little space and I miss her, but I get it and I want her but I shouldn't and—

And…

I am conflict.

But then she smiles.

At me.

Because she is hope.

"SHE ASKED ABOUT YOU TODAY," is the first thing Lachy says when he gets in my truck. "Which is weird, because she hasn't mentioned you at all since… you know… that night."

I force air into my lungs. "Oh yeah?" I try to play it cool but blood rushes to my face, and I'm white-knuckling the steering wheel so hard my fingers cramp. "What—I mean, what—what—what—" *Fuck*. I take another breath. "What did she say?"

Lachy's removing his sneakers, replacing them with his spikes, and I pull out of the spot, almost run down Old Lady Laura.

"Sorry, ma'am," I shout, my hand up in apology.

She glares, her lips pursed, finger waving at me. "You fucking Preston Punk."

I lower my window. "Yo. Watch your mouth, my little brother's in here!"

Lachy leans across me to shout, "You need penis in your life!"

I wind up the window. "Jesus, where the hell did you learn to speak like that?"

"Lucy," he says with a shrug. "That's what she always says about grumpy old ladies."

"You need to quit hanging around Lucy so much."

"Funny, that's what people used to say about you."

I don't respond, because my mind's already back to Aubrey, and now Old Lady Laura is giving me the finger and refusing to move.

I honk my horn.

She jumps, grasps her heart, then starts walking a snail's pace across the crosswalk. "Bless her," Lachlan says.

"So, Aubrey...?" I edge.

"What about her?"

"You said she asked about me. What did she say?"

Old Lady Laura drops her fucking old lady fruit all over the road, and Lachlan says, "Ah, fudge nugget!"

"Hop out and help her."

"No."

"Lachy."

"Fine," he whines, but he doesn't have to because a sea of scarlet appears, and I blink, hard, like I do every time I think I see her. Only this time it's not my imagination. Within seconds the road is clear and Aubrey is helping the woman across the street and safely on to the sidewalk. And then she looks over at us, or *me* to be specific, and she smiles. Again. She smiles, and my entire world unfurls, and Lachy says, "Why are you so smiley?"

I drive to the high school grinning like a fool, and I don't even care.

Because Aubrey's smile is my drug.

And I've never felt so fucking high.

I want to talk to her, even if talking means standing in front of her, mouth moving, spitting jumbled words and messed-up apologies. I want to talk to her because I've fucking missed her and because *she asked about me.* And even though I never found out exactly what it was she said, she still asked, which means she still *thought* about me. And that—that has my heart racing and my stomach flipping and goddammit, I've turned into Lucas.

YOU KNOW those stand-offs they have in old westerns? Where the good guy and the bad guy stand still, opposite each other, guns drawn, waiting for the other to make the first move? Well, yeah, that's happening right now. Only there is no good or bad guy. There's me and there's my dad. And we're not standing still. We're walking. And there are no guns.

Okay, so maybe it's nothing like those old westerns, but whatever.

He's walking toward me.

I'm walking toward him.

And right in the middle of us is Aubrey's shop.

We meet at the door.

I eye him confused.

He smirks.

"I thought you had something important to do," I tell him.

He says, "I did. Then Miss Red called, asked me to come by."

"Why?" I ask.

He shrugs.

And then we both open the door and try to walk through at the same time: an impossible feat for men our height, our size, but he's bigger than I am. Stronger, too, probably, and I get shoved back onto the sidewalk.

His chuckle grates on my nerves.

When we're both in the store, Aubrey's gaze flicks between us. Then she smiles again, and that one gesture sparks a longing I've tried so hard to push away.

"I'm glad you're both here," she says.

"You are?" I ask.

She nods. "I want to show you something, and I feel horrible for doing this, but I feel like I *have* to."

"Is everything okay?" Dad asks, concern dripping in his words.

Aubrey chews on her bottom lip, and I'm reminded of what that lip feels like, what it tastes like. I swallow hard, will my mind and my body not to focus on those thoughts. She walks to the corner of the room where a desk is set up, opens a drawer, and pulls out a sketch-book with a black cover. She flips through the pages while Dad and I make our way to her counter. When she returns, she slowly, carefully, as if the book will disintegrate with her touch, places it between us.

"You did this?" Dad asks, and I can hear the joy in his voice.

On the page is a sketch of a boy running—Lachlan—the world behind him a blur. It's in the form of anime, like *Pokemon* or *Dragon Ball Z*, and I frown, confused, because I had no idea she drew.

"I wish," she says, and she's the opposite of my dad. She sounds sad, and when I find the courage to look up, right into her eyes, they look as she sounds. "This is all Lachlan."

"No way," I whisper, gaze dropping, focused on the drawing again. I lift it to inspect it closer. "No way," I repeat.

"He draws?" Dad asks, and he's no longer joyful. "Did you know, Logan?"

"Not a clue."

"Why wouldn't he…" Dad trails off.

Aubrey says, "It takes him days to do one drawing. The first day, he sketches it out, the next he fine-tunes it, and on the last day, he adds color. And once they're done, he uses the shredder in my office to destroy them."

"Why?" I ask.

"Because…" she starts, then exhales loudly. "I've been taking pictures on my phone every night when he leaves, because I feel like they need to be kept and admired somehow. And I fought with myself over and over about whether I should show you, because I feel like…" Her voice cracks, and it's clear she's struggling to get through this. "I feel like I'm betraying my best friend." A calming breath and a slow blink later, and she's shifting her laptop screen to face us. "This is his work from last week," she says. I focus on the screen, on the drawing of Lachlan on a track, his hand gripping a trophy while a group of bodies holds him suspended in the air. There are no eyes on his supporters, no noses, just giant smiles. But that's not what I'm focused on. It's Lachlan—the drawing of him—*frowning*.

"I don't get it," I say, my voice barely a whisper. I clear my throat, ready the loudness of my voice. "Does he not want to run anymore?"

"Look at this," Aubrey says, switching to the next picture. This one is him, sitting front and center, legs crossed, a smile on his face, a pencil in his hand. He's holding it up as if it's a trophy, and in the background, the same supporting bodies, only their backs are turned. And it's not hard to figure out the hidden meaning behind this.

My inhale is shaky. So are my hands. "Does he not think we'd support him no matter what? He's nine years old, for Christ's sake, he can—"

"I don't think it's that you wouldn't support him, Lo." She called me *Lo*. "It's more that he loves the attention he gets from running. I mean, with Luke especially. It's like their *thing*... something only they share. And he said that y'all are there for every one of his meets, that y'all are proud of him. He mentioned that it's the only time you're together when you're not forced to be. I think he's afraid that if he stops, or if he's not as good as he is, all that will end."

"That's bullshit," I huff out, and then I realize that Dad hasn't said a word, and when I look up at him, he's staring off into the distance, color drained from his face. "Dad?"

He blinks, comes to. "Your mother..." he starts, then picks up the sketchbook. "Your mother was an artist. Like this."

"She was?" I knew she crafted. I knew she knit, scrapbooked, crocheted. I had no idea she drew.

Dad nods, slowly. "It was something she wanted to pursue in college, but her parents—your grandparents—wouldn't... they wouldn't support her, so..." he trails off. "So, she got her teaching degree. She wanted to teach art to kids. But then... then she had Lucy and Lucas and Leo and you and... well, we had planned... after Lachlan that—but then... so..." He presses down on his eyes with his thumb and forefinger, and there are very few moments I've seen him like this, and it's been a long, long time since I have. "I'm going to pick Lachy up from practice," he says, holding the sketchbook to his chest. He makes a move to leave but stops with his hand on the door. "Thank you, Aubrey, and I promise, no matter what happens, this won't fall on you. I'll make sure of it."

As soon as he's gone, I turn back to Aubrey. "So," I say.

She sighs. "You mind giving me a ride home?"

PHYSICALLY, it feels like the first time we did this: sitting in her driveway, neither of us making a move to leave. Emotionally, though? It's completely different. We spent the drive in silence. We're still silent. And I haven't stopped staring out the windshield. But then Aubrey sniffs, and my gaze moves to her. "I feel like shit, Logan."

"You did the right thing."

"I betrayed his trust."

"For good reason, though."

"He's going to hate me."

"He'll get over it."

"But what if he doesn't?" she says, facing me, those sad, sad eyes on mine. "He's, like, the *only* thing keeping me here right now. If he…" She exhales loudly. "Never mind." She gets out of the car, and I follow after her, walk her to the door. With her key in the slot, she turns to me leaning against her house, my head resting on the brick. "You okay?" she asks, poking at my stomach.

I muster a smile, but it's fake, and I shouldn't. So, I wipe it clear. She deserves more. "I used to spend a lot of time with him. I was just thinking, maybe if I still did, I'd know this stuff about him."

"He calls you his best friend, you know? He says you're his favorite sibling."

I nod, because I knew that. "If he came to me with this, I'd make it known it wouldn't change the way we feel about him. I just—I don't understand how he got to that headspace… and then my dad—hearing him talk about Mom like that…" I stop there, and push off the wall, tug on her sleeve. "Make sure you lock the door, okay?"

I STAND UP MARY, and instead, I go straight home, wait on the porch steps for Lachy to come back. It's more than an hour after his practice finishes when Dad pulls up, and Lachlan hops out, his head lowered, feet dragging. He looks up when I whistle, and he looks like he's been through the ringer. Dad, too. I stand when he gets close enough to touch and scruff his hair. "Grab your camping gear."

"But it's a weeknight!"

I look at Dad. "What say you, old man?"

"You make sure he gets to school in the morning?"

"Yes, sir."

Lachlan rushes up the steps. "Can we bring Chicken?"

"Whatever you want, buddy."

His frown reverses, his smile flipping my insides. Dad slaps my shoulder as he passes. "You're all right, kid."

29

AUBREY

Lachlan doesn't show up the next day. Or the next. The weekend passes, and *nothing*. I start taking photographs of my furniture to list online. I'll call my previous employer, see if they'll take me back. By Monday afternoon, all hopes of a future here begin to die. I look out the window, watch people walk by, and reminisce on all the ideals I had before I got here: the waves, the smiles, the warm welcomes that never came. I'm too lost in those thoughts, I don't even realize the door opens until Lachlan appears. I stand taller, hold my breath. My stomach drops when his eyes narrow, his glare directed at me. "I'm sorry," I rush out. "I just thought that they should know—" He busts out a laugh and drops his bag, practically runs toward me.

"I'm just messing with ya, Red!" he shouts, wrapping his arms around my waist. When he releases me, his smile is huge. "Dad's so proud of me. We spent all yesterday at the kitchen table, and he tried to draw like me, but, Aubs,"—he rolls his eyes, giggling as he does —"he's soo bad. And Logan—I don't know what's gotten into him, but he wants to spend all this time together. Like, seriously? Give me some room to breathe, bruh!"

My laughter feels foreign.

"We went camping and four wheeling and fishing and everything. That's why I haven't been to see you!"

"Oh, my God, Lachy, I thought you were angry at me."

"Sorry." He shrugs, removes his backpack and unzips it. "Anyway, while we were fishing, Logan asked me to draw something for him." He reveals a scrunched-up sheet of paper from his bag. "Here."

It's a drawing of *me*, my hair up in a bun, my eyes a bright green.

"It took forever for me to draw it. He made me change your nose, like, eight times. He kept saying *it's more upturned*! And then... oh, my God, don't even get me started on your freckles."

"My freckles?" I whisper, unable to take my eyes off... *me*.

Lachlan deepens his voice to mock his brother's. "*It has to be half the shade of her hair.*" Lachy sighs. "It's, like, I've hung around you way more than he has, but he's memorized every detail about you!" He's talking loudly, his voice filled with excitement. "Anyway." He grabs the picture from me. I try to take it back, but he hides it behind him. "No. This is his. You can't have it, and he'll be here any second."

"He's finishing work early today?"

"He started trade school today."

"Trade school?"

"Electrical."

"Electrical?"

Lachlan tilts his head to the side. "I don't know why you guys don't just sex again. This whole middleman thing is getting old."

"You're not the middleman."

He haphazardly shoves the drawing back in his backpack just as the store door opens. Logan smiles first at Lachy, then at me. "Red," he says, and it truly is a shame he's so repulsive to look at.

I say, nodding, "Lo."

Lachlan groans, so over-exaggerated it makes me giggle. He steps between Logan and me, points to his brother. "Logan." Then to me. "Miss Red." Then to himself. "*Middleman.*"

30

LOGAN

LAST WEEK, Lucas had to leave for a meeting during the day, which meant he had to change from his work clothes to a suit and tie in the office. While he was gone, Will, Dumb Name and I—*The Fearsome Threesome*—took the opportunity to create some Mayhem. I don't really know why Lucas had become our go-to target, but he's just too damn easy. Besides, it's his own fault for leaving his boots in the office to begin with. Removing the inner soles, screwing them down to the floor, and then replacing the inner soles is Mayhem 101. Child's play, really. But Luke must've been in a rush because when he came back and got changed, he shoved his feet in his boots, went to walk away, obviously couldn't, and then fell face first into the corner of Dad's desk and chipped his front tooth.

Oops.

He hasn't spoken to me properly since, and his girl, Laney—well, to say she's pissed is an understatement. I took the fall (credit) for the entire thing, not wanting Dumb Name or Will to get in trouble. But, somehow, Dad must've found out they were involved, because it's now first thing Monday morning, and all three of us are in his office, and my accomplices... they're sweatin'. Dumb Name keeps giving me these looks—like sad puppy eyes—and I keep shaking my head at him. *I got this.* Besides, the worst thing Dad's ever done is suspend my pay for a week for that time I covered Luke's truck with "I love cock" decals.

Dad sits in his chair, shifting papers on his desk. Without looking up, he says, "You boys are off the site starting today."

"Sir, I need—" Dumb Name starts, but Dad cuts him off.

"You'll be working a retail job. Logan, you're in charge."

The combined exhales of relief from Dumb Name and Will make my dad smirk, though I'm not sure the other two see it.

"Since when did we do commercial?" I ask.

"Since now," Dad replies, looking up at me. "Problem?"

"No, sir."

"It's a simple shop refurb." He hands me a piece of paper. "That's the address. Go."

"Now?"

"Yes, now," he says, his voice louder, deeper, sterner.

"Yes, sir."

Swear to God, I've never seen two grown-ass men try to leave a room as fast as Dumb Name and Will do. Dumb Name gets as far as opening the door before Dad's voice cuts through the air. "Gentlemen," he says, and it feels like the exact moment of calm right before the storm.

Will says, "Yes, sir—boss—Sir Tom—Mr. Preston Sir?"

"Kiss-ass," I murmur.

"Next time you want to pull that shit, don't do it on my time," Dad says. "I know my son's supposed to be your supervisor, so I'm putting this on him. Logan's getting his pay cut for a week. I'm splitting it between two charities of your choice." He puts pen to paper. "Name them."

Will and Dumb Name share a look. Then Will says, "RAINN, please."

Dumb Name scoffs. "Weather isn't a charity, bruh."

"It stands for Rape, Abuse and Incest National Network, *idiot.*"

"Oh."

Dad says, "And Dumb Name—I mean, Garray—your charity?"

Dumb Name doesn't skip a beat. "National Coalition Against Domestic Violence." *For Laney.*

Dad's lips press tight. "Good men," he says, then focuses on me. "You're paying for Luke's dental work."

I suppress my chuckle. "Well worth it, sir."

"Don't be a smart-ass, Logan."

———

Aubrey looks like autumn: tan boots, black leggings, dark green, oversized sweater, and a bright orange scarf. Want to know how I know? Because the retail joint we're working on is right opposite her shop. I'd say it was a coincidence, but I know the truth. *Preston, Gordon and Sons* have never worked a commercial site before. We've never even quoted for one. This is *all* Dad's doing, and he's doing it for me.

The following day, she sees me working, smiles and waves. I wave back.

The day after, she's dressed like a pumpkin. Orange from head to toe. I send her a text message that tells her exactly that. She writes back: *Perv.*

On the fourth day of working the site, all three of us grab a coffee from the bakery on our morning break, which means walking past her store. Twice. When I get back to the site, she sends me a message: *I like mine with cream and sugar.*

The next morning, I'm waiting for her outside her store with a coffee (cream and sugar). She says, "Thank you."

And I say, "You're welcome."

By lunchtime the same day, I'm about ready to rip off my ears because all I've heard all damn day is Will complaining about not getting his girlfriend Bree's one-year anniversary present on time. "She's going to kill me," he repeats, over and over.

"Just get her something local and tell her the real present was delayed," says Dumb Name. "It's not like you're lying to her."

And I say, because it's the truth, "If she's gonna be mad that you don't have a good gift, then she's fickle as fuck." Not that I really know

Bree all that well. The only link I have to her is Bella with the Boobies, and she's batshit fucking crazy.

"There's nothing good around here," Will whines. "It has to be amazing."

"Flowers?" Dumb Name suggests.

"Flowers won't cut it."

I roll my eyes.

"What about…"

I tune out and focus on my work, like they should be doing. A half hour passes, and they've gone through every single store on Main Street, and apparently, nothing is good enough for Bree. Then I look up, see Aubrey in her store, chin on her palm, elbow resting on the counter. She looks like she's daydreaming. "Does Bree like stationery?"

AUBREY STANDS TALLER when all three of us walk in, her eyes wide. "Red," I greet, holding the door open for the other two.

"Perv," she counters.

"Wow," Will laughs out. "Is there any girl in this town you've left untouched?"

"Shut up."

"This is new, right?" Will asks, looking around the shop.

"I've been here a while," Aubrey says. "Can I help you boys with something?"

Garray chokes on air, and when I turn to him, his face is red, his eyes on Aubrey. "You okay?" I ask, and he swallows, nods.

Will looks around the store while Aubrey trails behind him. Today, she's in all black, which does nothing to take away from her pale tone and scarlet, scarlet, scarlet. Garray nudges me with his elbow. "Dude," he says. "Is she—"

"Unavailable," I interrupt. It was supposed to be a whisper, but it comes out harsh, and both Will and Aubrey turn to us. Aubrey eyes me suspiciously, and I widen my eyes at her, like *what?*

Dumb Name nudges me again.

Aubrey turns to Will. "I take it this is a gift?"

Will nods. "For my girlfriend."

"How long has she been here?" Garray asks me. "She's fucking fire."

Me: "Fuck off."

Aubrey to me: "What?"

Me to Aubrey: "Nothing."

Will to Aubrey: "It's our one-year anniversary."

Aubrey to Will: "That's sweet. Congrats."

Garray to me: "Is this that Aubrey girl?"

Will to Aubrey: "Yeah, so I need to get her something good. I was expecting the *real* present to come, but it's been delayed, and…" *Blah. Blah. Blah.*

Garray to me: "It is, isn't it??"

Me: "Shut up."

Aubrey to Will: "Well, I don't know if I have anything that will suffice. One year is a big deal."

Will turns to Aubrey. "I didn't think so, but it was worth a try, right?"

Garray to me: "I think I'll ask her out."

Me: "No!"

Aubrey and Will: "What?"

Me: "Nothing."

Garray laughs. "Message received, bruh."

Aubrey: "What message?"

Me: "*Nothing!*"

Aubrey touches Will's arm, and I want to yank it from its socket and smash him over the head with it. Repeatedly. "You wouldn't happen to have a picture of you two together, would you?" she asks him.

"Like, a million on my phone," he says.

"I have an idea, but you have to trust me, and you'll have to leave it with me. What time do you finish work?"

"Four," he tells her.

She smiles at him, and I want to gouge out his eyes for being the receiver of it. "Perfect."

I GO with Will back to Aubrey's shop after work. Of course, Dumb Name does, too, because he's a shit, and he knows what's up, and I don't have it in me to deny it.

"Just in time," Aubrey says, and the first thing I notice is that her hair's changed. It's tied up now, away from her face. She's also wearing an apron, or a smock of some kind with paint splatters all over the front, all different colors. Her sleeves are rolled up, pale, porcelain skin a contrast against the black fabric. Her fingers and forearms look just like the apron. There's paint on her cheekbone, on her forehead, her temple. All on her arms, her fingers.

"Did you get into a fight with some paint?" Will jokes, and Aubrey giggles.

"Kind of." She jerks her head toward her office, down a short, narrow hallway. We form a line, Will first, then me, then Dumb Name, and follow her.

Will freezes in the doorway and squeals like a girl, and I'm lucky to be tall enough to see over him. In the small room is a canvas set on an easel with a painting of Will and Bree. It's... it's enough to make my breath catch and for Dumb Name to say out loud what I'm thinking. "Jesus shit. That's amazing! Did you just do that?"

"Is it okay?" Aubrey asks.

"Oh, my God," Will mumbles, stepping forward to take a closer look. Dumb Name pushes me aside and does the same thing. And I stand, my feet rooted to the floor, my entire world tilting on its axis, because I had no fucking idea.

Just like Lachy with his drawing, I had no clue that Aubrey could paint or that she *owned* the fucking shop we're all currently standing in. I stay silent, my hands in my pockets, while Will praises her work, offers her money, to which she declines, and Dumb Name...

Dumb Name asks her out.

And she says...

She says...

"Maybe."

And then we're all leaving the office, and Aubrey's walking us out, and we're exiting the store, but not before she tugs on my arm—not my hand—and asks, "Are you okay?"

I'm so lost in confusion and in my own self-destruction that I ask her, "How the fuck did I not know this about you?"

And she answers with the words that have me questioning who I am and what my life is: "Because you never asked, Logan."

IT'S FRIDAY NIGHT, and it's my first date with Mary since before what my dad likes to call an "episode." She's so deep in my lungs, in my blood, in my thoughts, in my mind, that I can feel myself losing to her, giving in to her touch, to the way her fingertips stroke against my flesh. She's whispering words in my ears, from all angles, all spaces. *Because you never asked, Logan.*

I've been to Aubrey's house, been to her shop, been inside and around and over her, and she's right; I never asked, but she's wrong, because she never told me. Never hinted. And that's what Mary's so good at; this mind space, these circles, and I can't get enough, because I inhale and inhale and chop, lick and roll, chop, lick and roll just so I can inhale and inhale and inhale some more.

Because you never asked, Logan.

"No," I say aloud.

Mary calls to me again, warns me of what's to come: *You're nine years old, and the leather cracks beneath your weight...*

"No!"

Your selfish and conceited and you only ever wanted one thing from her—sex—and it's the one thing I can't give you, and that's why you had her and that's why you miss her and that's why you think it's a good idea to get in your car right now and see her...

AUBREY

I'd be insane to open the door to someone at almost midnight. It could be a rapist, a murderer—I look through the peep hole—a Logan Preston.

I can't see his face, just his shoulder. A shoulder I clearly recognize... which may make me more insane than opening the door to someone at midnight.

I open the door.

He's leaning against the brick of the alcove, his hands in his pockets. His cap is pulled low, and I can't make out his eyes, but he smells like he's smoked enough weed to kill a small horse. "Do you have any more?" he mumbles.

"What?" I huff, sleepy and annoyed, and wrap my robe tighter around me.

"Paintings, Red," he says, head tilting back, red, raw eyes meeting mine. Worn and wary, he asks, "Do you have more?"

"Yes," I whisper.

"Can I see them?"

I open the door wider, because loneliness and need are the cause of my insanity. So is the boy stepping through the threshold. I lead him down the hallway, past the living room, the kitchen, and my bedroom. "I mainly paint in my sunroom," I tell him over my shoulder.

"I didn't even know you had a sunroom."

"You've never been past my bedroom."

He doesn't respond. And for the first few minutes of being in the sunroom, he doesn't speak. He touches. Not me, but everything around him. Paint brushes and paint droplets, the blank canvas sitting on the old easel. "What..." He clears his throat. "What do you do with them? Where are they all?"

"I have some around the house—"

"You do?" he says. "I've never..."

"Paid attention?" I try to smile, but it hurts to lie to him. "It's okay. It's not like I'm passionate about it or anything. It's just something I do in my spare time, Besides, I'm no Lachlan. I don't have his talent."

Logan blows out a breath, leans against the wall. "I don't know, Red. From what I saw today..." he trails off, as he slides down the wall until his butt hits the floor. It's as if he'd been struggling to stand since the moment I saw him.

I stand on the opposite side of the room, my back to the wall so there's as much space between us as possible. "You don't look too good, Logan. Are you—I mean… are you okay?"

He rolls his head back and forth. "I'm not okay, Red. I'm so far from okay and so fucking high that *okay* seems like a myth, like a lie. Am I…" His eyes squint at nothing in particular. "Am I self-centered? Because I didn't think I was, but lately… it's like I've been living in a bubble and I don't know shit about shit. Like with Lachlan or my mom or *you*. I know nothing about you."

"You know more about me than anyone else here."

"*Here*, maybe, and that's because I took away the only friend you had."

"No one put a gun to my head and told me to sleep with you, Logan. I'm a big girl. I make my own choices."

"Still."

"Does it matter?"

"I feel like I should know at least some things about you."

"Like what?" I ask, moving to a sitting position, my legs crossed, hidden beneath my robe.

"Like… what's your last name?"

"O'Sullivan."

His lips tilt up. "Irish?"

"Yes. What's your middle name?"

"I don't have one. What's your favorite color?"

"I don't have one. You?"

"Scar—" He cuts himself off, shaking his head. Then he asks, "Do you have any other family besides your mom?"

"Just my grandma on my mother's side."

"Why stationery?"

"Because I used to work in a store back home part-time, after school and on weekends. I thought I knew enough about it to open my own, but… but I was wrong. I don't. And I wasted all the money I'd inherited on it, so…" I shrug. "So, there's that."

Logan sighs. "Why here of all places?"

"Why not?"

"Has your mom come to visit you since you got here?"

"No."

"Why?"

"Because I don't... I don't really know why."

"Do you talk to her?"

I pick at a loose thread on the silk robe. "What is this? Twenty questions? You have a list in your head or something?"

"Yes."

I blink.

Once.

Twice.

He repeats, "Do you talk to your mother?"

"Sometimes. Maybe once a week?"

"For how long?"

"Logan, why are we doing this?"

"Because... because I need to know that I'm not a complete asshole and maybe asking these questions will help me determine that. Or maybe because I *want* to know these things about you. Does it really matter why?"

Yes. It matters more than the answers I give. "What's with your necklace?"

He reaches up, strums his finger along the gold chain. He doesn't pull out the pendant, the flattened penny I noticed the first time we were together.

Logan doesn't answer me. Instead he reaches to the corner of the room where I have a stack of smaller canvases piled high, face down. He pulls the top one down, a painting of Main Street viewed from my morning walk to work.

"Did you bring all your supplies here when you moved in?"

"No," I tell him. "I bought everything used. I came here with a single suitcase. I told you that the first night."

He nods, motions to the painting. "Did you set up on the street and paint this?"

I shake my head when his gaze meets mine. "No. I have it all in here," I say, tapping my temple.

He takes the next canvas from the pile. It's of his sex den with the four-wheelers parked next to it. His eyes widen, as much as they can when he's this lit. "This from memory, too?"

"Yes."

"It's almost perfect."

I scratch the tip of my nose with the back of my hand, wonder how much I should divulge, and if he'll even remember it tomorrow. "My mom burned everything of my dad's after he died. Literally, everything. I have nothing of his to remember him by. After he died, I thought I could remember parts of him, you know? Like certain facial features, but then I'd come to paint him, and it never turned out right. Never exact. So now I try to memorize everything in detail, just in case."

He nods, as if he knows what I'm talking about. But, there's no way he could possibly understand. His mother's memory is a thing to be cherished, the complete opposite of my dad's. "My therapist—" he cuts himself off.

My breath halts, my hands going to my mouth. Surprise and heartache linger in my chest, in my words, "Why do you have a therapist, Logan?"

He shakes his head, pulls down the next canvas. This one is of his lake. He doesn't ask about it.

"What's with your necklace?" I ask again.

He lifts his gaze.

"The penny on the end and the *K* stamped on it?" I push. "What's the *K* for? Is it your mom?"

After a long beat, he nods. Just once. "My mom's name is Katherine. *Kathy.*"

"And why the penny?"

"When's your birthday?"

"Why the penny?"

"Because I was a shit of a kid growing up, and whenever I was, she'd pull a penny from behind my ear, tell me it was magic—that it was *my* lucky penny and that I should carry one around with me always to remind me of just how lucky I am." He says all this with his voice unsteady, his eyes too low for me to see clearly. "The last time she did it was the night before she died." He reaches into his shirt, pulls out the penny pendant. Then, his voice barely a whisper, his emotions barely contained, "There's fuck-all lucky about it, Red."

I swallow the pain of his admission and rest my head against the wall. "Is that why you go to therapy?"

"Part of it."

"What are the other parts, Logan?" *What's beneath the bravado I'm breaking?*

Logan exhales, long and slow. "I started therapy after Laney got shot. She was in an abusive relationship, and then she got with Lucas. I was a freshman, and I was at their senior prom, and her ex... he came and he shot her and I saw it all go down. And I saw the blood and I heard the screams and I... I..." He clears his throat, rubs his eyes against his sleeve, refusing to look up at me. "That therapist was the first to tell me that I had... attachment issues, that I feared getting close to someone. Not because it would hurt me, that would be too easy, but because I hated seeing the hurt it caused other people. People I care about. First with my mom and all us kids, but my dad especially... he didn't take it too well. And then my sister and Cameron... they um... they lost a baby a few years back, before they were married, and I had to see how badly it affected them. They almost split because of it, and... God, Lucy... she was a mess. And the shit with Lane... she's like a sister to me, and Lucas... he nearly lost her. We all did. I don't... I don't like feeling that, like loss is... it's so big and so mean and so cruel and I don't—I don't like feeling like I can't control it. So, I'd rather not care about anyone, and I'd rather not want for anything than lose something I want so badly, and so maybe... maybe that's why I'm here, Aubrey. I don't know..."

I wipe the liquid heat from my cheeks just before he looks up to see it.

He asks, his throat bobbing with his swallow, "Did meeting me ruin your time here?"

I shake my head. "No. I mean, spending those few nights with you... I don't regret it, Logan. But it makes it hard knowing that my every day is so much less because of that time, you know?"

He nods. "Are you... are you homesick?"

I smile, but it's sad. "I don't know," I say, shrugging. "Which is really hard to admit considering how badly I wanted to get away from there. But I do miss it. I miss part of my life, and I think…" I wipe another stray tear, letting the constant ache in my chest control my words. "I think I miss my mom," I tell him, nodding at my truths. "I miss her even though our relationship was toxic by the end of it. I miss coming home to someone, and I miss just… interacting with someone. I miss feeling like I *am* someone."

"You *are* someone, Red. And if you don't believe me, you can ask Lachy. You've changed his life, and I'm grateful for that. Even if I don't show it."

My tears fall freely now, unable to control them.

He asks, "Why didn't you call me while I was gone?"

I shake my head.

"Why are you stubborn, Red?"

"To protect my heart. Why won't you hold hands, Logan?"

His face turns to stone. "Pass."

31

AUBREY

LOGAN FELL asleep in my sunroom. I left him alone. When I woke up, he was gone.

LOGAN

I fight all of Mary's temptations the entire Saturday, because I have plans, and I don't want her ruining them.

AUBREY

I put away all the petty cash in the safe and switch off all the lights, another work day done. When I go to lock up the store, Logan is outside waiting for me. He's leaning against his truck, his legs crossed at his ankles, his hands shoved deep in his pockets. He offers a smile that makes my insides turn to dust. "You missing your mamma, Red?"

I can't help but get excited. "Why? You want to take me to see my mamma, Lo?"

He opens the car door for me.

He opens the car door for me!

Once I'm inside and buckled in, he says, his finger running across my collarbone, shifting the hair away, "I'll take you wherever you want, Red, just as long as you want me to."

LOGAN

Okay, so I didn't have *plans*, so much as I had *a* plan, and that plan consisted of getting Aubrey in my truck. Last night she told me she wanted to see her mom, and I wanted to be the one to make that happen. Whether we were friends, friends by association, or friends on the brink of more, it didn't matter to me. What mattered is that she said *yes*. At least to this, if nothing else.

I got what I wanted, because she's in my truck, my navigation is set to her mom's address, and we're listening to music, creating a playlist of songs as good as our banter, back and forth, hers then mine, a collection of contrasts that make my heart and soul want to hide and heal all at the same time. Three hours fly by, and we've barely said a word with substance, which is fine; we have three more hours on the drive back.

Aubrey's mom's house is a standard suburban with a red SUV in the driveway. "I'll be quick. Like, fifteen minutes. Thirty at most. Promise I won't keep you out here waiting." She's grinning from ear-to-ear, one foot out of the truck already.

"Take your time, Red."

"Forty-five minutes. No longer. Swear."

"Red." I touch her wrist, make sure to hold her gaze. "Take as long as you need. Promise me?"

Another smile and she's off, running up the driveway and knocking on the door. A woman appears, her hair more ginger than scarlet. And then comes an embrace that has the woman's eyes widening, her lips lifting. She strokes Aubrey's hair, the way I want to, almost *need* to, and she looks up at me, and Aubrey turns, points, waves. And that heart of mine? That soul? The ones that wanted to hide and heal? They fight. And when the mother and daughter move into the house and I'm staring at a closed door, I make the choice for my heart and my soul.

I let them heal.

If not for me, then for Aubrey.

AUBREY

My mother is beautiful, there's no denying. If it weren't for her red hair, I'd question whether I was adopted. We have no common traits or quirks, but I've always put it down to her being absent when I was younger and being mainly raised by my dad. She's a recruiter for the Marines, and the strongest, most powerful woman I know. I admire her, but I don't want to *be* her, and for a long time, I wondered if that was the reason it always felt like there was a giant void between us. There's no void now, though, and feeling that, *knowing* that, makes me so grateful that Logan drove the three hours to get here.

Mom pours soda into a glass while I sit at the kitchen counter, listening to every word she's saying. She's telling me about her job, about the new neighbors, and I nod at all the right times, which makes her smile. And then she stops talking and takes me in properly, like mothers do. "I've missed ya, kid."

"You have?"

"Of course, I have. It's not the same here. The house is too big and too quiet, and I miss coming home from work and calling out to you, you never hearing me over the sound of those records you still have in your room. I'd walk in and you'd be elbow-deep in paint." She shakes her head, exhales loudly through her nose. "It's just not the same, Aubs. And you left in such a rush, you know? I feel like, like—"

"Like I'm only three hours away," I say, my voice low while my finger circles the lip of my glass. "You could always come and visit. My house is too big, too quiet. It's always empty."

"Always?"

"Always."

"What about that boy who brought you here…"

I shrug. "It's always empty."

"Friends?"

"Ma."

"What?"

"It's *always* empty."

"Well, then," she says, leaning on the counter, her hand reaching for mine. "I'll have to come and visit."

"Why haven't you yet?" I ask, my gaze lifting, meeting hers.

She shrugs, releases my hand as she stands taller. "I figured you wouldn't want me to. I thought maybe—maybe you left because of me…"

She's partly right but not completely. I shake my head. "I just needed a fresh start after everything with Carter."

"You shouldn't let a boy—"

"I don't need a lecture, Ma. I just need your support."

"Okay," she says, nodding. "Speaking of Carter, I ran into him at the store the other day. He asked about you."

My eyes go wide. "Did you tell him anything?"

"I just answered his questions."

"What questions?"

"He asked where you were living, what you were doing… Why? Was I not supposed to tell him?"

After keying *Pathetic Dick* into his car, I'd prefer it if he didn't know where I lived. Obviously, I don't tell her that. "It's fine."

She smiles again, only this time, it's half-hearted. "Well…" she says, looking around the kitchen. "Did you want to pack any more things now that you have a car to haul it in?"

I've been living out of a suitcase for six months and doing just fine. "I'm good."

"What about your records?" she edges. "Or more clothes? Or your painting supplies."

"No. I don't need them."

"Did you replace them?"

"No."

"Then… why?"

I sigh. "Because I don't know how long I'll be there."

"Oh, no. Why, Aubrey? What's happening?"

With a shrug, I focus on my pleated skirt. "I just miss you, too, I guess."

"Aubrey." There's no confusing the amount of pity oozing from her tone. "It has to be more than that. Talk to me, sweetheart."

LOGAN

After waiting outside for her for forty-five minutes, I send Aubrey a text, tell her I'm getting a bite to eat with Leo and to take her time. I lie about the meal but not about my brother. He meets me at a nearby intersection and directs me through the maze of his campus back to his dorm. It's the first time I've visited. It's his second year here. Just another reason I'm a sucky friend/brother/human. Ten p.m. on a Saturday and there are people, people, people every-fucking-where. Yeah. I for sure made the right choice. College is *definitely* not for me.

Leo leads me from a visitor parking lot toward a bright yellow building, up some stairs and then opens the door to a six by eight-foot prison cell. Or dorm room. Whatever. "Not that I'm not happy to see you," he says, waiting for me to step inside before closing the door. "But what the fuck are you doing here?"

His side of the room here is just like his one at home, the one next to mine. It's sparse, neat, tidy. Everything in its place. Books upon books on his nightstand. On the end of his bed. On the bookshelf I built him when he first moved out. No movie or music posters on the wall, but rather, inspirational quotes from whom I'm sure are dead poets and writers. Above his desk is a picture of us—his family—and on his desk is a framed picture of him and Baby Preston; Brian's son, Laney's stepbrother, and also his godson. Of all the Preston boys Brian could've chosen, he chose the best. *Really*. And there's no jealousy or animosity on my end. Maybe on Luke's, but that's a *whole* other story.

I stand in the middle of the room, hands in my pockets. "Nice digs."

"Nice deflect."

"No raging party to go to?"

"Eh." He shrugs. "You go to one, you've been to them all. Besides, I need to study."

"You're *always* studying." I drop to the floor, on my stomach, and check under his bed for any signs a twenty-year-old *actually* lives here and not a forty-year-old virgin.

"What the hell are you looking for?"

"That blow-up doll I sent you."

"I sold it on eBay."

"Had no use for it, huh?" I say, smirking when I'm back on my feet.

He jokes, "Flesh on plastic isn't the quietest sound in the world. My dorm mate wasn't loving it as much as I was. Speaking of girls, what the fuck are you doing here?"

"What does a girl have to do with me wanting to see me brother?"

He sits on the edge of his bed. "I don't know. I seem to recall a certain redhead living around here somewhere."

"Her name's Aubrey."

"And where is sweet Aubrey tonight?"

"At her mother's."

"Did you drive her here?"

I nod.

"Not one for meeting the parents, huh?"

I move a bunch of random shit off his roommate's bed and sit opposite him. "I'm self-centered, aren't I?"

He nods. "Fact as fuck."

"Jesus."

"Not always, though. I mean, Lachy worships you. No idea why. And the twins tolerate you. Lucy seems to think you have *some* good qualities."

"And Luke?"

"Luke hates you."

I chuckle. "Hate's a strong word."

"Nah," Leo says, leaning back on his forearms. "Sometimes I think Luke's jealous of everyone."

"Why? He has everything he's ever wanted."

"I dunno." He shrugs. "I think it's more about not knowing what *he* really wants. I mean, it took him years to decide not to go to college—"

"And here you are," I cut in, and Leo nods.

"And then with you—it's like, there's no pressure on you to do or be *something*. Like, no expectations, you know?"

"Because I'm a disappointment first and foremost."

"No. You're a *dick* first and foremost. The disappointment comes from your own expectations. What I mean is, you've never played by the rules or standards. You're just... you. But, one day, someone's going to expect something from you—a certain redhead probably— and that's when you're going to feel the pressure."

"I'm not changing for no one," I declare.

He laughs. "No one's asking you to, you *dick.*"

"Why are you so smart and level-headed?" I throw a pillow at his head. "I hate you."

He moves the pillow aside, laughing as he does. "So, how's the whole Aubrey thing working for ya?"

I shake my head at him. "I don't know. How's the whole unrequited love for Laney thing going for *you*?"

Leo sighs. "It gets easier every day, man. The distance helps."

"Sucks. If it makes you feel any better, I accidentally played a hand in chipping Lucas's front tooth."

"Mayhem?"

"Always Mayhem."

Leo sighs again, louder and more drawn out. "I miss Mayhem."

"I miss my sidekick."

"Awww," he says, reaching over and patting my shoulder. "You miss your big bro?"

I swat his hand away. "Fuck off."

"So... what should we send Lucas?" he asks, already on his phone. "Pets are out."

I tap my chin. "We should get, like, a hundred of those vibrating

Ben-Wa balls and hide them in his dash—get Cam's mechanic friend to help."

"Dylan Banks?"

"Yeah. He's like, the king of Mayhem, right?"

Leo nods, taps away on his phone.

I say, "I think you can control them from an app. So, you could partake in Mayhem from all the way over here."

"Solid plan, my friend."

"Thanks." I stand up to stretch. "It was his idea for you."

"Traitor." Leo scoffs. "Who should I send them to?"

I give him Aubrey's work address, then say, "Dad would be so proud to know you're spending all his hard-earned money on sex toys."

AUBREY

Mom waits out front with me for Logan to get back. It's almost midnight now, which means we won't get home until close to three. I almost offer for him to stay at my mom's house, in the guest room, but I'm not sure I'm ready for Mom to meet him *that* thoroughly. When Logan pulls up, Mom nudges my side with hers. "He's cute," she says, even though I can barely make him out in the dark.

"Yeah. He knows it, too, trust me."

"What's his name?"

I turn to her so I can give her a hug. "Logan."

Her arms tighten around me. "Logan what?" She releases me from her embrace but holds onto my upper arms. "What's his last name, Aubrey?" she asks, which is odd, because I'm pretty sure I was with Carter for a good two years before she stopped calling him Connor or Cody or Colin or any male name beginning with C.

"Preston." I shake myself from her hold. "*Jesus.* Why?" Her face is ashen, and she's staring down at my feet. "Mom? Do you— I mean—" I look over my shoulder at Logan, waiting patiently behind the wheel. "Do you know him or his family?"

"No." She shakes her head, her eyes wide when they meet mine. "Why? Should I?"

"You…"

Her eyes widen again, like a dare, or more like a lack of patience.

"Never mind."

"I just… I want you to be careful, okay? With your heart, Aubrey." Her gaze softens; so does the rest of her. "And I highly suggest you think about what we discussed." She turns on her heels and rushes back to the house, never once looking back. And I'm left in the middle, between my past and my present, with no definite future in sight.

LOGAN NUDGES ME, and I stir from my sleep, open my lazy eyes to his. He's smiling. "You're home."

"I'm a sucky passenger," I yawn out. "I'm so sorry I fell asleep." Truth is, it wouldn't matter if I fell asleep or not. Even when I was awake, I didn't talk. Couldn't. Because all my thoughts were filled with confusion about my mom's reaction to his *name*.

"You're cute when you're sleeping."

I roll my eyes, mumble, "You shouldn't say stuff like that to me." Then I step out of his car. He meets me by the hood and walks by my side all the way to the door. I leave the key in the slot when I turn to him. "Thank you, Logan."

"You're welcome."

"It means… more than you could ever know."

He shrugs. "You'd be surprised how much I know about missing a mom."

An ache instantly forms in my chest. "I'm sorry…" I reach up, wrap my arms around his neck and pull him down to me. "Thank you," I whisper.

"Are we friends now—no association?" he asks, rubbing my back.

"Yeah," I say through a smile. "We're friends."

When he pulls away, he keeps one hand on my waist. "Make sure to lock your door, okay?"

32

LOGAN

AUBREY'S COFFEE warms my hands while I sit on her shop stoop, waiting for her to show up Monday morning. Across the street, Dumb Name and Will watch, making pussy-whipping gestures that have me shaking my head. Pre-Aubrey, I would've done the same. Pre-Aubrey, there's no way I'd be in a situation that would have my so-called friends making those gestures.

Aubrey appears, on her bike, the end of that orange scarf from last Monday flowing behind her. She's half-peddling, half-wobbling, because the rear tire is busted. I stand when she comes to a stop, hops off the bike, and removes her helmet. It reminds me of the time she spent on the four-wheeler—when this all began. Her cheeks are red, wind burned, and she bites down on her lip when she sees me. "Hey," she says, her voice as warm as the coffee I'm holding. She locks her bike to the street lamp, as if someone's *actually* going to steal it. Then, in the following order, she:

Takes her bag from the handlebar basket, straps it across her chest.

Adjusts her jacket.

Pulls up her leggings.

Adjusts her skirt.

Then her hair.

And I watch, completely transfixed by her every move. "That was possibly the cutest thing I've ever witnessed," I tell her, handing her the coffee.

She rolls her eyes as she takes it from me. "Thank you, you pervert."

I chuckle under my breath, while she yawns the longest yawn in the history of the world. "Late night?" I ask, hands in pockets.

"Sleepless, more like it."

"Everything okay?"

"Yeah," she sighs out. "I just got a lot on my mind, that's all." She pats my arm. "I'll see you later?"

Nodding, I wait until her door's open and the lights are on before turning on my heels. Now Dumb Name and Will are pretending to go at it doggy style, tongues out wagging, and I'm so focused on getting to them so I can tell them to get back to work, that I don't even see the car coming until I've stepped onto the road. Luckily, the driver, a guy around my age in a polo with the collar up, stops just in time. I hold up my hand, say, "Sorry," instead of what I really want to say: that it isn't 2001 and we're not in a fucking Usher music video.

The guy rolls his eyes, motions for me to cross, and it takes all the power in me not to give him the finger, because fuck him and his stupid green BMW convertible, top down, and fuck his stupid clothes and preppy, rich boy bullshit. I take a calming breath and cross the road slower than Old Lady Laura. Just as I step on the sidewalk, there's the sound of glass breaking, and then an ear-piercing scream and tires screeching. My eyes immediately go to Aubrey. To her standing just inside her shop, her hands covering her head. Shattered glass surrounds her feet, and I'm running back across the road, shouting over my shoulder. I don't know what I say, but the words *cops* and *chase* are in there, and the next thing I know, my arms are around her and she's shaking, her eyes wide, distant. "Breathe, Red," I say, but she won't stop shaking, and now there are tears—tears I'm quick to wipe away. "Are you hurt?" I pull away so I can check for blood, her head, her hands, her entire body. There's no sign of blood, only scarlet, and I hold her again, say, "You're okay."

"I called the cops," Dumb Name says, and I nod at him while

Aubrey looks up at me, then outside, where a group of people have started forming, taking pictures on their phones. Will makes his way through them, struggling for air, and checks on Aubrey like I just did. When he sees she's unharmed, he turns to me, sweat dripping from his forehead. "I couldn't catch him. Honestly, I didn't even know what I was looking for."

Dumb Name picks up a brick from the floor—the weapon—and removes the note attached with an elastic band. He doesn't unfold it before handing it to me. I release her so I can read it:

Pathetic Pussy.

"Jesus Christ," I mumble, my hands trembling with anger. Rage.

"Carter," she whispers, and she's nothing but tears and torment and *fuck this guy.*

"Where does he live, Aubrey?"

"Logan, don't."

"His address, Red. I'm not fucking playing."

"No."

"He drives a BMW, doesn't he?" I should've beaten his ass when I had the chance.

Her eyes drift shut, and when they open, they're wider, clearer. She takes the note from my hands, scrunches it in hers. "Leave it alone, Logan." She looks behind me, to the nosy gossipers, then up to my eyes, her gaze pleading, her voice a whisper, "Make them leave."

"Are you okay?" Lucy cuts in, her hand on Aubrey's shoulder. "I heard the commotion, but holy shit…"

Aubrey doesn't take her eyes off me. "Please, make them leave."

"Who?" Lucy asks. "Them?" I don't know who she's referring to because I can't pull my stare away from green and agonizing. Lucy yells, "Don't you all have better shit to do? Go home and finger your buttholes or something! Shoo! Shoo! Go on! Get!"

LUCY CLEANS UP THE GLASS.

Dumb Name and Will go back to work.

Aubrey sits in the chair by her counter.

I squat in front of her, my hands on her knees.

If ever there was a time I could find it in me to hold someone's hand, this would be it.

I don't hold Aubrey's hand.

We wait in silence for the cops to show.

A text comes through on my phone:

Will: *Green BMW, right?*

I look up at Aubrey, but she's still staring ahead, lost.

Logan: *Yes.*

Will: *Punk's slow cruising down Main Street scoping out the scene. Motherfucker has a death wish.*

I shove the phone in my pocket, squeeze Aubrey's leg. "I'll be back."

She doesn't respond.

I tell Luce to keep an eye on her.

Then I step out on the sidewalk, lean against the lamp post where Aubrey's bike is chained. I shove my hands in my pockets, and I wait.

No more than two minute later, Dumb Name whistles from across the street, motions to the west side of Main Street.

Motherfucker *does* have a death wish.

I send Dumb Name a text as I step on the road: *Don't get involved.* Then I stop in front of the car again, this time on purpose. "Going somewhere?"

"Fuck out of my way, asshole."

Dumb Name and Will don't listen; they're by my side before I can respond.

"What?" Carter says, smirking. "Which one of you is she screwing?"

My fists ball. "Get out of the fucking car and say that."

"Make me, dickhead."

I round the car and lift him out by his stupid collar. He tries to fight me, but I'm bigger, stronger, and right now, I'm calmer than a Friday night with Mary. Because my mind's clear, and I want this guy to pay, want to him to suffer.

For all things scarlet.

I slam his back against his hood, get in his face. There are so many words, too many, and none of them make it out of my mouth before someone's pulling on my arm, telling me to stop. *Aubrey*. And because of her, and *only* her, I release the fucker, let him come to a stand. But I won't let him leave. No fucking way.

He laughs, looks Aubrey up and down while shaking his head. "You gone blue collar on me, Aubs?"

Dumb Name's next to me. "You don't take him out, I will."

"Just get out of here, Carter," Aubrey says, arms crossed, voice low. She doesn't look at him.

"You can't be mad about this, Aubs. I mean, you keyed *Pathetic Dick* across all four panels. Do you know how much that cost my dad to fix?"

Lucy cackles with laughter, and if I didn't know her, I'd tell her to shut up. "Pathetic Dick?" she laughs out. "Oh man, those *C*'s would've been tough. I'd question why it was pathetic, but then... your car... and *you*... makes total sense."

Carter glares at her. "Who the fuck are you?"

"Don't talk to her," I grind out.

Carter's eyes move from me, to Lucy, to Aubrey. He says to her, smirking, "I don't know what the fuck's going on in this hillbilly town, but if you left home to get away from me, and now you're seeing *this* guy, you may as well have stayed. Let me cheat on you some more."

Aubrey's face pales, her eyes going directly to his.

"Oh, what?" he chastises. "You didn't know? Yeah, I cheated on you the entire time."

I step forward.

Will stops me.

Carter keeps fucking talking, "It was impossible not to. I mean, look at me and look at you. You're the pathetic one here, Aubs. No matter how badly I treated you, you kept coming back for more. You loved me at my worst because I saved my best for everyone—"

"Shut up," Aubrey snaps. "Just shut up. You don't think I know that? You don't think I know about *every* girl you were ever with. You don't think I'd hear about it, or worse, have them tell me about it! I knew, Carter!" She cries out, a trail of tears streaking down her cheeks. The street's filled with people now, watching, waiting, but the world is silent, still, all while the girl who owns a part of me begins to crack, break. "I knew *everything*," she says, wiping at her tears. "I just didn't know *why*..." Her shoulders shake, and then she shatters, right in front of me, and the calm is no longer there. All I feel is the weight of the water, the ache in my lungs as they barely hold on, my mind telling me to float up, up, up to give my body what it needs: *air*.

But this time, I stay submerged.

And I let myself drown.

The fabric of the fucker's shirt tears at my fingers when I push him back down, my ears filling with the sound of his bone crushing against the metal of his hood. His eyes are wide, wild, restless, and I close mine so I don't have to see his pathetic last-second plea. My fist meets his jaw, then his nose, his chin, his chest.

The world is chaos.

The screams are loud.

My name is the loudest.

Lucy's screaming for Cameron.

Hands are on my hips, my arms, my chest.

"Stop! Stop! Stop!"

"Jesus Christ, Preston, you're going to kill him!"

"Lo! Stop!"

"Logan!"

"Lo!"

"Logan!"

My fist meets metal, over and over, while I hold him down, hear him cough up blood.

Sirens.

Louder and louder.

Car tires screeching to a stop.

More sirens.

And then hands on my shoulders, strong and determined, pulling me away.

"Holy shit." *Lucas.*

I can't stop hitting, fighting, punching my way through the water. I need air. I need to breathe. I need to *live.*

I'm being lifted off my feet, arms around my torso, pinning my arms to my sides.

"What the fuck happened?" *Cameron.*

I need to find the surface.

"It's okay, son." Dad's voice is right at my ear. "Just breathe, son. Breathe."

He leads me to his truck, puts me in the back seat, and slams the door shut.

My world is chaos.

Swirls of water.

Riptides of emotion.

My hand is busted.

And my heart... my heart is looking at me from the other side of the window wondering who the fuck I am and how the fuck she got here.

I close my eyes, tap at my empty pockets. *Mary, Mary, quite contrary, how does your garden grow?*

AUBREY

The world is a blur, and I am the core, the axis.

Mr. Preston locks Logan away in his car and makes his way back to us. He asks Carter if he's okay. Blood spills from Carter's mouth, making it impossible to comprehend his answer.

"Do you need me to call an ambulance?"

Carter shakes his head.

Two uniformed officers get out of their vehicle and meet up with a woman who has a police badge attached to her belt. They speak for a few minutes before approaching us. "What happened, Tom?" the woman asks.

"I don't know," Mr. Preston says. "I just got here." He has one hand on his hip, the other wiping his mouth. His eyes are filled with worry, and he looks over his shoulder to Logan—whose eyes are closed, head tilted back. Mr. Preston sighs, looks at the thick crowd around us.

The crowd, too, is a blur.

And I am the focus.

"Did anyone see anything?" Mr. Preston shouts.

He may as well be a drill sergeant with the numerous returns of "No, sir!"

"This is bullshit," Carter says. "I want that guy arrested!"

"Carter, you threw a brick through my window," I rush out, because right now, my focus is on Logan and Logan alone, and I don't want anything bad to happen to him because of *me*. I turn to the woman while pointing at Carter. "I want him arrested."

Tom sighs, then asks the crowd, "Did anyone see him throw the damn brick?"

Logan's workmates step forward. "Yes, sir. We saw it."

"Bullshit!" Carter snaps. "They didn't see shit!"

Lucy speaks up, "The security camera outside my store caught him doing it."

"It did?" asks the woman.

"Yes." Lucy nods. "It cut out right after, so without eyewitnesses, there's no real proof of what happens next."

Lucas Preston—a guy I've only ever seen in pictures—who's stood next to Mr. Preston the entire time, not saying a word, steps to Carter. "Look, I don't know what happened, but here's my card," he says, giving him a business card. "Just email the medical bills and whatever for your car. Attention it to Lucas. But right now, you need to get the fuck out of here, and don't come back, man, because I can guarantee, you ever try again to pull whatever shit you pulled today, my brother's not going to go so easy on you. And next time, we might not be around to stop him."

LOGAN

Dad doesn't say a word on the ride to the hospital. A couple busted knuckles, maybe some stitches from hitting the metal, but it's all shit that'll heal in time. It's definitely not broken, I know that much. But going by the look on Dad's face, I know he's not going to want to hear it.

Dad walks in with me through the emergency room doors, waits until I've given all the details to the woman behind the nurses' station. Then he says, "You don't come home until it's looked at. I'm going back to work."

"How am I supposed to get home?"

"You have legs," he says, and I know it's only part of my punishment.

I SIT in the stupid waiting room for a good two hours, alone, before my name's called. I wait another hour for an X-ray machine to become available. Another hour for the results I already knew were coming. I'm left alone to wait for someone to come back and stitch me up. My phone doesn't ring. Doesn't make a sound. A few minutes after the last doctor leaves, the door opens, and it's Aubrey. "You're an idiot."

I exhale loudly. "Save the lecture, okay? I'm going to hear about it enough when I get home. What are you doing here? *How* did you get here?"

"Garray gave me a ride. Nice guy."

"Yeah? Maybe you should date him. Oh, that's right. You said *maybe* you would. How's that going for you?" I don't know why I'm so pissed. The entire time I've been sitting here, all I wanted was her by my side. But I didn't want this: her clear disappointment.

"I'm not going to date him, Logan," she sighs out, stopping a few feet in front of me. She leans against the wall, her hands behind her back, and motions to my lap where my hand sits limp. "How bad is it?"

"They're coming back to stitch me up."

She shakes her head. "Why would you—"

"Leave it alone, Red."

"But... what happened? You told me you weren't a violent person."

"Yeah? Well, I've never witnessed anyone treat you like shit before, so..."

"Logan..." She sighs. Again.

"Why do you keep saying my name like that?" I ask, my eyes on her. "And why are you all the way over there?"

She takes a tiny step forward.

"Red."

"What?"

"Come here."

She exhales slowly before moving forward, her legs touching my knees. I brush my thumb against her thigh, rest my forehead on her chest. She smells like fall. Like pumpkin and cinnamon and raindrops. "Are you okay?" I mumble.

"I'm fine. A little embarrassed."

"Of me?"

"No, Logan," she says, holding my face in her hands and pulling away so she can see me. "Never of *you*."

With a nod, I tug on her legs until she's standing between mine. "What are we doing here, Red?"

"We're waiting for you to get stitched up...? Did you hit your head or something?"

My blink is slow, frustration simmering below the surface. "You know what I mean, Red. Can't we just go back to before? Don't you want that?"

Her hands slide down my shoulders, my chest, before they disappear completely. Then she steps back, away from my touch, away from me. Her gaze drops. So do her shoulders. She side-eyes the door. Then the floor.

I clear my throat. "I get it, Red. You don't need to say—"

"Say what?"

"That you don't want me like that."

"God," she says, eyeing the ceiling now. "I wish it were that simple."

"So, why isn't it?"

"Because I do *want* you, Logan. Like *that*." Her voice wobbles. "But I've done this before. I've *felt* this before. I've given up everything because it didn't work out. You saw how… you *saw* what happened today—"

"You're comparing me to him again," I bite out.

"That's not it," she says, stomping her foot like a brat. "I'm comparing *me to me* again!" She reaches down, her hand near mine.

Please don't.

My hand twitches, my resistance clear.

She runs her index finger along mine, then to the inside of my wrist, along my palm. She sniffs once, and when I look up, she's watching me, her eyes filled with tears. I grasp her finger, stop her from going any further. "Why are you crying, Red?"

"Because it hurts," she whispers, resting her forehead on mine.

I run my nose across hers. "What hurts?"

She sniffs again, and a tear falls, soaks into my cheek, into my skin, into *me*. She says, her words filled with pain, "I'm leaving, Logan."

I pull away, eyes wide and on hers. My lips part; so many words, so many questions. I release her finger. The door opens. Big Logan walks in, scrubs from head to toe. "Need me to come back?" he asks.

I shake my head, keep my gaze locked on Aubrey's. "No," I say. "She was just *leaving*."

33

LOGAN

I'm off work, no pay, two weeks.

Suspended.

Grounded.

Therapy three times a week.

And all I can think is at least I still have Mary.

It's ten in the morning by the time I wake up. My hand is throbbing. My head is worse. The house is quiet; no one's home. I throw the covers off of me, don't bother getting dressed, and part the curtains. Sunlight bleeds into my vision and I blink hard, fight against it. Thick and cool, I let fresh air fill my lungs when I slide my window up.

Mary calls to me from the pocket of my jeans.

I smile back at her.

Soon, baby.

The front door opens and closes, and my eyes narrow, confused. I kick my jeans under my bed, just in case. A knock sounds. *Lucy.* "Come in." But it's not Lucy; it's scarlet upon scarlet upon scarlet. I blow out a breath. "Stalk much?"

"Apparently." She shrugs. "I wanted to check in on you. I tried calling."

"I know." I've never had a girl in my room before—house rules—and the fact that it's a girl who wants nothing to do with me pisses me off.

She says, "Your dad gave me the code for the gate, told me where the spare key was."

I cross my arms, lean against the window while she stands in the doorway. "I have one question, Red."

She nods.

"You think about Lachlan in your choice to leave?"

Her features harden. "Lachlan will do just fine. He has all of you." She jerks her head toward my hand. "How's your hand?"

"It's fine."

"Can I see it?" she asks, and there's a desperation in her voice that cracks my facade, my need to hate her for leaving.

I lift my hand between us. "It's just bruised knuckles, small fracture, that's it."

She moves toward me, slowly, carefully, as if I'll pounce if she gets too close. Her hands are warm, soft when they meet mine. She lifts it higher, her eyes sad, her words sadder. "Does it hurt?" she asks, her thumb stroking over the stitches.

I shrug, pull my hand away. I don't want her touching me, because I don't want to miss it when she's gone. "Mary helps with the pain."

Her body goes still. Solid. And she makes a sound from deep in her throat. "Okay," she whispers. "Well, I'll let you get back to whatever…" She's crying, and she has no right.

"You can't do that, Red," I tell her, slumping down on my bed.

She's at the doorway again, slowly turning to me. "Do what?"

"You can't get mad because you think…" I sigh. "Mary's *marijuana.*"

"Like that Rick James song?"

"Yes." My mouth wants to smile. My emotions don't allow it. I shut my eyes tight, let out a frustrated moan. "Aubrey… I thought we were… I don't know… working toward something—you and me. I figured you just needed time, so I was giving you that, and then you tell me you're *leaving*. Where the hell are you going to go?"

"Home." She leans against the door frame, facing me. "The other night, when you drove me there, I talked to my mom about everything, about how I was feeling here. I thought she'd be disappointed in me, but she was really supportive. She wants me to—"

My bitter laugh interrupts her. I say, shaking my head, "I drove you there to get closer to you, and all it did was drive you away..."

"Logan."

I lie down, eyes on the ceiling, because looking at her hurts too much. "So, what happens now? You go home, you forget about this life, you forget about Lachy, about *me*?"

"If… if I stay here…"

"You think I'm going to treat you the same way as your ex—that I'm going to cheat and drive you out of town or something?"

"No," she says, her voice breaking. "But that's not to say I'm not terrified... And it's not even about the cheating, Logan."

"Then what is it?" I'm angry and frustrated and confused and hopeful all at the same time. I sit up again. "Explain it to me, because I'm having a really hard time understanding it."

"It's…" She pauses, regains her composure. "It's about giving my all to someone who can't do the same."

"What the hell are you talking about?" I'm practically shouting now. "I've given you more than I've given anyone, ever, and that might be hard to believe, but it's true!"

"Why won't you hold hands, Logan?"

My insides turn to stone, and my jaw clenches. "Fuck off with this shit, Aubrey." I shake my head, rub my eyes. "No."

"Then there's your answer."

I tap at my pockets, pockets that aren't there. *Mary, Mary, quite contrary.*

She adds, "Why do you smoke so much? It's not recreational, is it?"

"Stop, Aubrey," I grind out. "I mean it."

She pushes me further. "What are you trying to forget, Logan?"

I can't stop shaking my head, can't stop the thoughts flying through my mind. *I am nine years old…*

"See? You ask me anything, and I'm an open book. You can't even look at me when I ask—"

"What do you want me to say?!"

And then she pushes me over the edge. "The truth!"

I'm on my feet, in her face. "You want to hear the truth? I don't hold hands because the last person I fucking held hands with was my mom! I was nine years old, and I couldn't get to sleep one night. One random fucking night of all the nights! And I went to her room and climbed into her fucking hospital bed with her. She opened her eyes, smiled at me, pulled a fucking penny from behind my ear and told me she loved me." I ignore the heat behind my eyes, my nose, my *words*. "And I held her hand while my dad slept on the couch in there, and I rested my head on her chest, and listened to her heart beat. I listened to her breathing! And then she stopped. Her breaths. Her pulse. It all fucking stopped! I knew she was dead, and I didn't say shit. I didn't wake my dad to tell him! I just lay there, holding a dead woman's hand because I couldn't let go! Because letting go meant that I would never be able to do it again! So, you want the fucking truth, Aubrey? There it is!"

She's crying, loud and uncontrollable, and she tries to reach for me —this girl that pushes and pushes and takes and takes.

I slap her hand away. "Don't fucking touch me!"

"Logan, please," she cries. "I'm sorry! I'm sorry!"

"No!" I tug at my hair, swallow the ache in my throat from screaming too loud. I drown beneath the surface, my thoughts bubbles of air, rising, higher, higher... until they *burst*. I point my finger at her, let my anger control me. "You fucking come in here and you demand shit from me! You have all these fucking expectations, and then you make me feel guilty for not exceeding them! You don't even give me a chance! You never have! You just want want want, and you want it all right fucking now, and I've never once..." I take a breath. "Aubrey... I've never once wanted or needed anything from you. I've only ever wanted *you*!"

"God, Logan. I can't... I don't..." She wipes at her eyes, her nose, all signs of her pity.

"Get out, Aubrey! Just fucking leave!"

AUBREY

The front door slams behind me and I fall to my knees, my face in my hands. Sob after sob consumes me. My shoulders shake. And I can't quiet my cries. I can't forgive myself for what I've done. For what I've made him...

I can't take any of it back.

I'm clingy.

I'm needy.

I'm so fucking pathetic it makes me sick.

I brought a man to his knees.

I pushed and I pushed and I pushed until there was nowhere for him to go but down.

From his room, I hear the sound of bass pumping, music blasting —"These Arms of Mine" by Otis Redding—and I cry harder, louder. And then I smell it, *weed*. His Mary. The one who helps with his pain.

Why couldn't I be Mary?

Why couldn't I...

I get to my feet, rush through the front door and up the stairs. His bedroom door's closed, and I don't bother knocking. He won't hear it. His back is turned, the top half of his body outside the window. Dank smoke fills the air, fills my nostrils. "Logan," I cry out, and he shakes his head, refuses to face me.

"Close the fucking door!"

I close the fucking door. "Logan! I'm sorry, okay? I'm so sorry!" I scream over the music.

He turns, only halfway. "Why the fuck does it matter, Red?" he shouts. He brings the joint to his lips, inhales, exhales a ribbon of smoke.

"It matters!" I yell, my back to the door.

He shakes his head again, flicks the butt of his joint to the grass beneath him. Then he slides the window down, letting the glass rattle against the vibrations of the music. "It doesn't matter, because soon you'll be gone, and I'll be nothing but the guy you once fucked in a town you once hated in a life you once wanted!"

"That's not true!"

"Bullshit! When are you leaving?"

"Ask me to stay!"

"Don't you *dare* put that on me, Red." The music stops. Starts again. Same song. Repeat.

"Ask me!"

He shakes his head.

My eyes drift shut, my entire body weighted by the moments that brought us here. Every instant. Every memory. Every single word we've spoken, every touch, every bit of joy, of laughter. Tears fill my closed lids, and I hold back another sob. "Okay," I whisper, even though he won't hear it. "Okay." I turn around, reach for his doorknob.

Turn.

Pull.

LOGAN

It takes three steps to cross the room, slam my forearm against the door, and trap her body in with mine.

AUBREY

His breaths are as broken as we are, and each one of them lands on my neck, my shoulder, heated and fierce. Seconds pass, and we stay that way, his chest pressed to my back. He's keeping me here but hasn't yet said the word: *stay.* If he asked me to, I would. In a heartbeat. The music plays on, and I listen to the lyrics, let them control me. My tears don't stop. *Won't* stop. And my heart... my heart *hurts* in ways I never thought possible.

Logan's hand lands on my hip, begging with the gesture for me to turn to him. To look at him. But I can't, because I'm too afraid of what he'll see there: that I'm lost either way. "Aubrey," he whispers, and I don't know what he wants. I don't even know what *I* want. I turn to him, to tell him just that, but his blue-blue eyes are watching me. Waiting. And all words, all thoughts flee when he rests his forehead against mine. And then his lips… his lips press to me, so softly my breath catches. Logan likes to play, likes to tease, likes to go slow, but even during those moments, he's never soft. Never *gentle*. His hands cup my face, and every touch, every kiss, every swipe of his tongue along my lips is a plea. He guides me to his bed, lowers me slowly with his hand on my back.

"Aubrey," he says again, his hands sliding up my sides, taking my sweater with them. Then my shirt. Then my pants. Until I'm laid out in front of him in nothing but my bra and panties, and he's over me, kissing me, touching me, breathing me in. He lowers himself until he's on the floor, on his knees, his eyes on mine. A moment passes, my heart hammering… *What do you want, Logan Preston?*

His hard exhale warms my thighs, and then he's groaning, his head tilting back. "Why does this have to be so hard?" he murmurs. "I've never wanted anything as badly as I want you. I just want to be with you, and I want that to be enough."

I struggle to breathe through the pain etched in his words.

"I feel like you're trying to make me into someone I'm not."

I sit up, cross my arms over my stomach. "God, Logan. No," I whisper, reaching out to settle my hands on his shoulders. I wait for his eyes to meet mine before adding, "I don't want you to be anyone but you. I've wanted the same version of you that you've always been, and I wanted that before you even *saw* me like this, and you *know* that."

His throat rolls with his swallow, and he exhales again, this time into the palm of my hand.

I say, risking it all, "But I do want *more* of you. We hang out, and we make out a lot, and we have *incredible* sex, but I feel like I need to know that I'm more than *just* that to you… because you've become so much more than that to me, Lo. And I'm scared—"

"Because of your past?" he cuts in.

Nodding slowly, I answer, "And I know that's not fair to you, and I'm so sorry that I've pushed you this far."

Otis Redding croons while Logan sighs. "I hate..."

I look away, ashamed. "...Me?"

"No. Jesus, Aubrey. I'm fucking crazy about you."

My eyes snap to his. "You are?"

"You *know* I am. At least you should..." He licks his lips, tugs at his hair. "I hate that we keep ending up like this. Why can't it just be easy?"

"Because nothing good comes easily," I mumble, placing my hand over his when it settles on my leg.

"But we're not just good, Red," he says. "We're so much better, so much *more* than just good."

I nod, because it's true.

"Red?" he says, and the plea in his voice has my stomach twisting. "I don't know where we go from here."

"Me neither."

With a moan, he stands, then flops down on the bed next to me, his eyes on the ceiling, his hand behind his head. "Red?"

"Yeah?"

His hand circles my wrist. "Come here." And then he's pulling me down, down, down until I'm lying on top of him, my forearms resting on his bare chest. He cups my face in his rough, calloused hands, strokes my stray tears with his thumb.

His smile breaks through my walls, my defenses. He moves the hair away from my eyes, tucks it behind my ear, then his thumb moves across my cheek, to my lips, strokes once. Twice. On the third time, I kiss it. Bite down on it. And then his mouth is on mine, soft and gentle. I let him set the pace, expecting him to go further, but he doesn't. He kisses me with passion, with purpose. Every movement is slow, his lips, his tongue, his hands gliding up my sides, my back, through my hair. He's all over me, around me, inside me, and not just physically. "I'm glad you're here," he whispers.

"Me too."

We get under the covers, on our sides, face-to-face. We're still dressed in our underwear, just like the first night, but the way his eyes bore into mine, the way his hand settles on my hip, the way he continues to kiss me... I've never felt more naked in my life, more *exposed*. He pulls away, just his lips, but brings the rest of me closer. "You give good cuggles."

I throw a leg over his, press my face to his chest. "Cuggles?"

"It's how Lachy used to say cuddles. We all use it. Sometimes I forget that's not the real word."

"I used to call a vagina a jawatna."

He laughs, full force, rolling to his back and covering his eyes with his arm.

I move with him, lean up on my elbow to look down at him. "So... yesterday was intense."

He removes his arm so he can see me and mumbles, "Understatement."

"But Lucy"—I'm smiling—"telling people to go home and finger their buttholes..." And now I'm laughing.

Logan shakes his head against the blue of his pillow. "Lucy's... she's so inappropriate sometimes, and I used to think it was because she lived in a house full of boys, but now I think we got a lot of our traits from her." He curls his arm around my neck, pulls me down until my head's on his chest.

"Are we going to get in trouble... me being in your bed and all?"

He shrugs. "I don't know. I mean, Dad gave you the code, the key... he has to assume *something's* going to happen. Which is weird, because it's a house rule, no girls go up those stairs. Definitely not in the bedrooms."

I lie on my back, look around his room. "Your room's so different to what I expected."

"Yeah?" he asks. "What did you expect?"

I take another look around. The walls are bare. There's a desk. A computer. A bunch of parts that look like they once belonged in stereos, and his bed. A few clothes on the floor, on his desk chair. "I don't know. I guess I expected posters of girls in thongs and bikinis, bongs everywhere, cum stains on the wall."

He laughs under his breath. "Oh, no doubt there are cum stains on the wall. Probably the ceiling, too. Shit. I jerked-off so much when I was a teenager."

I giggle into his chest.

He adds, "I even taught myself to be ambidextrous because I kept getting hand cramps."

I'm practically howling now.

"I'm serious, Red. You get one of those white lights in here, it'll be just like a Jackson Pollock painting."

"Oh, my God." I press my face into his arm. "Is it weird that I *like* how gross you are?"

"Ah, fudge nugget," he says, and I laugh harder. He covers his eyes with his forearm. "Now I'm picturing you naked on my bed, getting yourself off."

"That's not going to happen."

"Why not?" he asks, his disappointment clear.

"What if someone comes home and sees that? Me, spreadeagle on your bed, fingers deep in my pussy."

"Jesus shit, Red. You keep talking like that, I'm going to add another stain to the ceiling."

"Sorry."

He sighs. "Besides, no one's going to come home. Kids are at school. Everyone else is at work. Dad might, just to check in on me, make sure I haven't left the house. But you'd hear him come up those stairs."

"Oh, yeah?"

He nods. "When we were kids, before the twins were born, Mom would let us know when Dad was going to be home, and all five of us would hide somewhere up here. Most of the time we'd just get under the covers in their bedroom. I was, like, three at the time, so I think I was still under the impression that if I couldn't see him, then he couldn't see me, you know?"

I nod, settle my head on his chest again.

Stroking my hair, he adds, "I remember all of us giggling, and Lucy telling me to be quiet, and the front door would open, and then Dad would be on the stairs, stomping his way up, and Mom would say…"

I look up at him when he stops, but he's too focused on the ceiling, on the memory, his smile lazy and carefree.

"She'd always whisper, 'Fee-fi-fo-fum,' like Dad was a giant, you know? And it always made me laugh. *Always*. And Dad—he'd pretend not to be able to find us. He'd go through all the rooms, and open all the doors. Sometimes, he'd even come into the room and get so close, and Luke—he'd have to cover my mouth with his hand to keep me silent. And then Dad would say, 'Welp. Can't find them. I must be too tired. I'm going to sleep.' And then he'd—" Logan laughs once. "He'd get under the covers and act all surprised that we were there." His breathing slows. "God, it was so stupid. I don't know how I remember that."

"It's good that you do, though. Those memories will last forever, and those are things that you'll probably pass down to your kids because you know how happy it made *you* feel." I swallow the pain, the realization that I don't have those types of memories.

He taps my leg. "The other day, I was thinking about what you said, about your dad and not having any memories of him. I don't think it's because you didn't pay enough attention when he was around. I just think… I mean, here, we're lucky. Luce was fifteen, and she was the closest to Mom, so she's always telling us stories. Saying things like, '*Remember when Mom…*' and that would spark the memory. It's not the same with you. It's not your fault."

I lean up so I can look down at him, feeling the burn behind my eyes, my nose. "Thank you," I whisper. "I really needed to hear that."

"Of course," he says, fingering a strand of my hair. "You have so much hair."

"I know."

"I like when you wear it up."

"Because it's less *hobo*?"

"Because it doesn't cover so much of your face. And your face is beautiful, Red. You shouldn't hide it."

I try to contain my smile when I take the hair tie from my wrist, wrap my hair in a high bun. "Better?" I ask, and he grins, runs the backs of his fingers along my jaw.

"Much." He leans up, kisses my mouth, my cheek, my jaw, then blows a raspberry on my neck.

"Ew!" I laugh out, wiping away his spit.

He chuckles, his smile unconstrained. "I think I like these moments with you the most."

"What moments?"

"Just this… existing with you. It's good."

"It's better than good," I retort, and he nods.

And then he's moving, his body shifting beneath the covers. His arm reappears, boxers in his hand. He throws them across the room. And because he's Logan, and I wouldn't want him any other way, I laugh when he says, "Enough with this shit, Red. Hurry up and fuck my dick off."

LOGAN

I bite down on Aubrey's hip bone, smiling when she squirms beneath me.

"Quit it," she whispers, her hands in my hair. "It tickles."

I move up her body, my tongue running along the slight bump of her belly, higher again, and kiss between her breasts, the tip of each nipple. She sighs. Content. I've gotten off twice already; she says she's lost count. We're both spent, but I can't seem to get enough of her. Her fingertips trail up and down my back, while I kiss the spot between her neck and shoulder, making her squirm again. "I said *quit it*," she giggles, but there's no fight in her words.

The same song's been playing on repeat, the soundtrack to our frustrations. I'd played it all night, fell asleep to it. Because the second she told me she was leaving yesterday, all I wanted to do was hold her, make her stay. But I pushed her away. *Again.*

I lean up on my forearms, look down at her. The sunlight beats through the window, reflecting off her hair, reminding me of Mary when I set her ablaze. Her eyes are half closed, her lips red from my assault. She's so perfectly imperfect, and perfect for *me*.

"What?" she whispers.

"You're so beautiful."

She shakes her head. "Shut up."

"You are."

Her hands are in my hair again. "*You* make me feel beautiful."

I lower my body, cover her completely. I nuzzle her neck. Sniff her hair. "You smell like fall," I mumble.

"You smell like man."

I chuckle. "Like sweat and body odor?"

"No," she says, "like strength and"—she sniffs the air—"semen."

My shoulders shake with my silent laugh. "That so *not* hot."

"It's incredibly hot."

I lift her leg, wrap it around my hip, ready for a third round, and that's when the front door opens. "Shit!"

"Shit! Shit! Shit!" she says, and she's out from beneath me, bare-ass naked in the middle of the room, spinning around trying to find her clothes. I find my boxers, slide them on. Then a pair of sweats.

Fee-fi-fo-fum.

"Get dressed," I whisper, find her clothes at the foot of the bed and throw them at her head. I open the door just enough to step out and find Dad on the top step. I shut the door behind me, keep my hand on the knob. "Hey," I say, but it comes out hoarse. I clear my throat, try again. "Hey, Dad. What's up?"

His gaze shifts from mine, to my door, over and over. "I know she's here, Logan. Her bike's still on the porch. Don't hide a girl like that. It'll make her feel as if you're ashamed of her. Are you ashamed of her?"

"No, sir."

"Then why are you hiding her?" he grumbles.

"The rules," I say stupidly.

Dad shakes his head. "You're nineteen years old, and you're grounded because you clearly can't follow the rules of *society*. The *laws*, Logan." He takes a moment to sniff the air. I'm sure he can smell the weed in my room, on me. He adds, "The rules of this house mean nothing to you. Now, get Aubrey and meet me downstairs. I need to have a word with both of you."

AUBREY SITS on the couch next to me, her hands clasped on her lap, her knees bouncing, her cheeks flushed. Dad sits on the coffee table opposite, glaring at the both of us. "This is the last time this happens," Dad says. He focuses on Aubrey. "I let you come over to check in on him because I knew you were worried." Then to me: "Now, I hope you discussed whatever you needed to and got whatever out of your systems, because grounded is grounded, Logan. That means no visitors. No phone. No Internet."

"Are you serious?" I huff out.

"As a heart attack," he answers, hand out waiting.

I murmur, "My phone's upstairs."

"Well, go get it."

I do as he says, hand it to him.

"When the twins get home, they're changing all the Internet and computer passwords. I'm boarding up your bedroom window. You will not smoke that shit in the house. And I'm changing the code on the house alarm. You will not leave the house while I'm not home."

"Savage," I mumble.

"Believe me, boy. You haven't seen savage, yet. And I can make it three weeks if you keep it up."

I look down at my lap. "Two weeks is good."

Dad clears his throat. "Are we all on the same page?"

"Yes, sir," Aubrey and I say in unison, as if he's the principal and we're in fucking elementary school. I say, "Can I... can I at least have five minutes with Aubrey, in private? We need to talk about—"

"No."

"Dad!"

"Rules are rules, Logan, and what is it that you kids are always saying? You play stupid games...?"

"You win stupid prizes," I finish for him.

"May I please speak, Mr. Preston?" Aubrey says, her voice meek. I shake my head, annoyed that Dad's put this level of fear in her.

Dad nods.

"I just wanted to say thank you for yesterday, for helping to board up my window. You didn't have to do any of it, and I can't thank you enough, Mr. Preston. And please say thank you to Lucas, too, for doing what he did."

My stomach drops. "What do you mean?" I face Dad. "What did Luke do?"

"Logan," Dad warns. "It's nothing. Don't worry about it." He's talking to Aubrey, but his words are meant for me.

"What did he do?" I press. "Don't tell me he fucking apologized to that motherfu—"

"Logan," says Aubrey.

"No. I'm so sick of him treating me like this, like I'm his responsibility. Like I need a babysitter. I smoke *weed*. I'm not out there selling my body for *crack*."

"Logan." Aubrey again.

Dad yells, his anger and frustration aimed right at me, "The last thing this family needs is *another* court case. Another chance of one of you boys spending time in goddamn prison for assault!" When he's really angry, a vein appears on his forehead. When we were kids, we'd all snicker about it, waiting for it to pop. It never did. It might now. After a few calming breaths, he adds, "Your brother fixed your screw-up, Logan. You should be thanking him."

My jaw tenses, and I refrain from saying anything more. I don't want to have this conversation. Not now. Definitely not with Aubrey right fucking here.

He says, "I'll give you a ride home, Aubrey."

"My bike..."

"Your rear tire is busted. Logan can fix it tonight when I get home from work. It'll be outside your shop tomorrow morning."

"Oh... okay, sir. Thank you."

Dad stands, says to me, "Lucas is coming home to take you to your appointment."

I stand with a groan, wait for Aubrey to do the same. Then I kiss her on the forehead.

"Appointment? As in therapy?" she asks.

Rolling my eyes, I say, "It's part of my punishment." I tug on a strand of her hair. "I'll miss ya, Red."

Dad asks Aubrey, "You know about his therapy?"

"Yes, sir."

I say, "Aubrey knows more about me than almost anyone."

Dad's smile is slight, hidden beneath his beard. "Good, good," he says, then leads Aubrey to the front door with his hand on her back.

She looks over her shoulder at me. "I'm sorry," she mouths.

I mouth back, "Me, too."

And then she's gone, taking our unanswered questions with her.

AT THERAPY, I write down one word, and one word only:
Hopeful.

34

AUBREY

It's AMAZING how getting a brick thrown through your window is the only way to get people in this town to actually know you exist. Even with the one window still boarded up, I show up to work Wednesday morning, fifteen minutes late, to see a line of people waiting outside for me to open. It's by far the busiest day I've ever had, and by lunchtime, I've sold more product than I normally do in two weeks.

After yesterday at the Preston house, I wasn't sure if Mr. Preston would still let Lachlan come around. I spend most of the afternoon watching the door, excitement then disappointment filling me every time the person entering *isn't* him.

Two hours after school lets out, Lachlan arrives, his eyes wide in surprise that people are actually in the store. "So, the rumors are true, huh?"

"What rumors?" I ask, clearing his desk for him.

"That some fudge nugget threw something through your window and Logan beat his face in? I heard my family whispering something, and I know Logan's on lockdown, but I didn't know *why*. Dad told me he did something stupid. When I got to school, everyone was talking about it."

I cringe. "I'm sorry you had to hear about it. People shouldn't gossip, though. It's not right, especially when they know who you are and—"

His shrug cuts me off. "Gossip is the only way this town runs. You'll figure it out soon, Miss Red," he says, removing his backpack and hanging it off the back of the chair. He unzips the top, reaches in, and pulls out a scrunched-up piece of paper. With a grin that splits his face in two, he hands it to me, says, "Logan paid me a hundred dollars to give this to you."

"A hundred dollars!" I gasp.

Lachlan giggles. "He must really want you to read it."

I narrow my eyes at him, playfully, and wonder what he could possibly have to say that's worth a Benjamin. "Wait," I say, eyeing the paper and then him. "You didn't read this, did you?"

Lachlan smirks. "Why? You think it's a dirty letter? I've read some of the stuff in Lucy's books. Trust me. I've seen *dirty*."

Pocketing the letter, I leave him with his sketches and attend to the customers in the store, my mind racing, dazed, all thoughts focused on Logan's letter. As soon as Cameron comes to collect Lachlan, I close up the store, sit in the office with the words that set my pulse, my heart, my world ablaze:

Sigh. My Pillows smell like you.

I can't ask you to stay, Red. Because asking you to stay would mean asking you to stay for me, and I can't do that. I won't. What if I fail you?

THE NEXT DAY, I plead with Cameron to pass on my reply to Logan. When he refuses, not wanting to go against his father-in-law, I turn to Lucy. "Please, Lucy. You're a sucker for romance, right?"

She sighs.

I beg some more.

Nodding, she silently takes the letter from me with the only four words I could think to write in response:

What if we try?

THE FOLLOWING DAY, the twins come to my shop. They've never been here before, so I'm already smiling by the time Liam pulls the same letter from his back pocket. "How much did he pay you?" I joke.

They laugh. "One fifty each."

That makes a total of $450 Logan's spent just to communicate with me.

The boy's an idiot.

My idiot.

I don't wait for them to leave before reading it.

What if that was all I could promise you?

AT HOME, I pace the living room, holding the letter to my heart. Hopefulness tears at my insides, and I try to push it away. To ignore it. But it's there. Every breath, every pulse is dedicated to that one feeling. I sit down at my coffee table and imagine him doing the same at his desk in his room. I wonder if he struggles to come up with words as badly as I do.

This time, I write down one extra word than the time before.

BY SATURDAY, I've folded and unfolded and reread the letter more times than I want to admit. By lunchtime, I start to lose patience. Then Leo Preston appears. "Home for the weekend?" I ask, trying to sound nonchalant, as if seeing him doesn't fill the hope bubble building in my heart.

Leo chuckles, just like the twins did. "For three hundred dollars, wouldn't you?"

"Jesus," I murmur.

Leo clucks his tongue. "Damn, girl. I don't think Logan's ever spent a cent on anyone before. He's fallen for ya, Aubrey. And he's fallen hard. Tomorrow, hell might freeze over."

I offer him the letter, and he takes it. "Have you spoken to him? Is he... is he okay?"

Leo smiles. "He's..." He breaks off on another chuckle. "Dad says he's been a pain in the ass. I'm just glad I'm not home to have to deal with him."

He leaves the store with my words of hope shoved deep in his pocket:

What if that was enough?

THE REST of the afternoon is crazy busy. It seems like everyone and their dog come through those doors. Literally, *their dogs.*

At 4:55, just as who I assume is the last customer for the day leaves the store, Mr. Preston walks in, fisting the letter Logan and I have been passing back and forth. "I think this belongs to you, young lady."

Blood drains from my face, my entire body. "I'm sorry, Mr. Preston," I plead. "I just couldn't... couldn't..." I trail off. *I couldn't keep away from your son.*

He sighs. "I think you can start calling me Tom, Miss Red."

"Okay.... Tom?"

"Besides, it's better than Silver Fox."

My body flames with embarrassment, and he chuckles, hands me the letter.

I hold it to my chest.

He asks, "Well, are you going to read it?"

"Have—have you read it?"

"Should I?" he asks, quirking his eyebrow.

I don't respond, simply unfold the paper:

I can't ask you to stay, Red... but please don't leave.
  - Logan.

35

LOGAN

"WHAT THE FUCK?!" I sit upright, bent at my waist, my eyes adjusting to the dampness leaking into them. This is the worst type of Mayhem: the ones that wake you from a deep sleep because it can take seconds, sometimes even minutes, to understand what the hell is happening. I open my mouth to speak, and that's when the powder is thrown at me: cocoa. "Fuck off!" I shout, and Lachy's laughter becomes the sound-track to my assault.

"Go!" Leo yells.

I barely get to wipe my eyes before I'm pounded in the chest with Nerf bullets, one after the other. It doesn't hurt, but it scares the shit out of me. I'm almost out of bed, ready to attack my little shit of a brother when Leo gets on me, pins me back down onto the bed and straddles my fucking chest. He forces something in my mouth, a nozzle of some sort, and then *cheese*. It fills my fucking mouth, and I'm gurgling, choking on a mixture of Eezy Cheese, cocoa and saliva.

Within seconds, I overpower my older brother, push him off me until he's on the floor. The loudness of his and Lachlan's laughter grates on my nerves and must wake the twins, because they come storming in, take one look at me, and join my other brothers. "Best day ever!" Lachlan shouts, and I should be mad, but I find myself laughing with them. It's the first time since Aubrey was here that I feel something other than annoyance and desperation. "You wait," I warn all of them, spitting cheese onto my already ruined bed sheets.

Dad calls the twins downstairs to help with Sunday Family Breakfast, and once they're gone, I strip my bed—minus the pillowcase... because *Aubrey*. Leo attempts and fails to open my nailed down window.

"That bad, huh?" I ask, already knowing why he needs the fresh air. It's not because of the cheese. Or the weed. It's because I haven't showered all week. I smell like shit.

Lachy sniffs the air, asks, "What's that smell? Is it that weed you smoke?"

My gaze snaps to his. "Where did you hear that?"

Shrugging, my youngest brother says, "Mitchell at school told me. He says you smoke weed and that it's illegal. He says you do other things, too, and that you're a junkie. That's why you beat the crap out of that guy, because you were coming down. What's a junkie, and what does coming down mean?"

"Logan's not a junkie," Leo tells him.

"But he said..."

I slump down on the bed, my previous jubilant expression replaced with dejection. Leaning forward, I tug on the front of Lachlan's shirt and pull him closer so we're standing face-to-face. Brother-to-brother. I look to Leo, as if I'll find the words I need written on his forehead. They're not. I go back to the kid we *still* call our baby brother. "You shouldn't listen to what everyone says, Lachy. This Mitchell guy—he sounds like a dick—" Leo's throat clearing cuts me off, and I recover, say, "He doesn't sound like someone who knows what they're talking about. His name's Snot Eater for a reason."

Lachy giggles. "But sometimes you *do* smell, and the smell is only ever in your room. It's not what it smells like now though. This *weed* Mitchell was talking about—is it like the ones in the garden? Do you just pull them out and then... how do you smoke it? Like Dad smokes ribs on the grill sometimes?"

I tug at my hair, my gaze back to Leo's for support. He tells Lachy, "Logan needs to shower now. Good job with the Mayhem, bud. I couldn't have done it without you." He offers his fist for a bump, and Lachy returns it. "Go set up the table for breakfast, okay?"

"Okay!"

I watch the door our brother just ran through. Leo watches me. "Fuck," I spit out.

Leo sits on my desk chair. "It had to happen sometime. I wouldn't worry about it."

I pick up a dirty shirt off my floor and wipe the water and cocoa powder mixture off my face.

Leo doesn't skip a beat. "So, Aubrey..."

"What about her?"

"Her ex is a piece of work, huh?"

"How do you...?"

"Lucas told me."

I rub my face, get cocoa powder in my fucking eyes. "Luke has a big fucking mouth."

"You need to cut him some slack, Logan. He does what he thinks is right. Always has. Always will." He starts to leave, but not before saying, "You need to shower, dude. Seriously. You smell like hipster farts and sweaty nut sacks."

I SHOWER AND head downstairs for breakfast. Everyone's already in the kitchen working away on their assigned tasks. I see the pile of pots and pans in the sink, on the counter, and sigh out loud.

Dad says, "Nice of you to join us."

"I'm here, aren't I?" I grumble.

Dad shakes his head.

A minute later, I'm elbow-deep in grease and soap suds, scrubbing at the fucking pots. I don't know how or why we use so many pots and pans for a forty-five-minute sit-down meal. We could just order from the diner, have someone pick it up. I'm grumpy, obviously, because I haven't left the house for a week, have had almost zero interaction with the outside world, physical or technological. Pre-Aubrey, I thought I wanted this life: to be left alone. But then Aubrey came along, and now Aubrey is all I can think about. Aubrey is all I want.

The letters, those few short words from her, they're the only thing I had to look forward to. Yesterday, when I'd given Leo my reply to the letter Aubrey and I had been passing back and forth, Dad had intercepted. He read it, and without a word, stormed out of the house. A few seconds later, Leo and I heard his tires screeching.

We have no idea where he went or what he did.

I don't know if Aubrey ever got my response.

The doorbell rings, and I roll my eyes. Great. The only person who would show up during Sunday Family Breakfast is Aunt Leslee—my dad's sister—the one with the stick up her ass. And that stick? It's the reason Dad sends me to stay with her every time I mess up. I haven't messed up in a while, at least not this bad, and I swear, if Dad's about to make me stay with her—"Answer the door, Logan," Dad says.

I drop the pot I'd been washing and turn to him, my sudsy hands out in front of me, eyes wide like *are you fucking serious right now?*

"Answer the damn door, Logan."

Without bothering to dry my hands, I stomp across the room, through the living room, cursing and mumbling under my breath the entire time. I'm a kid again. A brat. I should move out. Clearly, I'm being dramatic.

It takes three tries to turn the doorknob because I'm a stubborn asshole and refused to dry my hands. Finally, I get the door open, ready to plaster on a fake smile for Aunt Leslee. But it's not Aunt Leslee.

Aubrey's in tight, black jeans, ripped to shreds, and a granny cardigan different to the one she lost at the party. A bright red scarf wraps around her neck, the ends falling past her knees. I wait for my heart to settle before I even attempt to speak. "What—what are you doing here?"

Behind me, Dad booms, "Are you going to let the girl in or keep her out on the porch steps? What the hell is wrong with you, boy?"

AUBREY'S *HERE*.

She's here, and I don't know *why*.

During breakfast, my mind spins, questions upon questions upon more questions. I don't ask any of them. I won't in front of everyone. The meal is the same as it is every Sunday... only I don't talk. *Can't talk*. Because Red and Lachlan are acting as if nothing's changed, and she's asking all the right questions to all the right people. It's as if she *belongs* here. As if this is her home.

Does this mean she's staying?

Hope builds a home for itself somewhere deep inside me. But it's not the type that warms me. It's the type I dread: the wanting and needing and longing and disappointing.

I'm mad at my dad for taking the letter with him.

I'm mad at myself for getting caught.

I'm mad at her for not standing up right here, right now, and giving me an answer either way.

I face her sitting next to me, tap her leg with mine. She smiles, but it's slight, and she continues her conversation with the twins. When breakfast is done, she asks what she can do to help. I lead her by her cardigan toward the sink, start on my assigned task.

Dad hasn't asked her to leave.

I haven't asked her to stay.

"I wash, you dry?" I ask, and there's no mistaking the hope mixed with dread in my voice.

She takes a dish towel I offer and stands next to me at the kitchen sink, her arms brushing against mine every time I move. I wash the dishes as slow as humanly possible, just so I can be around her for a second longer.

When the room empties, besides the twins and Dad—who's reading the paper at the kitchen table—no doubt keeping an eye on us (or me, to be specific), I drop the rest of the dishes in the sink under the pretense of soaking them. It's loud and gets everyone's attention.

"You're so mopey," Lincoln says.

"I am *not* mopey," I huff.

"Yeah, you are," Liam responds. "You have been all week."

"You guys try being grounded for a week with *nothing* to do!"

"You've *totally* been mopey," Lincoln repeats.

And I groan. "I've been *frustrated*, not mopey."

Aubrey pouts up at me, her finger stroking my wrist. Those freckles move when she scrunches her nose, and God, I miss her. I don't have a single picture of her, otherwise I would've spent the week staring it. Or masturbating to it. Either one. I'll be sure to take a picture of her before she leaves... the house or the town, I don't know. She asks, "You've been mopey?"

"No."

Dad chuckles. "He's been mopey, Miss Red."

"Fine," I concede, hiding my smile. "I've been mopey." I tug on her hair. "I've just missed you, is all."

Aubrey bites down on her lip as she fingers the bottom of my shirt, smiling up at me.

I take her wrist, focus on her hand as I run my wet finger slowly across her palm. It's *so* close. Almost *too* close. And, fuck, I've missed this. Missed touching her and talking to her and being this close to her. With my voice low and my pulse rising, I say, "We never... I mean... you haven't said... are you...?"

She doesn't answer, and when I look up, her eyes are on mine. She inhales a sharp breath, as if she'd forgotten to breathe. Her hand trembles in my touch, but she doesn't pull away. She blinks slowly before saying, "I hear there's a really good autumn festival around here."

Random. But okay... I guess. "Yeah, it's a couple towns over."

She nods. Smiles. Wraps her entire hand around my fingers and squeezes once. "You should take me to it."

"It's not for a few weeks," one of the twins butts in.

Aubrey's grin widens. "That's okay. I'll be here."

She'll be here, and now I'm smiling like an idiot. The kind of stupid smile that makes you giggle. Fuck, I'm pathetic. This girl has *made* me pathetic, and I don't even care. "So, it's a date?" I ask.

And she nods, agrees, "It's a date."

Then Dad releases a long, audible breath that fills the entire room. "Goddammit, you two. One movie. Then Aubrey leaves."

"In my room?" I ask, standing taller, excitement filling me.

"Living room, Logan."

"Den?" I counter.

"Or she could go home now?"

"Living room it is."

Dad stands, rolls up his newspaper, and smacks me over the head with it. "No blankets. Hands where I can see them at all times. I'm not immune to the rumors about you, kid."

Aubrey giggles.

When the room has emptied and we're still taking our sweet time with the dishes, Aubrey bumps my leg with her hip, says under her breath, "You're such a little whore, Logan Preston. But you're my little whore now."

36

AUBREY

E𝚟ᴇʀʏ.

Second.

D r a g s.

During the second week of No Logan, I reached out to my mom, told her what all went down. I also told her I was staying. "For Logan?" she asked.

"For me," I responded.

"Be careful, Aubrey," she said. *Again.* And when I asked her why she kept saying that, she made an excuse to get off the phone. But now it's Friday afternoon and she's here, in town, visiting like she promised. I show her around the shop, not that there's much to look at, and she seems impressed. "I don't know how you did all this," she murmurs, and I roll my eyes.

"Seriously, Mom? You deployed four times, put your life on the line. This—" I say, pointing around us. "This is nothing."

"*I* could never do this. I wouldn't even know where to start."

"Well… thank you," I answer sheepishly.

"So, you said you had an office?"

"Uh huh," I nod, start leading her toward it. I pass the counter, and am halfway down the hallway when the bell chimes. "One minute," I call over my shoulder. Then to my mom: "It's just on your leahhhh!" I squeal when arms wrap around my waist, lifting me off the floor. I'd go on an attack, but I know who it is. I'd recognize these arms anywhere, know his scent from a mile away. My smile hurts my cheeks, and I'm giggling, smiling some more. As soon as I'm on my feet, I'm turning to him, my hands going to his face, and those blue-blue eyes I've missed so much land on my mine. I kiss him. I kiss him as if he's the only air left in the world, and I melt under his embrace, sigh with contentment, and then pout when he pulls away. He tugs on a strand of my hair. "Worst week of my life, Red."

"I thought you weren't getting out until Monday!"

"I wanted to surprise you."

"Oh, I'm surprised!" I can't stop kissing him. His lips. His cheeks. His nose. His entire face. "I've missed you so much!"

"I know. Prison blows."

Behind me, a throat clears, "You were in *prison?!*"

"Oh, shit," Logan rushes out. "You didn't tell me..."

I turn in his arms but keep him close. "Not *prison* prison," I tell my mom. "He was grounded, because of the whole Carter thing. I told you all this."

"Right." Mom nods, moves toward us.

Against my back, Logan is a brick wall. Rigid. Still.

"I'm Melissa," Mom says, hand out for a shake.

Logan puffs out a breath that hits the top of my head, then he moves around me, eyes me with a cheeky grin. He looks down at her hand, then at her eyes, then at me. He clears his throat, plasters on a megawatt smile that usually has me dropping my panties. "I'm more of a hugger," he tells her. My mom's eyes widen when Logan wraps her in his strong embrace, and then she, too, is laughing, just like I was.

I pull him away when it lasts a second too long and go back to hugging him. "Come back. I'm needy," I say, and he chuckles.

"So, you were grounded, huh?" Mom asks.

Logan nods. "No leaving the house. No visitors. No phone. No Internet. Which normally wouldn't have been so bad, but not being able to see your daughter was *The Worst*."

My arms are around his torso, his arm around my shoulders. We're still in the tight space of the hallway, and Mom looks between us, a frown pulling at her lips. "Maybe I should leave early then."

"No! Why?"

"Well, I'm sure he has plans for you guys. A date or something."

"Or something," Logan murmurs under his breath, and I elbow his side.

"You should stay," I tell her. "We were going to have dinner together."

"Yeah, but Logan—"

"It's fine, ma'am. I can see her tomorrow," Logan cuts in.

"Or later tonight?" I plead, looking up at him.

"Or," Mom says, "maybe… I mean, maybe all three of us could go out for dinner. You could show me around town, Logan?"

Logan is a statue. A monument. "Sure."

"You don't have to," I tell him.

"Why not?" Mom says. "It'll be fun."

"Yeah," Logan agrees. "It'll be *fun*."

LOGAN

"Dad! Dad! Dad!" I'm rushing through the house, opening every door to every room. "Dad! Dad! Dad!" My heart's racing and I need him and he has no life besides us so he should be here. I run back outside, down the porch steps and toward the garage. "Dad! Dad! Dad!"

The door to the garage apartment opens and Lucas is there, his eyes narrowed. "What the fuck is wrong with you?"

"Where's Dad?"

"Where's the fire?"

"Fuck off. Where's Dad?"

"How the hell should I know?"

"Dad! Dad! Dad!"

"Will you settle the fuck down! What the hell's going on?"

I stop at the bottom of the stairs leading to his apartment and settle my hands on my hips, try to catch my breath. "I have to take Aubrey and her *mom* on a *date*, and I have no idea what to do or where to go. Have you seen Dad?"

Lucas chuckles. "You're screwed."

"No shit, Luke! This isn't funny." I look around again. "Dad!"

"Calm down, Logan!"

"I don't know where to go. I don't know what to *wear*. And what the hell is wrong with my stomach right now?" I loosen my collar. "What's happening to me!?"

Lucas sighs. "You're nervous. That's all."

"But why?"

"Because you *care*, Logan." He opens his door. "Come on."

I SIT in his living room with a bowl of cornflakes, because cereal calms me down, okay? It has ever since I can remember, and somehow Luke remembers that, too, because he's the one who got it for me. He's sitting on the coffee table opposite me, and fuck, why did I let him take control of this? I tap my empty pockets. He sighs, knowing what I'm looking for. "So, you want to impress her mom, right?"

I nod. "I guess."

"So, food wise, have you thought—"

"I have no idea what I'm doing, Luke. You had it good. Brian already knew you before you started screwing Lane."

"Don't talk about her like that."

I drink the leftover milk in the bowl and set it on the table next to him. Then I slump back on the couch, let my head fall back. I rub my hands across my face. "I need a smoke."

"No, you don't. You just need to take a breath, okay? Aubrey—she obviously likes you for you—"

"Yeah, but her *mom*, Luke."

"So, go fancy. You can afford it right?"

"Yes."

"Go to that French place."

"I can't even read the menu there."

"So, fake it?"

"It's suit and tie."

"So?"

"So? I don't own a suit and tie! I have, like, the tux from Lucy's wedding, and that doesn't fit anymore. And whenever we see Mom, I always wear something of yours."

He shrugs. "So, wear something of mine."

IT TAKES a half hour for me to make his room look like a bomb exploded. Clothes, shoes, fucking socks.

I'm in a white tank and slacks, and I can't decide on a shirt and tie, because I look like an asshole in every one.

I look like Lucas.

"Just pick one, bro," he says through a yawn.

I notice his bed for the first time. The covers are disheveled on one side, as if he'd been sleeping. As if I'd woken him. "Did I ruin your nap time, you little bitch?"

"Yep," he says, stretching. "I haven't been getting a lot of sleep."

"Ew. Lane's like a sister, dude. I don't want to imagine that shit."

"I wish," he mumbles. "She's been having nightmares again. She wakes up sweating and completely out of it."

My stomach drops, because Laney *is* like a sister, and I care for her in that way. "Did—did something trigger it?" I ask. Personally, I don't have triggers, but I hear it's a *thing*. Plus, my first therapist asked the same question every time I mentioned nightmares. I never told her what the nightmares were about.

Luke says, "That fucker's lawyer reached out to her. Cooper wants to see her."

"No fucking way you're letting that happen, right?"

"It's not really up to me."

I lean against the door of his wardrobe, while I watch him cross the room to sit on the edge of the bed. His hair is a mess, his eyes are tired, his shoulders are slumped. He looks like Dad after spending half the night up waiting for me.

Luke adds, "Regardless of what you think, I don't have a need to control everyone's actions. And speaking of... I know you think I over-stepped with the whole Aubrey thing. And I know you won't believe me when I say this, but I just want you to be okay, Logan. I want you to have the best life possible. And if that meant apologizing to that asshole, I would've done it. Because Dad's right, we don't need anyone else in this family getting arrested."

I sigh. "That's not your weight to carry, Luke."

He stretches out his legs, crosses his feet at his ankles, and stares down at his toes. "Maybe not. But also, maybe. Dad shouldn't have to carry all that weight on his own. And I know I'm not the oldest, or whatever, but Luce—she has her own problems. She has her own family now."

I swallow down the meaning of his words, take them in completely.

When I don't respond, he says, "I don't think I've ever known you to even *like* a girl before."

"Can I ask you something?" I ask, ignoring his statement.

"Sure."

"Why haven't you asked Laney to marry you? I mean, we're all waiting."

He laughs once. "Because it's not time."

"Why not? Luce and Cam got married while they were still in college. They turned out fine."

"Because... I want to give her the same as I want for you: the best life possible. And I can't do that yet."

"You have a steady job, with a steady income. So does she. Isn't that enough?"

"No," he says matter-of-factly. "It's not just about us, Logan. It's about all you guys, too."

"That makes no sense."

He shrugs. "Maybe not for you."

He's treating me like I'm dumb again. "Whatever."

"The thing is... Dad—like, yeah, I don't expect him to retire anytime soon, but he will, eventually, and the job, that company, our livelihood, it's all going to fall on you and me. I don't want to do anything to bring it down or change our way of life. The twins, they'll be fine. But Lachy, he's still young, you know? I want to be sure that we can give him the same life that Dad has worked his ass off to give to us. I want him to be able to go to whatever college he wants—if that's what he wants—and not have to worry about any of it. And when I'm sure that I can do that for *all of us*, then I'll ask Lane to marry me. Because as soon as we say those vows, we're going to start popping out babies one after the other," he says, clicking his fingers. "And I want to be able to give our kids the same life we had, because —I mean, besides Mom dying—we had it pretty fucking good, Logan. Don't you think?"

I am nine years old, and the leather...

"Yeah, Luke. We had it real good."

37

LOGAN

BASED on Luke's final word of advice, I leave all the suits and ties in his apartment and dress in jeans and a button-up with the sleeves rolled up. I don't make a reservation at the French place. Instead, I decide I'll take them to my favorite place to eat—the concession stand at the sports park. Because like Lucas said: if I'm going to get Aubrey's mom to like me, she has to like me for *me*. And if it's not good enough—if *I'm* not good enough for her daughter, then I'll just have to find another way to prove that I am... that doesn't include eating snails and dressing like a jackhole.

I TAKE a single toke of Mary, just to take the edge off, before meeting back with Aubrey and Melissa at the store right before closing. "I hope you have comfortable shoes," I tell them. "Because the best way to see this town is hoofin' it."

Aubrey slips off her heels, claims she's going barefoot. Melissa smiles. "I'm excited to see the town through your eyes, Logan. Maybe it'll help get to know you better."

Our first stop is only two shops down: Lucy's store. "This is my sister's," I tell Melissa while Aubrey clings to my arm.

"I take it she loves books?" Melissa asks.

"She lives for them." I point upstairs. "The top level is her husband's office. We all work together. My dad has a construction company. Cameron's the architect."

"So it's a family business?" she asks, and I nod. "Are you planning on making that your future?"

"If I'm lucky enough, sure."

"And your sister," she asks. "How old is she?"

"Twenty-five."

"And her husband?"

"Same."

"Any nieces or nephews?"

I shake my head. "Not yet. Luce has issues with her girly bits, so the docs say she might not be able to carry a baby full term."

Melissa frowns. "Oh, I'm sorry."

I shrug. "I think they're full of fudge nuggets."

She laughs at that. "You don't believe your sister?"

"I don't believe the doctors."

"You think they're wrong?"

Another shrug. "I think she'll have a miracle baby. A girl. And she'll look just like Lucy. Like my mother." If Melissa wants to get to know me, I'm not going to hold back. "She'll be the cutest, sweetest little girl in the world, and my dad—he's going to love on her like no pops has ever loved on anyone."

Aubrey smiles up at me. "You really think that?"

"I can feel it in my blood, Red." And it's true. I really do. Because if anyone deserves a miracle, it's Cam and Lucy.

I point across the road. "That's the movie theater; it's pretty much all the entertainment this town has to offer. A few years back, Laney, my older brother's girl, she used to work there and sneak us all in for free."

Melissa says, "Aubrey tells me you come from a big family."

"Yep. Seven kids. I'm right in the middle."

"What are all their names?"

"I'll take this one," Aubrey says, her chin in the air. She rolls off their names and their ages and one random fact about each of them. She does it so easily, so effortlessly, as if she's known me forever. When she gets to Lachlan, she goes on and on and on about him. I'd be jealous but—okay, I'm a little jealous. Not because they're friends, but because they've spent more time together than we have.

When she's done, I tell them both, "That's actually where I had my first kiss, right in front of the ticket booth."

Melissa laughs. "How old were you?"

"Ten."

"And how did that go down?"

"It earned me a punch to the gut."

Aubrey cackles, patting my arm. "You let a little girl punch you?"

I shake my head. "No. Leo punched me. It was his girl. On *his* date."

I SHOW them around the rest of the town, which isn't much, but everywhere I bring them, Melissa asks questions. Lots of them. Mainly about what the places mean to me. She asks about my childhood, about my upbringing, and if I grew up *happy*. Which is odd, but she's her daughter's mother, so I expected a lot of inquisitive questions.

We eat the concession stand food like animals. Aubrey doesn't leave my side. Doesn't remove her touch from my arm. It's not exactly how I wanted our first date to go—not that I've really put a lot of thought into it—but I'm pretty damn proud of myself. *Pat on the back for you, Logan Preston.*

We head back to Main Street, where our cars are parked. Melissa and Aubrey get in Melissa's car, I get in mine, and we drive the couple minutes back to Aubrey's house so we can share a tub of ice cream and Melissa can see the house for the first time.

After the tour and the ice cream, Melissa gets back in her car to go home. We wave her off in the driveway, watch her car pull away, down the street, until her tail lights disappear, and I'm finally, *finally*, alone with my girl. I lift her off the ground, throw her over my shoulder, laugh when she squeals. I smack her ass. "You're in so much trouble, Red."

As soon as we're in her house and she's on her feet, her mouth's on mine, one hand undoing the buttons on my shirt, the other undoing my belt. I'm laughing into her mouth, and she's smiling against mine.

I rear back, just long enough to say, "I'm so fucking addicted to you, Red."

She doesn't bother with my fly, just shoves her hands down my pants and goes for gold. She grunts in my ear. "I want you to take that belt and wrap it around my neck, then walk me like a dog!"

I freeze. Pull away. "What the fuck?"

"No. That's not what—"

"You want me to *what?*"

"No! I meant…" She busts out a laugh.

"What the fuck, Red? How kinky are you?"

She's still stroking my cock when she says through a giggle, "I totally worded it wrong. I meant I want to do it doggy style."

I can't stop laughing, and she won't let go of my dick. "Don't try to talk dirty anymore, okay?"

She nods. "Deal. But will you still fuck me from behind?"

I kiss her again, chuckling when my tongue slides against hers.

"Stop laughing at me!"

"I can't help it."

"If you keep at it, I'll fuck *you* doggy style!"

"Jesus, Aubrey!"

She throws her head back with her guffaw, then grasps the back of my neck, pulls me down to her tits. "Shut up and eat my cookies already."

She's crazy and she's wild and she's everything I am, yet everything I'm not.

And the best part?

The part that blows my goddamn mind?

She's all mine.

38

LOGAN

I am nine years old, and the leather cracks beneath my weight. The car still smells new, even though I've been in it for months. The dash is gray. I can barely see over it. In the pocket of the door, there's a tube of hand lotion. It's pink. I wonder who it belongs to...

I sit up, gasping for air. I don't know where I am. Who I am. The covers are wet. Unfamiliar. A hand lands on my shoulder. I choke out, "Don't!"

The hand is gone.

The bed shifts.

I blink hard, try to settle the hammering in my chest. The dream is so vivid, too vivid, like the dreams that come to me when Mary's not around.

"Logan?"

The voice... the voice... I look around.

Four-poster bed.

Drapes of white.

And then I remember. I didn't fucking smoke. I didn't smoke, and I fell asleep with Aubrey beside me. I wasn't thinking.

Stupid.

Stupid.

Stupid.

"Logan?" Aubrey's next to me, her eyes wide, filled with tears. "Are you…" Her hand comes out again.

"Don't, Aubs." My feet land on the floor. I rub my eyes. "Just don't fucking touch me right now." Two fucking weeks without a single nightmare, a single flashback, and now this. With her. I hate that I'm here. That she's here. That she has to witness this.

"Okay," she whispers, and then she's off the bed, on the other side of the drapes. I try to inhale. Exhale. The air is thick. Sweat trickles down my temple, onto my jaw. I wipe it away. Aubrey returns, holding my cigarette case. She sits on the bed, an eternity of space between us. She spreads Mary's armor open, but Mary's not ready, not prepared. "Where…" Aubrey asks, and I shake my head. She's gone again, this time to get my jeans. She empties the pockets and she won't stop crying, won't stop shaking. I did this to her, to us. "Where the fuck is it?" she cries out, wiping her tears with the back of her hand.

I grip the edge of the mattress.

"Jesus Christ, Logan, you're shaking."

She's naked, and I'm naked, and I want nothing more than to touch her, to feel her, but she won't take away the memories. She won't take away the pain. My throat closes in.

I am nine years old…

"Your keys," she rushes out. "Where are your keys, Logan?" She doesn't wait for me to answer, and that's good, because I can't. I can't fucking speak. Can't think. Can't breathe. I tug the ends of my hair.

I am nine years old…

Aubrey's slipping on my shirt and leaving the room. The front door opens, and through the pounding in my chest, I hear my truck door open, close.

The weight of the water presses down on my shoulders, fills my lungs. Aubrey's back with a baggy and she's ripping it open, pulling out papers and spreading Mary open for me. She's back on the bed again, trying, trying, trying to roll me a joint, to give me the girl who takes away the memories. She's frustrated she can't get Mary right, and she curses her frustration through sobs that tear my heart to pieces.

Mary is sloppy, fat, crooked, but it doesn't matter, because she feels like heaven between my lips. Aubrey stands, sparks her to life. I inhale, inhale, inhale my need into my lungs, into my muscles, into my memories, my nightmares. Aubrey sits next to me again, her knees up, forearms resting on them.

She hasn't stopped crying.

Hasn't stopped shaking.

I take another hit of Mary.

Then another.

"One day…" Aubrey whispers. "I'll be your Mary, Logan. I'll be the one to take away your pain."

Her words are bubbles of air formed beneath the water, appearing out of nowhere. Saving me. Filling me.

And then Mary speaks: *She can't give you what you need, Logan. Only I can.*

Aubrey begs, "Say something, Logan."

I close my eyes, push off the bottom of the lake. Hit the surface. I tug Aubrey to me, put my nose to her neck. I inhale and inhale and inhale some more.

She can't give you what you need, Logan. Only I can.

"One day," I whisper, kissing her jaw. "There won't be any pain."

39

AUBREY

LOGAN'S not in bed when my alarm wakes me the next morning. My phone lacks any text messages from him or anyone else. Last night… last night was so perfect… until it wasn't.

I force myself not to think about it, because thinking about it brings up questions, and I don't want to drown in those questions like I have in the past.

I don't want to push him away.

I don't want to lose him.

I stumble out of bed, my eyes half closed, ignoring the throbbing between my legs, a reminder of last night's activities. I shower, brush my teeth, and slip on my robe before heading to the kitchen. Then I stop in the doorway, let my smile, my emotions, consume me.

Logan's by the sink, looking out the window, sipping on a steaming mug of coffee. He's in his boxers and nothing else, and the boy is a work of art. *Really*.

"Morning," I say, and his gaze lazily moves to mine.

"You sleep like the dead, Red." He's smiling, as if last night's terror never happened. I'll let him think it, let him feel it… as long as he *stays*.

"I thought you left," I say, my voice hoarse from sleep.

He shakes his head, crooks his finger at me.

Gravity pulls me toward him.

Right into his waiting arms.

He gathers my hair in his fist. "So much hair," he says. And then he kisses me once. "Listen, about last night…"

"We don't need to talk about it," I tell him. "Unless you want to."

"I don't," he sighs out. "Believe me, that's the last thing I want."

I nod into his chest.

"Thank you for…"

"Not pushing you?"

"For not asking about it. For handling it the way you did. For knowing what I needed."

He needed *weed*. He didn't need *me*. "Can I ask one question?"

"I don't know, Red…"

"Does it happen often?"

He pulls away with a sigh and takes my finger in his grasp. "I have a surprise for you," he says, deflecting.

I smile through the hurt. "Is the surprise your penis?" I try to joke. "Because I'm pretty sore right now."

His eyebrows shoot up. "You are? I'm sorry."

"Stop it. I practically begged for it."

"Actually, you *did* beg, and damn do you look good on your knees." He bites down on his lip, stares at my breasts. "How sore are you?"

"Sore, Logan," I warn. "And I have to get to work, so…"

He scoffs. "Work is for sissies."

"Says the boy who works, goes to trade school, and is getting his GED."

His eyes narrow. "How did you know about the GED?"

"Lachlan."

"I haven't even—"

"Downloaded the forms? I know. They're on my coffee table." I smack his butt. "Get to it, school boy."

He smirks. "Will you be my tutor?"

"I can do that."

"I was kidding, Red."

"I wasn't."

"Hmm." I'm in his arms again, and he's kissing my neck, my jaw. Into my ear, he whispers, "The other day at your work, you were wearing this skirt and these high socks, and all I could picture was bending you over the counter and lifting that skirt and shoving my face between your legs, licking you slowly from your clit to your—

"Logan!" I shove him away, ignore the instant throb building between my legs. "You keep talking like that, I'm going to be late for work."

His hands glide up my legs, under my robe, until his fingers squeeze my butt. He bites down gently on my jaw. "Seriously, Red, how sore are you, and can I kiss it better?" He doesn't wait for a response before shifting his finger, moving my panties to the side to dip inside my wet pussy. "Jesus Christ, Red." Then he's behind me, pushing me to the kitchen table and bending me over at my waist. My chest lands softly on the table top, and when I look over my shoulder, he's sitting down on a chair, peeling my panties lower, lower, lower. I help him to remove them completely, smiling when he pockets them. His eyes meet mine, a smirk pulling on his lips. "So fucking hot," he says, and then the tip of his tongue is exactly where he described, exactly where I want it. I press my cheek into the wood, grip the edges of the table while he works and works and works at kissing me better.

I'm dizzy and deluded and he's passion and perfection, and I'm screaming my release into my closed fist, my pleasure soaking on his tongue. His cocky chuckle vibrates against me, the way it always does after every one of my orgasms—as if he's just won a prize he knew was his all along. The chair scrapes when he stands, his need tenting his boxers. He wipes my pleasure off his mouth with his forearm.

I flip over so I'm on my back, my legs spread. "Are you going to give me what I want, or are you going to make me beg again?"

He runs the tip of his finger between my folds, then slides all the way in. My eyes roll back, my breath caught in my throat.

"You're going to be late," he says, tugging on my legs until my ass is on the edge of the table. "Maybe you should take a sick day."

"Tempting," I whisper, and then he's inside me, filling me.

We moan at the same time. "I could do this all damn day, Red." And then he's undoing the tie of my robe, revealing every part of me.

His mouth covers my nipple, while my hands find his hair, and he's going slow, slow, slow, and I can feel every inch of him, every—

"Shit! Condom, Logan."

"I'll pull out," he says against my neck. "I promise." He's back to worshipping my breasts, his movements faster now, rocking the table with his movements. He bites gently on my breast, murmurs, "Cookies and pussy: breakfast of champions."

And I can't help but laugh, my entire body shaking beneath him. I tug on his hair, giggle when he grunts in pain. I wait until his eyes meet mine before saying, "You're an idiot."

"You're the idiot for wanting me."

And then he's moving again, fucking me harder, faster. The table creaks beneath me, then cracks. "Logan!" I tap his shoulder. "Logan, the table's going to break!" But his eyes are closed, and he's so focused on his task that I don't think he hears me. "Logan!" He pumps into me harder again. "Logan!"

"That's it, baby, say my name!"

"Oh, my god!" I laugh out, wrapping my arms around his neck, hoping he can hold me up.

And then the table gives way, breaks in half, and I'm holding onto him while he lifts me, tries to steady me in his hold. "Did we just break the fucking table?" he laughs out, his cock still deep inside me.

"I tried to warn you!"

"I was having too much fun."

"You owe me a table."

He carries me, effortlessly, from the kitchen to the couch, and sits down, never once shifting our connections. With my knees bent on either side of his hips, he grabs onto my ass, starts setting the pace. "You feel so fucking good," he says into my neck, and then his hands are on my hips, stopping me from moving. "Fuck, Red. I'm gonna come if we keep going. We need to slow down."

I start riding him harder, faster, the way I know he likes it. The way I like it. I set a steady rhythm, feel my insides start to build, build, build until my head throws back, my arms reaching behind me, hands on his knees for leverage. His mouth is all over me, kissing my breasts, my neck, my shoulder, all between whispered words filled with filth and encouragement, and I come all over him, cursing at the ceiling, screaming his name.

"Fuck," he laughs out, kissing me. "I'll never get tired of that. Ever." Then he links his fingers behind his head, smirks at me. "Now take care of your man."

My head throws back with my laugh, and I salute him. "Yes, sir."

And then I take care of *my* man.

WE SHOWER TOGETHER AFTERWARD. He can't keep his hands off me, and I can't stop touching him, looking at him, kissing him. *My man.*

When we're both dressed, I ask, "So… about my surprise?"

"Right." He smiles, leads me by my finger down the hallway and toward the sunroom. For the second time this morning, I freeze in the doorway. Sitting in the middle of the room is a brand-new easel, larger than my old one, definitely better quality. A canvas sits on the stand, blank besides the words *You + Me* written in thick black marker.

It's not the most eloquent of words, and definitely not a declaration of his love, but it's *You + Me* and it's all I ever wanted and needed from him. I face him, my eyes wide, my jaw unhinged, my breath caught in my throat. "You bought me an easel?"

He smiles, his cheeks warming, and never in my dreams did I ever think I'd see Logan Preston blush. "I *made* you an easel, Red."

"Shut your stupid face." I rush over to my surprise, pulling on his arm to follow, and run my fingers over the wood. It's made to perfection, every inch, every joint. "You made this?"

"Your other one's old, Aubs. Like, falling-apart old. Besides, I had a lot of spare time these past two weeks."

"Yeah, but…"

"Don't make a big deal of it, okay? I got bored, I made it, it's stupid."

"It's not stupid," I tell him. "You're stupid for thinking it's stupid, *stupid*."

He wraps his arms around me from behind, presses his lips to my shoulder. "So, you like it?"

I run my finger across the words he'd written just for me. "This is my favorite part," I whisper.

He laughs. "It took me forever to come up with it."

LOGAN DRIVES me to work a half hour late. There are people already lining up outside. He stops in the middle of the road, giving zero shits about the cars behind us. "Thanks for breakfast," he says, and I bust out a laugh. "I need your keys."

"For what?"

"To fix your table."

"You don't have to—"

A car honks behind us. "Keys, Red."

I hand him the keys.

HE SHOWS up to work fifteen minutes before I close. There are still customers in the store, so he busies himself by tidying my stock. He leaves for a minute, returns with a measuring tape, and starts measuring things in the store. The windows first, then the floor. He looks up at the ceiling, then at the walls, and then he's on his phone, but I'm too distracted with my customer to hear his conversation. Five minutes later, Tom and Luke show up with a giant ladder. They wait outside until my last customer leaves. Logan lets them in and sets up the ladder.

I tug on his sleeve, and he turns to me. "Hi," I say, the first word we've spoken since he walked in.

He smiles. "Hi." And then he kisses me on the lips, chaste and perfect.

"So… what are you doing?"

"Just checking something."

"What exactly are you checking?"

He pats my head, as if I'm a kid.

Tom says, "We can get you a new window by Tuesday."

"The insurance money hasn't come in yet, so…"

"So, you can pay for it when it comes in," he says.

"Um…"

"Or," Lucas cuts in. "If you let us put a company sticker on the window, we could write it off as advertising."

"That's a good idea," says Tom.

"No, it's not," I tell them. "You have a shop two doors down with a giant *Preston, Gordon & Sons* sign on top."

"Yeah, but that's high. Not pedestrian level. We need pedestrian marketing."

"You can put your sticker there, but I'm paying for the—"

"It should work," Logan cuts in, and he's already on top of the ladder, his head poking through a board he's removed.

"How much?" Tom asks.

"A good ten feet."

"Structural?" Lucas asks.

And Logan sighs, glares at his older brother.

"Right," Lucas says. "Sorry."

I narrow my eyes. "What are you all talking about?"

"I could probably get this part done in a day," Logan states, ignoring my question.

"I'll help you out after hours if you help me with the house a couple Sundays," bargains Lucas.

"Sundays are Red's only days off. Can we do Saturday?" Logan asks, climbing down the ladder.

"Deal," Lucas states, while Logan folds up the ladder again, and his dad takes it from him.

"Help with what?" I ask.

Tom says, "Jot down the supplies you'll need. Luke can order them Monday morning."

"What supplies?!" I almost shout.

Lucas laughs. "LTT night at the house, you guys coming?"

Logan looks to me, his eyebrows raised, as if he's waiting for my answer. I don't even know what the question was. "What's LTT?"

"Lachlan's Tasty Tacos," Tom says. "We'll see you there."

"Okay," I say, having no idea what I just agreed to.

Logan drives us to his house where we all have Lachlan's Tasty Tacos for dinner. Pancakes with candy. He lets me choose what candy to blend to make the sauce. Apparently, it either goes really well or really, *really* bad. Mine goes down well.

The Preston house is such a contrast to mine. It's so full of people and love and laughter, and I never want to leave. I tell Logan that, and he smiles, kisses the tip of my nose.

I wave to the Preston crew, all standing on their porch, while I sit in the passenger's seat of Logan's truck. When we get back to my house, Logan doesn't wait for an invite to come in, to stay the night. He doesn't need one.

My kitchen table is gone, and when I ask him where it went, he tells me it's in pieces in the back of his truck. I didn't even notice. He leads me by my sleeve into the garage. I think he's going there to smoke, but instead, he shows me what he's been doing all day: *building* me a new table. There are power tools all in my garage—a garage that's basically sat empty since I moved in. "It'll be sturdier than your old one," he says. "I just need to finish up on the edges and then sand it down. We can go to the hardware store sometime this week so you can choose a finish."

"You don't need to do all this," I say, my stomach flipping, my heart beating for the boy wrapping his arms around my waist. "I could've just bought a new table."

He holds me to him, walking me backward until my butt hits the edge of the table gently. Then he lifts me, as if I'm nothing but an exhale. As if I weigh the same. I sit on my new, unfinished table with him between my legs, his hands coasting my thighs. "I have a secret," he tells me, and I smile, nod for him to reveal it to me. "I *like* doing this stuff, Red. And I especially like doing it for *you*."

"You do?" I ask, biting my bottom lip. Heat blooms in my chest at his admission, at the tenderness in his voice.

"I have another secret."

My hands make their way up his abdomen, to his solid chest. They stay there, while my smile widens and my feelings for him deepen. "What's that?"

"I'm excited, Red."

"For what?"

"For everything."

"Like...?"

"Like that autumn festival you want to go to."

I laugh, not because it's funny, but because of the nerves swarming my insides. This... this is what it feels like to be content, to be sated, physically and emotionally. "It could be lame."

He clucks his tongue, throws in an eye roll. "Things are never lame with us."

"That's true. What else are you excited about?"

"*Everything.*"

"Like what? Tell me."

"Like, Sunday Family Breakfast tomorrow."

My eyes widen. "You want me to go to your family breakfast?"

He nods, so sure of himself and the words he's speaking. "And every Sunday Family Breakfast after." He shrugs. "I'm just excited to be with you, Red."

I can't stop smiling.

"You know, there have only been two things in my life I care about enough to *try*. My family and work. And now there's you. I might not be the best guy for you right now, and I know that, but I'm going to *try*, Aubrey. I'm going to try really fucking hard to be the guy you deserve. Because you're *here*. For *You Plus Me*. And that makes every-thing worth it."

I lose my breath somewhere in between his words. "You know, for a guy who thinks that romance is dead, you sure are romantic, Logan no-middle-name Preston."

His hands land on my hips. "Only because you *believe*, Red."

"In romance?" I ask.

He shakes his head. "In *me*."

PART 3

40

LOGAN

AUBREY DRESSES FOR SEASONS. And I'm not just talking like how fashion labels release a new line of clothes every season. I mean, Aubrey dresses *as* seasons. It took all of fall and all of winter—when she smelled like chestnuts, wood fires, and pine trees—for me to realize this. It's also the length of time it took me to realize that I was wrong about being with her. The way things started off with us, I was sure we were destined to fail. But... being with Aubrey is easy.

Cheesy? Yes.

Truth? Also, yes.

We spend every night together, every spare second.

I don't know how we got to this point. It's kind of like Lachlan with Mom's chair. There was no conversation. It just kind of happened. One day, she called me while I was at work, asked what I wanted for dinner. She didn't ask if I was coming over or what time I would be. She just assumed. And she assumed right.

The best part, though, is that somehow, Aubrey's managed to replace Mary. The night after I had my first "flashback"—so the therapists like to call them—I smoked every night I was there. Then I noticed I started to run out. I smoked less and less. On the first day I was dry, I left work with every intention of seeing Denny, my dealer. I ended up at Aubrey's instead. I haven't smoked since. Because Aubrey —she knows what to do, how to settle me. She doesn't touch me. Doesn't ask me what's wrong. She… makes me a bowl of cereal, waits until I'm settled enough to breathe properly, and then she helps me get back into bed and curls up next to me. Then she sings me a song, as if I'm a goddamn baby: *"My balls, my balls, put it in your booty hole, my balls, my balls…"* Her version is so much better than the original. And she—she's so much better than I ever thought I deserved.

During the second week of my grounding, I found one of Laney's books in Dad's office about dressing up homes to sell or rent. She's a realtor who sells a lot of the houses we flip, so I knew it was hers. There was a section in the back about retail stores and storefronts, and that's when I got the idea to update Aubrey's shop. She didn't do a lot to it when she set up, and prior to her, it was a pet store. So, it didn't really suit what she was trying to sell.

Luke and I worked after hours and on Sundays to get it just right. And when it was done, I spent Saturdays helping him build his and Laney's forever home on the property.

Dad was surprised at how well her shop turned out and asked me if I'd one day be interested in running *Preston, Gordon & Sons Commercial*. I told him I'd think about it.

I'm still thinking about it.

Aubrey spent Christmas morning with her mom, then they drove up here to spend Christmas evening with my family. She got me a new stereo for my car. I got her a matching bra and panty set—cookies— and the first *Preston, Gordon and Sons* jacket I ever owned. Everyone thought it was stupid, but Aubrey—she knew what it meant. That day, Melissa took charge of the cooking, and we all did our best to chip in… besides Cameron, Lucas, and Leo, who did their best to keep Lucy *out* of the kitchen. Melissa had met my family a few times prior. The first time was when Lachy had a track meet in Raleigh. The second was for my birthday—when she gave me a picture of Aubrey as a kid. Missing teeth, fiery-red hair, too many freckles. I don't think I've ever laughed so hard. Then Dad showed Aubrey a picture of me as a toddler, taken from behind. I'd obviously removed my own shit-stained diaper, my bare ass proof, and I held it in both my hands, looking up at the spinning ceiling fan. Dad says the picture was taken about a second before I tried to throw it up there. I didn't get enough leverage, so he says, but the picture was solid proof that even as a toddler, I was a pain in the ass.

NEW YEAR'S DAY was the first time I got Aubrey behind the wheel of my car, tried to teach her how to drive so she didn't have to peddle around everywhere. Swear, it was easier teaching Lachy how to drive the go-kart, the four-wheeler, the jet skis, and the boat than it was to get Aubrey to understand that the brakes are pressured and pressing down on them full force means being jolted out of your seat. I'd promised myself to try to get in an hour of practice with her every day. I gave up within the hour. The following day, I went to the only person I thought could help: my dad. So far, he'd taught six of his seven kids to drive. Laney, too. Hell, I could drive by the time I was twelve. Within a month, Aubrey had her license and Dylan—Cam and Lucy's friend—helped her purchase a used car. My old man's a miracle worker, and if he and Coach Taylor ever went head to head, I'd put my money on him.

Now it's the start of spring, and Aubrey's been smelling like citrus and flowers.

Spring might be my favorite season of all.

It's Chicken's second birthday, and we're all celebrating it as if he were a human kid. Lane made him an outfit. Aubrey made him a cake. Dad thinks the party is the dumbest thing in the world. He refuses to sing "Happy Birthday" to a "damn pig" and we all laugh at how unreasonably grumpy he is about all of it. All eleven-three of us are out in the front yard after Sunday Family Breakfast with balloons and party poppers, and I ask Dad, standing next to me, "Is there such a thing as male menopause?"

He playfully smacks the back of my head.

Chicken shoves his snout into the cake, and we all cheer.

Lucy puts a party hat on the pig.

Dad rolls his eyes, then nudges me with his elbow. "We need to talk."

"About what?" I ask, smiling when Aubrey takes the leftover cake and smears it all over Lachlan's face. He squeals, then warns: "You know I'm fast, right?"

"Oh crap," she says through a giggle.

"I'll give you a thirty-second head start."

Leo yells, "Hide and seek!"

"Yes!" Lucas shouts, and then they're all running in different directions. Besides Lucy, who takes a book from her back pocket and sits down on the porch steps. And I realize now, that Lucas was right all those months ago. We did have it good—us kids. We always had someone to play with, always had toys and enough yard to have the most epic hide-and-seek games that lasted all day, all evening. I smile at the realization, then laugh under my breath when I see Aubrey attempt to climb my truck and hide in the bed.

Dad answers, "We need to talk about your wage."

I face him. "I can take a pay cut if you need the funds somewhere else. I don't mind."

He shakes his head. "No, I was thinking a pay raise."

"Nah." I shrug, shove my hands in my pockets. "I don't need a pay raise, Dad. You pay me enough."

"Yeah, but things have changed now. You pay rent and bills and—"

"What?"

His eyes narrow. "What?"

"What are you talking about?"

"Your rent," he repeats, slowly, like I'm hard of hearing. "And bills…"

"I heard you the first time, Dad. But, I don't pay—"

"You don't pay rent?" he shouts. "You live with the girl and you don't—"

"I don't *live* with her. I mean, not technically." *Do I?*

"Do you have a key?"

"No."

He sighs. "I can't even remember the last time you spent the night here."

I scratch my head. "Neither can I..."

"Here's a piece of advice, Logan. Whether technical or not, you're living with the girl. You use her electricity, her water, probably eat all her food."

"I buy food," I state. *Stupid.*

"When was the last time you were even in your room?"

"I don't know."

"You don't know the twins have turned it into their office?"

"What?! No! What the..."

He chuckles to himself, shaking his head. He clasps my shoulder. "Do the right thing, Logan. Get your name on the lease. Start paying rent. Pay bills. At *least* half, if not all." He starts walking away.

"Wait!" I call out. "Aren't you going to miss me?"

"Son, I thought you moved out months ago!"

BACK AT AUBREY'S, she sits on the couch, her legs over mine, watching a movie. I tap her leg, wait for her to look at me. "Did I stealth move in here?"

She giggles. "I think so."

"When?"

She shrugs.

"How come you haven't asked me to pay rent or anything?"

Another shrug. "I like having you here."

"But I should be paying rent."

She sits up, turns off the TV with the remote, and sidles up next to me, her hand on my stomach. "I don't want you to feel like you're contractually obligated to be here. If you want to stay as a guest in the house, then I'm more than happy with that. Like I said, I just like having you here."

"I'm going to pay rent," I say, fingering a strand of scarlet. "You should probably get a key cut for me."

"I already have one," she says, reaching for her bag sitting on the coffee table. She hands me the key. "I didn't want to give it to you until you said something."

I flip the key between my fingers, stare down at it. "Am I a sucky person for not offering earlier?"

"No."

"Am I a sucky boyfriend?"

"Shut up."

"No, Aubs, I'm serious." I lift both her legs until she's sitting sideways on my lap. "It's just… being with you is… it's like being with my best friend, you know? So maybe I'm not thinking about all the things I should be doing as your *boyfriend*. I've just been cruising along with all of this, and…" I break off on a sigh. "And maybe I've just been too casual about everything."

"You're overthinking things," she says. "Are you happy, Logan?"

"Of course, I am, babe."

"Good, because I'm happy. I don't think I've ever been as happy in my life as I am when I'm with you. So, I really don't think you or I, or *we*, should be doing things any differently. And your family, they…" she trails off, her voice breaking.

"They what?"

She licks her lips, looks down at her thumb stroking her bare leg. "They make me feel like I'm part of something, and that… that means a lot to me, so…" Her voice ends on a whisper, and I lift her chin, make her look at me. Her eyes are clouded with tears, and I frown, hating that I caused them.

"My family adores you, Red."

She smiles, but it's sad. "I wanted to ask you to move in a while ago, but I was kind of scared."

"Of what?"

"Of *pushing* you too far, of wanting things you may not want."

I laugh once. "Aubrey, you didn't have to be scared to ask. I mean, why would I not want to come home every day to the girl I love?"

Her eyes widen, her gaze right on mine. "What?"

"What?" I look down at her warily.

"What did you just say?"

"You know what I said. I love you, Aubrey, and if you didn't know that already, then I'm clearly a sucky boyfriend."

Her shoulders shake, and then she's crying, calling me an idiot. I can't help but laugh, which is horrible, because no guy should laugh when their girl is crying. Her arms wrap around my neck, her face pressed to my chest, drowning out her quiet sobs. I rub circles into her back, press my lips to her temple.

"When did you know?" she asks, looking up at me.

"That I love you?"

She nods.

I inhale deeply, exhale slowly. "It was a Sunday," I start.

"You know the *day*?"

Smiling, I run my hands through her hair, try to contain its wildness. "It was a Sunday morning, and I'd woken up after you had. You were in the sunroom painting, and you were in my shirt and nothing else. You were all bare legs and bare feet, and your hair was this wild mess on top of your head. You were doing a painting of my house to give to my dad for his birthday—"

"I remember that," she whispers.

"And I just remember standing there, watching you, thinking if I could wake up to this—to you—for the rest of my life, I'd be a damn happy man. And then you turned to me, and you had no make-up, no jewelry, and you were so perfectly flawless that for a second, I actually stopped breathing. Then you said, '*Don't come back until you have my coffee.*'"

She laughs now, the sound filling every empty space within me.

I add, "I probably loved you a long time before that, but that was the first time I actually *knew* what the feeling was. I just kept it to myself in case… in case…"

"In case what?"

My insecurities force me to look away. "In case you didn't feel the same way."

She fingers the penny hanging around my neck, while silence settles between us. Minutes pass, and I start to worry that maybe—

maybe I've pushed *her* too far. Finally, she speaks, her voice low, soft, *sweet,* "Do you remember our first night?"

"I remember it well, Red."

"Maybe, but I'm sure you don't remember it like I do."

"How do you remember it?"

She exhales her breath right into my chest, into my heart. "I remember standing waist-deep in your lake. And you brought me there because... because you wanted to show me the stars. I always thought that you hated me, but that night... there was something about the way you looked at me, the way your eyes settled over mine. You know that I'd crushed on you before that night, but standing with you, with the stars above us, it was the first time I actually hoped to get to know *you,* and I remember asking myself, *What's beneath the bravado, Logan Preston?*"

I clear my throat, push back my emotions.

"Logan," she says, looking up at me with those tears she refuses to let fall. "I never thought that we'd be here. *Together.* And I never, *ever* dreamed that I'd be lucky enough to find what was beneath that bravado... or that I'd fall so fast, and so hard, and so *deeply* in love with every single part of you. Bravado and all."

41

LOGAN

I ALWAYS FINISH work an hour before Aubrey does. It used to mean finding something to kill time for that hour before she got home to let me in. But for the past two weeks, I've had a key. Because for the past two weeks, I've "officially" moved in. The day after we talked, told each other how we felt, I went to the bank and withdrew the cash I needed for rent, as well as rent and bills for the past few months I've been staying here. When I gave it to Aubrey, she said she always wanted to make love on a bed of cash. So… that's what we did. I kind of feel bad for anyone who has to handle that cash from now on, because seriously? Body fluids are no joke.

I park my truck in *our* garage and leave the door open so I can bring in the trash, check the mail, because I'm domesticated as fuck.

Bills.

Bills.

Bills.

I can't believe she never made me pay this shit before. Now I know what Destiny's Child were whining about all those years ago. I *am* a trifling, good-for-nothing brother. A motherfricken' *scrub*. Wait, that wasn't even Destiny's Child.

Whatever.

Among all the bills is a single letter, no name, just the address. No stamp either. I pocket the other mail and drop the trash can, my eyes narrowed when I rip open the envelope. Inside is a photocopy of what looks like a police report and a photograph. I look at the photograph, and my stomach turns, my heart stops. My breath... my breath doesn't exist.

I am nine years old, and the leather cracks beneath my weight...

"No." My eyes are frantic, as frantic as my mind, my heart, and I don't want to read this... don't want to know...

My hands shake, turn to fists.

I blink hard, see red.

Not red.

Scarlet.

Missing teeth and crazy hair and too many freckles... "No," I breathe out. "No..."

I tap my pocket, but my reprieve isn't there. She hasn't been for months.

I run to the garage, check behind the stereo on the bench where I used to keep my stash.

Nothing.

I am nine years old, and the leather cracks beneath my weight. The car still smells new, even though I've been in it for months...

I grasp my hair, my heart pounding.

"Shut up. Shut up. Shut up!"

The letter's still in my hand, and I find an old lighter, set it ablaze and watch it burn, burn, burn on the concrete floor. If it doesn't exist, it won't be true. *Can't be.*

My stomach churns, and I know what's coming.

I run into the house, search every pocket, every corner, every hidden space.

Nothing.

Then I run back outside and bypass my car, too worked up to drive.

I am nine years old, and the leather cracks beneath my weight. The car still smells new, even though I've been in it for months. The dash is gray. I can barely see over it. In the pocket of the door, there's a tube of hand lotion. It's pink. I wonder who it belongs to. "Are you all buckled in?" he asks, looking down at me…

I throw up at the memory of his voice, all over the front lawn, then I sprint the few blocks to Denny's house. My hope answers, his eyes narrowed at me.

I try to catch my breath. Can't. "You still dealing?"

"You still using?"

"Watcha got?"

"Whatcha need?"

I need something to settle my heart, my thoughts, my nightmares. "I need Mary."

AUBREY

Logan's truck is in the garage when I get home.

The roller door's up, which is strange. He never keeps it up because he stores his work tools in some new, fancy toolbox that's just begging to be broken into. The trash can is by the mailbox, and the mailbox is open.

I enter the house, call out to him.

He doesn't respond.

I go through every room in the house.

He's not here.

I call his phone.

He doesn't answer.

LOGAN

Sweet Mary.

She's the same as she's always been, but nowhere near strong enough.

I'm four joints in and sitting on Denny's couch, my body numb, but my mind won't stop. This bitch used to be able to make me forget, take the agony away. She's forgotten about me… about what I need from her.

You left me, Logan.

"I didn't."

"What?" Denny asks, and I shake my head.

You left me for her.

I shake my head again.

You're nine years old…

"Shut up!"

It's so easy to mess with you, to screw with your mind. That's what happens when you think you can replace me, Logan.

"Shut. Up!"

"Dude," Denny says, pulling on a bong. He exhales a ribbon of smoke, and I watch it float up, up, up. He points to me. "You're trippin'."

"I'm fine."

I wrap Mary in her home—Rizlas provided by Denny—before I even finish the joint between my lips.

"Slow down, man. You're hitting it too hard."

"I've paid you, right?"

Denny sighs. Nods.

"Then what's the problem?"

"Nothing, man."

On the couch opposite me, Denny's roommates sit, watch me take control of Mary like the whore she is.

A half hour later and I can't get that picture out of my mind, out of my goddamn eyes. I pull at my hair, frustrated.

This is what happens when you abandon me, Logan.

My head rolls to the back of the couch, and I try to focus on the lights reflected from the television, try to see something other than scarlet. It doesn't work. I close my eyes. That doesn't work either.

You're nine years old, and the leather cracks beneath your weight…

My phone rings: Aubrey's ringtone.

I reject the call.

It rings again.

I shut off my phone.

"That your girl?" Denny asks.

I blow out a breath, feel the full effects of Mary control every muscle, every move. *Why can't she control my thoughts?* "It's not working," I mumble.

Denny laughs. "You need something stronger, bro."

Yeah, you do, Mary agrees. *Have you met my friend Acid?*

AUBREY

By midnight, concern and anger wage war on my emotions. I pace the kitchen, my phone gripped tight in my hand. I stopped trying to call him a few hours ago, when every call went straight to voicemail. Panic swirls in my veins, scratching at my flesh from the inside. I stop to attempt a calming breath, right before I hit dial on my phone, bring it to my ear.

Tom's voice is quiet, short. "Aubrey, everything okay?"

"Hi, I'm um…" I'm pacing again, chewing on my thumb.

"What's wrong, sweetheart? What happened?"

"Did Logan— was he… was he at work all day?"

"Yes. Why?"

"Because he hasn't come home. I mean, he has, but…"

Through the phone, I hear Tom shift, as if he's getting out from under the covers. "Where is he?"

"I don't know, Tom. His car's here, but the garage door was left open, and it's like… It's like he was here and then he was gone, and I don't—" I break off on a sob, fear overtaking all other emotions.

Tom stays quiet a moment too long. Then: "Did you kids have a fight?"

"No," I tell him, certain. "We didn't have a fight or even anything close to it. I don't know what happened."

"Okay," he says. Then repeats himself. As if he's speaking to the both of us. "Look, Logan—he does this sometimes. Disappears for a few hours and doesn't come home until the middle of the night."

"He does?" I ask, my heart slowing.

"He's never done this around you before?"

"Never."

"I'll get in my truck, drive around a bit, see if I can find him. If I do, I'll send him right home to you, okay?"

"Okay, sir... yeah."

"Aubrey?"

"Yes, sir?"

"Please try not to worry," he tells me, but I can hear it in his voice; he's as worried as I am.

I SPEND the next few hours the same way I spent the last few. Pacing. Worrying. Frustrated. At 4:30, my phone rings. I jump for it, praying it's Logan. It's not.

"Anything?" I ask Tom as soon as I answer.

"No. I take it you haven't heard from him?"

"No."

He exhales into the phone. "Let me make a few calls. You stay put in case he shows up. Stay by your phone, okay?"

"Yes, sir."

DARK TURNS TO LIGHT, and I've flipped the house upside down looking for any clues as to where he might be. At this stage, I'd almost be happy to find another girl's number in any of his pockets. I'd call the number, calmly, and ask if he was with her. I just need to know that he's okay. That he's not dead in a gutter somewhere. There are no numbers, no signs of other secrets he might be hiding.

I call Tom at 6:30, when I know Logan usually goes to work. Tom isn't at the site, but Lucas is, and there's no Logan.

Not at 7:00.

Not at 8:00, 9:00 or 10:00.

By lunchtime, my stomach is growling, begging for food.

Eating is the last thing I can think about.

I run through the past few days in my head, try to come up with reasons why he might just up and leave. There are no reasons. No answers.

At two in the afternoon, there's a knock on my door. I pray for Logan, but he has a key. He'd come right in. Because this is his house. *Our* house. Lucas and Laney look as worried as I feel. Laney hugs me. "Have you heard—"

"Not a single thing, and his phone—"

"Goes right to voicemail," Lucas finishes for me. "I know, I've been trying all day."

Laney says, "Lucy and Cameron checked out his shack. Cam even took a bolt cutter to the lock on the shipping container. It doesn't look like he's been there for months."

"The twins went through video footage of the security cameras around the house and by the front gate," Luke tells me. "He hasn't been there."

My stomach drops at their news, and I cry into my hands. "Where the hell is he?" I sob.

Laney takes me in her arms again. "We'll stay here with you until we find out *something*."

"Have you checked his truck?" Luke asks, and I shake my head, rush out to the garage with them right behind me. We search through his car frantically, looking for any clues. There's nothing there.

Laney asks, pointing at the floor by Logan's workbench. "What's this?"

I make my way around the car to see what she's pointing at. *Ash.* Not the normal kind I used to find back when Logan smoked every night. There's more of it, and it's thicker. Lucas squats down, runs his finger through it. "It looks like burnt paper." He looks up at me. "Do you know what it is?"

"I have no idea."

At 5:26 in the evening, Laney's phone rings and we all jump at the sound. "It's Misty," she says. Her stepmother. The town's Senior Deputy. The one who was there the day Carter was here.

"Oh God," I breathe out, the worst possible scenarios running through my mind.

Laney answers, but the news Misty has for us is neither good, nor bad. It's *nothing*.

LEO COMES HOME FROM CAMPUS, and that's when I know it's bad. That this isn't one of Logan's episodes where he disappears for a few hours and comes back as if nothing happened. Leo's presence in my house replaces Luke and Lane's. He enters with a bag of food from the diner. "Dad said to make sure you were eating."

"Could you eat if you were me?"

"I can't even eat, and I'm *not* you," he sighs out. His eyes are red, raw, tired. I wonder what I must look like. "He'll be okay," he tells me. "He has to be."

"How do you know?"

His throat rolls with his swallow, then he sighs. "I don't, Aubrey. I'm sorry."

Day turns to night, again, and I can't stop the constant tears filling my eyes or the constant dread filling my soul.

Leo sits in the armchair.

I sit on the couch.

We watch our phones.

Watch each other.

We don't sleep.

Can't.

I ask, "Does Lachlan know?"

"Not yet. We don't want to worry him until we know."

"Until we know *what*?"

He rubs at his tired eyes. "I have no idea. I'm just trying to stay positive. Aren't you?"

I cry harder.

He gets up to sit down next to me and holds me through every sob, every inconsistent beat of my heart.

"God, Leo, I'm so worried."

"Me too," he says. "Fuck, Aubrey. Me too."

LOGAN

I wake up in the back seat of a moving car, and I have no idea how I got here. Denny's driving. His roommate is in the front passenger's seat. Next to me is a girl: hair darker than dark, longer than long. Black denim clings to her legs, white tank, black leather jacket. Her window's down, and she's smoking a cigarette, blowing cancer out the window. She turns to me, smiles. "Nice to see you're still alive," she says.

At her voice, my head throbs.

It takes a minute for me to register who she is. Charlie. A brat through elementary school, a troublemaker through middle school. By the time she was expelled from high school, she'd been suspended too many times to count. Her most infamous ordeal included an attempt to set the school on fire. She's me on steroids, minus a dick. "I thought you left town," I mumble.

"I did. Now I'm back." She offers me a drag. I decline.

I attempt to stretch my legs, but the car is too fucking small, and every muscle in my body rejects the movement. "Where the fuck are we?"

Denny chuckles. "You said you wanted to go with us."

"Go fucking where?" I reach into my pocket, feel Mary's needy grasp light hope into my lungs, and I no longer care where we're going, just as long as I have my bitch by my side.

"Acid's a trip, huh?" Charlie asks.

I spark the tip of my joint and roll down my window. Then I pull Mary inside me, my head rolling when I feel her warmth cover me, her legs wrapping around me.

Isn't it good to have me back, Logan?

"So good," I mumble.

Charlie giggles. "If you think acid's good, you should try ecstasy," she says, dropping a bag of pills on my lap.

"I'm good," I tell her, staring down at the pills.

Mary laughs right in my goddamn ear, cynical and sinful. *You don't want to be nine years old forever, do you, Logan?*

AUBREY

Logan: *I'm safe. Don't let anyone worry about me.*

As soon as Leo gets the text from Logan, he tries to call him, but his phone's already off again.

At least we know he's alive.

At least there's that.

Leo calls Tom, who calls Misty, who calls Laney, who calls me.

And I have no one to call but my mom.

She shows up a few hours later, followed closely by Lucy. We sit silently at the kitchen table that Logan had made me, the table we spent days sanding and staining in the garage, laughing and dancing and happy to just exist together.

I pick at a knot in the wood until my fingers ache.

"Aubrey," Mom whispers, covering my hand with hers.

I look up at her, but she's barely visible through my never-ending tears.

"What are you feeling, honey?"

I inhale a shaky breath, because breathing through this level of heartache feels impossible. "I feel... selfish for feeling insignificant." I get to my feet, start pacing. "He contacted *Leo*, who doesn't even live in the same house or the same fucking town!"

"Leo's his brother, Aubrey," Lucy says, her tone full of pity. "And they're very close."

"They don't *live* together!" I cry. "They haven't planned a future together! He *has* to know! Logan has to know that I would worry about him, that I would—" I break off on a sob, drop my head in my hands.

And for a moment, just one, I let anger overpower concern, let the single emotion control me. "He knows I *love* him! And he doesn't care about what he's done or how it would make me feel! If he didn't want to be here with me, he could have told me! He didn't have to run away like a fucking pussy!"

"Aubrey," Mom says, now on her feet, trying to console me.

"No, Mom!" I shake my head, keep her at arm's length. "I knew this would happen. I knew it. I knew it was too good to be true. *He* asked to move in. *He* told me he loved me first. I did everything I could not to push him away. *Everything*. Because I wanted him to stay, because I didn't want to lose him. And now…" I can't breathe through the pain, through the constant stabbing in my chest. I cry and I cry. Mom's arms are around me, and I fall into her, unable to stand. My sobs are loud, my tears fat, each one landing on her shoulder. My body shakes with agony. I can barely breathe, barely speak. "He's gone, Mom. He's gone even though I *tried*. I tried so fucking hard to keep him. And he's gone…"

LOGAN

I'm in Myrtle Beach, in a random guy's house, on a random strip of road, surrounded by random people. The music blares, pounding at my eardrums, and the walls are moving, warping. I've spent the entire day with Mary between my lips, letting her fill my mouth with her pleasure. She tastes so damn good, and I can't fucking get enough. We're back to the way it was, the way it should be. We use and abuse and set each other off just to bring each other down. Up and around and around and around, but always high. Always.

I leave the dark bedroom where I've just had a fucking four-way with her and her friends, Acid and Ecstasy, and I'm so fucking high I can barely walk, but I don't care.

Who needs to walk when you can fly?

There are too many people in such a small space and just enough drugs in my system to tolerate it. Denny's in the kitchen, drinking straight from the keg, and Charlie's in the living room, tapping on her phone with a bank card. Three lines of coke stay put on her screen when she looks up, catches me watching her. She smiles, motions for me to join her on the couch.

Mary takes my hand, leads me into the room.

"I don't mind sharing," Charlie tells me.

"And I don't mind taking."

She snorts two lines, passes it over to me. I finger the rolled-up Benjamin and close my eyes. *Scarlet upon scarlet upon scarlet.*

When I'm done, I rub my nose, sniff the leftovers on my hand. Charlie climbs onto my lap, her warm hands pressed against my nape. She scoots closer, closer, closer, closer. Her cunt's on my cock, and she licks up my neck, whispers in my ear, "I've wanted to fuck you since high school."

I push her off of me, watch her fall to the floor. "I have a girlfriend."

AUBREY

I sit in the middle of my bed, my legs crossed, my entire body and mind begging for some form of stillness. It's been three days. I don't remember sleeping, but I'm sure I have. At some point, after hours and hours of worrying and waiting and anger and more waiting, something has to go numb, right? Numb enough to sleep?

Mom's still here.

She's the only one left.

Surrounded by white drapes, I stare up at the canvas, hanging over *our* bed. At the words *You + Me*.

I remember when I'd asked him to hang it. It was about a week after his grounding had ended, and he'd spent every night of that week with me. I'd sat right where I'm sitting now, staring up at him. He was shirtless, in sweatpants, and I kept making him move it from side to side, not because I wanted it centered, but because I liked watching the way his body moved, the way his muscles curled, bulged in areas. It took a whole five minutes for him to realize what I was doing, and when he did, he was on me, verbally, physically. He lay over me, his forearms keeping the top half of his weight off me, his bottom half between my legs. "I'm not a piece of meat, Red," he'd said, kissing my neck. He loved kissing my neck. My shoulder.

My gaze lowers, and I look at his side of the bed, at his pillow that hasn't been slept on in days.

I smile through my tears as the memory plays on. He'd tickled my side then, made me squirm. He'd said, "You little pervert." I'd laughed uncontrollably.

Logan always made me laugh.

My smile fades when my insides turn to stone, and the single bubble of hope I'd held onto bursts. Because... I'm thinking about him in the past tense.

As if he no longer exists in my life.

Or maybe... maybe he never truly existed at all.

I thought I'd broken his bravado.

But I was so, *so* wrong.

LOGAN

I am nine years old, and the leather cracks beneath my weight. The car still smells new, even though I've been in it for months. The dash is gray. I can barely see over it. In the pocket of the door, there's a tube of hand lotion. It's pink. I wonder who it belongs to. "Are you all buckled in?" he asks, looking down at me.

I nod, and he smiles.

"So... how are things at home with your mother?"

I gasp for air, having passed out in the bathroom. My pants are around my ankles, my cock out, and the last thing I remember was coming in here to piss. I'm higher than high, but the memories keep me beneath the water's surface. I pull Mary from my pocket and bring her to my mouth, spark her to life. White ribbons emit for my lungs, and my mind brings me visions and moments of white drapes and freckles half the shade of her scarlet hair. She's in a long skirt, white tank top, and an oversized granny cardigan, and she looks like a hobo. But she's *my* hobo. Her laughter fills my ears, my heart, and I can feel myself weakening.

See what she does to you, Logan?

"Leave her out of this. She didn't do anything," I whisper, tugging at my hair. I bring Mary to my lips, shorten her lifespan just to shut her up.

As soon as I exhale, she's talking again. Laughing. It's sinister and it's deranged, and if she doesn't quit it, I'll flush her down the goddamn toilet. *You think she didn't know? Of all the towns in all the world, she moved to yours. Why do you think she went after you? Why do you think she stayed with you? You know, Logan... You know...*

My eyes drift shut, my jaw tensing. Mary burns between my fingers as my mind plays havoc with my emotions, tugging my heart in all different directions.

In my head and all around me, Aubrey replaces Mary's laughter.

Then Mary replaces hers.

On and on.

And on.

And on.

You're nine years old...

"Quit it!"

I'm your whore, Logan. Now and forever. Tell me what you want. Tell me what you need, baby.

"I need you to quit this shit," I whisper, my eyes filling with tears. "Please," I cry out. "I need you to stop. I can't fucking take it anymore. Please. Stop."

You're nine years old, and the leather cracks...

"Make it stop," I plead, liquid heat streaming down my cheeks, to my jaw.

But then Aubrey: "*...or that I'd fall so fast, and so hard, and so deeply in love with every single part of you. Bravado and all.*"

And Mary: *She knew, Logan. You know, deep down, she fucking knew.*

I swallow, thick, and plead with Mary for something *more*, something else. Something to take it all away.

She helps me with my pants, leads me out of the bathroom and back through the living room and toward the kitchen where the party plays on, clueless to my downfall. At the table, strangers sit. On the table are needles and powder and lighters and spoons and Mary taps my shoulder, whispers seductively in my ear, *Have you met my friend, Heroin?*

She presses down on my shoulders until I'm sitting with the strangers, and then she runs her hands through my hair, tells me to find her in one of the bedrooms when I'm done.

THE HIGH THAT comes is instant. Every inch of me warms, every memory disappears. Every thought. I'm walking on clouds. Floating. Opening every door to every room.

Mary, Mary, quite contrary, how does your garden grow?

I find my whore on a mattress in one of the bedrooms, laid out and waiting, her legs wide open for me. I climb on top of her, feel my heart slow when her fingers comb through my hair. Mary's fingertips tap, tap, tap at my spine, her warmth surrounding me, caressing me.

I think I'm in love with Heroin, but Mary doesn't seem to mind.

Mary loves me for loving her friends.

Mary loves me for me.

Pressure builds in my cock, her hands grasping me, begging me to give her what she wants. What we both want. She's whispering in my ear, words I'm too far gone to make out. She licks at my flesh, at every inch of my body. I'm naked and needy, and she's my dirty little slut, so wet, so desperate.

Mary is my comfort.

My *joy*.

I fuck Mary until she screams.

My Mary, Mary, quite contrary...

When I'm done, I pass out next to her, covered in a cold sweat, my mind, my heart, my soul finally empty.

I AWAKE to movement next to me, and I realize I'm naked. I groan when I sit up, stirring the person next to me. My brain's trained to see scarlet upon scarlet upon scarlet.

My heart stops when it's not.

There's no fucking scarlet.

No upturned nose.

No freckles.

And Mary? Mary's nowhere to be seen.

Hair darker than dark shifts on the pillow, her murmured words making my stomach flip: "You want a repeat of last night, huh, baby?"

I flip to my side, puke all over the carpet. Sweat coats my skin, fear pricks at my flesh, regret… regret empties the content of my stomach for the second time.

"Jesus, Logan," Charlie mumbles. "Learn to handle your shit."

I dress. Find Mary in my pocket and leave the room. The house is quiet. Bodies everywhere. I take whatever illicit drugs I can find. I'll need them as much as I need Mary. I'll need them as much as Mary needs me.

Sunlight burns my eyes when I step out of the house.

I wish it would burn me entirely.

I walk, having no idea where I am.

Who I am.

I pull out my phone, switch it on, and fall to my knees the instant I read her single message:

Aubrey: *Whatever it is, Logan, we can get through this. I love you so deeply. Always have. Always will. Forever yours, Aubrey.*

42

AUBREY

THE MOOD in the Preston house is somber, filled with dread. Tom had gotten a call from Senior Deputy Misty Sanders, and she has news— news she wanted to tell him in person. As soon as he got off the phone with her, he called me. Now I'm here with my mom, along with everyone else who shares/once shared/will share the Preston name.

Everyone besides Lachlan.

He's nowhere to be seen.

I sit with my mother, let her take my hand.

I don't belong here.

I'm not his family.

Right now, I truly believe I'm not his anything.

Maybe it's a defense mechanism.

Or, maybe the past four days have ruined me completely and I'm dead, dead, dead inside.

When Misty arrives, everyone stands. I stay in my seat, grip my mom's hand tighter. She gets straight to business, speaking to everyone. "Logan's been arrested for possession down in Myrtle Beach. I have an old friend working at that precinct, and I called in a favor. His charges stand, but he can deal with the consequences here."

"Possession of *what* exactly?" Lucas asks. "Marijuana?"

Misty inhales deeply, exhales the same way. "I wish that was all it was, Luke."

"How bad is it?" Tom asks.

"Cocaine and heroin."

I stop breathing.

Tom runs a hand across his face. "Jesus Christ."

Leo says, "He's never done this before."

"That we know of," Luke replies.

Misty adds, "You can pick him up from the station whenever you're ready."

Tom grabs his keys, slips on his shoes. Lucas and Leo are right behind him. They don't ask if I want to come.

"You shouldn't go," Lincoln says, freezing everyone to their spots. All eyes turn to him.

"What did you say?" Tom asks him.

"You shouldn't go. Not right away. Let him rot in there. Think about what he's done to all of us! We've all sat here for days praying he wasn't lying dead somewhere, and now we find out he's on some kind of bender? No, you guys. It's not good enough." He shakes his head. "It's not good enough for us, and it sure as hell isn't good enough for Aubrey!" He points to me. "I mean look at her. Look at what this has done to her!"

I hold back my cry, but I can't do the same for my tears.

"If you want to go get him, then go, but understand that when he gets back, I'm not going to coddle him. I'm not going to hug him and be grateful that he's here. And I won't support him. I just won't."

Tom sighs, looks to Lucy.

She's crying silent tears beneath silent heartbreak.

Tom asks Liam, "Is this how you feel, too?"

Liam hesitates a moment, then nods slowly. "Yeah, Dad. It is."

"You guys," Lucas says, his eyes wide in disbelief. "This isn't up for discussion. We *have* to go. He's our brother. Our blood."

It takes approximately five hours to drive to Myrtle Beach. The same to drive back. Take in another couple hours for stops and whatever they need to do to get Logan out, and we're looking at a twelve-hour wait.

The twins have locked themselves in their rooms.

Lucy and Cameron whisper quietly to themselves.

Mom leaves and comes back with food.

I eat what I can. For her.

On the eleventh hour, Lachlan comes home accompanied by his Aunt Leslee, a woman I've only met twice. He lies down on the couch, rests his head on my lap. "Is it true?" he asks. "Logan's coming home?"

I nod, unable to speak.

He wipes a stray tear off my cheek with the tip of his finger. "You remember what I told you about him, right?"

I nod again, and this time, I wipe away my own tears with the back of my hand. I can barely look at him. Blue-blue eyes and dark-dark hair, and he's the reason we're here—Logan and me. If it weren't for him shoplifting all those months ago...

"He's self-destructive, Aubrey," Lachlan says. "It's just the way he is."

Opposite me, Mom sniffs back her own cries. Whether she's crying for me or crying for Logan, I don't know. I don't ask. "Maybe there's a reason for it all," she says. "Maybe..."

"Maybe what?" I push.

Lucy answers, her gaze unfocused, "Maybe the twins are right."

––––––––––

IT'S 3:30 in the morning when the Preston men return, and I see my heart's desire for the first time in four days. But he doesn't look like Logan, not the Logan I know. He's still in his work pants and work boots and a plain white shirt with too many stains. His eyes are blood-shot, dark circles beneath them, days worth of stubble cover his jaw. Lachlan wakes from his position on my lap, and everyone stands.

Waits.

Lachlan cries.

Lucy cries.

My mother cries.

And I… I am dead, dead, dead inside.

"I'm glad you're alive," Lachlan says through a sob, and then Lucy is moving forward, her arms open for Logan.

He lets her hug him but doesn't return the embrace.

Leo shakes his head.

Mom says, "It's been a long few days and a late night for everyone." She attempts a smile. "Why don't we get you and Aubrey home?"

Logan's gaze lifts for the first time, his eyes right on her. "Did you know?" he asks, and my gaze snaps to Mom's.

"Know what?" I ask.

My mom's shaking her head, lips parted, eyes wide.

"Know *what*, Mom?"

"Know what?" Tom repeats.

Logan shakes his head. "I'm going to my room. Nobody wake me for, like, five days. I'd really appreciate it."

He climbs the stairs two at a time, while I watch him and Lachlan watches me. "That's not his room anymore," Lachlan says, his voice low so his brother doesn't hear. He looks to his father. "This isn't his *house* anymore!"

"Let's go, Aubrey," Mom states. "I'm sure this family has a lot to discuss."

I start for the door, my legs heavy, my mind numb. Lachlan takes my hand, looks up at me with those eyes so similar to The Boy Who Destroyed Me. "I want to go with you, Aubrey," he struggles to say though his withheld cry. "I don't want to be here."

"You can stay with us, Lachy," Cameron says. "We can watch movies, eat junk food. Whatever you want, buddy."

Lachlan holds my entire arm to him. "I said, *I want to go with Aubrey!*"

MY MOM COULD ONLY STAY for so long. After Logan came home, she dropped Lachlan and me back at my house and headed home herself.

Lachlan lies on Logan's side of the bed, his head on Logan's pillow. On the wall behind us are the words I once lived by, words I no longer believe in.

You + Me.

Lachlan turns to his side and faces me. "You should try to get some sleep, Red."

"I can't," I whisper.

He asks, "Want me to tell you a bedtime story?"

"Sure."

He clears his throat. "Once upon a time, there was a superhero with fiery-red hair. Some people described the color of her hair as scarlet. She had an upturned nose with freckles all across it. In her village, she was known as The Red Raven…"

I finally give in to fatigue and fall asleep to Lachlan's words, my liquid pain hidden beneath my closed lids.

43

AUBREY

Tom picks Lachlan up for school.

I go back to bed, lie under the covers and stare up at the ceiling. Occasionally, I'll hear noises outside and stop breathing, just so I can hear them clearer, make sure the sounds are real and I'm not just imagining them. I'm always imagining them. His car is still here. So are all his clothes. At some point, he'll come for them. Truth is, I don't know if I want to be here when he does.

At midday, there's a knock on the door. Hope pulls me out of bed, forces my legs to move, one foot in front of the other. Hope dies when I open the door to a dark-haired girl with clothes too tight and eyes too wide. She takes a drag of her cigarette, the end lighting fire in my vision. Then she exhales the smoke into the house, onto me. I choke out a breath, wave it away. "Can I help you?"

She drops the butt onto the ground, stomps it with her black leather boots. "Yeah, I need you to open the garage door."

"Why?"

She rolls her eyes, fishes keys out of her pocket. She holds them out between us, gripping the plastic keychain containing a picture of Logan and me. His car keys are there. So are the keys to this house. "Logan asked me to pick up his truck for him."

"And you are…?"

She quirks an eyebrow. "The girl he's been with the past few days. Who the fuck are you?"

I slam the door in her face. If she wants his truck, she can break the fucking garage door down. If Logan wants his truck, he can come here and face me.

I am no longer The Girl Who Breathes.

Or The Girl Who Blinks

Or The Girl Who Is Pathetic.

I am *The Girl He Destroyed*, and I let that destruction carry me to the bedroom, where I jump on the bed, take down the stupid canvas and bring it to the kitchen. I drop it on the table he *made* me and rip it to shreds with the biggest, sharpest knife I own. I tear through his words, his declarations, his promises. I pull at the fabric, ignoring the red that bleeds through the canvas. I cry. I cry so loud my throat aches with the force of it. Tears fall too fast, too free. And when I've worked on it long enough to make his words disappear, I take the knife to the table, scratch and stab, until the days of sanding and staining and laughing merge into my brokenness.

I cry.

I stab.

I spear.

I cut.

I tear.

I wound.

I sob at every word. Every memory.

And then I stop.

Drop the knife.

Hold my hand to my chest and fall to my knees.

I drown in my emptiness, and I don't come up for air.

LOGAN

I managed to escape the prison cell of the house under the pretense of a nonexistent therapy appointment.

Instead, I go to Denny's place.

Mary is here.

But her friends are not.

Apparently, Denny doesn't want me playing with them.

Apparently, I took things too far in Myrtle Beach.

Apparently, me being here could get him shut down. Not just shut down but jail time.

Apparently, none of that mattered when I showed him the wad of cash I had ready to buy back my whore.

Charlie and Denny left Myrtle Beach the same day I did. If I'd waited a half hour, I would've been in the car with them. Maybe. Either way, I wouldn't have passed out on the fucking sidewalk and been picked up by the cops. I was too out of it to know what was happening. I didn't even fight back when they searched me. I don't remember the police station or the holding cell or even Dad and my brothers coming to get me. It wasn't until I walked into the house and saw Aubrey that I realized where I'd been, how long I'd been gone, and what the consequences were.

I couldn't face her.

But most of all, I couldn't *look* at her.

Because I was too damn scared of what I might see.

Nightmares are one thing.

But when those nightmares are real...

Denny's front door opens, and Charlie walks in with her usual zero-fucks swagger. "She wouldn't open the garage," Charlie says, dropping my keys on my lap. "You still owe me a hundred."

"What do you mean she wouldn't open the garage? Did you actually speak to her?"

Charlie flops down on the couch beside me, takes my joint without permission. "She slammed the door in my face, dude. I don't know what you want me to say."

"What the fuck did you tell her?"

Charlie shrugs.

I take back the joint, stand, and shoulder my backpack, where the majority of Mary is hidden from view.

"What about my payment?" she calls out once I'm at the door.

"Fuck you."

THE HOUSE I briefly called home looks the same, but my feelings toward it are completely different. Even before Aubrey and me became *Aubrey and Me*, I had always felt comfortable. Always invited.

Now, I hesitate.

My keys are in one pocket; Mary's in the other.

Fear and restlessness cause havoc on my mind, but for once I ignore Mary's voice. As lit as I am, even I know that the sooner I do this, the quicker Mary and I can be alone again. And right now, that's the only thing I want. The only thing I need. Because Mary is right: Aubrey had to know. There's no other reason she'd end up here, with me, pulling me into her hell, into her destruction.

I use the key to enter the house, expecting Aubrey to rush at me, but the house is quiet, still. *Perfect.* I head to the bedroom and pull out the same bags I used to move in here. As fast as I can, I throw in as many clothes that will fit and take one last look around the room. Something is different. Something has changed. I spend way too long trying to work out what it is. Mary calls to me from my pocket, *I need you, Logan.* And I forget everything but my addiction.

I rush through the bathroom, the living room, and stop in the doorway of the kitchen. Splinters of wood are all over the place, bits of canvas torn to shreds. I make out the black marker used to scrawl the words I spent hours thinking up. My heart slows. Stops. And then I see the table, the mars of angry scars running along the wood. Recollections of her laughter fill my ears, my heart, and I look down to the bags in my hands, get lost in the memories: *hot pink boots and tiny shorts and a flannel shirt tied just under her breasts. Her pale stomach on show, her hair up, hidden beneath a bright red bandana. She looked like a 1950s poster girl for Girl Power, ridiculously adorable, and when I told her that, she grinned from ear-to-ear, told me that it was the look she was going for. And as cute as she looked, as hot as she was, I didn't feel the need to strip her naked and take her right away. We blasted music through the stereo, back and forth with our alternate song choices. We sanded, we stained, and she taught me how to slow dance. She'd laughed when I messed up, and so I messed up some more just so I could hear that sound again and again and again.*

I realize I've stopped breathing, the memory knocking all air from my lungs. I drop the bags, run my finger along the indents on the now ruined table, and ignore Mary's plea to leave, to get me alone, to have her way with me. A knife sits on the table, the point ruined, and *what the fuck did you do, Aubrey?*

And then I see red.

Not scarlet.

But blood.

Droplets on the table, leading to the floor. I follow the trail toward bare feet and bare legs and the face of a girl who once bared her soul.

My eyes fill with heat, my heart pounding, kick-starting my shallow breaths. She sits in the corner of the room, her back against the cabinets, clutching her hand to her chest. Bright crimson seeps into white cotton, and I drop to my knees in front of her. "Jesus fuck, Aubrey, what the hell did you do?" I find what little courage I have and look up at her. Mouth open, eyes wide, dried tears on her cheeks, wet tears in her eyes. She stares into nothingness, the same nothingness that's plastered all over her face.

I look away, because if I look at her any longer, I might recognize the source of my nightmares. "Aubrey." I don't touch her. "Did you slit your wri—"

"No."

"Do you need me to call an ambu—"

"Did you fuck her, Logan?"

The content of my stomach rises, rises, rises some more, and I swallow it down, down, down.

"Did you?" she whispers. Her voice is as broken as she looks, and Mary taps on my shoulder, whispers, *She deserves to be broken.*

"I don't fucking remember," I mumble.

Aubrey clutches her stomach with her blood-covered hand and

cowers farther into the corner, her sobs slicing through the air, through her heartbreak, through my armor.

"I'm sorry, Aubrey," I plead, my words cracking. "I was really fucking messed up…"

Her shoulders shake, her eyelids closing, releasing tears Mary won't let me touch. "Make sure you get everything you need, okay?" The strength in her voice weakens my own.

"I got it all."

"Good. And leave your key. I don't want you coming back here, Logan. I don't ever want to see you again." She keeps her eyes closed as I remove the key from my set, place it by her feet. And she stays silent as I gather my bags, walk past her and into the garage where my truck awaits.

I sit in the driver's seat, start the engine, Mary's pulse beating in my pocket. I wait for the roller door to rise, and when I reverse out of the garage, I see the remains of the single piece of mail that brought us here.

I am nine years old, and the leather cracks beneath my weight. The car still smells new, even though I've been in it for months. The dash is gray. I can barely see over it. In the pocket of the door, there's a tube of hand lotion. It's pink. I wonder who it belongs to. "Are you all buckled in?" he asks, looking down at me.

I nod, and he smiles.

"So…" he says. "How are things at home with your mother?"

I frown. "She's getting worse."

I DRIVE to a skeazy motel on the outskirts of town and pay for a week in advance. When I get to the room, I crash onto the bed, Mary in my hands, on my mouth, all around me. I let her fuck with my mind, my body, all while I ignore the sounds of my sobs and the tears that accompany them.

44

LOGAN

WHEN MY WEEK at the motel is up, I pay for another week. I don't go to work. I don't answer anyone's calls besides Lachlan. I'll always talk to Lachlan, my best friend. He's the only one who uses the home phone, so I know it's safe. He wants to meet up soon. I tell him I want that, too. I miss the kid. I miss Aubrey.

Misty calls.

Messages.

Court dates.

Hearings.

Probation.

Rehab.

I ignore every one.

I do everything I can to make sure the rest of my family give up on me. Mary said it was for the best, and Mary is always right. We don't leave the hotel room. Don't let anyone in. I breathe her into my bloodline until she's part of me, until she becomes me. I pass out, wake up, pass out, wake up, and every second my eyes are open, so are Mary's legs, begging, pleading to be fucked.

Sometime during the second week, Mary wakes me from my sleep, her hand squeezing my heart. *I miss my friends,* she tells me. *Don't you miss my friends, Logan?*

I raise my hand against the bright sunlight weaving into the room and murmur, "You want to see your friends?"

Yes. And you want to make me happy, right?

WITHIN HOURS, Mary and her friend, Cocaine, have used and abused every inch of my body. When I wake up, the sun is setting. I have no idea how long I've been out, but my stomach is screaming and my mouth is dry, and so I slip on my sweats, grab the loose change sitting on the nightstand. I tell Mary I'll be back and open the door, stop in my tracks. "Luce?"

She looks into the room, then up at me. "Who are you talking to?"

"No one." I close the door behind me, attempt to look as straight as I physically can. "How did you know where to find me?"

"Small town, Logan."

"What the hell are you doing here?"

Her features flatten, and she takes me in from head to toe, slowly. "You don't look so good."

I wipe under my nose. Sniff once.

"Jesus Christ, Logan," she whispers, stepping back and crossing her arms over her chest, shielding her body away from me. As if I'm a threat. She's my goddamn sister. I love her beyond words. I'd never fucking hurt her. I'd never hurt any of them. I only ever hurt myself.

"What are you doing here?" I repeat.

"I came... I—" She breaks off on an exhale and shakes her head, then starts again, her head higher, her voice stronger. "I came here because I know Lachlan asked to meet with you tomorrow."

"Yeah, and...?"

"And I see you now, and... and I don't think you should do it, Logan. I don't think our baby brother should have to see you like this!"

I roll my eyes, frustrated, and brush past her toward the vending machines. Over my shoulder, I say, "Our mother's dead, Lucy. You're not her."

She follows behind me, nipping at my heels. "Do you even know why he wants to see you?"

I push coins into the vending machine before making a choice. "Why?" I ask, distracted.

"Aubrey's leaving, Logan."

My stomach drops.

"She's leaving for good. Tomorrow night, we're taking her out to dinner to say goodbye. Lachy was going to ambush you, try to get you to come so you can convince her to stay. I think, in a way, I came for the same thing, because Aubrey—she's become a really good friend to me, and while you were together, she became part of our family…" When I don't say anything or even make a move to face her, she adds, "Did you know that Lachlan thinks he killed Mom?"

"What?" I huff out, stabbing at the buttons of the vending machine. "That's dumb, and he's never once mentioned that to me."

"Me neither," she says, "but he told Aubrey, and Aubrey told me. And when Cameron and I confronted him about it a few months ago, he said that it didn't matter anymore. That he had Aubrey. He said that he always felt like he'd missed out on so much, that sometimes he hated us for being able to remember Mom in ways that he can't," she cries out, and all the way from the motel room, Mary squeezes my heart again. She squeezes so hard, I cringe in pain, so much pain my eyes water. "He said that we all got to see her in the kitchen baking or got to sit at the table while we drew pictures and she'd watch over us. He didn't get any of that. Not until Aubrey."

I shake my head, ignore Mary's painful twisting and prodding. "Aubrey and I broke up. It happens. What do you want me to say, Luce?"

"Nothing," she murmurs. "I don't want you to say anything, Logan. And I don't want you anywhere near Lachlan and Aubrey. Not like this."

45

LOGAN

OBVIOUSLY, I stayed the fuck away from all things Lachlan and Aubrey. I don't know if Lucy ratted me out to the motel owners, but that night, I got kicked out. Of all the fucking people that went in and out of that place—hookers and Johns, pushers and junkies—they honed in on me. I was so fucking high when I got in my truck, I *barely* made it to Denny's house. It was the only place I could think to go where people would leave me alone.

It's been two weeks now, and Denny's made it more than clear that I've overstayed my welcome.

Denny pushes my feet off the couch—my bed—and sits down in their place. He pulls some weed from my paid stash and starts chopping a bowl. "I thought your girl left," he says.

"Mary?"

His eyes narrow. "Who the fuck is Mary? I meant Aubrey."

"She did."

"Huh."

I sit up, start prepping the papers for him. "Why?"

"I saw her in town just now. She's with her mom, I guess. They're packing up her store. Boxes fucking everywhere."

Don't you dare, Logan, Mary warns, already knowing what I'm thinking. *We've been through this. You don't need her. You have me. And you've been doing so well.*

For the first time in a long time, Mary is fucking *wrong*. I haven't been doing well. Ever since we left the motel and have been staying here, Mary's all I've had. She swears she's all I need. But every fucking time I close my eyes, I see scarlet. I see her in her house. In her sunroom. I see her hair set ablaze by the sun. I see her in her shop. In my home. In the yard feeding Chicken his fucking birthday cake. I see her by the lake, riding the four-wheeler. I see her walking the shore, my baby brother's hand in hers. I see her looking over her shoulder, smiling at me, and I die every time she smiles. Every damn time. And then Mary—she's the one to bring me back to life. To my scarlet-less reality.

I grab my keys off the coffee table.

You're nine years old, and the leather cracks—No, Logan! No! Don't you dare leave me!

AUBREY

"Tell him to leave," I tell my mom. "I don't want to see him."

"I can't do that, sweetheart."

"Why not?"

She sighs. "Because it's a free country, and he's not doing anything wrong."

I look over my shoulder, out the window. Across the street, Logan's standing by his truck, staring into the shop, a lit joint alternating between his lips, his fingers. "Call the cops, then. That's not a cigarette he's smoking."

Mom follows my gaze. "If you want to call the cops, go ahead. I'm not doing that to him."

I moved back home two weeks ago, and during those two weeks, I've spent almost every day trying to convince my mom to come here on her own and pack up my inventory to send back to suppliers. Laney, being a realtor, has found someone to take over my lease at the house. Now, we're just waiting for someone to do the same for the shop. Until then, I'm paying the rent for a place I don't use, in a town I don't live in, in a past I want nothing more than to forget. Mom—she hasn't made the forgetting part easy. "Maybe you should go out there and just talk to him, Aubrey. I *know* Logan, and what he—"

"No, Mom. You *thought* you knew Logan. We both did. And I don't understand how you expect me to go out there and talk to him… as if the break-up was easy on me. You *saw* me. You *know* what that did to me."

"They're fresh wounds, Aubs," she sighs out. "Besides, I don't think he plans on leaving until you at least acknowledge he's there."

I turn around, give him the finger.

He drops his gaze.

I look back at Mom. "Happy?" I ask, but she's shaking her head, her features sad. Her eyes—her eyes fight to hold back tears. "Why do you care so much about him, anyway? You didn't care this much about Carter."

"Carter was an entitled little shit. You were always too good for him."

"And Logan's a cheating motherfu—"

"You don't know that for sure, Aubrey."

"Yeah, because he was too high to know himself!" I yell, my emotions getting the best of me. For days after he got home from his bender, I dealt with sadness and regret. Most of all, I dealt with the hurt, the longing for what once was. Now, I'm beyond all that. Now I'm just pissed.

Mom sighs, swallows loudly. She looks over my shoulder toward The Boy Who Destroyed Me. "Please, Aubrey," she begs. "He needs someone in his corner right now."

"So, *you* go be that someone."

"I can't," she says.

"Why not?"

"I just *can't*."

"Fine!" I turn on my heels, push open the door with the palm of my hand and march over to him. He stands taller when I approach, drops the joint by his foot and stomps it out with his heel. He keeps his head down.

I cross my arms. "What do you want?"

He shoves his hands in pockets, his shoulder lifting. He doesn't speak.

"Look, my mom—she made me come out here and talk to you because she doesn't think you'll leave until I do. The thing is, I don't know what to say to you, Logan. I'm so mad at you," I say, my voice wavering. Because as mad as I am, as strong as I try to be, standing in front of him brings on a new wave of memories I'd tried hard to forget. Physically, the boy standing in front of me is not the Logan I know, the Logan I fell in love with. He's... *less*. So much less. Skin and bones and pale flesh, he's nothing but a ghost of who he once was. But I'm still drawn to him, in the worst possible ways, because he looks like the boy who's just woken up in the middle of the night gasping for air. The boy who doesn't want to be touched. The boy who blinks and blinks and blinks and tries to push away whatever it is the nightmares are made of. I want to rush to the kitchen and make him a bowl of cereal and hold him in my arms and sing him a stupid song until he falls back asleep with his head on my chest and his arms and legs around me. I want to be that girl for him. I *would've* been that girl for him. But he didn't come to me. And there's only so many times he can find comfort in something else, or *someone* else, before it becomes too late.

He clears his throat but refuses to meet my eyes. "Does Lachlan know you're here?"

Lachlan. Our common ground. "It's better if he doesn't."

Logan nods, as if he's agreeing with me. "Have you spoken to him?"

"I need to go, Logan." I'm weakening. I can feel it in my bones, in my blood, in every heartbeat. "Take care of yourself, okay?" I start to leave, but he says my name, and I pause, my back to him.

"I have one question. Just one. And then I'll leave."

My mom's outside the door, her eyes on us, listening to every word we say.

Logan asks, "Did you know who I was before you moved here?"

I turn back to him, my eyes narrowed. "What are you talking about?"

Logan's gaze lifts, his focus somewhere behind me. Footsteps sound, closer, closer. Mom steps in front of me, as if she's a shield. As if I need one. "What are you talking about, Logan?" I repeat.

Logan switches his gaze from me to my mom. His eyes on hers, he pulls out a fresh joint, sparks it right in front of her. He inhales long, hard, and exhales with a shake that takes over his entire body. In front of me, my mother is still. Logan jerks his head at her. "Did you know?" he asks, and there are tears in his eyes, but no cry to accompany it.

"Logan," she whispers.

And then Logan shouts, pointing at her, "Did you fucking know?!"

"Mom!" I cry out. My heart thumps against my ribs, and I tug on her arm, try to get her attention. "What is he talking about?!"

Mom wipes at her face, exhales a puff of cold air into the stillness of the night. "Not while it was happening," she cries out. "I swear to you, Logan. I had no idea…"

Logan nods, his jaw set.

"What the hell is going on?" I shout, stepping between them, my gaze switching from one to other.

Logan pulls on the end of the joint, once, twice, and he doesn't stop. Not until the entire thing is gone. Then he flicks it to the ground, his stare on my mother's the entire time. "Fuck you," he says to her. Then looks right at me. "Fuck you both!" And then he's in his car, the engine revving.

My pulse beats wild in my eardrums, and I run to him, reach into his open window, and try to take the keys from the ignition. He shouldn't be driving. Not like this. "You're going to kill yourself, Logan! Don't!"

"Get the fuck out of my way, Aubrey."

"No!" My hands are on the keys. His hands are on my wrist. "Mom! Help me!"

Logan tears my hand away from his keys, holds it roughly in his grasp. Desperation clings to my lungs, to every cell. "Please, Logan," I cry. "Don't drive away. Please!" Tears fall from my eyes, heated and heavy. "Stay. Talk to me! Tell me!"

"Tell you what?" he shouts. "That you're the cause of all my fucking nightmares?!"

"She doesn't know, Logan!" Mom yells. "She doesn't know about any of it!"

My gaze snaps to my mother. "What the hell are you talking about?!"

Logan pushes me away so hard I fall back a step. And then he presses down on the accelerator, his tires screeching, burning. Smoke fills the air before the truck jolts forward. He swerves, left, right, and I watch in horror as he sideswipes a parked car. "Get in the car, Aubrey!" Mom yells, already opening her car door. I rush to the passenger's seat, buckle in, and hold on to the dash as my mother speeds through the streets, following Logan's taillights. My mind is racing, my pulse erratic, and my heart—my heart is behind the wheel of a speeding car, out of his mind, gripping to his death wish.

LOGAN CRASHES through the iron gates of his family home, and the metal flies behind him, smashing into our windshield. He's going a million miles an hour, and we're struggling to keep up. Mom maneuvers the car with both hands on the wheel, and I cry into my phone the second Tom answers. "He's at your house, and he's driving and there's something wrong with him and I don't know…" I drop the phone when Mom takes a hard turn, and I don't bother trying to reach for it again. I grip the dash with one hand, press down on the button for the window with the other. I call out after him, beg him to stop. He's doing donuts on the lawn, smoke rising from his tires, and then he's off again, gaining speed, and Mom's cursing and she's crying and I try to speak through my sobs, but nothing forms on my tongue. Logan drives through the property, toward Cameron and Lucy's house, the path surrounded by trees. Terror builds in my gut as the trees become thicker, thicker, and *this is how my dad died*.

Head-on with a tree.

He'd been drinking.

Who knows what the hell Logan's been doing.

We get jostled in our seats, and Mom hangs on to the steering wheel with one hand, dries her tears with the other. Lights appear behind us, more than one car, and then the trees disappear and it's the wide-open space of the lake. *The lake.* I scream, and Mom hits the brakes, but Logan... Logan speeds up, *up,* **up** until he's driving on the dock, but the dock is too narrow, and then the truck is on its side and then it's **down,** *down,* down...

46

LOGAN

I AM EIGHT YEARS OLD, and my mother is holding my hand. We're walking on the shore of the lake. Her belly is big, but not as big as it was with the twins. She says she's going to name the baby Lachlan. I tell her I think it's a silly name, and she giggles, bends down to my level and says, "It can't be any worse than Garray." I laugh so hard my belly aches. We walk back to the dock, where my brothers and sister are jumping off the edge. Lucy dives. Lucas cannon balls. Leo belly flops. The twins swim circles around each other. I grip my mother's hand tighter, because I know what she's about to tell me. "The water can't hurt you, Logan," she says, squatting down in front of me. She holds her stomach in her hand as if the baby will fall out of it before it's fully baked. "See, the twins are littler than you, and they're okay."

I look down and pout. "But... I'm scared," I say quietly.

She lifts my chin with her finger so my eyes are on hers. She smiles. "What are you scared of, sweetheart?"

I wipe the sweat off my brow and scrunch my nose. "Drowning and dying."

"Hmm..." She taps her chin. "What if we get you private swimming lessons."

I shake my head. "The others," I say, pointing at my siblings. "They'll make fun of me."

"What if... what if we say that you're doing something else, and they won't ever know about it."

"What will you tell them?"

She grins from ear-to-ear. *"What about... if I tell them that you've been selected by Tony Stark to be the next Marvel superhero?"*

My eyes go wide, my smile wider. *"Yes!"*

"Yeah?" she asks.

I nod.

And then I'm in her arms, and she's so warm, so... so... dripping wet...

"Logan!"

"Logan!"

"Oh, my God, Mom! Do something!" Aubrey screams.

"Come on, son!" Dad shouts. "Please!"

Pressure builds in my chest, in my lungs.

"You have to save him, Mom!"

My mother pulls away from the embrace, holds a penny up between us. *"Look how lucky you are, Logan..."*

47

AUBREY

FOUR SEPARATE CARS followed the ambulance to the hospital. Tom rode with Logan. We haven't seen either of them since.

My mother is offered scrubs to change into from her cold, wet clothes. She was the first to jump into the lake to get Logan out of his truck. He'd left the windows open, but the doors locked. By the time Lucas found a crowbar and jumped in there with her, Logan had already been submerged for over two minutes. It was four minutes by the time Mom and Tom pulled him out of the water. Her military training provided her with the CPR knowledge she needed to bring him back to life.

Lucas is still drenched.

Lachlan hasn't stopped crying. Neither has Lucy. Neither have I.

The difference? My cries are silent and formed with guilt.

Lucas is pacing, his bare feet squeaking on the worn linoleum.

The twins sit side by side, Liam with his head in his hands, Lincoln with his arms crossed, his knees bouncing. "This is bullshit," Lincoln murmurs.

"We're not giving up on him," Lucas snaps.

"How much more are we expected to take?"

"That's enough, Lincoln," Tom booms, entering the waiting room.

Still in his damp clothing, he looks around at all the waiting faces. "He'll be okay. The doctors are running some tests, checking to see if he needs..." he trails off when his gaze catches my mother. "Melissa, I can't thank you enough..."

Mom holds up a hand, shakes her head. She hasn't stopped crying either. Like me, hers are silent.

Laney's parents arrive, baby Preston in tow. "What can we do?" Misty asks. Laney's Dad hugs her, and she sobs into his chest. He hugs Lucas, too.

My mom hasn't touched me.

Has barely looked at me.

Tom says, "Can you take Lachy home with you?"

Lachlan puts up a fight that lasts all of two seconds. Our embrace is weak. As soon as they're out the doors, Lincoln stands. "I'm going home."

"You can't leave!" Lucy cries, and her husband holds her to him.

Lincoln's eyes narrow when he spits, "This is bullshit, Luce!"

"Enough!" Tom snaps.

But Lincoln isn't done. "You remember the last time we were all in the hospital like this?" He points to Laney. "When *she* took four bullets from a guy who wanted to *kill* her!"

Lucas sighs.

Lincoln goes on, "She didn't *choose* to have that happen to her! And the time before that? It was for Mom. She didn't *choose* to get cancer, and she sure as hell didn't choose to die! Logan—he *chose* to do all this shit! He chose this path! And now he has to deal with the consequences." He crosses his arms, widens his stance. "I'm sorry, but I'm not going to sit around and feel sorry for him because he's so high on whatever drugs that he can't see straight. That he drives his truck right into a goddamn lake. He could've killed someone! Jesus Christ, Lachy could've been out there playing with the pig when he sped through the yard, and we're supposed to sit here crying about it?! No! No effing way am I wasting a single tear on that jerk. For all I care, he can—"

"Stop!" Mom cries out. "Just stop!" She covers her face, muffles her loud sobs with both her hands.

I stand, finally find my voice, find the words I'd been too scared to ask. "What the hell do you know about him that you're keeping to yourself?"

"Melissa…?" Tom asks. "What is she talking about?"

Mom sucks in a breath, attempts to steady herself. "You should sit down, Tom."

"I think I'll stand," he says, his jaw clenched. "Start talking."

Mom wipes at her tears as she falls into the seat opposite me. There's no color in her face, no hesitation in her words. "Logan was molested as a child." She looks at me. "By your father."

48

LOGAN

I AM NINE YEARS OLD, *and the leather cracks beneath my weight. The car still smells new, even though I've been in it for months. The dash is gray. I can barely see over it. In the pocket of the door, there's a tube of hand lotion. It's pink. I wonder who it belongs to. "Are you all buckled in?" he asks, looking down at me.*

I nod, and he smiles.

"So... how are things at home with your mother?"

I frown. "She's getting worse."

"Is it sad being at home?"

"Yeah," I whisper, my toes kicking at my swim bag.

Mom used to take me to my private lessons before she got sick. Then Dad did it for a while, but it became too hard for him with all the other kids. Mom says I have to keep going. That life has to keep moving. So I go. My Aunt Leslee takes me to the lessons. Coach Murphy brings me home.

His hand settles on my leg, and I look up at him. He smiles again, but this time, it's different. It looks fake. "Do you want to go home, Logan?"

I shrug. "Not really."

"Why don't we go back to my house for a bit? We can watch a movie. I'll let you eat whatever you want."

"You got nut-free candy?" I ask.

"I would think so. Why don't we check?"

A smile tugs at my lips. "Okay."

I DON'T KNOW *how long the car ride to Coach Murphy's house is, but he doesn't live in our town. There are no stairs at his house like there are in mine. He leads me into his kitchen where he opens the pantry and tells me to choose from all the candy. I choose one of everything I know doesn't have nuts. He's smiling at me when he pats my head. "Why don't you go to the TV room and wait for me there?" He points to a room on the other side of the hall. It's small. Like my bedroom. There's a TV and a few toys. Girls' toys. Nothing I want to play with. I push the red-headed doll off the couch, watch it fall to the floor. In the kitchen, I hear Coach Murphy talking on the phone. "Hey, Tom. The people in the pool before us went overtime. We're still here. We'll be running a little late."*

I don't know why he's lying to my dad.

I don't ask.

When he comes into the room, he's not wearing a shirt. Or pants. Just boxer shorts. I ask, taking the drink he's offering, "Why did you take your clothes off?"

He chuckles. "We just do things a little differently in this house. Besides, it's not like we haven't seen each other like this before. We swim together all the time."

"I guess."

"And it really is comfortable. Why don't you take your clothes off for me, Logan?"

49

AUBREY

My DAD WAS drunk behind the wheel of a car that crashed head-on into a tree. That was my last memory of him.

The memory is real.

The events are real.

But the circumstances *surrounding* it? The lead-up? They were all things I didn't know about. All things my mother tried to keep hidden from me.

His death happened exactly a week after the detectives knocked on the door of our family home two towns over from where we currently are. It's the same town that holds the yearly autumn festival. The festival Logan had taken me to. The boy who made the allegations was from the same town. My father had been his swim coach.

He was ten years old.

My dad had written Mom a letter before getting in his car.

She calls it a suicide note.

I call it an admission of guilt.

In the letter, he'd admitted to what he'd done and named all his victims from oldest to youngest.

There were five names.

Logan's name was last.

After his death, we moved to Raleigh, where she went through the process of changing my name, homeschooling me, blocking all access to anything that might reveal who he really was, and burning anything and everything that could possibly remind me of him. She kept me sheltered, hidden from his actions, and was grateful I was still too young to ask questions.

She did it to *protect me.*

She tells us all of this in an unoccupied, private room of the hospital where a clock ticks too loud, and my pulse is too thick, and everyone's sniffs and sobs are constant.

I sit on the floor in the corner of the room, holding on to my knees. I rock back and forth, back and forth, her words replaying in my head like a broken record. "I burned his letter, but I've memorized the names, and I've spent the past ten years trying to find each one of them, trying to make sure that the actions of a monster I once called my husband hasn't ruined them," Mom says. "For the past ten years, I've been paying for therapy for the first boy who came forward. There are two who want nothing to do with me, who swear they don't know what I'm talking about. One of them is currently deployed in the army. I was about to find Logan when... when he brought you home that first time." My mom cries through her words, her heartache.

Toms stops pacing. Starts again.

"Aubrey, honey," Mom says. "Say something."

I shake my head, press my cheek to my leg, and rock harder. Faster.

I am empty.

I am void.

I am eight years old, and Dad's letting me sit in the front seat of his car for the first time. He'd bought the car when Mom was deployed. He didn't ask her if he could buy it, and I heard them arguing about it the first night she was home.

I reach into my backpack and sift through my clothes.

"Put your seatbelt on, sweetheart," Dad says.

I find the hand lotion Grandma gave me and do as Dad asks.

"How was your sleepover at Grandma's?" he asks, reversing out of the driveway.

"Good," I say, looking up at him. "How was your night?"

Dad smiles. "I had a lesson that ran a little late. Besides that, it was the same old boring night." He taps my knee with his finger. "Don't tell your mom, but I had candy for dinner."

I laugh to myself as I rub the lotion into my hands. I try to put the tube back in my backpack, but with my seatbelt on, it's impossible to reach, so I drop it into the pocket of the door. I sniff my hands, and Dad says through a chuckle. "That's really smelly, Aubs."

"It's nice," I say. "It smells like summer. Like sunshine and cut grass and strawberry milkshakes."

"It smells like poop," he says, scrunching his nose.

I sit on my hands, saddened by his words. My fingers brush something flat, something cold. I pull out a penny from between my butt and the leather seat and hold it up in front of me. "Where did this come from?" I ask, looking at the coin.

Dad glances at it quickly, then back at the road. "One of the kids I coach was in my car last night. It must've fallen out of his pocket."

"Aubrey," Mom says pulling me from the memory.

I gasp, get to my feet.

Whatever reaction is on my face has Cameron stepping toward me. "You're in shock, Aubrey. It's okay..." His hands settle on my shoulders. Strong. Defiant.

I shrug out of his touch and aim my glare at my mother. "You wanted to *protect* me?" I growl, my anger and hatred directed at her. "You may have protected me then, but you didn't protect me now, and you sure as fuck didn't protect Logan!" My heart pound, pound, pounds, then stops. Drops. I scream, "You *knew*! This entire time, *you knew*, and you didn't say a thing!"

"Aubrey," she cries. "I tried. God, I tried. But, how could I? How does one..." She falls into a heap on the bed, her head in her hands. "I tried, Aubrey," she repeats. "And then I got to know him, know his family, and he seemed fine—"

"Fine?!" I shout, throwing my arms in the air. "How the hell is this *fine*?!"

"He told me he grew up happy, I assumed—"

"Why the hell didn't he say something?" Tom says, his tone

breaking my already dead heart. "Why wouldn't he come to us... why..."

Lucy lets out a sob. "Because Mom was sick... and we were all... we were going through so much that he... he..."

I run out of the room, her words slicing at my soul, killing me from the inside. I race down the hall, ignoring the heavy footsteps behind me. I can't deal with my mom right now, and I sure as hell won't force the Prestons to be in my presence for a second longer.

My heavy legs carry me to the exit, where air hits my lungs, and I bend over myself, my hands on my knees. My stomach lurches, my entire body convulsing with the force.

I clasp the penny in my palm, look up at my dad. "What's his name?"

"His name is Logan."

I giggle. "Is he cute?"

I empty the content of my stomach into the bushes by the front door.

"Aubrey." I recognize the voice as Lucas's, but I don't turn to him. "Don't, Luke," I cry out, my mouth covered in spit and tears and turmoil. "Don't come near me!" I start to walk away, my phone gripped tight in my hand.

"Where are you going?" he calls out after me. "You can't leave him, Aubrey. He needs you now more than ever!"

I freeze in the middle of the road, my shoulders tense. Then, slowly, I face him, his dejected figure blurred by the tears that won't fucking quit. "He needs me?" I repeat, my voice breaking. "Lucas... how can he ever look at me the same? Every look we've shared, every touch... God... how can he look at me and not feel sick to his stomach?"

"Because... because he loves you, Aubrey."

"Love isn't enough anymore! He can't... he can't pick and choose the parts of me that will settle his mind. That's not how this works. No..." I cry, walking backward, giving me the distance to breathe. "He *can't* love me. Because I'll always be my father's daughter, and my father will always be the man who molested him."

Behind me, Leo's voice echoes through my agony. "What is she talking about, Lucas?"

50

LOGAN

THE FIRST THING I do when I come to is pull the fucking tube from my throat and sit up, searching for somewhere to empty my stomach.

Dad's next to me, holding a trash can beneath my chin.

I puke and I puke and I puke until I can no longer breathe.

My head pounds. My heart does the same.

Dad strokes my head, my back. "Let it out, son."

Doctors and nurses and too many people fill the room, and I fall back on the bed, call out for Mary.

She isn't here.

Neither are her friends.

The only one here is Misery, and Misery becomes my poison, weakening all my senses.

I close my eyes, let her destroy me.

THE VOICES ARE HUSHED but loud enough to hear through the fog of my mind.

"It makes sense."

"He was always acting up, but it got worse around that time."

"I think we all assumed it was because of Mom getting sick."

"Why wouldn't he say something to us?"

"Be glad that motherfucker's already dead."

"What do we do about Aubrey?"

Aubrey…?

My jaw tenses.

They know.

They all know.

Melissa… she must have told them…

My shoulders shake before the sound of my cries fall weakly from my throat.

Tears land on my pillow, wetting my temple.

"You're okay, son. We're here. We're all here for you."

Dad reaches for my hand.

I pull it away.

HOURS PASS. I stay semi-lucid. The door of the hospital room is forever opening, closing.

People come in.

People go out.

Laney cries.

Lucas comforts her.

Leo stands by the door, his hands behind his back, his head lowered.

The twins whisper to each other but never to me.

Lachlan isn't here.

Neither is Lucy.

Dad sits in a chair next to the bed. He never leaves my side.

I don't want them here.

I only want Mary.

And she's nowhere to be found.

Cameron enters, stands with Leo.

Still no Lucy.

I remember the steering wheel shaking in my grip, the bump of the seat as I sped through the property. I remember seeing the lake. And I remember wanting to be submerged…

I'm twenty years old, and all I wanted was to hear my mother's voice.

"Dad?" I whisper, and he leans forward, his eyes wide. It's the first time I've spoken. "I'm sorry."

He shakes his head, his tired, worried eyes on mine. "No, Logan. No one is as sorry I am. I'm sorry I didn't know. I'm sorry I wasn't there for you. I'm sorry—"

"Stop it!" Lincoln cries. "We're *all* sorry." He walks over to me, stops next to Dad. "God, Logan. We're *so* sorry."

The doctor comes in, someone I don't know. He has a clipboard and stethoscope. They all do. He asks about my medical history, my allergies, my past intake of drugs. That's when I lower my gaze, ask everyone to leave. I don't have the energy to hold on to secrets, and so I tell the doctor about my unconditional love for Mary, about her friends, about the good times we all had together.

When he leaves, no one else takes his place.

I lie in the bed, stare up at the ceiling, the beeps of the machines sound around me—another playlist, just one song, one genre. In my head, I title the playlist "The Downfall."

TIME PASSES TOO SLOWLY, and then the door opens and Lucy appears. "Hey," she says, her voice low. Her short legs shuffle across the room and toward me, where she stops at the foot of the bed, her eyes on mine. She's in flannel pajamas, the type Mom used to wear, and she looks so much like her that it rips at my heart.

I try to respond, but my words catch in my throat.

Then Lucy's trying and failing to get onto the bed with me. I reach to the side, where the controller sits, and lower the bed for her, let the electronic whir fill the room. When it's completely down, she climbs on and settles in next to me. I start to move to give her more room, but she asks, "Stay close?" And so I do.

She settles onto her back, I do the same, and then we let the silence bleed into the atmosphere. Regret stretches time, and time stretches pain, and I roll my head to the side, watch the single tear streaking down my sister's temple.

For the year before my mother died and the few months after, Lucy became the strength that mom's cancer had left behind. I reach up, wipe away her liquid sadness with the back of my finger. "I'm sorry for putting you through—"

"Shut up, Logan," she says, her jaw unmoving. "Don't you dare—" She breaks off on a sob that clogs my throat. Then she turns to her side, both hands under her head. The direction of her tears change, and I wipe all of them away. "I love you so much, and I'll never stop loving you. Ever. And I'm so, so sorry that you—that you…"

"I know, Luce. We don't…" I shut my eyes tight and count to five, before opening them again. "I don't want to…"

Nodding against the pillow, she says, "I understand. And I won't make you, Logan. I won't ever make you do anything you don't want to." She rolls onto her back again but keeps her eyes on me. "But, I have to tell you something…"

"Okay…?"

Her lips tremble with the force of her exhale. "I'm not going to lie, Logan. I worry about you, especially now, knowing what we know, I worry that you—that things are going to get worse with you and that you're going to fall into this cycle, and we—Dad and us—we'll have no choice but to watch someone else we love slowly die…"

"Lucy," I whisper. "It's not that bad…"

"For you, maybe," she says, looking down at the space between us. "But for us… it's the same, because we can't control it. We can't control *you*."

The struggle for air squeezes at my lungs, at my throat.

"You know," she adds, "before Cam and I lost that baby, we would always talk about our kids, about our future…" Her tears come faster now. Freer. She glances up at me, then back down.

If I could hold her hand, I would.

"I always had this picture in my head," she says, "this one scene where we'd come by the house and y'all were there. I'd open the car door, and our daughter would be in her seat—blue eyes and pigtails—

and as soon as I had her unbuckled, she'd be off running toward her Uncle Logan, her *favorite* uncle…"

My heart skips a beat. Two. I struggle to ask, "I'd be her favorite?"

"Yeah," Lucy says, nodding. She looks up, right into my eyes, and keeps me pinned to her stare. "I mean, when you think about it, she'd be a pretty lucky girl to have all those uncles looking out for her. But with Lucas, he'd be her protector, you know? And Leo, he'd be the serious one. The one trying to teach her all about morals and"—she rolls her eyes—"how to be a lady."

I can't help but smile.

"But you, Logan—you'd be the *fun* uncle. The one who'd skip out on work just to take her to the zoo. You'd be the first to dress up as a fairy if she asked you to. You'd for sure be her favorite, and she'd love you beyond words, and in my mind, in that scene, I'm always smiling when I see you waiting for her with your arms spread, lifting her off the ground the second she got to you. She'd call you Uncle Lo… and you… you'd call her your Little Princess."

I wipe my eyes on the pillow, and Lucy reaches up, cups my face. "Can you see it, Logan?"

I nod against her hands, sniff back the sorrow.

"Can you see it if you're too high to see *her?*"

My chest rises. Falls. "Lucy—"

"Because I'm *pregnant*, Logan," she cuts in. "It's a girl. We're going to name her Katherine, after Mom. Katie for short. And I want you to be around to watch her grow up. I want Katie to have her favorite uncle in her life," she cries. "But I'm scared… I'm scared that you…"

I can't breathe. "What do you need from me, Luce?"

She muffles her sobs into my chest.

I hold her face in my hands and plead with her. "I'll do anything, Lucy. Just tell me…"

"I need you to get help, Logan."

And I say…

I say…

"Okay."

51

AUBREY

I FORCED my mother to give me the names of the five boys. I don't know *why* I needed to know or what I even planned to do with the information once I had it. A part of me wanted to reach out to them, to apologize for the actions of a man I'd once loved. I could do that. So long as I never used the words "I get it" or "I understand" because being the daughter of a pedophile is *not* the same as being a victim of one.

I don't eat.

Can't.

And when I close my eyes, I see the twenty different pictures of Logan hanging on the wall next to the staircase in the Preston house.

I do my best not to close my eyes for too long.

FOR THE FOURTH day in a row, I sit in the confines of my room, on my computer, in a bomb shelter made of boxes that once filled an entire house. I type in their names, one after the other, multiple search engines, numerous filters.

Mom says I shouldn't obsess over it.

My mom can fuck off.

Because as much as she likes to think that she somehow did the right thing, my dad died *ten years ago*. For ten fucking years she's known about it, and she was just *recently* looking for Logan. No. That doesn't make sense. She could've found them within minutes had she tried. My dad *coached* them. Their details would've been under the same roof we called home. She could've reached out to the parents then. She could've done so many things. Instead, she was a coward, and now she's using *me* to defend that cowardice by saying she did it all to *protect* me. There were five boys out there who needed the protection more than I did.

I go through pages and pages of searches and sites and don't come up with anything solid. And so I rely on my last option: social media.

I log onto Facebook for the first time since Logan's return from Cambodia. I don't expect many notifications, if any. But there's one. A status update from Carter that he'd tagged me in:

> *When you drive three hours to slip a letter in a mailbox... Revenge is a bitch, Aubrey O'Sullivan. Enjoy the hate.*

My eyes narrow, my mind confused, and I try to think if I'd seen anything come from him. I look at the date he'd posted, and my breath, my pulse—all of it stops.

I rush downstairs, ignore Mom calling after me, and grab my keys from the entry table. I get in my car and let rage drive me, let it control me.

MY HANDS ARE fists at my sides while I walk from my car into the office of the BMW dealership owned by Carter's dad. I hear him before I see him, his laughter grating on my nerves, building my anger. His office is surrounded by floor to ceiling glass, and he's lazing back in a chair behind his desk, having no clue to the fury I'm about to unleash. A couple is sitting opposite him, signing paperwork, and as soon as I open the glass door, I tell them to get out.

Carter's eyes are huge, and he's on his feet, making his way toward me. "Jesus, Aubrey, you don't look so good." He's smirking, cocky, and I wish I had the strength to wrap his stupid tie around his neck and choke him to death.

He holds up a finger to his clients. "One minute," he asks, holding the door open for them.

They leave his office.

Carter closes the door behind them.

He's still smirking.

I say, doing my best not to cry, "What the fuck was in that letter?"

His eyes narrow. "What are you talking about?"

"That letter you put in my fucking mailbox!" I shout. "What was in it?!"

"Keep your fucking voice down," he utters. "That was, like, *weeks* ago."

I shove his chest. Hard. "What. Was. It?"

He grasps my wrists. "Feisty," he says. Laughs. "I like this version of you, Aubs."

"Fuck you."

He rolls his eyes. "It was a police report about your dad, okay? Oh, and a picture of you two..." He smirks. "You always wanted to find a photo of him, right?" He shrugs, releases my wrist. "You should be thanking me, really. I gave you what you finally wanted. Did you know Daddy Dearest was a kiddy fiddler? Did he ever... you know..." He wags his eyebrows.

I try. Honestly, I do. But the tears fall, his words weakening my determination. "What is wrong with you, Carter?" I cry out. "You ruined so many lives with..." I trail off, unable to speak through my sobs. I don't lower my head, my gaze, because I want him to see me. See what he's done to me. "Why would you want to hurt me like that?"

His features fall, and he steps toward me.

I take a step back.

Shaking his head, his voice is as weak as I feel when he says, "Fuck, Aubrey, I'm sorry. I wasn't... I don't..." He takes my hand. *Holds it.*

I snatch it away, bile rising to my throat. I whisper, "You have no idea what you did." I leave his office, my torment building cement walls around my chest. I should just leave, because there's nothing left to say, nothing left to do. But then I hear him behind me, "Don't you feel better for knowing?"

I stop in my tracks, scream so loud my throat burns. A bomb explodes inside me, shattering the walls that had just been built. I pick up a metal chair, throw it at him. Pick up another. Throw it through his office walls. Glass falls to the floor, as if in slow motion, and I picture Logan opening that mail... try to imagine the look on his face when he was reunited with a past that destroyed him...

Weeks of silent sobs force themselves out of me. I cry. I cry so loud my lungs, my throat, beg for me to stop. But I can't.

I can't stop.

I run for my car, and when I hear Carter coming after me, I run faster.

I get into my car, lock all the doors, and start the engine. I should leave, just drive away, and forget this day. Forget Carter. Forget every single moment from my past.

Logan included.

Logan.

And then I remember the pile of ash sitting on the garage floor, the burnt remains of Logan's history.

Through my rage, my agony, the never-ending tears blurring my vision, I see Carter's Pathetic Dick of a car parked in front of the office. I don't think. I just do. I put the car in gear, hit the brake and accelerator. I hear the tires screeching, smell the burn. My head lands on the steering wheel when I crash into the side of his car head-on. I check behind me. Reverse when it's clear. Then I hit the brakes. Put the car in drive. I don't close my eyes when I smash into the BMW again. And again. And again. I ignore the sirens blaring and the shouting from outside. But most of all, I ignore my own screams. My own cries. My own pain. My own mind telling me that I should've worn my seatbelt, that I shouldn't give into the darkness.

52

AUBREY

Four months later

Time heals all wounds. At least the physical ones. I ended up with a concussion, a few stitches over my eye, a fractured wrist, collarbone, and a couple bruised ribs. Carter paid for the damages I'd made at the dealership from his own pocket. The last time I spoke to him, it was to tell him that there was no way I'd be paying him back a single cent. He told me he hadn't expected me to.

As soon as my injuries healed, I went looking for a job. I now work full-time cleaning rooms in a mediocre hotel. Once I'd saved up enough money, I got the hell out of my mother's house and moved into a share house with two college girls. They leave me alone. I leave them alone. Laney is the only person I've spoken to from my old life, and it was only so she could inform me that she found someone to take over the lease at the shop. Lucy's called a couple times. Leo, too. I don't answer their calls. I'm ashamed. For so many reasons. Not just because of what my dad had done, but my mom… after what happened with Carter, I sat in a hospital room with her while she stared at me, concerned, and I looked at her, and the only thing I felt was *ill*. Sick to my goddamn stomach. How could she do what she did?

How could she not say anything? And then when it came to saying something, how could she do it the way she did… just spitting it out to get it out of her system, with no regard for how the Prestons might feel. How *Tom* might feel. How *Tom* might want to handle it when it came to the other kids. My mom is selfish in the most slyest, most vindictive way, and she doesn't even realize it.

She calls every now and again.

Occasionally, I'll answer her calls.

Some days are good.

Some days are bad.

But every day, I think about *him*.

I wonder how he's doing.

I wonder if time will ever heal *his* wounds.

Those days, I cry myself to sleep, clutching onto the work jacket he'd given me for Christmas. It was the only thing of his I kept.

Some nights, I can still smell him on it.

Those are the nights I live for.

53

LOGAN

"Well, it was really nice meeting you, Logan," the girl sitting next to me says. Her name's Courtney, a twenty-two-year-old in her final year of college. Her major: marine biology. I know all these things because for the two-hour flight from West Palm Beach, Florida to Charlotte, North Carolina, she hasn't shut the hell up.

I'm pretty sure she's flirting, or at least trying, and I'm also pretty sure that I'm annoyed by it. Or, maybe I'm just not used to it because I've spent the past four months in a detox, rehab, and intense therapy treatment facility where the only people I really spoke to were the therapists themselves.

Lucy and Amanda were the ones to find it. According to Amanda, it was one of the best treatment facilities in the country. Thank God I never went to college, because the four months there cost my dad the same as four years of education at the University of North Carolina. He says it's money well spent, and honestly, I agree.

The treatment was only supposed to last two months, but Dad made it known prior that if I felt like I needed more time, I shouldn't hesitate to stay. So, I stayed.

I had to make sure I was ready.

The extra two months helped me with that.

The only rule at the center I struggled with was no contact with the outside world, bar one person of my choosing who had to be approved by the therapists.

Of course, I chose Lucy.

She's the reason I was there.

Well, her and my unborn niece.

Now, I keep my eyes on the seatbelt light, waiting for it to switch off, and murmur, not looking at Courtney, "You, too."

As soon as the seatbelt light is off, I get out of my seat, shoulder my duffle bag—the only luggage I have—and practically run down to the exit. I told Lucy I didn't want to make a big deal of my coming home and made her promise not to bring everyone with her. I didn't want to create a scene at the airport with eleventy-three people. And the tears. God, I don't think I could handle seeing my family cry any more than I have. My family—their reaction to everything—it was one of the reasons I stayed back those extra months. I wanted to be sure I knew how to handle their questions, their concerns, their unconditional love for me. It took all four months for me to accept that last one. For me to finally believe that I was worthy of it.

My heart beats wild in my chest while I look at the waiting faces outside the gates. I search and I search, and it seems to go forever. People walk left, walk right, walk right into my vision, and then, like in those sappy movies, the coast clears and I see her. She's on her toes, biting her bottom lip. Lachlan is on one side. Leo on the other. Her belly… oh, my God. I find myself smiling, laughing to myself, and I slow my steps as I move toward them, taking in every single moment. My lucky penny shifts against my chest with every step, and I smile wider. I *truly* am lucky.

Lucy squeals when she finally sees me, starts running/waddling and I drop my bag, make sure I can catch her. She throws her arms around me, and I keep my lower half at a distance that won't suffocate the baby. I don't know how that stuff works, but I'm pretty sure any impact is *bad* impact. When she pulls away, I say, "Holy shit, Luce, you've gotten big."

She glares.

I backpedal, "Not, like, *fat*. No, that's not—"

I'm shaking my head, and she's pursing her lips, and then an old lady approaches us and says, "You guys are such a sweet couple."

Lucy drops her hands from my neck, sticks out her tongue and makes a gagging sound. "Ew! He's my brother, you creep!"

"Luce!" I laugh out, then apologize to the woman on her behalf.

When the woman's gone, Lucy says, "Pregnancy 101, Logan. You can pretty much get away with saying anything." She smiles, so much like Mom. "How are you feeling?"

"Good, Luce." I exhale, look over her to see my brothers walking toward us. "Honestly, I've never felt better."

"Clean teen looks good on you," she says, hugging me again.

I rear back so I can look down at her belly. "How's my little princess doing?"

"She's a feisty little one," she says, letting go of me to rub her stomach. "She won't stop kicking."

When Lucy told me she was pregnant, she didn't say exactly how pregnant she was. I didn't find out until she was driving me to the airport that she was sixteen weeks. *Four months.* She said I was the first person she'd told. She'd been too scared to tell anyone in case there was a repeat of last time. Then she showed me her bare belly hidden beneath her loose shirt, and there was no doubting she was either pregnant or had just eaten way too many tacos. So, basic math... she was four months pregnant four months ago, which means she's eight months now... and this baby of hers, my little princess, she'll be arriving real soon.

Lachlan gives me a hug that challenges the strength of any hug I've ever received. He holds back tears that bring on my own. "I'm okay, now, Lachy. I promise."

Through the weekly phone calls with Lucy, she'd told me about Lachlan. About how they all sat down with him and told him everything about me, past, present, and future. It wasn't just so he understood what all I went through, but so that he knew if anything, *anything*, ever happened to him, he should feel comfortable enough to talk to someone about it. To not keep it inside. That no matter what was going on in anyone's lives, we'd all be there for him. Always.

Leo gives me our standard bro hug—this one lasting a little longer than most. "You didn't have to leave campus for this," I tell him, picking up my duffle again.

He side-eyes Lucy. "She didn't tell you?"

"Tell me what?" I ask, settling my hand on Lachy's shoulder as we walk toward the exit.

"I quit school, man."

My steps falter. "Not for me, right?"

He shakes his head. "You don't need a college degree to join the police force. And honestly, I faked it for as long as I could, but I *hate* school."

I stop to stare at him, to look right in his eyes. We've spent enough time together that I know his traits, his downfalls. His eyebrows rise when he lies, and as soon as he's done, he chews his bottom lip, like he's doing right now. I should call him out on it, but what would be the point? Instead, I laugh under my breath and shake my head, "Welcome to my world."

Lachlan says, looking up at me, "So does that mean I can quit school, too?"

"No," Lucy, Leo and I say in unison.

Lachlan's laughter fills my ears, my heart.

Once we're out of the airport, I stop to breathe in fresh air as if I'd been locked away for years. Someone calls my name, and I turn to see Courtney. She hands me a piece of paper—her number—and says, "You should call me. Maybe we can get together sometime."

I take her number, shove it deep in my pocket. I won't be using it. Won't be needing it. "I'm really not looking to get involved right now," I tell her.

Besides, my heart isn't really mine to give away…

Leo drives back home, Lachlan in the front seat, Lucy and me in the back. When we get to town, my gaze searches—scarlet—and my mind wonders—scarlet—and I turn to Lucy, my eyes pleading. Her frown gives me the answer before her words do: "I'm sorry," she mumbles, shaking her head. "She's gone, Logan."

My family is all waiting for me on the front porch when we get to the house. I smile when I see them. Lucy grasps my arm, squeezes once. Leo turns to me. "Welcome home, little brother. We missed you something fierce."

I try to hold back on my emotions through every hug from all my siblings, through their words of encouragement and pride that humble my heart. I keep it together for as long as I can, but when I'm standing in Dad's office, alone with the man who's believed in me beyond words, beyond reason, and I look into his eyes—eyes filled with tears, *I break*. I fall apart in his arms—arms of pure strength—and I grasp on to the back his t-shirt, apologize for everything I've put him through. He keeps his hold tight, unwavering, and I am six years old…

I am six years old and I'm lying in bed, terrified, the blankets pulled to my chin. I stare at the strip of light under the bedroom door, my eyes widening when I hear the sound…

Fee-fi-fo-fum…

A second later, the door opens, and Dad pokes his head inside. "I knew you'd be awake."

"How did you know? I ask.

The mattress dips when he sits on the end of the bed. "Lucas shouldn't have shown you the movie with the scary clown."

"I not scared!" I shout, lying through my teeth.

"Oh, I know," he says, his voice low so he doesn't wake the other kids. "Can I tell you a secret?"

I nod, start to get out of the covers. "You can tell me anything."

He dips his head, his mouth to my ear. "I'm scared, Logan. And I knew you'd be awake because you'd know that, and you'd worry about me. Right?"

I settle my hand on his huge leg. Nodding, I say, "It's okay, Daddy. I'm here now."

"But… I'm still scared."

So am I, I don't say. Because I want so badly to be just like him: brave and strong. "What can we do to make you feel better?"

His eyes wide, he asks, "Can you come downstairs with me… maybe eat a bowl of cereal?"

"I can pour the milk!"

On his shoulders, I giggle all the way out of the room and down the stairs, where it's completely silent besides the clicking of Mom's knitting needles. She's sitting in her chair, her fingers moving but her eyes on us. "The rest of the kids are in bed," she tells us, but she's smiling. Not as big as I am. I don't think anyone could ever smile as big as I am. Mom asks, scowling at us, "What are you two up to?"

Dad helps me down from his shoulders, holds my hand in his as we walk toward the kitchen. "We're having some quality man time." He ruffles my hair. "Just me and my boy."

54

AUBREY

My mom doesn't know where I live. She does, however, know where I work. So, when I get a call on the radio telling me I have a visitor at reception, I know it's her.

I leave my cleaning trolley outside room 302 and take the elevator down to the ground level. Mom stands a few feet from the desk, wringing her hands. She's nervous. She should be. Whenever we're together, things are hostile at best. When I get to her, she asks, "Have you got a break coming up?"

"No."

"Maybe I can come back—"

"No."

"Aubrey."

I drop the facade. "I'm on the clock, Mom, so I can't really talk... what are you doing here?"

She reaches into her bag, reveals two envelopes. "You have mail."

I take them from her, recognize the handwriting on both.

Mom says, "I thought you should have them right away. They look personal. Do you know who they're from?"

My pulse spikes. My hands shake. "Thank you for bringing them to me," I say. Then I turn around, shove the letters in my back pocket, and promise to keep them there until I'm home, alone, where I don't have to hide my reaction... or my emotions.

AFTER WORK, I go straight to my room, where I sit in the middle of the bed, legs crossed, drapes of white satin surrounding me. I stare down at the letters, trying to decide which one to read first or if I should read them at all.

One is addressed to *Aubrey O'Sullivan*.

The other: *Miss Red*.

I pick up the letter from Logan, hold it to my heart, then to my ear. I shake it. I've known that there was something more than just paper in there since the second Mom handed it to me. Curiosity filled my mind the entire day. Fear filled my heart.

"Just do it, Aubrey," I whisper to myself, my eyes closing. I unseal the envelope and reach inside. Metal. Cold. My eyes snap open, and I empty the contents onto my palm. I hold the flattened penny under my nose, my eyes widening when I read the words etched into the metal, etched into my soul: *You + Me*.

Dear Aubrey,

I'm sorry for everything I've put you through. I don't think I realized until too late that my actions and mistakes have consequences on anyone other than just myself. The past seventy-two hours in this hospital room have helped me see that. My family—they've helped me through it. I don't know who's helping you, but I hope someone is. And I hope that someone is there to help you realize that you're a victim in this, too. Maybe not in the same way I was, but still... you are. And there's nothing wrong with feeling that.

Lucy and Amanda, my therapist, have found a treatment center for me to attend. It's in Florida. Apparently, I won't be able to call or write or keep in touch with anyone besides Lucy. I don't know if that's something you expect or even something you want. For me, I'd like to know that you're doing okay. Selfishly, I'd like to think that you'll think of me sometimes and wonder the same. Even more selfishly, I'd like to believe that you'll never stop loving me. Because as hard as I've tried, as much as I've fought it, I'm still crazy in love with you, Aubrey. And I don't know what that means or if there's anything I can do about it.

I'm going to be taking this letter with me to the treatment center. My therapist says I can use it as a journal to look back on my progress. If I send it to you, it won't be until after I get out. If I send it to you, it means that I want you to read it.

It's been two weeks, and I want nothing more than to see you. Or to call you. I'd give anything just to hear your voice. The detox is killing me, the rehab... I don't even know. I think the worst part, though, is the therapy. There's so much of it so many times a day, and right now, I feel like all it's doing is making me face my mistakes. Every day, the people here are trying to force me to come to terms with all the events that led me to where I am now. I wish I could say that it's been easy, that the path was written before I knew there was a path...

While talking about it all, I realized that you—you probably have no idea what happened, what set it off, what triggered all of this.

On the day I left you, there was a letter in the mailbox. It was a police report with your father's name on it... a kid had come forward, someone I didn't know... I didn't read the whole thing, but just enough. His name—your dad's—made my skin crawl. I thought that was bad enough, but then I flipped the page over and there you were... hair too red and too wild and missing teeth and too many freckles and you were in his arms and your mom was there and I knew... I knew who he was to you...

You don't have the same last name and I don't know why.

I thought you lied to me about it.

I thought you knew about me.

I thought you came into my life to ruin it like he had done.

I thought so many things, and all I wanted was to stop thinking.

So I went to the source of mindless thoughts, to my dealer's house, and I suppose that's where it started. It was a whirlwind of desperation and destruction and...

I wasn't lying the first time you asked me if I'd slept with someone else and I told you I don't remember. I didn't then.

I do now.

I don't think I'll ever be sorrier for anything in my life than I am for doing what I did. And I know it won't make sense to you, that you won't ever be able to forgive me, but... and this is where I get really fucking selfish, Aubrey... I didn't do it to hurt you. I did it to hurt myself.

And I sit here in this empty room, and I picture you in your kitchen... the way you were... the way I destroyed you... and I realize that it was never about me.

Because you + me, we were never about just me.

And now it's too little too late, but I'm sorry anyway.

Aubrey,

I started group therapy today. We were supposed to talk about one thing we looked forward to when all of this was over. People were talking about their kids, about holding them, loving them. I talked about our very first night together. It felt pathetic in comparison, but those people—they don't know...

All it took was one girl.

One night.

For you to ask yourself one question.

I showed you what was beneath the bravado that night.

And you fell in love with me because of it.

Now I'm in my room again, and I can't stop thinking about you.

Strands of scarlet wrapped around my fingers, and I lifted my gaze to your green-green eyes. The warmth of your nakedness coated my skin, and your forearms pressed down on my chest, your toes tickling my legs. My fingers crawled up and down your spine as the morning light bled through your bedroom window, turning scarlet to sunshine. "I like your bed, Red," I told you.

You looked around. "Yeah?"

"I like the drapes, the way they surround us like this. Like there's nothing and no one else. It's just us, in our own little bubble. In our own little world."

You smiled at me, the freckles on your nose shifting with the movement. Your fingers toyed with the lucky penny hanging around my neck, and you said, "Maybe you got this wrong..."

"The penny?"

You nodded. "Maybe it wasn't about you finding luck, Logan. Maybe you are the luck. Maybe... maybe it's meant for the person who finds you. Because I found you, and I feel pretty damn lucky that I did."

I bit down on my lip, moved the hair from your eyes, and kissed the tip of your nose. You caught my lips with yours. Kissed me once. Then you settled your head on my chest. "I feel like I was destined to find you," you murmured.

My fingers paused on your spine. "I feel like you were destined to save me."

Aubrey,

I've been here for two months now, and every day this letter sits folded in my pocket. Every day, I read it. Every day, I realize that nothing's changed. I don't know if that's progress. I don't know what it means. All I know is that I think about you all day. I dream about you all night. I wake up, and you're the first and only thing on my mind. My pillows don't smell like you, and I hate that they don't.

I'm going to stay, Red. I'm going to stay for you, for my family, and maybe even a little for me. Because I don't want to fail anyone. I don't want to fail you, Aubrey.

Red,

I made you a penny.

It's not a lucky penny.

It's a penny filled with hope.

My hope.

You + Me.

55

LOGAN

I STAND on the marble floors, my finger itching at the space between my collar and my neck. I'm in a suit and tie, and I feel like a jackhole. Probably look like one, too. "Tell me again why I'm dressed like this?" I ask Dad, but he's too busy talking with Cameron about the architecture and age of the building.

Lucy rolls her eyes at them and stands in front of me. Her belly presses against my leg when she reaches up to adjust my tie. "Quit messing around with it. And you're dressed like this because... because I don't know why. But it's a big deal for Lachlan, so suck it up, Princess Asshole."

We're standing in the foyer of St. Luke's Academy, the only private school within a fifty-mile radius, waiting to get into the theater. During the four months I'd been gone, Lachlan's started entering some art contests. He's been doing as well with his art as he does with his running. This contest, according to Lachlan, is his most important one yet. He submitted his own work—work no one in the family has seen —and it made the final cut. Tonight, they announce the winner.

Lachlan's already in the theater, on his own, getting judged. They do this in private because, and this is crazy, the organization fears that parents will sabotage the competitions' pieces. I can't even deal with how ridiculous that is. I stare down at Lucy, still fiddling with my tie. "Can you not be an annoying, over-the-top parent?"

The door to the theater opens before she can respond, and all the guests form a line to file through one by one. "The tickets are allocated seats," Dad says over his shoulder. "Lachlan arranged them." He stops by the door to reach into his pocket and pull out a wad of tickets the size of my head. He starts rambling off our names, one by one, handing us the tickets with our names written in blue pen. "Lucy, Cameron, Lucas, Laney, Leo, Lincoln, Liam."

Behind us, people start complaining that we're holding up the line. Lucy glares. "Would you chill the fuck out?"

The asshole behind me says, "Nice. You plan on kissing your baby with that filthy mouth, sweetheart?"

If you ever want to see the fear in a man's eyes from the threats of six men over six feet tall, get him to say something shitty to the men's daughter/sister/wife. I step forward, "Say that again."

Dad takes my arm. "Forget him. Here's your ticket."

A woman mumbles, "Damn Preston Punks."

Lucy yells, "Whore!"

And then we're being ushered to our row, a discombobulation of bodies all trying to find their allocated seats.

"Ten minutes until it starts," Dad says, sitting down next to me. "Let's try not to get into any verbal or physical altercations, okay?"

I stand to remove my jacket, loosen my tie. Too many people. Too little space. I feel like I'm suffocating. Luckily, the seat next to mine, an aisle seat, is empty. I hope it stays that way.

Fifteen minutes later, the lights dim. A few minutes after that, Lachlan, along with five other kids, walks onto the stage. It takes a few seconds for my family and me to realize that we're the only ones standing and clapping. So... this is nothing like Lachlan's track meets. *Noted.*

An old man with a gray beard waits for us to be seated before adjusting the microphone on a podium. "Welcome to The Fifteenth Annual—"

The door to the theater opens, shuts, the sound echoing through the room. The old man sighs into the microphone. "We're on a schedule here, young lady."

Lucy, on the other side of Dad, whispers, "Someone should really remove the pole up this guy's ass."

Dad shakes his head.

I push his elbow off the armrest. "That'll be you in a few years, grumpy old man."

"No, it won't."

"Hey, Luce," I whisper yell and wait for her to lean forward, past Dad, to look at me. "Should we start planning Chicken's third birthday party?"

Dad grumbles.

I laugh.

The woman in front of me turns, glares, tells us to pipe down.

Lucy opens her mouth to retort, but stops, her eyes wide and focused on something behind me. "Oh, my God…"

I look over my shoulder.

Scarlet.

Upon scarlet.

Upon scarlet.

56

AUBREY

THE OTHER LETTER my mother had given me included a ticket and single flier with three words written in bright red marker.

The flyer was for an art contest, and Lachlan's name was listed as one of the finalists. I told myself I wouldn't go, that it would hurt too much, that nothing good could possibly come of it. I was still telling myself that on the three-hour drive here. When I got here, I'd sat in my car, watched each and every one of the Prestons, people I'd once considered my family, enter the parking lot, get out of their cars, meet by the front door, and walk into the building together. I stayed in my car, tried to convince myself not to come in. But then I looked at the flier again, the invite from a little boy who owns a piece of my soul and the words he'd written... the only three words he knew he'd need to get me here:

Please, Miss Red?

And now I'm here, sitting next to a boy who owns every piece of my heart, and I struggle to breathe. Struggle to keep my emotions in check. If I'd known I'd be sitting next to him, I would've stayed by the door, watched it from a distance.

I keep the hood of my coat over my head, try to hide my face. The last thing Logan needs is to see me, to realize that the freckles half the shade of scarlet, the upturned nose he loved so much… they were things I got from my father.

The man on stage is talking, but my fear has tuned me so far out of reality that I can't even comprehend what he's saying. In a daze of emotion, I keep my eyes forward, focused on Lachlan, and fist my hands on my lap. My heart pounds, pulse beating in my ears. I'm covered in goosebumps, and my stomach is rising, falling, flying, head-diving. I can't breathe. I look behind me, back at the door I came in from.

I could sneak out.

Make another scene.

It wouldn't matter; I'll never have to see these people again.

But then Lachlan's name is called, and I'm watching the stage again, my entire body lifting with anticipation. When he gets behind the podium, a step stool is offered to him, and the audience laughs. He's the youngest one here, the others in their late teens, and the idea of his greatness brings a smile to my lips, a tear to my eye.

He says, into the microphone, "I was told that I had to say something about myself before I talked about the work I'd submitted. I don't… I don't really know what I'm supposed to say…" He shrugs. "I'm just a kid who likes to draw."

I smile wider.

Lachlan adds, "I'm also a kid who likes to run. At one point, I thought it had to be one or the other… but then someone really special to me said something really important… she told me that I never had to stereotype myself. That I am who I am and I like what I like and that I never had to choose. It meant a lot to me—what she said—and I guess that's why she became my muse for the artwork I submitted."

My breath catches in my throat, and I find myself sitting forward, my hands shaking, my heart racing.

On the stage, a giant projector screen lowers behind Lachlan, and the lights dim, and then the entire screen is filled with what looks like a comic book cover. The girl on the drawing seems to be floating high above the buildings, bright blue leather covering almost every inch of her body, the letters *RR* across her chest, and enough red hair to fill half the screen. She's holding a pen, a laser shooting out of it, directed at a body below her—a body of a boy with something strapped to his chest.

My mouth opens, and I force an inhale, hold it there.

Lachlan clears his throat, the single sound haunting the entire room. "Once upon a time, there was a superhero with fiery-red hair. Some people described the color of her hair as scarlet. She had an upturned nose with freckles all across it. In her village, she was known as The Red Raven..."

I choke on a sob, cover my mouth with my hand to muffle the sound.

"In the same village as Red Raven lived a boy. A boy who had a past that no one knew of, no one spoke of. A boy who hurt in ways no one could ever understand. This boy would spend nights alone in his bunker, tinkering with his tools, pulling apart electronics just to put them back together again. Sometimes, he'd incorrectly rewire the units just to see the destruction it would cause.

"One night, he gathered an old alarm clock, a camp stove, and a stereo and pulled them all apart. When he was done, he started the task of joining them all together, wiring them all wrong. But before he could, the boy gave in to fatigue, and instead of packing up all the parts, he fell asleep on his bed with all the parts next to him. When he awoke the next day, the pieces of his broken project had somehow attached themselves to him. Right across his chest.

"He startled as he sat up, confused, and that's when he heard the tick, tick, ticking of the clock. When he looked down, he noticed that everything had been wired wrong. *Too* wrong. In his sleep, without his knowledge, his creation had become a ticking time bomb... right over his heart. The boy got up, stared at himself in the mirror, his blue eyes scared. And he knew that without meaning to, without wanting to, he'd become *self-destructive*."

My eyes drift shut, allowing the silent tears to fall along with my silent cries.

"Meanwhile, The Red Raven watched the boy from just outside his window. She could hear the bomb ticking but could see no change in the time of the clock. There was no exact hour, minute, second. There was no countdown. All she knew was that at some point, at *any* point, the boy was going to explode. She looked down at her pen, her super-power, and knew that with a wave of the pen, a scan with the laser, she had the power to remove the bomb, to rewire it, to rewire *him*. But the problem was, she didn't know him... this self-destructive boy who looked so broken, so sad..."

I wipe furiously at my tears, try to contain my cries as best I can. My hands settle on my lap, shaky and wet, and I inhale, exhale, too quick, too sharp, and I can't catch my breath. Then a single sound echoes through the room, through my entire body. Logan sniffs. And I'm too afraid to look, too scared to watch.

Lachlan goes on, "And so she made a promise to herself to get to know the boy, to see if he was worth saving..."

I can't see through the tears, can't breathe through the heartache. And then a stroke of warmth flows across my wrist—Logan's finger. My throat closes, and my eyes drop to the connection. He shifts my hand until the back of it rests on my leg. The tips of each of his fingers connect with mine, dragging them up, up, up, opening my hand for him, revealing the Hope Penny I'd been holding on to since I got here. His heavy breath lands on my head, and then his fingers are sliding through mine, lacing, joining, curling, and then...

Then he holds my hand.

He holds my hand and everything inside me breaks, crumbles to ashes. A second later, his lips are on my temple and my eyes are closed, and I feel all the broken pieces, the leftover ashes formed by our destruction, get swept away with the touch of his hand, and I'm being rebuilt, rewired from the inside out, and Lachlan continues: "The self-destructive boy glanced out his window and saw The Red Raven watching him. Their eyes met, and they held each other's gaze: the boy's pleading, the girl's concerned. And then the boy blinked, pulled them out of their stupor. He walked to the window, lifted the glass, and said the few words that would forever change them...'*Save me, Red.*'"

57

LOGAN

As soon as Lachlan's off the podium, Aubrey and I stand and walk out of the theater with my hope held between our hands.

She leans against the wall just outside the theater door, her head lowered, face hidden. She's in a red coat, the hood still on, and I joke, "You look like Little Red Riding Hood. The porno version we watched that time."

She laughs once but keeps her head down.

I notice a scar across her eyebrow I swear wasn't there before. I lift my free hand, run my thumb across it. "What's this?"

Her shoulders lift.

Fall.

I sigh, squeeze her hand. For months, I've thought about this moment, dreamt about it, and every time I did, she was looking at me. *Seeing* me. She's not seeing me now. "Why won't you look at me, Red?"

"I'm scared," she whispers.

"Of what?"

"What if... what if you look at me, and you see *him?*"

"Aubrey," I breathe out and lift her chin with my finger until her tear-filled eyes are on mine. Air fills my lungs for the first time since I saw her, and I take her in completely: all the pieces of her that I love, that I miss. And then I tell her the truth I'd been dying and hoping to say, to *feel*: "I don't see anyone but you. Even in my lowest, darkest moments, Aubrey, I only ever saw you."

I hold our joined hands behind her back, bring her closer to me. She smells like summer, like late nights and lake water and star-filled skies.

She says, holding back tears, "But... what if... what if one day that's not what you see? What if—"

I lean forward, cutting her off. "What if we *try*, Red?" I kiss her neck, her jaw, her cheek, all the parts of her I've missed. I ask, repeating the words that were once written with hope, "What if we *try*, and what if that was all I could promise you? Will that be enough?"

Her eyes drift shut, her lips finding mine, and then we're kissing, touching, and there's a calmness in the moment, as if we *know*...

We know that this is our future. Right here. Right now. Each other. And we can't ever let the people in our pasts, and the pasts we created, define who we are and what we stand for, what we live for. What we *love* for.

Her tears fall against my cheek, and she whispers the words I've held on to, the words I imagined hearing as I lay in bed at night, thinking of her, lost in the stillness, "I love you, Logan."

I rear back so I can look in her eyes. "God, Aubrey, I love you so much. Please *stay*," I beg.

"What?"

"I'm *asking* you to *stay*, Aubrey. *For me*..."

And she says...

She says...

"*Okay*."

EPILOGUE

LOGAN

"My Girl" by Otis Redding plays through the entire house, and I hold my niece in my arms, pull a penny from behind her ear. "What's this?" I whisper, smiling back at her the way she's smiling at me. She grabs my chin with her chubby little fists, and I spin us around the living room a little too fast for Dad's liking. "Take it easy, Logan. She just ate."

"I got her," I tell him, then look back into her eyes—eyes just like my mother's. "Your uncle Lo's got you, doesn't he, Princess?"

Exactly a year ago today, Baby Katie was born. It wasn't easy on Lucy, and I'm saying that as someone who has absolutely zero knowledge of the labor process, but Lucy, probably the strongest of us all, struggled. Bad. She was in labor for fifteen hours, completely drug-free —because that's how Mom had done it—and she wanted to be just as strong as Mom. When it got time to push, things got worse, and Katie —she was beached. No. Bitched. No... wait... *breeched*. Yeah, that's it. She was upside down or something, probably facing the butthole instead of the vagina—gross—but anyway, they had to do a last-minute emergency C-section.

Swear to God, I've never seen Lucy that scared.

When they wheeled her out of the room, we were all waiting for her in the hallway. She wouldn't stop crying, and it wasn't the physical pain that made her that way. She kept saying she couldn't do it, that she'd failed as a mother... and then, the saddest part of all, she kept crying out for Mom. Broke my damn heart. Dad's, too. I gave her the lucky penny from around my neck, told her it was Mom's, and that Mom would be in that room with her. She looked up at me, cried some more. "But it's yours," she said, and I shook my head, told her it was going to be Katie's, anyway. It was. I'd planned to give it to her the minute she was born. Besides, I don't need luck anymore. I had Aubrey. Who sat by my side the entire night, holding my hand, and telling me everything would be okay.

An hour after Lucy was taken into the OR, Cameron came out, covered in scrubs from head to toe, and *blood*. So much blood. I thought that something horrible had happened. And then he broke down in tears and said, "She's so perfect. God, she's so perfect."

And she is.

My baby niece.

My little princess.

"My turn!" Lachlan shouts, arms up, reaching for Katie.

I set Katie on the floor, make sure she's steady on her feet before letting her go. "Be careful, okay? She's only little."

Lachy rolls his eyes at me. "I'm not a dummy, Logan! Jeez, you gotta give me room to breathe, bro."

Lucas sways past, dancing with Laney, and smirks, "You play stupid games..."

I shake my head. "Shut up."

Dad smacks the back of my head as he walks to kitchen. "Don't talk to your brother like that."

And then Leo's coming down the stairs. "Yeah," he says. "Don't talk to your brother like that."

"You don't even know—"

"Everything's good to go," the twins shout, their heads poking through the front door.

I look at my watch. "What time does the party start?"

"In an hour," Cameron says, picking up his daughter. "Where's your girl?"

"Wherever yours is."

The song ends, the back door opens, and Aubrey walks in: hair down, long summer dress with palm leaves, flowers in her hair. I ask her, "Have you seen my friend, Wilson?"

"Who?" she says, making her way through all the people to get to Katie. She kisses her cheek, then wipes off the lipstick she left behind.

"My friend, Wilson," I repeat. "Because you look like a castaway."

Cameron shakes his head, chuckles. "Poor effort, dude."

"You're an idiot," Aubrey tells me. "And why are you still in your underwear? The party starts in an hour." She flicks her wrist, shooing me out the door. "Go. And you, too, Lachy."

I grasp both her hands in mine and smile; I can't help it. "My clothes are up in my old room." I kiss her quickly. "And I was kidding. You look beautiful."

Had it not been for Aubrey's four-poster bed, her move in to the garage apartment with me would've been just as stealth as my move in with her.

She hasn't left my side.

I won't let her.

Neither will my family.

And, sure, we could've gotten our own place, but truthfully? I don't want to be far from my family—my support system—and after the first night of *You + Me 2.0*, when Aubrey caught me up on everything going on in her life, it was pretty clear she needed a support system of her own. And my family—my dad especially—was more than happy to be that for her.

She now runs Lucy's bookstore.

"Why do I have to dress like this?" Lachlan asks, fidgeting with his tie. "I feel like a jackhole."

I sit on the edge of my parents' bed and shake my head at him. "You hang around me way too much."

"Not by choice," he says. "You're just wherever Red is, and I actually like her."

Aubrey giggles as she buttons my sleeve.

"Why can't I just wear jeans?"

"Because..." I start. "Because it's Katie's first birthday and Lucy wants to get some nice pictures of all of us today."

"That's dumb," he mumbles.

"Listen, Lachy," I say, my voice firm. "Lucy and Cameron—they were told they'd never have a baby, and it's something they've wanted for a really long time. Besides, Lucy and Cam—we owe them a lot. I know..." I look down, a knot forming in my throat. "I know you were really young when Mom died, but afterward, Dad—he didn't take it too well, and if it weren't for Luce and Cameron and Cam's mom, we might not even be here."

"What?" he says, his eyes narrowed. "Like, we'd be eaten by zombies?"

"No," I laugh out. "I mean, we wouldn't be here, all together like this. We may have been separated. And could you imagine that... all of us living in different places?"

"No," Lachlan mumbles. "That would suck."

"Right? So, I think we can dress like penguins for one day a year. I think Cameron and Lucy deserve that. Don't you?"

He nods.

Then Katie cries, and I look to the door, to Lucy and Cameron standing there, watching us. "You're a jerk," Lucy cries out, wiping at her tears.

Aubrey sniffs, and she's crying, too.

I sigh.

Lachlan does the same. "Girls are so weird."

"They're not that bad," Cameron says, laying Katie down on the bed. She's in a frilly purple dress, my lucky penny hanging from a gold chain around her neck. Blue-blue eyes and dark brown hair and more cheeks than you can squeeze between your fingers.

"You make good kid," I tell Cameron.

He nods, his eyes doing that crazy distant thing whenever he looks at his daughter for more than a second. "Fuck, yeah, I do."

Lucas says, walking into the room with Laney right behind him. "At some point, we're going to have to cut it out with all the swearing. She's going to start picking up on it."

Laney laughs, her head throwing back. "Remember that time Lachlan thought pussy-whipped meant that you didn't like cats and you whipped them?"

Everyone laughs. Everyone but Lachlan. "Wait. That's not what it means?"

The twins come in then, all of us around the king-sized bed, looking down at Katie. Lincoln says, "Aunt Leslee just got to the gate."

We all groan.

"Guess who's with her?"

"Who?" Lucy asks.

"Vagina."

"Ew!" Lachlan squeals.

"Virginia?" I ask. "Our old nanny?"

"Uh huh," says Liam, but he has that sly smile on his face that can only mean one thing.

"Wait," Lucas says, unable to hide his smirk. "Does that mean Mia's here, too?"

Liam nods. "Yep."

All eyes go to Leo, who's covering his face. "Nooooo!" he whispers into his hands.

"Who's Mia? And why is Leo..." Aubrey trails off.

"Mia's Virginia's daughter, and she fucking loved Leo," I say through a chuckle.

"Loved?" says Lucy. "She was *infatuated.*"

"How long do I have to stay at this thing?" Leo mumbles.

"Remember that time she made Leo a cake with her face on it?" Lucas laughs out.

I say, "Oh, my God, and it was at that *really* bad stage. When she had that—"

"Brace face!" Liam shouts. "And acne."

"Oh, my God, so much acne," Lincoln adds.

"Didn't Virginia send her to fat camp?" I ask.

The room goes silent.

"We're such assholes," Lucas says.

"Yeah," Lucy agrees, frowning down at her daughter. "We're the worst."

"The worst," Liam agrees.

"She was a really nice girl," I add. "Like, super sweet."

"We're the meanest, most judgmental bunch of whorefaces in existence," says Lucy.

Leo sighs. "I mean, yeah, we are, but still... if y'all could be my buffer, I'd appreciate it."

"You're on your own, bud," Lucas says, slapping his shoulder.

We all go quiet as we stare down at Katie. "If anyone treats her the way we just treated Brace Face—I mean Mia..." I rub my hands across my face. "Jesus."

"Kids!" Dad calls from downstairs. "You have visitors!"

Lucy exhales, frowns some more.

"Kids!"

No one moves.

Voices sound from downstairs.

Then Dad's footsteps, thumping.

Lucy whispers, *"Fee-fi-fo-fum."*

I chuckle. Lucas's eyes go wide. "Quick!" he whisper-yells. "Everyone hide."

Lucy takes Katie off the bed, and then I'm lifting the blankets while everyone tries to fit on the bed. Legs off the edges, arms bent, hands in places they shouldn't be. Aubrey settles on top of me, giggling into my chest.

Katie coos.

"Shut it, Katie," Lachlan jokes. "The giant's coming."

Fee-fi-fo-fum!

"Kids!" Dad yells, and then the bedroom door is opening, and it's silent besides Lachy giggling, Lucas's hand covering our baby broth-er's mouth.

"Welp," Dad says. "Can't find them. I must be too tired. I'm going to sleep."

And then the blankets are lifting and we're laughing, squealing like little kids again.

AUBREY

The Preston property has been converted into a scene from a fairytale, and to everyone here, Katie is the princess. I don't think I've ever met a little girl so spoiled with love and affection. And no one showers her with more love and affection than her Uncle Logan. I watch him holding her, walking around to the party guests one after the other, a giant smile on his face.

It took a while for that smile of his to return after everything that had happened. There was no denying our initial emotional connection, or *re-connection*. But it was the moments after that led us to the strength we have now. We were both wary of our feelings and the feelings of those around us. While the Prestons made it known they had abso-lutely no issues with me, that they supported and loved me regardless of what my family ties were, their feelings for my mother was some-thing else. Tom held the same disdain toward my mother as I did, and I couldn't fault him for that. While I wish things were different between my mom and I—I still can't look at her and not feel sick to my stomach that she did so little to save those boys, now men.

In my eyes, she's neither a victim nor a villain. She is, however, a bystander, and that's something I don't think I can ever truly accept.

It doesn't mean I don't miss her, though.

It was all those things combined that led me to Logan's therapist.

I see her twice a month. One session alone, one with Logan. We'd see her more if Logan's schedule would allow it, but with him working full-time, going to trade school, studying for his GED *and* ticking off the hours for his court-ordered community service, he barely has time to breathe. I learnt that during his four month stint at the treatment facility, his family, along with Senior Deputy Misty Sanders, Judge Nelson (the town's only judge who also handled Lucas and Laney's cases against her ex), and Nathan Andrews (a lawyer and family friend) fought his charges. It was another six months before we were able to get Logan's final sentence. No prison time was the outcome we all hoped for. We were beyond thrilled with the decision.

Now, Logan's stopping to talk to the lady I'd been introduced to as Virginia, their old nanny, and her daughter Mia… who is *nothing* like they'd described.

I nudge Leo standing next me, then wince in pain. The man's a brick wall, muscles in too many places. He's spent the past year and a half—since Logan's downfall—working construction and *working out*. Next week, he's off to the police academy.

With a chuckle, he throws his arm over my shoulders, brings me into him. "You're weak, Red." All the Prestons call me Red.

I look up at him, but he, too, is watching Logan. Logan and *Mia*. "Mia grew up, huh?"

"No shit," he laughs out.

"You gonna talk to her?"

"And say what? Hey, I leave next week, but wanna sex?"

I shrug. "Why not?"

"Because I'm not *Logan*."

I elbow his stomach made of stone.

"I meant, Pre-Red Logan. *Obviously*."

Right on cue, Logan appears, no Katie. "Get your own girl," he says, pulling me out of Leo's hold. He takes my hand, walks me to an open patch of grass. Then he stops, turns me to him. He says, his arms around my waist. "I finally found it."

"Found what?"

He smirks, motions to Linc and Liam working the stereo. "Our song."

I try to get out of his hold, but he's too strong. "No, Logan. Not now."

"It's a good song," he laughs out.

"No. Last time you said that, it was 50 Cent's 'Candy Shop'!"

He pins my arms behind me, holds my hands tight in his. Then his mouth is on my neck, my jaw. "I promise, this is it."

The song starts, and I'm already rolling my eyes in anticipation. Logan starts to smile when my features soften. "Lucky" by Jason Mraz and Colbie Caillat plays through the speakers, through my heart, my entire body. I let the lyrics fill every part of me.

"Was I right?" he asks, slowly releasing my hands. They go behind his neck, fingers linked. We sway, back and forth, his blue-blue eyes right on mine.

"You were right," I tell him, my cheek pressed to his chest. "This is perfect."

"*You're* perfect, Red. And this life, what we have, what you've given me... it's all perfect."

We rear back at the same time, just so we can see each other. He's smiling from ear-to-ear, like a giant goofball. "I'm the lucky one," I tell him, grasping the Hope Penny around my neck. *You + Me.* "And I'm kind of crazy in love with you."

"The feeling's mutual, Red." And then his lips are on mine, and everything fades with the swipe of his tongue, with the way his fingers grasp at my waist. I tilt my head to the side, bump the side of my face against something. *Katie.* "You guys are so cute it makes me sick," Lucy says in a high-pitched voice. She's squatting down, hiding behind her daughter.

Logan shakes his head.

Lucy giggles, stands to full height and holds Katie on her hip. "We're about to light the lanterns for Mom," she tells us. "Let's go."

I let go of Logan, let him be with his family, because I know how important this is to all of them. They did it for Cameron and Lucy's wedding, and they plan on doing it every year for Katie's birthday. Lucy and Logan are two steps away before they both turn, in sync, and narrow their eyes at me. "You coming?" Logan asks.

"You guys go," I say, shaking my head. "It's a family thing."

Lucy scoffs, comes back to me, and pulls on my arm until I'm being dragged behind her. "You'll realize soon," she says.

"Realize what?"

"That you *are* family, Red."

Logan wraps me in his arms, then lifts me off the ground, throws me over his shoulder. He smacks my butt. I squeal, try to get out of his hold, while my world flips. Everything is upside down. Wired wrong. Perfect. And then Lachlan's running up to me, handing me a sky lantern. He smiles his gap-tooth smile. "Let's set the skies ablaze, Red!" And Lucy's right. I feel it. Only the time isn't soon. It's *now*. And all the people watching us—they have it wrong. Katie's not the princess here. *I am*. And I'm living my own fairy tale. My own Happily Ever After.

When we get to the end of the dock, we light the lanterns, watch them float high, high, high into the sky. Logan takes my hand in his, and I feel the familiar sensation of the cold metal against my palm. I take the flattened penny from between our touch, my heart racing as I lift it to my eyes:

You saved me, Red.

WANT MORE?

Want more of Cameron and Lucy's story? You can find out all about them in the More Than Series, particular More Than Forever (can be read as a standalone).

MORE THAN SERIES

- More Than This
- More Than Her
- More Than Him
- More Than Forever
- More Than Enough

PRESTON BROTHERS NOVEL

- Lucas

ALSO BY JAY MCLEAN

THE ROAD SERIES

Where the Road Takes Me

Kick Push

Coast

COMBATIVE TRILOGY

Combative

Redemptive

Destructive - Coming Soon

BOY TOY CHRONICLES

Volume One

DARKNESS MATTERS

Darkness Matters

ABOUT THE AUTHOR

 Jay McLean is an international best-selling author and full-time reader, writer of New Adult Romance, and skilled procrastinator. When she's not doing any of those things, she can be found running after her two little boys, playing house and binge watching Netflix.

She writes what she loves to read, which are books that can make her laugh, make her hurt and make her feel.

Jay lives in the suburbs of Melbourne, Australia, in a forever half-done home where music is loud and laughter is louder.

For publishing rights (Foreign & Domestic) Film, or television, please contact her agent Erica Spellman-Silverman, at Trident Media Group.

Connect With Jay
www.jaymcleanauthor.com
jay@jaymcleanauthor.com

Made in the USA
Columbia, SC
31 July 2020

15093736R00236